PRINCIPATO

PRINCIPATO

TOM McHALE

NEW YORK ❧ THE VIKING PRESS

First published in 1970 by The Viking Press, Inc.
625 Madison Avenue, New York, N.Y. 10022

Published simultaneously in Canada by
The Macmillan Company of Canada Limited

SBN 670-57697-2

Library of Congress catalog card number: 71-104134
Printed in U.S.A. by The Colonial Press Inc.

PRINCIPATO

ONE

In the street before the San Giorgio Baths, his father's red Thunderbird was already parked, and Principato drew alongside, to be instantly saddened, as always, at the reflection of himself and his car in the T-bird's sleek side. Both looked held together by threads somehow: a sham on an unsaid American tradition that a son ought to look infinitely more prosperous than his father.

He parked his car in the San Giorgio lot and pushed through the revolving doors to the marble-covered entranceway, where the vague fecal odor of the place hit his nostrils almost immediately. An unchangeable smell that had been sharply impressed on his senses from the first time that, as a kid graduated to the ranks of men, he had gone to sit small and naked in the steam room beside his great and naked father.

Charlie, the old man who handed out towels and soap and robes, acknowledged him with a grunt, though he never actually spoke to him, since Principato was of the new generation of weight losers for whom Charlie had only an enduring contempt.

In the lockers he undressed quickly, slipped into a robe, then walked in clogs toward the steam room, past the pillared lounge that he always called the Roman Senate for its collection of draped and lazing small-time politicos. He entered the steam room behind a small naked man across whose buttocks was imprinted the mesh pattern of its benches and squinted through the fog for his father. An occasional pair of hairy legs and kneecaps stared back at him, but none he recognized immediately as his father's with the purplish scar on his left shin.

"Pop?" he called.

"Who is it?" came a voice from the top row.

"Principato."

"Your old man's been here and gone. I think he's in the pool right now. For Christ's sake, don't let him take too many laps around that bathtub. He looks like the living death today."

"He's got to watch that heart. It can go on you faster than that." A finger snapped somewhere in the steam above the twitching white feet.

"The heart's the least of his problems with the bad liver and the kidney the way he's got it. Once the old liver goes you're finished. Spreads poison all through your system," said a slow, sad voice from a top-row corner that sounded as if it knew what it was talking about.

"Does he still have the ulcer, Pato?" asked the first.

"Yes."

"Well, it's the goddam Defiance that brought that on. If a man's got something like your old man eatin' away at his insides for years, he's bound to have an ulcer sooner or later," said the second.

"I hate to be critical," said the third, in a tone even slower and sadder than before, "but I never could understand why he couldn't lie down and take it like the rest of us poor sheep."

"Because he's Principato! Life is an eternal waltz with unerring principles! Vive la Defiance!" sang a gravel voice that Principato recognized as Agostini, still his father's partner. "He's the only pape in America who gets to telephone in his sins at eleven-thirty on a Friday night because they haven't been able to coax him inside a church in thirty years!"

"You're kidding! It's thirty years now he hasn't been to the mass?" said a new speaker.

"Exactly. It's so long that if you asked him he wouldn't even be able to remember how the Defiance got started. The important thing

4

is to keep it going. I'm telling you"—Agostini nearly wept—"if I had it to do all over again, it would be with a different partner. We could have made three times as much money in that coffin racket of ours if it wasn't for Principato's arch high principles."

"Yeah, and then you'd be in a lot worse trouble with the law than a simple morals charge. Are you still laying sly hands on the flanks of young girls?" said a voice that Principato was no longer certain was the first or second or third.

Relieved, he left the steam room as the overweight doom chorus of his father's friends turned blessedly to heckling Agostini and walked quickly to the pool, where he saw the great, sad hulk of the old man alone and naked in the shallow end, his thin arms jutting out from his huge body and slowly churning the water as if he were propelling a whirlpool that could ease away the collective ills of his ulcer, kidney stones, and bad liver that living with the Defiance had brought on. As always, he puffed on a cigar.

Principato removed his robe and jumped in at the deep end, swimming a slow breast stroke toward his father, who turned and flicked his ash into the poolside overflow gutter. When his feet touched bottom, the water line that ebbed about his father's waist crept up and down on the son's narrow thigh. Naked, and side by side, they were both a shambles, each in his own distinct way, Principato thought morosely.

"How does your brother, Rocco, seem to you today?" was the first thing the old man asked.

"Same as usual."

"Not cured, huh?"

"What were you expecting?"

"Nothing. Not a damn thing." He spat disgustedly into the gutter. "When his mother gets that weepy look in her eyes and asks me for two thousand bucks to take him over to Lourdes, what can I do but pay? She's back at the house all last night trying to tell me how much good it did him so I won't think she took me for something."

"Maybe it did her some good," Principato said, deploring any attack on his mother's own brand of dervish Catholicism.

"It must've done her some good. She made a couple hundred new friends just as screwy as herself, I think. Her and your Aunt Lucrezia were up before dawn writing out those Visit Philadelphia post cards to everybody they met over there. Then she gets on the phone to all her gang in town to tell them about some guy Rocco saw get up out of his wheel chair. When she got as far as Jenny Rindelli she was crying so hard I thought her face was going to slide off. Whew! I was glad to get out of that place and over to the hospital."

At the mention of hospital, Principato felt his chest tighten. He watched as the familiar film of exasperation that came into the old man's eyes whenever he spoke of his wife's religiosity appeared. Then his father jammed the cigar between his teeth and chomped on it heavily.

"Come on, Pop, let's take our little swim, O.K.?"

"O.K.," his father answered. Obediently he set out with Principato to make their slow turns about the pool as they had done every Saturday for years. The old man, possessor of the Defiance, and his son Principato, who sensed then with certainty that in a few months he would be heir to everything of his father's—except, of course, the Defiance. For how, he wondered, could you bequeath that to someone like himself, for whom small angers had always been sufficient?

"What did the doctor have to say, Pop?"

"Throat cancer, all right," he said, breaking stroke to put a finger to his neck. "These babies finally caught up with me, I guess." He held the cigar over the water in front of him as if he were seeing it for the first time.

"But they can fix you up, right?"

"Too late now. If they caught the bitch before, even two months ago, they might've been able to do something with it."

"Cripes, no," Principato said in a low voice. Then he began floundering toward the side.

"Keep swimming," the old man commanded. "I told you before what it might be. It's nothing to go to the bottom over like your old lady would."

"How long, then?"

"Nine, ten months. Maybe a little longer."

"Nine months only. Do you think you might at least give up the cigars for that much time?"

"She's fine. Only tell me everything you remember about Raymond. Some members of my family have been asking."

"Pato, Pato," the uncle urged, "we came here to discuss your poor doomed father."

"First Raymond, then my poor doomed father," Principato said, his voice quivering. After eleven years of marriage to a Corrigan, he at last had the family to the brink about something. He turned to glance at Cynthia. There was a new kind of hatred in her eyes.

Then Principato stood up, thinking that he might somehow dismiss his six missionary antagonists by simply hobbling out. But youngest brother Jim sprang to the doorway. His great hand circled Principato's arm.

"Our uncle wants to talk with you about your father," he said, enunciating carefully while tightening his grip.

"My father and I question the validity of your family's right to interfere here. We, for example, have always had our doubts about your Raymond." His voice quivered by octaves now, he imagined. Sweat poured from his body, soaking his shirt.

"Jim, Jim, this is not the Catholic way," the uncle said, getting up from his chair. He placed the biretta back on his head as he advanced, with apparent kindness in his eyes, and removed his nephew's hand.

Cripes, thought Principato involuntarily in the midst of his fear, he's really over the hill now. He was going blank in the middle of lectures when I was in college, and that was eleven years ago.

"Pato, can't you sense our sincere concern about your dear, only father?"

"Yes, Father, I can. But you must understand that, as the missionary target, we're not all that sure you come to us with unstained credentials."

"Ah, that," said the priest. He began walking a slow circle about Principato, his hands clasped behind his back. "Well, I suppose it had to come out in the wash like anything else. You see, Raymond was not an ordained priest, only a brother of the order. And he had the misfortune . . ."

"He had no misfortune at all, Mr. Principato," the old lady corrected. "Father is entirely mistaken about what happened."

15

"Yes, that's right. Father has it all wrong," echoed Matt, standing quickly with his brothers to corner the honest old Jesuit and herd him from the house. Their mother came right up behind them.

"Raymond was a good Corrigan and a good missionary," she said emphatically, jabbing a long bony finger into Principato's diaphragm so hard that he lost his wind for a moment.

"Don't you ever dare doubt that for a minute, Mr. Principato," she told him.

Then they were gone in a soft hum of limousine transmission, the uncle sitting in the padded back, looking as if his legs had been cut out from under him.

Thus began the impasse that would continue through the remainder of the summer and into the fall. But chiefly at night, with Cynthia lying rigid and closed in the next bed and threatening to find a technicality for annulment, but occasionally changing her tack to taunt her husband through the darkness, "Think of him going to be judged!" Her voice, a plaintive whisper in normal conversation, assumed an apocalyptic quality. Instead of a bed, he was lying in a basket of saw grass and being eaten by soldier ants.

Often, hearing her in the night, he tested the Defiance. The ancient doubts about the Christian myth were down there all right. He hoped they would come rushing to the surface with enough strength for him to tell her off with a succinct and final "Bullshit!" But they did not. The equally ancient fears, well ingrained, of slandering the Christian myth were there in greater array. Toward the end of the month he slinked off downstairs to the refuge of a living-room sofa, waking often during the next few weeks from the nightmare of his wife, her uncle, brothers, and mother, all sad-eyed and ethereal in long white robes, approaching from a black abyss. Cynthia carried an object in her hands: it was an urn.

"How'd you ever get tied up with an outfit like that?" the old man often asked him as they plied the Saturday waters of the San Giorgio pool. This question about the Corrigans bothered him constantly, since he had never been quite certain whether his son leapt into his marriage willingly or was somehow coerced. Principato was not entirely certain either.

16

In his senior year at Midwestern Gonzola University he discovered he was flunking theology with "Sleepy" Corrigan, arch purveyor of conservatism, who had a, by now, legendary marriageable niece named Cynthia back in Philadelphia. Predictably, the uncle got to him. Handing back a third, and really flunking, test paper, he asked quietly, "Where do you come from, Principato?"

"Philadelphia, Father."

"See me after class."

The day, properly chosen perhaps, was quickly darkening and raining. The old priest pressed his face against a fogged-up window, leaving the sharp impression of his nose, his eyes gazing intently at the outside as if he could see a troupe of morbid bachelors parading past with drooping shoulders and slick, dripping hair. But there was only a sad-eyed Jesus statue, his mantle being washed clean of excreta by the rain. Then he turned to face Principato.

"Have I ever spoken to you in this way before, Principato?"

"No, Father."

"I'm glad. There have been so many. My memory seems to fail me so often now." He raised his hand to the side of his head and began massaging as if he might knead his roving memory back into the proper slot.

"Good-by, Principato. Perhaps, then, we'll hear of you over the Christmas holidays."

Their first date was to be a candlelit dinner for two in the Corrigans' great old home. In the afternoon, hours before he was expected, he drove out to look the place over, and discovered to the rhythm of a quickening heart beat that he was some sort of opportunist. The house was a Georgian brick, white-trimmed, in a distant, rambling suburb and was surrounded by acres of lawn and trees. Principato walked around it four times. With each circuit, the notion grew stronger in him that a place like this should be filled with great hunting horses and aristocratic dogs. There was a stable behind the house where they were probably kept. The fifth time around, he cut into the Corrigan property and sneaked along a line of fir trees to the side door of the stable.

Inside, instead of horses, there were hearses. Four of them parked in a row, each labeled CORRIGAN FUNERAL SERVICE in neat gold letters.

"The sight of these four carts always gets 'em," said a bull voice behind him. "I don't know what the hell they expect to find in here."

Principato spun around to see a heavy-set woman in a kerchief holding a broom.

"Who are you?" he asked.

"I'm Stella, the household drudge. Who are you? Tonight's Sir Galahad for my lady Cynthia?"

"I guess I am," he admitted with an embarrassed laugh. "I was just looking around."

"Most of 'em do. Dear Cynthia's been watchin' you walk around all afternoon through binoculars from her bedroom window. What's the uncle got on you out there at school?"

"I'm flunking his theology course."

"Well, I'd take the goose egg, kid, before I'd ever get mixed up with this gang. They'd take the sweat from the poor dead Jesus," she said, crossing herself furiously.

"What's Cynthia like?" he asked. He felt a rapport with the woman.

"How old are you, kid?" Stella asked, sitting down heavily on a barrel.

"Twenty-two."

"Well, she's twenty-six. That for a start. Then she's got big feet, cold hands, and she's been on a cryin' jag since I can remember. Also . . ."

"Forget it. Don't you like any of them?"

"Nuts to 'em all, except the old man, that is." Her face brightened at the thought. "He's a sweetie. But he had a stroke a coupla years ago and he goes around in a wheel chair now. They probably won't even show 'im to you tonight. Only bring 'im out when it's absolutely necessary. They're just dyin' for 'im to kick off."

"He's got all the money, huh?" Principato said, drawing himself onto the fender of one of the hearses.

"Naw, they got it all. The old lady and her three killer sons. But as far as they're concerned, the old man's just a pain in the ass to have

18

around. Boy, you should've known 'im before the stroke. A real Irish-man. When the wife'd clear out in the afternoons for some society party she was always crashin', me and him'd sit down in the kitchen with a bottle and get loaded. No funny stuff, of course. . . ."

They heard a door slam at the house, and then approaching foot-steps.

"Quick, kid, hide against that one by the wall!" she urged. Princi-pato ducked behind the last hearse as one of the brothers came into the stable.

"Have to go to work," he said to Stella, who still sat on her barrel. Then he opened the door of one hearse and climbed inside. Princi-pato watched him through a line of windows. It was Jim Corrigan, who had been captain of the Gonzola football team when Principato was a freshman. He seemed larger, if possible, now than then.

He started the hearse and drove out. Stella stood up and spat after him.

"Well, see you tonight in the great hall, kid," she said, waving her broom at Principato.

That evening, in a setting that had deep roots in romantic history, he encountered Cynthia for the first time. Soft pink lighting, an im-mense regal room, portable gypsy band and Bach on the corner rec-ord player. From the table, a profusion of dishes and silverware stared up at him. The total, however, was not sufficient distraction. He was stricken at the sight of her: a thin, willowy creature with soft downy hair, wearing a strapless white dress that seemed presumptu-ous and unnecessary in the area of her small, athletic girl's breasts. Her nose had the crooked suggestion of a fracture found out too late then allowed to heal on its own. Her eyes were not hers entirely. They were the eyes of her great-uncle Linus, the bishop, whose scowling portrait hung in innumerable places about the house. Her character was implied in their weepy, frustrated cast.

Her brothers were in the next room, pained at the lack of conver-sation. They kept running in, dressed in their bowling-league shirts, to shake his hand, ask after old teachers out at Gonzola, and pour him continuous drinks to celebrate the fraternalism in having once been Jesuit charges also.

In time, Cynthia dismissed them irritably, and the two of them sat down, Principato remembering at the last moment not to tuck his napkin bib-fashion into his shirt. She rang a little bell. On signal, Stella, his friend from the afternoon, charged through the door, resplendent in her new maid's uniform. The sight of it pinned up behind her suddenly heartened Principato, allowed him to see through the lie. She gave him a broad wink.

Later, when she served them a cold Bulgarian soup from her international cookbook, she also gave him an exit pass. In truth, the soup was sour cream, garlic flavored. Cucumber slices floated on top like diminutive lily pads. What matter that it might prove unpalatable? It was foreign. The first spoonful came away tasting like a gruel of anisette.

"I don't think I can finish this, Cynthia."

"Why?"

"I have an allergy to sour cream," he lied.

A strange, helpless look came over her face. Which was probably the main reason for his marrying her, he often reflected later. There was, all notion of being opportunist aside, a ready pity in the Principatos for a face like that. He could not imagine it going anywhere in life under its own sail. It would have to attach itself to someone.

Between them, a long silence set in. From the corner record player, the Magyar band scraped and wailed its way into his brain. He realized his body had lapsed into some contortive accompanying rhythm. At length Cynthia got up, the tears starting from her eyes, and ran through the door into the kitchen. A period of fierce whispering followed, broken occasionally by the bull-voiced Stella who lamented, "Aw, you poor kid," over and over again. Then the maid came through the door. There was a look of conspiracy in her face.

"Mr. Principato, I hope you'll excuse her, but our Cynthia isn't feeling very well this evening." Then she came near. "All right, kiddo, you got your ticket outta here. If you never did a smart thing before, you'll head for the door now."

Gratefully, Principato let her help him into his coat and bolted for the car, Cynthia's helpless face perfectly remembered in every detail. . . .

The first day back after vacation, Corrigan caught up with him in the hall.

"What happened?" There was a look of earnest puzzlement in his face. Principato felt an arm around his shoulder.

"I don't know, Father. She got a little upset at dinner that first night. I tried calling her afterward, but there was never any answer."

"No answer? That's very strange," the priest responded. But that was all he said.

After first-semester finals when a diarrhetic Principato picked up his transcript, he found a withheld grade in theology instead of the D or failure he had anticipated. He crept up to Corrigan's office.

"Mr. Principato, what can I do for you?"

"You've given me a withheld grade on my transcript, Father."

"Ah yes, that," the priest shook his head sadly. "I'm afraid you took gas on the final, as the saying goes. But I always end up being more than decent to our Philadelphia boys. A geographical weakness on my part, Pato. By the way, did you manage to see dear Cynthia over the semester break?"

"No, Father. I tried calling again, but nothing," he lied. "But I intend to drive out and see her over spring vacation."

"Good! Good to hear! And we'll make some arrangement about retaking that final. Can't have one of our Philly boys deficient in theology, of all things."

"No, Father, certainly not that," he agreed, retreating unhappily from the office.

When Principato, still deficient in theology, arrived home for spring vacation, the three Corrigan brothers were waiting outside his home in one of their great funereal limousines. They climbed out at his approach.

"Hello, Pato, how's things? We came by to get you this time," Matt, the eldest, said. His tone was friendly and disarming.

But Edward, the second, struck the sinister note. "Yeah, Pato. In case you called and couldn't get an answer with mother and Cynthia and Stella and the old man and usually one of us at home all at the same time." He spat into the gutter. Jim, the third brother, said nothing.

Principato merely shrugged. "Wait until I put these suitcases in the house."

Inside, his father was waiting. "Is this a good thing or something?"

"They've got lots of money, Pop."

"Well, the way they were in here this afternoon taking inventory, I thought they were trying to marry some."

But his mother had been impressed. "Somebody named Linus was a bishop, honey. And they've got two priests in the family right now."

"The hell with their bishop!" the old man said. "You don't forget to tell them your Aunt Lucrezia's a millionaire. Only don't tell them how she got her money. By the way, what's the girl look like?"

"She's O.K.," Principato said dully, then he left his own people to go off with the Corrigans.

After that, he might have given up on Cynthia a thousand times, the withheld grade notwithstanding. But he had committed himself to a kind of vocation and the recognition of it grew stronger with each passing month. Compensating, he substituted this for the tragedy of love. Without himself in her life, he decided, she was automatically banished to the high and separate station of maiden aunt. He had a great sense of how her loneliness would be: pouring at endless sodality teas, afternoons spent doing volunteer work in hospitals, meeting occasionally to open the floodgates of her soul with a sensitive, well-read young man who would probably turn out to be a homosexual anyhow. He needed to save her.

Cynthia, for her part, was disbelieving. During their quiet formal dates in the Corrigan living room she watched him intently, as if she expected him to bolt for the door at any moment, never to return. And in the background her family worked with fierce intent. They were imbibing him after a fashion, he realized dimly as he was going down.

The summer after his graduation from Gonzola, no longer deficient with an A in theology, and back home in Philadelphia, his days spent with the brothers seemed to him a single, great incursion into the small dishonesties of the Corrigans' dual professions. To the old lady, for her part, went the task of family historian. The Corrigans had a mania for preserving the past. She led him into every room of their museum of a home, stood weeping, to his embarrassment, before the retouched portraits of dead heroes and heroines, dug out old stacks of photographs for his benefit. He spent long hours staring at the hazy daguerreotypes, gaining a sense of the Corrigan ancestry. In their early American past, they had been hod carriers and brewery workers to a man. One had helped dig the Broad Street subway. With a shovel. Only the intense, anemic-looking Linus seemed to be thinking beyond Saturday night's glass of beer.

Once she thrust open a door and said savagely, "This is my husband." An old man sat in a wheel chair and tried to smile at Principato. Behind him, Stella stood running a hairbrush through his great lion's mane. Principato felt a sharp pity for this person the rest of the family considered just a pain in the ass to have around. He picked up a limp hand and shook it.

"This is Cynthia's beau," the old lady said. Principato watched her husband's eyes go liquid with sorrow. They seemed to be pitying him in turn.

"Mr. Corrigan had a stroke and can't talk," his wife explained.

"Yeah, but the tales he could tell if he could talk," Stella said. "Huh, kiddo?" She jabbed the old man in the shoulder with her elbow. Then she kissed him on the forehead. He smiled appreciatively.

"That will be enough, Stella!" Mrs. Corrigan said, then she closed the door. Outside she told Principato, "We expect Mr. Corrigan to die any day now."

"It's just as well," Principato heard himself say.

Finally into the inner sanctum. Linus, the bishop, had become the pinnacle of the family. In this special room, his fierce, ugly portrait stood on an easel, a spotlight fixed over it. The place lacked being a shrine only because Linus was buried elsewhere under six feet of earth. But its commemorative function was easy to see.

Mrs. Corrigan went to a tall closet, unlocked it, and slid back the doors. Inside were a bishop's copes and mitre. Next she opened a small cabinet to reveal a jeweled chalice. Then she sat down on a straight-backed, uncomfortable-looking chair, her hand gripping the frame of Linus's portrait. Principato remembered the scene. An early evening in August with the fiery glow of sunset coming through the old wooden slats of the blinds.

Before him sat the mother, frail and incredibly white-skinned. Cynthia's weepy-eyed cast came from her. He saw it all now. A half-

23

refined, delicate sort of woman, hardly looking like the mother to three sons who chiseled barflies in colored ghettos. He waited for her to speak.

"Our family, Mr. Principato, did not leave Ireland because we were starving." "Our family" meant the Corrigans. This surprised Principato. Cynthia's mother was a Mulhaney. Evidently she considered herself completely assimilated.

"No?"

"We were kicked out for stealing horses." It was no confession. He sensed it in an instant. She had a firm kind of pride in the Corrigans' having once been horse thieves back on the Auld Sod. Perhaps she offered it as an explanation for their New World ambition, almost predatory, that built this great house and acquired their chains of barrooms and funeral homes. He was only casually impressed. His own Aunt Lucrezia had done them all one better in her living American present, he reasoned.

Then, a week after the visit to Linus's shrine and the dark revelation about the Corrigan past, they gave him a test. He drove up to the house on a Sunday afternoon to find brother Matt wringing his hands on the front porch, a mask of anxiety on his face. Beside him, brother Jim chewed frantically on a thumbnail.

"She's gone, Pato," said Matt. He meant Cynthia, of course.

"Gone where?"

"To Florida, near Tampa. She left a note saying she wanted to get away from everyone to think."

"Well, don't worry," he had said, patting Matt's arm, "she'll be back. Cynthia's a sensible girl." A faint hope sprang up in him that perhaps Cynthia would not return.

Behind the brothers came her uncle, the Jesuit, assisting her mother across the porch. With her liquid eyes and a wrung handkerchief, the old lady had been waiting all her life for this role.

"I'm afraid something will happen to our Cynthia, Mr. Principato. Please bring her back to us."

"Look, Pato," said Matt, "at least we know where she is. Take my car and find her, O.K.? Bring her back. You can make it to Florida in two days easily."

He pointed to his Oldsmobile under the carport and pulled two hundred dollars out of his wallet. Numbly, Principato took the keys and money, the four pairs of eyes watching.

Then he heard a tapping sound. At his bedroom window, the old man held a sign against the pane while Stella motioned for him to come up. Matt turned to investigate, then ran across the porch and into the house. Brother Jim took Principato's arm.

"You'd better get going, Pato," he said.

Two days later, tired and unshaven, his mind still traveling the endless ribbon of Southern highways, he found her having a drink with the owner of a hotel at which her mother spent a month every winter.

"You took a long time," she said. But in mock triumph. The hotel owner, her mother's friend, was obviously in on the game. He moved over to make room for Principato.

"I want to talk with you, Cynthia," he told her sternly. She had gotten up and led the way to a corner of the lobby.

"Well?"

"We're going to bed together down here or you're taking your brother's car back to Philadelphia alone."

She regarded him for a long minute, eyes spaniel as always, but the rest of her evincing a strange calm. She had a curious way of screwing up the corners of her mouth when she considered something, first one side then the other, as if two warring opinions lived in either cheek. He had seen it all before, of course. Lately, their talk had gotten around to the imminent loss of her virginity. An analytical sort of thing, with heavy medical overtones.

"All right," she answered. Evidently it made sense to her. Effort deserves its reward. You did not send a prospective husband on a down-country love chase and expect him to be satisfied with lollipops at the end.

"Here's the room key. I'm going to need another drink for this. Take a shower."

Later, when she lay beside him, broken and crumpled-looking, as if some life force within her had snapped along with the tautness of her hymen, the telephone rang. It was Cynthia's father. She continued to snore, her mouth open wide.

"I thought you couldn't talk," Principato whispered.

"All right, don't speak to me for the next ten years. How long do you know this outfit? Less than a year, right? This woman's been working for them for twenty years."

"Yeah, but the day after they get around to buryin' that sweet old father of theirs, I'm through," Stella said. "And listen, kiddo, if you ever need a battle-ax to beat this gang off with, just ask them what ever happened to Raymond. All's not so holy in the holy family," she advised him with a bleary wink.

Principato digested the tip about Raymond, storing it somewhere deep inside him, and moped back to his new wife across the ballroom. He was pregnant now with a special sorrow. Like that accompanying the end of a twenty-two-year innocence, perhaps. The old man and Stella had given a quick death to the hope that he would ever learn to love Cynthia. They had put it down to the level of a contest, even provided him with an ace for the time he would need it most.

He watched his father and the Corrigans' drudge cutting up in the midst of a tango and jealously yanked Cynthia to her feet to dance. Her warm, slightly fecal breath flooded into his face. He thought, self-pitying, that she would probably demand he make love to her that very night.

After their honeymoon trip to Europe that lasted all of a harsh cold winter and assured Principato that his marriage was indeed loveless, they returned home to an aging Victorian pile from which the Corrigans had recently evicted some tenants. A singular gift. Huge, as if of itself it might inspire dreams of empire in their new brother-in-law. Instead, it frightened him. Overfurnished, incredibly ugly, it was profaned inside and out with gargoyles and all manner of stained-glass windows. The miles of plumbing connecting four bathrooms hissed and gurgled ceaselessly.

He spent most of his time outside in the beginning. A particular cast of late-afternoon shadows had him seeing fleeting figures at the upstairs windows. Outside was the safety of white light; inside a host of hues from hanging pink and violet lamps that might have done better service before tabernacles or the dim insides of bistros.

In the old days it had belonged to some biscuit king. In the lo

"I can, but I pretend I can't. This way I don't have to argue back. Only Stella knows."

"Why did you call?"

"To warn you, son. Don't marry that bitch of a daughter of mine and get tied up with this family. In a couple of years you'll think your name was always Corrigan. There won't be anything left of the old you except that sallow, woppy complexion of yours. I don't think they can find a way to get rid of that."

"You're crazy. No father ever tried to warn someone away from his daughter for that reason."

"Well, I'm glad I got to be the first one then. Listen, son, get smart. I know what your motive is. It can't be the money. There isn't enough in Philadelphia to buy a husband for that beast. It's pity, isn't it? That's exactly the way they want. . . . They're coming. Good-by!"

Principato put the phone down. It made a loud click and brought Cynthia to life out of her tangle of sheets.

"Again?" she asked timidly. He felt her cold fingers touch his naked leg.

They set the wedding for a Saturday a month off, only to have her father die the night before. The final protest, Principato thought. But that stopped nothing. His wife and sons simply had him embalmed and stored away until they had time for him. The next day they were married by an ancient bishop who had been an auxiliary to Linus before a divided audience of light-skinned Corrigans and sallow Principatos.

But not before the Corrigans got their first real taste of the Defiance. Conspicuously absent beside his henna-haired wife and sister-in-law and shawl-covered mother in their pew, the old man waited outside in his convertible, cigar jammed between his teeth, for his chance to throw confetti and rice. Before the ceremony, the three Corrigan sons had hastened out by turn to implore him to come in. How was it going to look to their family and friends? In the sanctuary, Principato and his best man nervously watched the three conferring with their mother, then saw her leave her seat and stalk down the carpeted center aisle. In a moment, a blare of car horns rolled

into the church. His father was trying to drown out C mother.

The old bishop finally compromised the issue. Glancing in his watch in the sacristy, he asked Principato, "What's the

"My father, I think. He doesn't go inside churches."

The bishop shrugged, then walked down the aisle to the

"Isn't the world going around in the Corrigan orbit t growled loud enough for the whole congregation to hear. better get inside before the victim decides to flee and tha the catch he's already gotten you."

Afterward, at the dismal wedding reception, Stella got stood in a tight little knot of Principatos denouncing her occasionally stopping to dance with Principato's father certain-looking mother. Far across the ballroom, the C took turns dancing with their mother when she was not Lucy in her nun's habit.

"Don't this just pull the rag outta the bush?" Stell poor sweet old bastard of a father of theirs dead and la ice and they're here celebratin' the fertility rites." temptuously on the floor.

"Kiddo, I love you like a son," she said, throwing around Principato's neck. "I know what you're like. V kind of people. I know the sweet pity in you that m that wreck!" she shouted, pointing to Cynthia, wh midst of her eight bridesmaids. "But you're nuts, k lived with this mob for the last twenty years."

"Listen to this woman," his father said. "She k talking about."

"But, Poppa," his mother said, "they had a bish and a couple of priests, and they got another bishc today. We could never do that for any of our daugh to marry off."

"The hell with their bishops and priests again. kid is nuts."

"Listen, Pop, I can't have my father talking to wedding day."

ceilinged attic, where shingle nails punctured the roof and Principato's head too, he found, amid the usual dust-covered junk, a bundle of letters from the biscuit king's mother. Apparently, he too had been afraid of his house. His mother in Cincinnati prescribed leaving the gaslights on all night, or hiring extra servants to do watchman's rounds of the house and stables. In any event, she cautioned him not to lose his sanity, or the neighbors (who seemed to have something on him already) would know for sure. Society is always judging, she said. Principato sat long hours under the cover of shiny roof nails, reading and rereading the letters, his heart swollen with sorrow for the poor, young biscuit king. In the end, he learned from his neighbors, the McGinchy sisters, the king had hanged himself from a stable rafter.

"It was that house, Mr. Principato," they said. The news came as no surprise to him. After it, he took an extreme, fatalistic view toward his own duration therein. At night, lying in bed, he was comforted, cheered even, at his imaginings that all the shiftings and creakings of the old place were the biscuit king and his servants and bakers going about the business of living again.

Along with the house came his watchdog, Mrs. Phillips, a mammoth-busted crony of Cynthia's mother's who had worked for years since her husband's death as a housekeeper for priests in various Philadelphia rectories.

"She's a bargain at three times the price," his mother-in-law informed him conspiratorially, though price meant nothing to Principato, since the Corrigans were paying Phillips's salary anyhow. What bothered him was that her capacity in his Corrigan-owned home was never exactly defined from the first day that she swept haughtily past as he waited at the entrance, and superordered his life with her rigorous schedule of risings, meal times, and laundry days. To Cynthia she was plainly an ideal daytime companion, and his wife spent hours in the kitchen with her listening to all the rectory dirt that Phillips's broad memory encompassed—and that was constantly being supplemented by phone calls from her girl friends in the rectory-housekeepers corps.

Principato himself would, out of simple charity, have declined to call her the watchdog, except that he began listening on the telephone extension to conversations between Phillips and old lady Corrigan, who obviously did not care whether they were overheard or not. In their dialogue, his code name was the Italian.

"The Italian didn't get home from his Holy Name meeting until eleven-thirty last night," Phillips informed her buddy on one occasion. "Marion Kee told me today that the meeting was ended by ten o'clock and her Jack was in by ten-fifteen."

"But I had a flat tire," Principato said in his defense.

"Well, we mustn't be too suspicious," the old lady counseled, oblivious to the flat-tire excuse. "I dare say there's no other woman involved with the likes of our Cynthia to keep him amused."

Which was true in one sense, Principato conceded as he replaced the receiver in its cradle. The first year of their marriage was an endless revelation for him. Cynthia thrived in the great, ugly house with her new husband and friend Phillips, earnestly believing it to be the only kind of house worth living in. He watched mystified as his twenty-six-year-old wife shrugged off her whining nature, straightened out the pitiful bend in her back and added new pounds to her thin frame until she seemed taller and heavier than he. The notion that he was becoming shrunken and diminutive in turn became an obsession. He discovered himself constantly sidling up to her for comparison. He was convinced her arms were longer than his. Her feet were certainly larger. It affronted some part of his maleness that his wife should have longer arms and feet. In bed she became insatiable, leading him down long, strange sexual avenues that seemed to him neither properly Catholic nor even Western.

During the summer of that first year he came to know his in-laws better: a wealthy tribe of shanty Irish who arrived at frequent barbecues in Principato's back yard in a hearse loaded down with kegs of beer. The relationship between mother and sons was uncanny. A delicate old creature, she sat primly near the smoking fireplace, sipping her plum liqueur, while her three boys, red-faced and sweating, drank beer until they became sick, vomiting noisily behind Principato's garage. Their mother and Cynthia went on talking as the brothers curled up in fetal positions on the lawn and went to sleep. Later, with Cynthia, the old lady, and one of their drivers who came especially for the job, Principato helped load the three into the hearse for the trip home, their mother sitting soberly up front with the driver.

When the uncle was transferred from the Midwest to Philadelphia, Principato had an eager hope that the Sunday-afternoon drink fest would be canceled. But nothing changed. He arrived in the trim black Ford from the Jesuit motor pool a half hour after the hearse to sit beside Cynthia and her mother, taking a small, clerical portion of beer while his nephews continued to vomit and pass out on the lawn.

To Principato, it was the uncle, in fact, who became the worst offender. He monopolized them, when the summer barbecue season was ended, at interminable Sunday-afternoon dinners. Then, as always, he was preoccupied with the notion he was going to die. For some reason, he expected to pass away on the morrow. Wished it, perhaps; Principato was never able to make the distinction. He came weekly to pluck at his niece's and Phillips's ready heartstrings, to share with them his last, graying hours. A kind of funereal shroud seemed to descend on the huge, decaying house when he arrived.

One Sunday afternoon, looking outside to where the sun was shining and the two old McGinchy sisters, youthful into their eighties, ran about the lawn playing croquet, Principato decided he could stand it no longer. He ran for his car and headed for Fairmount Park.

There, on a lawn, next to the riverbank, some Negro boys were playing football. Principato went up to them. "Will you let me play with you?"

Most were unwilling. Their lack of acceptance pained him. But one, the leader perhaps, kinder and wiser than the others, sensed his terrible need to play.

"O.K., mista. You on their side."

Side meant nothing to Principato. He could make little distinction. Instead, he ran screaming up and down the field for an hour, joyous in his exultation over living. His lungs burned; his clothes clung sweatily to his body. Finally, someone thrust the ball into his arms and pointed out a direction. Gamely, Principato charged along until the kind-wise leader brought him down with a body block. Lying on the grass, he was filled with heroic agony.

"I think my leg is broken," he said simply.

Kneeling beside him, the leader nodded sagely. Apparently he expected as much. The others sat around him in a ring, exuding much sympathy. A runner was sent for a park policeman. In ten minutes a red ambulance bounced onto the lawn, its driver and interne moving him gently onto a stretcher, then carrying him to the vehicle. Inside, Principato, a nonsmoker, asked for a cigarette. His Negro teammates waved through the ambulance windows. Their kind-wise leader handed him the battered football.

"You was a good player, mista. We wants you to have this football."

Principato accepted gratefully, taking a long, painful drag on the cigarette as he had seen a succession of heroes do on late-show war films. Then the ambulance bounced off toward Philadelphia General Hospital, its siren wailing in the afternoon.

Later, after passing out at the hospital, he awoke gradually to the cold touch of fingers on his eyelids and ears and knew that he was being given last rites. He was not frightened. Some distant part of himself had been waiting for that touch with a special earnestness lately. Only now the distant part seemed to be laughing ironically that perhaps he had beaten the old uncle to the gates. He tried easing his soggy mind back into the pool from which it had come, a happy place filled with laughing Principatos and maidens with properly Catholic and Western sexual preferences. But no good: he was out of it now.

His eyes opened to the six Corrigans and Phillips sitting in a half circle at the end of the bed. Instead of weeping, Cynthia only looked at him curiously. Brother Jim actually frowned. Principato stared at them for a moment, then felt his eyes fill with self-pitying tears.

"I think I want my family," he said, emphasizing the "my" as best he could.

"I think you're going to need them," Cynthia said. "Cripes, are you crazy! Playing football with a bunch of coon kids in the park at your age. I wish I knew what I was getting into when I married you!"

"Cynthia, Cynthia," he countered, the tears flowing down his cheeks, "don't let me explain to you why I married you, O.K.? Do you know what you turned out to be? A saprophyte!" he yelled, proud of remembering the name from some long forgotten biology text. "You put on pounds and get yourself decent-looking for the first time in your life and I start wasting away. Well, now you're ready to grab off some guy on your own. Do you want a divorce? You can have it. All I want to do is go back to South Philly."

Cynthia stood up calmly, and the rest of the Corrigans with her.

"We're Catholics, remember? Catholic people don't get divorced. Never. Never ever." She glared.

"Your marriage is sanctified, Pato. Become the perfect Catholic father and husband," the uncle urged him, then slammed his biretta on his balding head like an exclamation point. At a click from the mother, they turned and walked away.

The tone for his marriage was set: all illusion stripped away. Even when the children began coming with good old-fashioned Catholic fertility.

THREE

One Saturday morning Principato drove far out of the city to the Good Shepherd Home for Paraplegics to see his brother, Rocco, who had been hauled back from Lourdes some weeks before. The first thing he noticed about Rocco—after he beat his way past old and Irish Sister Winifred, with her habitual stern warning against any kind of drama—was that his brother was still not cured. He had plenty of time to reflect on this, sitting across from the eternal invalid still festooned in leg irons and planted firmly in his wheel chair, for Rocco hated him and rarely spoke to him except under extreme provocation. Then he could be counted on to shout the house down: a well-rehearsed litany of abuse for his elder brother, who walked ably under his own power and understood the secret rhythm of making love to a woman. This last was a particularly sticking point with Rocco, age nineteen and waiting, Principato suspected, with a continuous erection in the area of copious cloth where his massive torso tapered off into two spindly legs.

In any event, the result of Rocco's tirade was always the same. In moments the clacking of rosary beads and pounding of stubby-heeled nun's shoes would be heard in the long hallway, and Sister Winifred, Rocco's champion, would burst into the room and begin jostling a vainly protesting Principato toward the entrance, swearing in her sanctimonious old nun's way that he would never be allowed to enter again. And each time, Principato simply resigned himself to her feeble blows and half curses and ended up being finally shoved through the front gate with never a thought to striking her. For, all things considered, how could you hit a nun?

Otherwise, when Rocco was not up to haranguing him—as apparently he had not been that morning—and to show his hatred was still operative, he kept the cold silence and always held audience with Principato in the hallway outside his room and dangerously near the staircase in a way that made him suspect all Rocco wanted from him was a little nudge. But Principato was not a willing dispenser of gratification either. If Rocco would not consider going over the edge himself, then his brother sure as hell would not help him.

The lack of any cure was not, however, a real disappointment. Principato had not expected anything so conclusive as to see a Rocco reborn and playing stand-up center in mockery of the paralytic fraternity zooming around them in a full-court, wheel-chair basketball game in the gym at the end of the hallway. Rather, some naïve and still-Believing Catholic part of himself wished for a change in Rocco —any change—after exposure to that distant center of the hopeful. Anything, he had considered angrily, looking at his brother busily rummaging through his box of Pepsi-Cola bottle tops, to wipe away the sad, anemic smile Rocco used in anybody else's presence to conceal the self-satisfaction of a kid who knew he could liquefy eyes and plunge voices into whispers at the rattle of a leg brace.

The day turned dismal, though, when a boy who had tried a hook shot and missed had been framed for a moment in the doorway of the gym. Principato saw the word form on Rocco's lips before it hurtled down the hall.

"Gunner!"

Delighted, Principato echoed the loud word, then slapped Rocco's arm.

"Hey, kiddo, why don't you play a little basketball with the rest of the boys sometime?"

"Why don't you drop dead, kiddo? Huh?"

Principato absorbed this sting and returned to contemplating the pictures of martyrs hanging in the hallway, some smiling, some anguished, depending on their natures, when he heard the familiar clacking of rosaries and pounding of stubby-heeled nun's shoes from a hallway at right angles to the one in which they sat.

"Now what are ya doin' to that poor child?" Sister Winifred demanded, about to reach for Principato and shove him toward the door.

"Nothing, Sister. We were only cheering the basketball game," Principato said, backing away from her.

"He's right, Sister. He's behaving this time, so far," Rocco offered as a complete surprise to his brother.

"Are ya sure, Rocky?" Winifred begged in her special plaintive brogue, using Marciano's Christian name since she had never quite caught on that Rocco's name was Rocco and not Rocky. "Are ya sure he hasn't threatened ya with harm if ya was to tell me?"

"Yes, Sister, he's been good. Really."

"Well, it'll certainly be a change for him. Because he hasn't been good on some past occasions that we can remember, has he, Rocky?"

"No, Sister, he hasn't," Rocco agreed sadly as Winifred turned to go. She took a few steps—Principato ground his fury with his teeth—then turned around.

"Did ya see the postcard your poor dear brother sent me from the shrine at Lourdes?"

"I guess I haven't, if he sent it to you."

"Well, I don't know if I should show it to you, then, if you're gonna be so smart."

"Please show it to him, Sister," Rocco said, "because I didn't send him one and I want him to see what he missed."

"Well, all right," she said, reaching somewhere deep inside her habit. "But don't get it dirty, mind ya."

Principato took the proffered card, being elaborately careful to hold it on the edges and not soil it, and saw an aerial view of the Lourdes basilica on one side. He read the writing on the reverse:

Dear Sister Winifred,
    Today a man across from me got a very strange look in his eyes, unbuckled his leg braces, and stood up from his wheel chair. I think it was a miracle. I wish it could have been me.
                                            Your friend,
                                            Rocky Principato

36

"Did ya see what he wrote me?" Winifred said. "The child saw a real miracle at the shrine."

"Did he really stand up?" Principato asked, the still-Believing Catholic part of himself hungry and rushing to the bait.

"Yes, he really did," Rocco said. Just then a buzzer called Winifred away, and she snatched at the post card and scurried down the hall.

"But listen, Rocco, what happened after the guy stood up?" Principato asked.

"He fell flat on his ass. What do you think happened?" Rocco laughed so hard that he shook all through his heavy torso and into his spindly legs. Principato resisted the urge to break him in two at the junction of those two anomalies.

"I don't suppose you got any feeling like that, you sarcastic bastard?"

"Do I look like the kind that wants to fall flat on my ass?"

"You probably spent the whole three weeks laughing."

"Only some of the time. For the rest I sat in a line of paraplegics and played cassino with Mother while Aunt Lucrezia prayed, or with Lucrezia while Mother prayed."

"I guess you didn't condescend to talk with anybody? To ask anybody else why he had come there?"

"Yeah, I did. I spent about ten days talking with a kid from Germany in the next wheel chair when they left us alone, and we both decided we wanted to stay in our chairs for the rest of our lives. If you think I have it good with Mother and Lucrezia to take care of me and Pop footing the bills, you should've seen this kid. He had about ten people with him."

"Boy, I've heard it all. There goes a few thousand smackers down the drain."

"What the hell were you expecting for your money, a new race horse? I didn't ask to go on that little trip. Mother and loony Lucrezia whizzed in here one Saturday and told me they were taking me to Lourdes in a week. What am I supposed to say from the helplessness of my wheel chair?"

"Helplessness, my ass! Why didn't you just say no?"

"And spoil their pleasure in taking me to that circus over there?"

37

"You've spoiled everybody's pleasure plenty of times before. What stopped you now?"

"I needed the vacation," Rocco answered, then turned casually and dumped his box of Pepsi caps on Good Shepherd's gleaming tile floor. Principato stared at the disarray of tricolored buttons that he had always supposed his brother was saving by the boxful in case the world's monetary standard were arbitrarily shifted from gold to Pepsi caps.

"Somebody's going to have to clean that up before we leave, or Winifred will make sure you don't get in here again," Rocco said after a time.

In a moment Principato was on the floor, anguished in the perfect company of the hallway's collection of anguished martyrs, scooping the mess back into the box. He looked up at the scornful invalid.

"Tell me one thing, Rocco. Why do you think you hate me so much?"

"You couldn't guess with those two legs to walk with and a wife to throw into the rack every night?"

"So that's it."

"I guess it is."

"What do I do to overcome the debt?"

"You really want to know?" Rocco asked, leaning toward him so that Principato feared the wheel chair might fall forward.

"Yes."

"Get me a woman."

"You're joking," Principato said.

"You think there's no woman in the world who would make it with a paraplegic? Farragan in the next room has a book with ladies who even do it in boots and with whips and chains, too. I'll show it to you." He propelled himself quickly down the hall to Farragan's room, while Principato, still on his knees, wondered where, indeed, such a woman might be found: a dispenser of favors to paraplegics in leg braces of steel and leather that Rocco predictably equated with a perversion. Not that he doubted the existence of such a woman, but as for contacting one . . .

"Here it is. This one puts your foot into that thing and crunches your toes if you want her to," Rocco said excitedly, handing Principato a black-bound directory of Hamburg prostitutes wherein booted and belted hags with often-repeated names like Madame X or Lady Pain flailed and crunched and stomped along for fifty pages.

"You shouldn't have a book like this," Principato said.

"It's not mine. It's Farragan's."

"I ought to give it to Winifred. She'd fix you guys pretty fast."

"Don't be stupid. She'd never believe you. We'd have her convinced you brought it in to get us in trouble."

"Where did Farragan get it?"

"His brother brought it back from the service in Germany."

"He's lucky he didn't get caught then."

"They're slick in that family. Not like some families I know. Now, have you decided if you're going to get my woman or not?"

"What am I supposed to do? Put an ad in the paper?"

"Make up your mind. And if it's no, then I don't want you to come here and see me again. Ever. This is the only thing I ever remember asking you to do for me."

"All right, I'll try. I promise," Principato said as he got up to leave. But, my God, the task! he thought, feeling it was somehow unclean. Behind him, Rocco leafed intently through Farragan's book of perversions.

On the first floor, near the entrance in front of the reception desk, old Winifred was waiting for him.

"Well, did ya manage to have some screamin' with that poor child after I left so that I'll have to go up and calm him down?"

"Sorry to disappoint you, Sister, but he seems reasonably calm on his own."

"Well, it's a wonder. Ya should've seen him in the past when ya had your drama with him. Weepin' and cryin' so I had to hold his poor head in my arms to make him stop."

"I'm sure he won't be crying any more, Sister. He seems to have gotten a new goal since the Lourdes trip."

"Well, perhaps," she agreed, suddenly warming. "And who wouldn't after seein' the miracle like he did? It'd be enough to give anybody some hope who was confined to their chair like poor, dear Rocky is all these years."

"Uh, Sister, if you could stand just a little criticism . . ."

"What kind of criticism?"

"Well, I don't think you should baby him as much as you do. After all, he's nineteen now."

"Yes, he is. And for how many of those nineteen years have you been taking care of him? I'm the one who knows what he needs. Not you or your mother or anybody in your family."

"Well, that's not the point . . ."

"What's the point?" she asked angrily, grabbing Principato by one arm and grinding her heel into the toe of his shoe.

"Sister, Sister, stop it, please. There's no need to do this!"

"I'll stop when I'm good and ready! And don't ya dare think of raisin' your hand against me!"

"Ow, I wouldn't hit a nun, Sister."

"Well, that's good to hear," she said, releasing him with a rude shove. "No matter how bad ya seem to me at times, I can see ya had a good Catholic upbringin' at least. Now, get out of here and telephone me to see if it's all right before ya ever dare come back here again."

Then, laughing for the first time Principato had ever seen, she walked quickly along the hall toward the elevator while he held onto the reception desk and hopped and moaned on his one good foot.

After his father's revelation, Principato began telephoning him daily at the coffin factory. Long, conversationless calls sustained by his father's wheezing breath on one end and the son's desperate effort to find something to say on the other. Usually though, nothing came out. Each time, for the mere sake of hearing words, Principato was tempted to tell his father about Rocco's request for a woman, but he kept silent, unable to recall a single precedent that would determine how the old man would react. Simply, he decided, he needed no shouting from the other end of the line, and contented himself with sitting and gripping the receiver, and listening to the incessant tapping of hammer and chisel etching out the names and

40

dates of the newly dead in the workroom outside his father's cubby-hole office, just as the old man must be listening to the clack of type-writers behind his son at the Holy Family House for the Protection and Care of Unwed Mothers. At the end of ten or fifteen minutes at most, they hung up with a series of grunts, Principato instantly sad-dened anew at his failure.

Once his father had started to say something, then his voice fell away to a hoarse whisper, and Principato thought of the cancer and wondered, despite the doctor's prediction, if it were an instant killer like a heart attack that could roll a man out of his chair dead onto the floor while his son waited for a response on the other end of the tele-phone. The notion had terrified him and he had shouted, "Pop! Pop!" into the receiver so that others in his office had turned to look at him. But his father had barked back, "What the hell's the matter with you?" in a clear voice, ending with, "Idiot!" and a loud click in his son's ear.

The calls ended though, the day he remembered to tell the old man about the visit of the Corrigan mob to the house and how he had recourse to pull Raymond out of the closet.

"Good boy! You got the Defiance in you, all right. Put it to those bastards every chance you get. Old Stella really knew what she was talking about years ago when she told you not to forget Raymond. I wonder what that guy did anyhow."

Principato pictured his father with his forehead wrinkled in con-sternation at the mystery. He had a surprise quality like bitchiness that would puzzle excessively over Raymond's deed.

"I still don't know," Principato said. "The uncle was about to tell me when the rest of them shut him up."

"Maybe he took off with some little black chicken over there in Af-rica," his father speculated. "Or maybe he sold the gold altarpieces from his church. That sounds like something those Corrigans would do. That's right down their alley, all right. Yeah, I got it all now. He sold the altar stuff and took off with the black chicken."

"Where do you think he went?" Principato asked, laughing.

"How do I know? Maybe France. Your mama told me she saw a lot of mixing over there when she was at Lourdes, and nobody cared too much. She probably walked right past Raymond and his girl and didn't even know it."

"Lucky she didn't know it."

"Yeah, lucky for him," the old man answered. But that was all he said.

Then there was the usual silence for minutes, the clack of typewriters and the tap of hammer and chisel streaming over the wires toward each other.

"By the way," the father said, "Nick Malatesta's home. He was over at the house yesterday to say hello. He wants you to come see him."

"Huh, that gigolo! Back from the wars. What's he doing now?"

"He's running an amusement park in Jersey someplace. Your mama's got the address."

"An amusement park?"

"That's what he said. Why don't you go and talk with him for a while, kid, and give your old man a rest. If this whore of a cancer decides to dry up and go away, I'll telephone you first before anybody. I promise," he said, putting the phone down so gently that Principato seemed to hear the tapping still.

But it was a Sunday, a full month after his father relayed the word about Malatesta, that Principato got around to seeing him. Not that he had not considered it sooner. It was simply that all of Principato's thoughts about Nick were two-headed monsters that made for indecisiveness and delay. One perpetually, righteously screaming that he wasn't worth the effort and let him go to hell; the second, a dark, scheming curiosity, anxious to know how far the decline of his friend the gigolo, to whom he had once held open limitless possibilities for success, had progressed. Being a Principato, bitchy son of his bitchy father, the second had the victory from the very beginning. But not without a fight. Up to the last minute he tried hard at putting obstacles in the inevitable pathway.

After dinner that Sunday he went into his back yard and began swinging a listless golf club at a Wiffle ball. Then he stretched out on the living-room sofa in front of the TV set. On the screen fat, undoubtedly precocious little girls tap danced artlessly in a children's review, all staring at the camera eye. Silently he thanked heaven that Cynthia had been spared the mentality of aggressive mothers who thrust their children into dance studios and piano lessons from infancy.

Otherwise, he reflected, he rarely had reason to thank her for anything. She sat now in the kitchen with Phillips and the Jesuit uncle, their low conversation covering the harsh approaches to salvation. The priest spoke slowly of death. Ironic, thought Principato, and the tears of frustration sprang to his eyes: eleven years after the wedding and the old bastard was still weaving his shroud. He decided in that instant that the priest was never going to die. He would live forever, become a symbol of Catholic Christian immortality that the Jesuits would exhibit each time a new pope was installed, the way they brought out the Civil War veterans and Indian chiefs for the Presidential inaugurations in Washington.

Principato listened and heard his father and the urn brought into the discussion, with Cynthia's occasional hot bursts of anger. Then he got up from the couch, flicked off the set and pushed through the door.

"I'm going over to Jersey to see Nick Malatesta."

"Isn't he the one who broke up the assembly out at school that time?" the uncle asked.

"Yes, that's the one."

"I'm really surprised you would continue to maintain a relationship with someone like that, Pato. I wasn't aware of this." A look of dismay passed between the priest and his niece. Incredible: she had never even met Malatesta. She knew of him only from her uncle and brother Jim.

"I think I'll take Terrance, Sean, and Noreen along for company."

"I don't know . . ." Cynthia looked to her uncle.

"What Cynthia means, Pato, is that she's a little worried about that car of yours."

"What's wrong with that car of mine?"

"Well, after all, it is eleven years old."

"My father gave me that car for a wedding present."

"We know that, Pato. He gave it to you when Cynthia's family gave you this house. Yes, we remember exactly how it was."

"Listen, Cynthia," he said, "are you going to let me take the children or not?"

"Oh, all right. But for God's sake be careful in that old wreck, will you? They're out in the back yard."

He pushed through the screen door onto the back porch, suddenly realizing that with the almost separate ways of their lives, Cynthia had not been in his car in years. Usually she left the house by cab or in one of the limousines her brothers sent around at her request when business was slack.

His three eldest children were sitting under a tree beyond the garage. As always, they preferred the shade. A choice that grieved their father, who believed fervently in the curative powers of the sun; as babies, if they were put out on the lawn, they would crawl away into a shadow, as if their sallow skins and strange russet-colored hair had marked them out to be some special breed of night people. Groping in the dark for a hallway light switch, he often found them walking easily about, their blue liquid eyes glowing in the darkness. Occasionally, he even thought of them as moles.

Principato prayed they would be receptive to the idea of going over to Jersey.

"Hey, who wants to go to an amusement park this afternoon?"

No answer. The three looked at their father without enthusiasm. He wondered what the hell it took to get them moving. Once, at the invitation of a man he met in the subway, Principato had taken Terrance, age ten, to a Cub Scout meeting. Little boys in blue uniforms and yellow kerchiefs had leapt and screamed their delight over a potato-sack race. Terrance had sat watching silently, then demanded that Principato take him home. Now he began to stir. "Will there be shade or is it in the open?"

"Oh no, there's plenty of shade," he said, lying. "Everything is covered." Their lonely father wanted very much for them to go with him. Perhaps they would even talk with him.

"O.K., we'll go. But there'd better be shade."

He loaded his sallow-skinned, russet-haired children into the old De Soto, waiting patiently while their mother ran from the house to whisper something to Terrance, who passed it to eight-year-old Sean, who passed it to seven-year-old Noreen. Then he released the brake and started the car rolling gently forward down the driveway. He threw it into second and popped the clutch. Faithfully, the engine caught and gave out a cloud of dark smoke.

Driving slowly through the quiet suburbs, he considered dimly what his neighbors might be up to. There were no children anywhere. No dogs, no sidewalk strollers, no cars in the driveways even. Only the dumb sentinel of an overgrown maple standing hugely before each home seemed to have life in it: thousands of sparrows inhabited each tree, making the sidewalks beneath gray with their droppings.

Cattily he suspected they might all be over in civilized Jersey. Sneaking thirstily away from Pennsylvania, panting under the cross of its Sunday Blue Laws, to pour alcohol into themselves and revenue into the coffers of that already fat little state. None of it made any sense to Principato, who admittedly understood little of politics. Yet he sincerely wished the governor in Harrisburg and all his legislators well, even to the extent of occasionally including them in a formula prayer in his special intention when he lit a candle before mass: Lift the scales from their eyes, O Lord, and cause them to put all those patronage jobs under Civil Service. Amen.

He left the Expressway at City Line, opting to drive the twisting road through the park, instead of the superhighway that would land him easily on Vine Street near the Franklin Bridge. Close by, on the river, Penn oarsmen were streaking upstream in a long shell. The fronts of the boathouses were ganged with sports cars and madras clothes. The familiar curiosity arose in Principato to know something of these young people who went idly off to college in sports cars. As always, when he passed here, he was tempted to stop and introduce himself. The image of himself standing in a circle of madras girls with sleek little asses and grabbing sly handfuls delighted Principato. Somehow, he imagined, from the very brightness of their clothes, his jaundiced skin and stooped posture would be instantly transformed.

The traffic eased past the museum into the Franklin Parkway, then Logan Circle, where, in front of the cathedral, a delegation of Negro women in great hats was alighting from a line of cars. Out of the corner of his eye, Principato saw Terrance sit bolt upright.

"Are they Catholics?" the boy asked, real astonishment in his voice. Principato stiffened. Have I ever taught my children a prejudice? he asked himself. He looked at the three in the rearview mirror. They had already taken refuge in a kind of "we-they" mentality. The first promptings had not come from the wind, obviously. They were home all day with their mother and Phillips, a veritable sludge bucket of opinions.

"Yes, they are Catholics," he said.

"I didn't know colored people were Catholics. I thought they were Protestants."

"No, some are Catholics."

"How come there are never any in our church?"

"Well, no Negroes live out where we live."

"Why?"

"I don't know."

"Principato . . . ?"

"Yes, Noreen?"

"Who's this guy we're going to see?"

"He's the guy who broke up the assembly when Principato was in college," Terrance informed her. "And Uncle Jim punched him because he tried to make a revolution against the Jesuits."

"Who told you that?" Principato asked.

"Father-uncle and Mother talk about it a lot. Father-uncle said he tried to save his soul because Malatesta had a bad girl friend, and that he deserved the punch Uncle Jim gave him since he wouldn't let Father-uncle save him."

"What else did Father-uncle say?" Principato demanded testily.

"He said that you and some Jewish guy were his only friends, and that you were probably lucky Uncle Jim didn't punch you, too."

"That's not true. I had nothing to do with it, Terrance. I was only one of the crowd at the assembly," Principato said in vain protest.

"Father-uncle doesn't think so. You and the Jewish guy were Malatesta's roommates. He says you had to know what was going on, and your duty was to go to the dean and tell him what Malatesta was going to do."

46

"Yeah," said Noreen, "and Mother told us not to talk with this man today, because he had a bad girl friend."

"That's right," Sean said. "Her name was Magdalene."

"That's right," echoed Principato, thinking that if Malatesta's letters from Europe were to be believed, he had had about a dozen Magdalenes since the one the old Jesuit remembered. Then he tromped down on the accelerator and raced the car onto the Ben Franklin Bridge faster than the speed limit allowed and the old hulk was meant to go. Fleeing across the Delaware from Philadelphia toward the Camden ugliness and the symbolic freedom that lay beyond: no Corrigan lived on that side of the river.

In the beginning of their freshman year at Gonzola, three had been assigned to what was actually a two-man room. When Principato entered, carrying his luggage with the aid of his father, Malatesta and Mermelstein, the other two, were already there. The former sat on a bed with a sleek, fortyish-looking brunette whom Principato knew was no relative of Malatesta's since the boys had attended a Catholic high school together in Philadelphia before Nick's mother sent him off on a windup tour of highly corrective military academies. The woman lazed back on the bed with one leg almost fully extended. With all the impressions he had from innumerable films, Principato fully expected her to purr. From their rapt gazes, it seemed Mermelstein and his henna-haired mother sitting on another bed, may have expected the same.

"Hello, Mr. Principato," Nick greeted them, getting up and shaking hands with the old man, whom he had met previously.

"How are you, Nick? Who's this? Your aunt?"

"No sir, this is my girl friend."

"Slick. Pretty slick," the old man acknowledged, looking at the woman as if she were on an auction block. "This one," he pointed to his son as he addressed Mermelstein's mother, "doesn't have the fuzz burned off his ears yet and they put him in with an operator."

"They have to learn what it's all about sometime, I guess," she answered. "I just wish they had let me get in and out of here before the lesson started. A mother could have nightmares about things like this back at home."

"What do you think? That I come with the college like a course?" the woman said. "Your two little boys don't have a thing to worry about, believe me. This is the one for me." She caressed the side of Nick's handsome face.

Mermelstein spoke for the first time. "I don't want you guys to think I came to a Catholic school just because I couldn't get into a good university."

"It's true," his mother said. "He always wanted to come to a Catholic school. He's been talking about it for years."

"He'll fit in fine, just fine," Principato's father said, then he turned to Malatesta's woman. "Hey, miss, where do you live? here in town?"

"My name is Terry, and yes, I have an apartment in the city. I work as a travel agent."

"That's nice," he congratulated Malatesta. "You've got a good thing going here with this lady. Hang on to her and don't mess it up, kid. Little study, little girl, little beer, moderation in everything, then you won't have the liver and the kidney and the ulcer off and on like me." He belched. Even then he had the tripart malady.

"I don't mind if the boys come over now and then for a bit of home cooking," Terry offered. "If I had to eat every day like we had at lunch today down in the cafeteria, I'd be dead in a week."

"Isn't she nice?" Mermelstein's mother suddenly said. "And here I thought I was going straight home to write a letter to the dean about her."

Mermelstein's mother may have forborne from writing her letter, but Principato later suspected that it was Mermelstein who, from a growing jealousy, tipped off "Sleepy" Corrigan, their dorm proctor that year, for Cynthia's uncle could never have been expected to make the discovery on his own. With typical Corrigan single-mindedness, he began cornering Malatesta in week-night visits to their room to denounce his attachment to the woman he persisted in calling Magdalene, as if he failed to appreciate that Mary Magdalene had long since been given Church clearance.

"You can't parade that Magdalene about this campus in mockery of its sainted intention!" he ranted, for Malatesta often met with the fortyish Terry in the dorm lounge and ate with her in the student union.

48

As the weeks progressed, so did the level of elocution.

"You slander your precious manhood in becoming a slave to the charms of that heinous trollop!" the harangue continued at Malatesta and his Magdalene, completely ignoring the presence of Principato and Mermelstein in the room.

"I shall be taking you before the disciplinary council with a recommendation for expulsion," the priest informed Nick sadly one night. When he left the room, Mermelstein broke the silence. "I'd protest his infringement on what I call a strictly personal matter."

In short hours, it seemed to Principato, the dormitory grapevine had gathered the protest group, a collection of seedy fringe cases who began congregating in their room to plot and conspire. For the most part, they were perennially failing and anticlerical and seemed willing enough to accept the handsome, charismatic, Malatesta as their leader.

A petition was circulated to protest the proposed appearance of Nick before the disciplinary council. Two thousand signatures were easily gathered and the petition was forwarded to the university president, whose secretary returned a polite note to Malatesta stating that the petition had been pleasurably received and would be given due consideration in the near future.

But, the letdown unnerved Mermelstein, who kept pressing for some small token violence, although, even as the confessed son of former anarchists, he had no idea where to proceed next. The seedy fringe cases were equally at a loss and considered it best to wait on further word from the president's office. Mermelstein countered that the uneasy waiting game was a cornerstone of famed Jesuit diplomacy and he demanded that they unsettle the administration with a surprise rebellious act. The issue smoldered until Principato unwittingly helped it to a head.

Ashen with fear, he walked into their room one night after dinner. "I need help."

"What?"

"I think I have the clap."

"Oh." There was a kind of reverent silence in the room. Then Mermelstein put on a jacket, sighing wearily as if he had spent half his young life leading clap cases to a secret clinic for the cure. They drove in his convertible, Principato weeping quietly, to an obscure brick development where a cousin of Mermelstein's had his doctor's office. Inside, amid a profusion of chromium fixtures and antiseptic smells, Principato forced a urine sample through his pain.

In a little while the cousin came back from his analysis. "Not clap exactly, but like it," he said simply, then gave Principato a buttocks injection of penicillin while Mermelstein and Malatesta looked on.

"He'll be O.K. in a couple of days," the doctor said to his cousin as Principato heisted his pants.

"By the way, how's your mother?"

"Good."

"And the father?"

"Good."

"And the sister, Nancy?"

"Good."

Mermelstein put on his jacket to leave.

"The fee's ten bucks."

"Ten bucks? For what?"

"Analysis and penicillin. That stuff doesn't grow on trees, you know."

"No, just nearly, though. Keep your money," he said to Principato. "This is my treat."

Outside in the cold darkness Mermelstein picked up a clod of frozen earth and threw it against the house. It shattered into a flurry of small chips.

"They're all out to screw me, even my own relatives! Cheap bastard!"

The screen door suddenly flew open with a rattle of its retarding chain. The cousin appeared on the front porch, shaking his fist.

"What'd you do that for? I've got to make a living too!"

Enraged, Mermelstein had picked up another clod to throw. But not before Malatesta had put a rock through a huge picture window. Tinkling slivers of glass rained onto the sidewalk in front.

"How's that for a rebellious act?" said Malatesta, his head flung back in a kind of exultation.

There was a long silence, broken only by the creak of a tree bending in the wind. A neutral Principato watched Mermelstein turn slowly toward Malatesta. The look on the former's face frightened him, caused him to move away a few yards.

"What kind of rebellious act was that? In my opinion that was plainly anti-Semitic," Mermelstein said. Then he lunged at Malatesta, who sidestepped, pleading, "Not my face! Don't hit the face!" then tripped Mermelstein to the ground. Principato and the doctor cousin looked on while Malatesta labored gleefully over Mermelstein's face and head with his thick right hand on which he wore two blunt, heavy rings. Then he pulled Mermelstein to his feet.

"I said that was a rebellious act!"

"Anti-Semitic," countered Mermelstein. There were tears in his eyes. Blood flowed down his chin from a cracked lip.

"I dismiss it as elementary vandalism," offered the cousin. "What do you think?" he asked Principato.

"I'm not sure," he answered. "It could be one or it could be the other." Then he was instantly shamed when he saw the doctor's young wife stuffing the jagged hole with a blanket.

"Come inside and we'll talk this out," the doctor said. "We can all use a cup of coffee."

At the kitchen table, Mermelstein wrote an impassioned speech extolling personal freedoms in the face of Authoritarian Mother, the Church, that he goaded Malatesta into promising to deliver from the audience at the next student assembly. Plans were made for the inclusion of a professional photographer who would take a series of shots to blackmail Father McGonigle, the university president, whom they were all hoping might race down from the stage to punch Malatesta. Mermelstein and Principato were relegated to the initial, important task of erupting into anti-Jesuit catcalls and hisses when the riot broke loose. Afterward, they would lead the doubtless sympathetic, larger element of the student body in wrecking the assembly hall and library.

Mermelstein speculated that, since it was to be a sports assembly, the athletic teams might remain faithful to the Jesuits. But Malatesta quieted his fears with stories of the three teams' dissatisfaction with the athletic department. They would be in the first rush, he promised. Then the three left the doctor's home early in the morning, in arms-linked camaraderie of anticlerical revolutionaries.

51

The riot turned out to be a fizzle, though. Nick, for courage, began drinking after breakfast, and by two p.m. had to be helped into the assembly hall with his bull horn. On stage, Father McGonigle stood in his awesome thinness, his long right arm awkwardly jabbing at the illusion of a thousand defeated enemies to come. Jim Corrigan, football team captain that year, sat large and dumb-looking on the stage behind the president. Then in his senior year, he was a hero of such epic proportions that he had no idea who Principato, his future brother-in-law, even was.

In a lull, after a dutiful cheer, Malatesta stood up in the audience, the bull horn clasped in his hands.

"Hey, McGonigle, you black-robed simpleton!"

The words slurred loudly through the hall. After them, a kind of tittering laughter arose. Confused, Principato and Mermelstein, who were sitting together, refrained from making their anti-Jesuit catcalls and hisses.

"Hey, Mac, they ought to put you in a uniform next year!" Nick laughed through the horn, delighted at his own sudden wit. On stage, McGonigle's arm fell to his side as if he had been shot. His face was shocked; no voice came forth.

In the audience, the conspirators look at one another perplexed. None of this was the impassioned speech extolling personal freedoms that Malatesta had rehearsed for days. Still, it seemed not to matter so much. The student body was in chaos, laughing and clapping for more. On stage was another kind of bedlam. Jim Corrigan had turned reactionary. McGonigle and the athletic director held him from rushing down and murdering Malatesta.

Then the arch stroke. Nick stood high on a chair and surveyed the audience, supremely contemptuous. He mocked into the bull horn, "You are all a herd of shitty sheep!" The laughter died away abruptly and a low, angry rumble took its place.

"Keep your eye on this," said Mermelstein to Principato. "Nobody craves a mirror flashed in front of him like that." They watched as Malatesta suddenly had the chair yanked out from under him, then disappeared into a hail of fists, pleading, "Not the face! Don't touch the face!"

Loyola was a soldier. After him, the Jesuits became diplomats.

Now, considering the moment proper, they released captive Jim Corrigan, who hurtled from the stage into the center of the fray with an animal scream and disregarded Malatesta's plea about not assailing his face. Then for a minute, with a kind of hurt dignity common to social workers and other flagellants, they watched Nick get the hell pounded out of him. A day later Malatesta was axed.

"He's finished," said Mermelstein. "Now maybe we can get some work done around this damn place. Let's put his bed out in the hallway."

Later in the day they drove a stiff and pain-racked Malatesta to the airport. He was covered with cuts and welts, his lips cracked and swollen and one eye blackened as a testimony to Jim Corrigan's defense of the faith.

"Good-by, you guys. I'm off to Europe if I can beat the Army."

"Good-by," said Principato.

"Good-by," said Mermelstein.

At the dorms again, Mermelstein, unaware that Principato was within hearing range, phoned the doctor cousin.

"It worked out better than I hoped. Instead of the speech I wrote for him, he shot off his mouth and a gang of guys beat him up right in the assembly hall. It's going to be quiet around here now. The kid with the clap is O.K. You just have to get rid of the charismatic types."

Then he hung up. Principato, pretending not to have heard, was saddened at the revelation that he had been only a pawn in a second and certainly more skillful conspiracy.

In Jersey, after Cherry Hill and the quick succession of terrifying circles, he urged the De Soto along an unfamiliar highway. Long and straight and lightly traveled, it passed for miles through a sea of three-foot scrub pines that grew right to the road's edge—an evil sort of woods, with roots like tentacles encroaching upon the concrete ribbon. He guessed that a great fire had swept through the original stand like a tidal wave. Now the only break in the level new expanse was Malatesta's amusement park. Principato was shocked at the sight of it. He sensed immediately, even from a distance, that it was in tatters, the broken-down remnant of tired old carnival equipment. The location was strangely unreal: like coming upon an empty circus unexpectedly in a cornfield or the middle of a steppe. Then, suddenly, with relief, he saw it all as a great laugh. Typical of the old joker in Nick to stick his park here, stark and forlorn, and pipe the standard variety of merry-go-round music hauntingly into the wind. Calculated to draw the symbolists in for a fleecing. Well, Principato the Catholic was no less a symbolist than any other man, he thought, as he turned off the road.

"There's no shade. You said there would be shade," began Terrance.

It was true. Before them, a miniature coaster and airplane rides and tiny wooden horses straining their traces before tiny wooden carriages all sat baking in the sun.

"Well, listen, a little sun isn't going to kill you for an hour."

"I don't care. I'm not getting out of this car."

"Me either," said Sean.

"Me either," said Noreen. "And don't bring that man over here to see us."

"Knowing as much as he does about your mother, he may not want to come and see you. I don't think you have anything to worry about." He opened the car door. Then he stopped at the sight of a tall, erect woman riding in a kind of Toonerville Trolley beyond the miniature coaster. Dear Lord! He was unable to believe in the possibility of such a coincidence. It was Jedda McMahnus, his supervisor from the office. Her impeccably clean VW was parked at the other end of the lot.

"Shh," he warned his children. "Stay quiet for a minute. There's a woman I know out there and I don't want her to see me."

"Who is it?"

"Miss McMahnus, my supervisor." Poor McMahnus. Who lives alone. The truth will out. Tomorrow McMahnus will sit down at their conference and begin, "What a lovely day I had yesterday," and launch into a ten-minute tale about the tea she attended with her girl friends or her visit to the seashore with the gentleman of irreproachable good intentions. After eleven years of alternating her girl friends and the irreproachable gentleman for his benefit at Monday-morning conferences, Principato would weep for the embarrassment it might cause McMahnus if she were to see him here.

A boy emerged from an old house trailer at one end of the oiled down lot and walked toward the control box for the trolley. It stopped abruptly and McMahnus clambered out, rumpled the boy's hair and started her VW. Principato stretched quickly out on the seat as the supervisor moved past in a high-pitched whirring of gears, counting on her poor eyesight not to recognize his car. When he sat up again, the boy was walking toward him, his sneakers squeaking on the oiled ground.

"Good afternoon, sir."

"Good afternoon. Is Nick Malatesta around?"

"Yes, he is. Are you Mr. Principato?"

"Yes, I am."

"He said you might come and see him. I've been watching for you for more than a month. He doesn't have too many friends, so I guessed it might be you when you asked for him by name."

Principato regarded the boy for a long minute. Behind him, in the back seat, he sensed Terrance stirring to life at the threat of competition. The kid outside was handsome, but not that bland, tow-headed cuteness of young boys that turned suddenly mediocre in their late teens when their hair became darker. The thin face and intelligent eyes of this one would ward off that risk. His diction was perfect, Principato noted, not the usual lazy jargon of a kid. Certainly, this must be Malatesta's son of fabled genius. His mother was the Gonzola Magdalene.

"How old are you, Jon?"

The kid seemed startled that Principato knew his name. "I'm fourteen, sir."

"My son Terrance is ten." Principato jerked a thumb back at Terrance, who was cringing again in a shaded corner of the car. Then he stifled the urge to reach back and smash him.

"Where's your father?" he asked, getting out of the car.

"He's in the trailer sleeping off a hangover. Eva brought him home from a party in Philadelphia at about three this morning and he just fell into bed. He'll probably wake up at five o'clock or so."

"Who's Eva?" Principato asked. They were walking across the lot

55

toward the trailer. The scrappy ends of old newspapers and candy wrappers swept past their feet in the breeze. Horseflies buzzed around their heads. Principato sniffed the odor of hot grease from the rides and a garbage dump not far enough from the trailer.

"Eva is Father's new girl friend," the boy answered. Then he opened the screen door of the trailer and held it back for Principato.

Inside, in a tiny, hot compartment, Nick, whom he had not seen in years, lay huge and disheveled on a bed. Sweat oozed from his face and coursed down the thick folds of skin around his neck, soaking the pillow. His chest heaved slowly up and down to the accompaniment of a ragged snore, and a sly dribble crept from one corner of his mouth over a crust of what must have been last night's vomiting. A pointy-toed, un-American-looking loafer clung to his left foot; the other foot was clad only in a black sock.

"Poor guy," the kid said, as if he could read Principato's thoughts, "he's really over the hill now. Just look at him. There won't be too many more women with all that fat. Did you ever see this picture of him?" he asked, digging in his wallet for a frayed photograph of Nick taken during his first year in Europe.

"Yes," Principato said. "Giulietta, your grandmother, showed it to me years ago."

"He was twenty then. I wonder if I'll ever look like this when I'm twenty." The ragged condition of the picture told Principato it had been studied at great length. He watched as the boy unabashedly picked up a hand mirror and considered his own features in contrast.

"Does he do this often?" Principato asked.

"Yes, pretty often. He's got an awful conscience for a gigolo," the boy said matter-of-factly. "You'd think, after fourteen years of trying to get by without working, he'd have everything straightened out by now. But, from what Mother tells me, Catholics make the worst gigolos. Their guilt complexes are something terrible. When they get the chance at the brass ring, they always muff it."

"Well, I'm not so sure it's all that bad," Principato said, chuckling at the serious analysis. "But you're not a Catholic, huh?"

"No, I'm currently unaffiliated."

"Oh."

"Do you want a beer, sir?"

"Thank you, yes."

Nick's unaffiliated son opened the refrigerator and removed a can from a six-pack. Principato sat on a second bed, and the boy returned with two glasses.

"Father always lets me take a little," he explained, pouring a full glass for Principato and half for himself.

"How long have you been here, Jon?" Principato asked. The kid looked to him as if he had just settled down to a life of being shipwrecked. He wore a faded blue pullover, and frayed Bermudas that had obviously been cut from a pair of jeans. His sneakers were ragged and dirty.

"About three months now. Mother agreed to let me come east for the summer to make a study of Nick's decline from his old albums. She's afraid I'll consider gigoloism romantic and try to imitate my father. My time isn't that far off, you know. I'm fourteen now."

"Well, when were you planning to enter the field?"

"I thought I might give it a try when I'm about eighteen. From what I've learned, I can certainly capitalize on my father's mistakes and turn the venture to a profit."

"Has Nick been that complete a failure?" Principato asked. Some vague prompting like loyalty to Nick crept out to spit at this kid.

"Oh well, it's been up and down, but mostly down. He's done the whole circuit," the boy said knowledgeably, "Cannes, Biarritz, San Sebastian. He's had a few good chances in the past to make a lot of money, but he blew them because of the conscience. That's not what he says, but you don't pick up and run away for no reason at all. Now, of course, he has a lot less to bargain with than in the old days. This woman he has now gave him a few extra duties to make up for it. That's why he lives out here. He's the recruiter for Neutral Corner."

"What's Neutral Corner?"

"That's something his girl friend Eva started over in Philadelphia. She's very wealthy and has nothing in particular to do, so she has meetings at her house for people that are having trouble with their marriages. She bought this old carnival for him and got a lease on the land out here. When families come in Nick's supposed to talk with the parents and invite them to come to the sessions on Tuesday nights and Saturday mornings. His quota is twenty for each two-month series. But I've ended up doing most of the recruiting so far. I got my twenty people for the last series, but I'm three short this time. I'm afraid Eva's not going to like that. Business had better pick up out there," he gestured toward the empty lot, "or she'll cut off Father's allowance. Then he won't have any support."

The kid shook his head sadly over his father's outstretched form, then turned to Principato.

"Here, have a Neutral Corner brochure. From what Nick tells me about your marriage, you might benefit from the sessions."

"Why has Nick told you anything about my marriage?" Principato asked.

"Because I asked him. I needed a contrasting study, and you seem to be the only one he keeps any contact with from the old days. Sort of his anchor back in Philadelphia. You were particularly good because you haven't had the mobility he has and you've been static on the same job without advancement for years."

"I beg your pardon, but my life has not been a failure!" Principato protested. "I'm happily married and have five children."

"Well, I'm not saying it's been a failure, Mr. Principato. But your marriage can't have been so happy, considering you were conned into it by your wife's uncle."

"That's not what happened at all. I don't believe Nick said anything like that."

"Now come on, Mr. Principato. Your father told Nick that after you were married."

"Jesus Christ and Mary! My own father!" Principato wailed. Then Nick, who must have been faking for at least part of the conversation, leapt from the bed, obviously released from his hangover.

"Get out of here, you little bastard!" he raged, grabbing his son's arm and shoving him toward the door. "No wonder I'm loaded all the time, with the spirit of Relentless Truth living with me for three months. That kid never heard of diplomacy or polite lying. He hits you straight in the face with the pie every time he can. I think his mother sent him here to get even with me. If he thinks I'm a failure as a gigolo, wait until he hits the circuit. He couldn't make a bend in the road if his life depended on it."

58

"He's a real bastard, all right," Principato agreed. "How soon are you going to be able to get rid of him so I can afford to come and see you again?"

"In about two weeks, when his school starts. Then I can go back to social drinking. Christ, when he first came here I sat like a fool and pretended he was the Delphic oracle going to straighten out my poor errant life all by himself. Now I'm praying to get back to it."

"I wish him a bitch of a success," Principato said, swigging the last of his beer.

"Yeah, all kinds of women at his feet. Like an acid bath," Malatesta added, taking two more beers from the refrigerator. "Here, have another. How have you been, Pato?"

Principato reached greedily for the beer, anxious to dilute the spirit of Relentless Truth. "Pretty decent, Nick. How about yourself?"

"O.K., except for the wrath of my son and my new girl. How's the family?"

"Same as usual."

"Medium to miserable, huh?"

"That's about it."

"Oh well. Let's go outside to the circus, Pato. It's getting too warm in here."

Outside, the breeze had died and heat waves rose from the oiled surface of the lot. Malatesta's son hung inside the window of Principato's car, talking with his three children.

"Look at him now," Malatesta growled. "He's trying to psychoanalyze those kids of yours."

"I think he's met his match. If they find out he's not a Catholic, they won't even speak to him."

"Huh. Let's get on the horse-and-carriage ride, Pato, and we'll see if we can't get up a little breeze."

"Why not?" Principato said, grinning. He chose a seat and held Nick's beer while the other pressed some buttons on the control box then swung aboard. Before their carriage, two horses began suddenly to bob up and down in rhythm to the merry-go-round music. Malatesta pulled on the bell rope. A rusty bell that Principato thought might have done better service on the near-by miniature fire trucks began clanging over the horses' heads.

"So you see, things haven't changed that much," Malatesta said. "From the glittering carnivals of Europe to the glittering carnivals of New Jersey. You really didn't have to come to see me after all."

"I have a motive, Nick. I need a favor."

"What kind of favor? Wait a minute. I need another beer for this. Hey, Jon," he yelled, "bring us two more beers."

Principato kept silence while the boy obediently left the car and walked to the trailer. When he returned with two fresh cans, Nick snagged them from his hands as they whirled past.

"What's on your mind, Pato?"

"I need a woman for my brother, Rocco."

"Rocco in his wheel chair?"

"Yes."

"He can do it with the legs like that?"

"He's going to give it a try if I can get the woman. I promised I'd look. But I don't know where to start. You don't put ads in the paper for this one."

"Uh huh. This is going to be a toughie. I've been out of Philly for a long time and the contacts are a little rusty. If it was Cannes, maybe. . . . I used to know a guy in a chair who got it once a week. Real nice-looking girl, too."

"Will you help me, Nick?"

"O.K., Pato. I'll give it a bash. But I want a little favor from you, too."

"Speak."

"How about showing up for this Neutral Corner bullshit a week from Tuesday night? The kid's right. He has only seventeen signed up and none of them are men. I might be safe with eighteen, as long as one of them's a male. Otherwise, it might be a long, hard winter with Eva."

"I understand. It'll be cheap enough if you can come through on Rocco for me."

"Cripes, you sure love that kid, don't you? I always thought he was a miserable little shit, even though he is in a wheel chair. Maybe a piece of ass is what the doctor ordered. By the way, how's the old man? I saw him a month ago, and he told me about the cancer. Very nonchalantly standing in the kitchen, he informs me he's got about nine months to live."

"What do you expect from him? A man who tells you his son was tricked into his marriage isn't going to bother with ceremony."

"Sorry about that, Pato. I put my own kid onto that just so he'd take off after a new scent and leave my mistakes alone for a change. I'll switch him back to Malatesta, Failed Gigolo, for the next two weeks if my brain can stand the Scotch treatments."

"Thanks Nick. I'd appreciate that." Beneath them, the horses and carriage leapt and rolled on through their swift circle, producing a small, cooling wind. In the west, toward Philadelphia, the first fire of sunset had begun to appear. Principato's children and Malatesta's son stared at their fathers revolving on the ride, beer cans in their hands.

"I'd like to stay on here for the next two weeks until that kid of mine goes home," Malatesta said. "That way I wouldn't have to talk with him."

"I know what you mean," Principato agreed. He had been covertly sticking out his tongue at his children each time the ride turned on their side. "It's like suspended animation."

"Yeah, except that it's making me dizzy as hell. Jump off quick, Pato, and stop the damm thing!"

Principato stood up, preparing to jump, then decided the centrifugal thrust would either hurl him roughly to the ground or dash him against the near-by miniature coaster. Declining heroics, he screamed for Nick's son.

"Jon! Jon! Turn this off! Your father's going to be sick!"

Still half standing, he watched as the boy came across the lot to press a single large control button. As the ride began slowing, Nick retched violently over the side onto the wooden track.

"That's twice today," Nick's son said as the ride halted.

"Good-by, Nick. See you next Tuesday," Principato called as he fled across the lot from Relentless Truth. In his car he fumbled with the keys, then quickly started the engine and moved toward the highway.

"Who's that stupid kid, Principato?" Terrance asked.

"A real little bastard, that's who!" Principato told him, believing this to be the first time he had ever cursed in front of his children.

"I thought so, Principato," Sean said. "You should hear the questions he was asking us."

"Yeah, Principato," said Noreen, "he was asking me if I still make pee in my bed."

"Do you still make pee in your bed, Noreen?"

"Yeah, but I wasn't going to tell him nothing."

"Well, you just go on making pee in your bed, and don't listen to anything that boy has to say," Principato said. Then he hastened the old De Soto back toward the safe, predictable misery on the Corrigan side of the Delaware.

FOUR

They met Kababian after mass a week after Principato's visit to Malatesta. Or rather, Cynthia had stalled on the church steps, pawing the sisters McGinchy until he came out. Inside, when he had emerged from somewhere farther back to strut up the aisle for Communion, she had knelt suddenly upright, the Sunday-morning slouch going out of her back, and shamelessly, hungrily, followed him with her eyes.

Jesus Christ, Cynthia! Principato wanted to scream. Instead, he jabbed her with his elbow, feeling in it some token vindication of himself. She slashed back: a hard, vicious thrust that caught him in the forearm and made him drop his rosary. Bending to retrieve it, he looked up at her. Her jaw muscles were quivering with a fierce anger, her eyes arched over the rows of heads in front of her, seeking out Kababian at the altar railing. He watched as she struck her breast three times in rhythm to the intonation of the priest who held the host above the chalice.

So, all this was to start again, he thought wearily. Adonis was home. Since the beginning of the summer, when Kababian had gone away to a lifeguard's job in Virginia, that problem had gradually diminished in Principato's mind, become superseded by others. Occasionally they had received a post card from the young god—appropriately addressed: Mrs. and Mr. Principato—which Cynthia promptly wedged into the corner of her dressing-table mirror. But the airplane view of massed, sweating bodies cluttering Virginia Beach had done little to remind Principato of his powerful rival, except for making him think gleefully that Kababian was probably overworked and underpaid and, by now, thoroughly detesting that high-chair existence he was looking forward to so eagerly in the spring. Also, Principato wished for the daily appearance of sharks off that crowded coast.

Four years before, on a Sunday afternoon, he had come home early to find Cynthia crouched down on the upstairs porch, her huge feet plugged into her boatlike house loafers, watching the sweat-suited, fourteen-year-old Kababian lifting weights on the patio below. Even Principato had noticed this "mulatto" of mixed Greek and Armenian parts turning into a hero. He had arms like a dock worker's and had heisted the front end of his mother's Volkswagen only a few days before.

Above, Cynthia's eyes had the intense look of a huntress. She did not know her husband was watching. Below, Kababian stood curling a weighted bar, the veins standing out in his neck and arms. Accompanying him was a rapid Armenian cacophony of screeching and banging from a portable tape recorder. Flutes and reeds wailed, a drum pounded lustily. BBs rattled in a tin can and water spilled on a sheet of metal, it seemed to Principato.

Kababian began a kind of post-exercise limbering dance. Squatting down in kazatsky position, he circled the flagstone twice, then leapt into the air, falling flat out into a long series of pushups, clapping his hands with each rise and fall. Shrieks and yelps issued from his lips. Life, vitality flowed through him. Cynthia began actually to tremble. Principato, unable to stand it any longer, whispered throatily, "Cynthia!"

She turned, but not fearfully or ashamed, as he had expected. There was an excited but challenging look in her eyes: Match that if you can, skinny.

"What a man that fourteen-year-old kid is going to be," she said evenly. Below, the exhibition continued.

64

Stricken, Principato had stepped quickly inside to their bedroom mirror. Always sallow, with the drawn face of the pessimist he had become, he felt he lacked only some prop like cobwebs around his ears to complete a recognizable type. His clothes seemed suddenly faded and shapeless. A thin arm inhabited the toga sleeve of his jacket. The too-large shirt collar was bunched and spreading around his neck. His tie was a wide-bottomed leftover from the Truman era.

In truth, something was gone from him, blown or wasted away since the old days in college when he had been skeletal yet optimistic about fattening up in married life. But now look at him! He knew himself immediately and called himself by name. He was his own Uncle Niccolò. Gray, beaten Niccolò, who dug graves in the Italian cemetery. The grayness came from within. Uncanny phenomenon. A chemical secretion perhaps, like sweat, that permeated his flannels and denims after the first wearing. The Chinese launderer and Niccolò had long ago come to terms. Nothing could be done. The yellow man sadly handed the gray man his clothes and took his money in return.

"Them clean, Niccolò. Velly clean. The spilit dead. . . ."

Days later, on an afternoon when Cynthia was away at the Corrigans', Principato jumped over the hedge to ask Kababian if he might try to lift the barbells. There was a fierceness in his demands, and poor Kababian could not know why. He offered Principato the weights, his great doe eyes kind, eager to be helpful. Principato, unwilling to be taken in, glared at the young giant. This was the enemy, even if he did not know it.

The bar was transferred. His hands supinated, Principato held it tightly. The great weight threatened to tear his arms from the shoulder socket; it pressed inward on his groin. Now that he had it, he was uncertain as to what to do with it. He thought with sudden embarrassment that there would be two great rings of sweat on the bar where his hands had clenched when he handed it back to Kababian.

Remembering that he had seen Kababian lift it outward and upward, he exerted a mighty force, then looked down disbelieving as it rose to the level of his stomach. It stopped. To get it to the level of his chest would be impossible. He tried jerking it upward. No good. The tonus was draining from his arms. He recognized it from their

65

sudden trembling. He was becoming lightheaded from holding his breath.

Kababian, infinitely kind and pitying, took the bar back into his hands.

"It takes a while to work up to this weight, Mr. Principato. You should start with something lighter."

"Yeah, I guess you're right. Sorry to bother you."

"No trouble, Mr. Principato."

Principato turned and hopped the hedge back into his own yard. Behind him, he sensed the pitying eyes. He walked slowly, controlled, onto the back porch and into the kitchen. He was crying now, weeping over the unfair parceling out of large bone and heavy muscle that had overlooked Principato and left him instead anemic and shrunken.

"Thin men make the best lovers," he had insisted to Cynthia at the beginning of their marriage. But she had long since proved him incorrect on that score. Having sapped her husband's strength and energies, she cast an enticing eye across Kababian's low hedge into that Hellenic province of barbells and flex.

But the young god was on to nothing so far in these four years. Principato was sure of it. He had absolutely no awareness. After mass that Sunday, with the McGinchy sisters in tow, all the neighbors had walked slowly home, Cynthia holding Kababian's bicep between her hands. Her friend played football for some remote Catholic high school, and Cynthia, who devoured the sports page looking for his name, spoke knowingly of long pass, short pass, quarterback sneak. Their communion was uncanny. Kababian asked her if she thought he should go to Notre Dame or Iowa. Cynthia replied he should stay in the city. Penn or Temple perhaps. After all, there was his mother to consider.

"Yeah, you're right, Mrs. Principato. I didn't think of that." His look definitely suggested he was ashamed.

In front of the house Kababian left, shaking hands with Principato. He turned, and Cynthia's shoulders fell forward. Her eyes took on that watery, frustrated glaze her husband saw only rarely these days. Her hands grew cold. She trooped dejectedly inside to check with

Phillips on the roast in the oven. In a few minutes her uncle would come, the talk between them covering death, salvation, and, undoubtedly, Principato's father and the urn.

Principato went straight downstairs to the cellar. Kababian's rivalry drove him to it, he realized even while negotiating the steps. Far back, where the walls were always damp and hidden crickets chirped in the summer, he kept his virility center. In a kind of frenzy, he fished for his keys, then unlocked the tall metal cabinet. The camphor odor of moth balls rushed out at him, a smell that assured him that his 286 bags of hair were in prime condition. He took out the first and the last. The design was the same, although eleven years separated their contents: a red-and-white peppermint-striped bag with the words BISBING'S BARBERSHOP in block letters on the front. Every one in the cabinet was the large size. Suddenly he began to feel strengthened. Society's real judgment of Principato, he thought, comforting himself. He touched the bags almost reverently to his lips.

Bisbing's was the world's most bizarre barbershop. It was, in fact, the local weekly judiciary, but far more interesting than a court or confessional. With all the aloofness of a divine-right monarch, Bisbing clipped your hair, then stuffed it into either a large or a small peppermint-striped bag. Men waited long hours to be shorn. The place tingled with a heightened expectancy, like, sadly enough, the expectancy of a wolf pack waiting for one of its own to go down.

The large bags were for those who lived their lives in—how could he say it?—seeming equipoise or balance, perhaps. Principato refused to think of it in terms of mediocrity. But success counted heavily too, like a Calvinist motive in Bisbing. Judge Garvey always got a large bag. Old Murray Rosen, rich in retirement, and returning once a year from California to see his grandchildren, had the meager clippings of his monk's tonsure handed him in a large bag.

The others took home a small bag. Frank Morris's son committed suicide. Principato was there when Bisbing handed him the prize. There were tears in Morris's eyes.

"I don't know how I failed him, Bisbing. I had nothing to do with it."

"Nevertheless, he's dead," the barber had answered. But that was all. Strangely, disturbing to himself, Principato had felt no pity. Only a kind of relief that he had no son old enough to be seriously considering suicide. On the occasional day he witnessed somebody's going down, he received his large bag as a special commendation. Gratefully clutching it to him, he exited smiling. After the first year he no longer thought it strange that Bisbing was in his neighborhood. He decided that if he were to move, Bisbing would certainly follow. Be in any place he chose to live.

As to Bisbing the man: who was he? Where did he come from? It was a mystery to everyone. Often, sitting in the barber chair, Principato thought of opening a conversation with him. But Bisbing talked only weather. And looking into the mirror at the eager faces of his neighbors sitting about the room, he decided against even that. In the same way they all decided against it.

Only once had Bisbing actually spoken to him. Or about him, really. Handing him his large bag and taking Principato's money in return, he proclaimed gravely to the barbershop, "Principato is a good man. A simple man."

Around the walls, the seated mob of political appointees and small-time businessmen had nodded sagely in agreement. Choked with emotion, Principato had staggered from the shop, remembering in his delirious joy to stop in church and light a candle for Bisbing on the way home.

Today, he sifted through the contents of the first and last bags, examining them minutely in the half light. Beside the fact of Bisbing's judgment, there was another association. Hair and virility had connection since Samson. Except that his own had grown straighter, nothing had changed since his marriage. The color, remarkably, remained the same. A dark, lustrous black, pride of Mediterranean types. He thought with sudden satisfaction how Kababian might look after eleven years of marriage. Muscular people went easily to fat. His hair seemed to be thinning already. With luck, Kababian might be completely bald at thirty-four.

"Bisbing," he prayed as he replaced his prizes, "send me many large bags of dark, lustrous hair." Also in the cabinet, along with his framed, autographed picture of Rocky Marciano, was the scarred football the Negro boys had given him the day he broke his leg. He took it out and whipped through the motion of a quick forward pass, thinking of how he had lain in heroic agony on the lawn waiting for the ambulance to come. Then he heard the slight cough.

"Principato, Cynthia wants you to come for dinner."

It was the Jesuit uncle. Principato, instantly embarrassed, mumbled something like O.K., stuffed the football inside, and slammed the door. How long had he been watching? Did he see him kiss the bags of hair? Suddenly, Principato felt worn and deflated again as he climbed the steps after the old priest.

"She's always calling me neurotic. Am I so neurotic, really?" Principato wondered aloud as he drove to work the next morning. In the car, struggling with traffic into the city, he was fond of conversing with himself.

"I'm whole. I'm entire," he said, touching himself in several places. "It's just that no one thing is up to perfection. But there has to be something wrong with that Kababian. It can't all be up to perfection. Maybe he's a young impotent and lifts weights to make up for it." The idea delighted him. Then, blinking, he saw his rival hitch-hiking near the expressway entrance. Principato pulled over to the shoulder.

"Mr. Principato, hello!"

"Good morning, Nikos."

"Boy, am I glad you came by! Nobody wants to stop with all this rush traffic getting into work. I've been standing here an hour."

"Where are you going? All the way to town?"

"Yes sir, I've got a little shopping to do," Kababian said as he climbed in. Principato drove back into the flow of traffic.

"Back-to-school shopping, huh?"

"No, Mr. Principato, I have to buy two presents."

"Ah, girl friends, then?" Principato asked hopefully.

"No, sir. One's for my mother and the other's for Mrs. Principato."

"For my wife? Why would you want to buy something for my wife?"

"Well, I talked it over with Mama and she thought it would be very nice after all the chocolate brownies Mrs. Principato sent me down in Virginia."

What goddam brownies? What was the kid talking about? Diplomacy, Principato, he cautioned himself.

"Oh well, she didn't send you that many chocolate brownies, did she, Nikos?"

"But don't you remember, Mr. Principato? She sent me two boxes every week."

Two boxes every week! No wonder there had not been a single chocolate brownie in the house all summer! Principato and his children starved for something they could not name, and Nikos Kababian had two boxes a week of it down in Virginia. Basta!

"Was it really two boxes each week? It didn't seem like so much to me."

"Yes, sir. Like clockwork, every Monday and Thursday. That's why I want to get her the present. Mama said she'd probably like some perfume and she gave me the name of a store where I could get some. Do you think she'd like perfume, Mr. Principato?"

"Well, yes, I guess perfume is always a good bet," he answered lamely. But then . . . "You know, Nikos, you've just given me an idea. How much were you planning to spend on Cynthia's—that is, Mrs. Principato's—gift, if you don't mind my asking?"

"No, sir, I don't mind. I thought about ten dollars."

"Ten bucks, huh? Listen, there's a statue in a religious-goods store on Arch Street that Cynthia has always liked. I wasn't going to get it for her until Christmas, but since it's you and she's so fond of you, I wouldn't mind making up the difference. She'd be thrilled at getting it with your name on the card."

"Hey, that's a good idea, Mr. Principato. But you wouldn't have to pay so much extra, would you? Do you remember what it costs?"

"It was about thirty dollars, I believe."

"Then I'll pay fifteen. All right, Mr. Principato? I don't think it's very nice for you to have to pay more than fifty per cent."

Fifty per cent? He would pay ninety-nine per cent of thirty thousand dollars to have that atrocious pink-and-blue sequined Virgin delivered to the house with Kababian's name on the card. And he would moonlight to augment his time payments on the thirty thousand principal until, an overworked and cadaverous old man, he had

70

no recourse but to fall dead into a coffin, he thought, as he gripped the wheel hard to conceal his giddiness.

"That's decent of you, Nikos. I don't have a conference until ten o'clock, so we can drive there right now and buy it. I'm sure they'll deliver it this afternoon."

In the religious-goods store, where the sequined Virgin stood four feet tall in a corner, an aging nun who reminded him of Rocco's Sister Winifred waited on them. Her huge feet, bound up in the sandals of her order, reminded him of Cynthia's own.

"It's that one you want?" she asked Principato. "You're not with any circus or carnival show that would want to defile Our Blessed Lady, are you?"

"Oh no, Sister," Principato protested, thinking that whoever had made the thing had done a pretty good job already. "No, it's nothing like that. The young man here wants to get a present for a lady, and she's had her eye on this particular statue for a long time."

"What sort of lady is she?" The nun was still doubtful.

"She's this man's wife, Sister," Kababian said.

"But is she a good woman?"

"Of course she's a good woman," Principato said. "She's a good Catholic, the mother of my five children. Her uncle is with the Jesuits. Another uncle, now deceased, was a bishop. Her family gives plenty of money to the Church every year. Maybe you know them? Her maiden name was Corrigan."

"Corrigan? No, I don't know them."

It's a goddam wonder, thought Principato, trying to decide whether or not to advance to the full theatrics of getting on his knees to the nun to convince her to relinquish the statue.

"But, Sister, I don't understand. Why are you asking these questions?"

"Simply because I could never believe that anyone would buy such a mean representation of Our Lady without malicious intent. I've always tried to keep it from being taken away. You've heard of black masses and all this shady kind of business?"

"Well, yes, Sister. We've all read about that nonsense taking place in England on the moors. But, after all, this is America."

"We are sometimes a naïve people," she said, shaking her head sadly. "We want to believe in universal loving kindness and inherent goodness in all men. It just isn't so."

"Sister," he said, motioning toward Kababian, "he's only a kid."

"Yes, I understand. I'll have it wrapped and the delivery truck will take it to your home this afternoon."

"What's the price on that, Sister?"

"It's tagged at thirty-one-fifty. But I'll make discount it to twenty-four-fifty for you. You seem like a good man to me."

"She's a nice nun," Kababian whispered. "That means I only have to pay twelve-twenty-five. I hope Mrs. Principato likes it."

But there was no real doubt in Kababian's tone. Apparently, he either found the statue agreeable or was completely lacking in taste. But then, Principato conceded, for some people the thought in giving was all-important. He believed he had a real purist beside him now.

"I'm sure she will, Nikos."

Outside Principato shook hands with Kababian, leaving him to buy a present for his mother, and drove quickly to his job at Holy Family House. He parked in the agency lot and entered the building as Jedda McMahnus, his supervisor, sauntered past.

"Ten-o'clock conference," the tall woman reminded him, and Principato nodded. At ten he slipped into McMahnus's frosted-glass cubicle. She began according to form: "How was your weekend, Principato?"

"Fine, Miss McMahnus, and your own?"

"Oh, I had a lovely weekend. Yesterday after mass I drove down to Margate with a gentleman friend for a picnic. His name is Thomas Butler. Perhaps you've made his acquaintance in the past."

"No . . . I don't believe so, Miss McMahnus."

"Well, it's your loss entirely, Principato. Let me assure you. A gentleman of irreproachable good conduct. It's a relief for a single woman like myself to know that a person of such good intentions exists."

"Yes, I can appreciate that. What does Mr. Butler do, Miss McMahnus?"

"I don't understand, Principato."

"I mean what sort of job does he work at?"

"Oh, that. Well, he's a teacher. A teacher at a very respectable girls' college near the city. A biology teacher, in fact," she said, her face screwed up into multiple wrinkles—at the arduousness of creating a fib, Principato suspected.

Alas, Jedda, sweet lying supervisor, thought Principato as he smiled back at her. Last week I saw you on a Toonerville Trolley in Jersey. You swept past me in a screaming of Volkswagen gears while I hid on the front seat of my car. Really, he wondered which of them would be more embarrassed if the truth were known. Then he drew his chair within range of Jedda's chlorophyll-scented morning breath.

"Well, Principato, we've got something of a small emergency in your case load today."

"Really?"

"Yes, I took the liberty of pulling a record from your files before you came in this morning."

"Sorry about being late, Miss McMahnus. I had a flat on the expressway on my way in. Who's our problem child?"

"Myra Phee, Principato."

"Myra Phee? What's up?" he asked warily.

"We received a letter from her this very morning informing us that at long last she has ascertained the name of the father of her second —that is, the half-white—child."

Principato blanched. Keen, swift justice. Retribution had come instantly for daring to involve the Holy Virgin in a revenge plot. Doubtless the letter had been written, posted, delivered, and read all in the short time he stood in the religious-goods store wrangling with the old nun for the right to purchase the sequined atrocity. Resignedly, Principato slumped down in his chair.

"Whom does she accuse, Miss McMahnus?" he asked, his voice a hoarse whisper now.

"A white man, as we knew, by the name of Milton Eisenberg. He sounds like a Jew to me."

Milton Eisenberg, the father of Myra's half-white child, and not Angelo Principato! Thanks be to God and especially his Mother Mary, who must indeed have consented to be the tool of Principato's own justice! Restored, he sat up in the chair again.

"Yes, the name does sound Jewish. Does she give any details?" Principato asked.

"None beyond the name. I had my secretary phone a neighbor of Myra's this morning who promised to tell her that you'd be dropping by this afternoon. I want you to get right on this and direct Myra in getting in touch with this Eisenberg, wherever he may be, on the matter of support for the child. Instruct her on court procedures if it comes to that, too."

"Yes, I understand, Miss McMahnus," he said, rising. Then suddenly, smiling down at her, he understood how this McMahnus had achieved the necessary balance in her life. From a long work week of wading armpit-deep through a mire of illegitimacy and fled paramours like Milton Eisenberg, she went to her weekends with a mythical, well-intended gentleman. Thomas Butler, biology teacher, symbol of her vague hopefulness for the human condition. In that moment, seeking redemption, Principato might have admitted that he was Myra Phee's Milton Eisenberg. Instead, he turned and walked from the office, carrying Myra's case record.

Larkin was the only one in the coffee bar. He wore his usual rumpled seersucker, the pants cuffs wide like a sailor's bell bottoms over the shapeless black loafers, and white socks.

"How was good mother Jedda this morning?" he asked. His voice betrayed contempt for their supervisor, who had slapped Larkin down in his bid for a promotion the month before. Principato's loyalty to McMahnus prevented him from telling his coworker about seeing Jedda in an amusement park.

"Same as usual," he responded.

"Boy, that dame burns me up!" Larkin said furiously.

Good, thought Principato, and silently he rejoiced in the other's displeasure. This Larkin was an ex-seminarian and long-time friend of the Corrigans' to boot. In an age when housewives chattered in the language of psychology, Cynthia's family still viewed their pal as living miserably in a dark cocoon: the spoiled priest. The mention of his name was greeted with a kind of voice-lowering reverence and a sad shaking of heads. Old lady Corrigan prayed loudly that he might give up on this present self-castigating interim of his life and either flee back to the priesthood or marry the piteous-looking Grace Marie,

74

a cousin of Cynthia's who had been one of her bridesmaids at the wedding eleven years before.

For his part, Principato had distrusted him mightily since the day they were graduated together from Gonzola. Often, paranoically, he felt Larkin knew more about his life and problems than Principato himself, even that this friend was being subsidized by the Corrigans to stay at his job and spy on their in-law. Once, unprompted, Larkin had even dared to speak about Principato's father and the urn.

"I heard Malatesta is back," said Larkin.

"I guessed you would by now." Principato dropped a dime into the computer-looking Mr. Coffee machine, pressed REGULAR on the top row of buttons and EXTRA SUGAR on the second. A watery brew shot into the cup and tried to mix with the cream extract that instantly curdled. Principato began drinking it anyhow.

"When did you hear about Nick, Lark?"

"Last night. I was talking to Big Jim Corrigan about ten o'clock or so."

That was slow, Principato considered ruefully. Some hitch in communications somewhere. Normally, channels were open and flashing within minutes after anything important broke.

"What did Malatesta have to say?" Larkin asked, trying to sound casual. He was peering slit-eyed over the rim of his plastic hot-chocolate container, the near-Mongoloid shape of his head with its thick brush-cut covering of red hair reminding Principato of some Irish simian creature sent especially to interrogate him.

"Oh, we talked about the day you broke your nose in the student union out at college. Remember that?"

Larkin would never forget it. The cup came away from his mouth and his hand went instinctively to touch the purplish scar across the bridge of his nose. Larkin had been a cheerleader. Once in their freshman year, during a rally in the student union, a chair had collapsed under him. Like a log, he had fallen forward and connected with the end of a table. Geysers of blood, it seemed to an easily nauseated Principato, had erupted all over the place.

"You know, Pato, I still think it was that bastard Malatesta that kicked the chair out from under me. That guy really hated the big men around school. A real jealous weasel. He had a perfect opportunity with all the noise and confusion."

"Look, Lark, I've told you a hundred times, Nick was standing with me and Mermelstein at that rally, all the way across the room from you. It was probably another enemy of yours who did it."

"Now, what other enemy did I have, Pato? You've got to admit that, for being a wheel, I never stepped on very many toes out there at school. Who was ever more diplomatic than myself? For a guy like you, it was easy to figure you'd never be into it with anyone. You were quiet, you kept to yourself. But for somebody who did as much moving as I did around campus, it was just a miracle that things were so rosy."

Ah me, thought Principato, and he felt the familiar nameless exasperation flooding into him. He had to stifle the urge to throw the last of his curdled coffee at this idiot Larkin, whose memory still sped through the half-lit Jesuit hallways filled with intrigues and counter-intrigues and the affable but distinct relationships of the big men and the small men. Larkin had not been a big man. Only a carrot-topped lout following slavishly after another lout named Jim Corrigan. Greatness by association. Really, the only miracle Principato recognized about Larkin was that some crusading aesthete had not yet struck him down in anger over his ugliness. A long silence ensued while Larkin waited for an answer. There was none.

"Listen, Pato, do you want to go on a retreat this weekend up at Saint Malachy's? Our Holy Name Society's going up and I've got a paid ticket that somebody can't use."

"I'm afraid I can't, Lark," he answered.

"Come on, Pato. It's only a weekend, and you haven't been on retreat in years. Three years exactly, as a matter of fact. It's not like it's going to cost you anything."

"Has it been that long really, Lark?"

"Yes, it has, Pato. You're about due for another."

Principato's eyes swept through the door of the coffee bar into the main office, where women, white and Negro, sat at desks set in long, precise, bureaucratic lines clacking away on typewriters. At nearly every place were the familiar props of women workers: Kleenex box, rolls of Life Savers, packs of cigarettes. Except for Principato's, the barren oasis of a man who worked among women and made certain of his masculinity by neither smoking, nor crunching Life Savers, nor recognizing any reason to incessantly pull Kleenex from a box and crush it tightly into a ball in his fist.

Then his mind was at the retreat house, remembering its glossy varnished miles of wood paneling and the ever-lingering presence of incense that seemed to dispel even the cooking odors in the kitchen. Fragrant ghosts of past secret prayers and petitions. He had an instant vision of himself crowded into the gilded chapel with other men, lulled to sleep by the slow, Latinized words of the retreat master exalting the Catholic home and family. Principato would shut his mind to that bullshit or stand to tell the priest about Cynthia and her children and close the matter for the weekend. It was only for the meditation periods he decided he would go. The long hours of walking alone and absorbed about the grounds or sitting in his tiny cell of a room, thinking about his father, who would soon die. He would talk to his father also—seriously, persistently—to demand if there were any way in his lifetime that the son, Principato, had failed the old man and could not be forgiven for it. Also, he would take him to task for telling Malatesta his son was tricked into his marriage. He had not forgotten that either.

"O.K., Lark. Count me in."

In the afternoon, Principato walked toward the subway on his way to visit Myra Phee. He descended into the tunnel at Walnut Street, leaving the city's awesome heat above him. Below, it was replaced by the subway's cool dampness, the persistent smell of urine. In the concourse, before the turnstiles, water seeped down the white tile walls, dragging chromatographic lines of green stain behind it.

Beneath him, a southbound train screeched into the station. All the cars but one were newly painted in the imitation red of London subways. The exception was a dirty old Philadelphia green, coupled ignominiously to the end. For a moment he smiled in a kind of nostalgia at the sight of it. American feeling for the underdog. In front of him, people began running, charging the turnstiles, hastening down the steps toward the cars. In their wake came a prancing bum.

"Hey mister, could ya spare a dollar for a poor soul?"

"A dollar? I thought the standard tap was a dime."

"Ah yes, sir, that was during the Depression. But now there ain't so many of us on the bum, and everything costs more these days."

"It certainly does," Principato agreed. Covertly, he was trying to draw away from the man's foul-smelling breath.

"How will a quarter be?" he asked hopefully.

"That's all you can spare?"

"Look, pal, I've got a wife and five kids, and not the world's highest-paying job either." His amusement at the first sight of the prancing bum diminished. He started moving off when the man's partner came skipping up. Principato was shocked at the new arrival: a huge fag bum with giant lips and lewd, bloodshot eyes. He felt a hand moving lightly up his arm. Staring at the man's lips, he could not remove the word "fellatorism" from his mind. Or was it "cunnilinction"? He would look it up later in the dictionary.

"All I asked him for was a dollar, and he wants to give me a quarter," said the first bum.

"A quarter!" An unbelievably high-pitched scream echoed through the concourse. A disparaging laugh followed it. Principato saw the woman in the token seller's booth turn sideways to watch them. A hot flush coursed through his body.

"Well, I know how to make him give us a dollar." His face with the bloodshot eyes came very close.

"Ask her for the key to the men's room, mister," he said, pointing to the woman in the booth. "She'll give it to you."

"Are you crazy? Get your hands off me!" His voice had become suddenly husky. He felt the sweat coursing into his palms. The huge man's arm had somehow gone around him. His face was very close to the other's reeking armpit. Principato looked down. Layers of filth and grime had worked their way into the concrete floor. Green, ugly wads of sputum glittered under the ceiling lights.

"I'll call the police if you don't beat it!" Principato broke away, walking quickly to the change booth.

"Oh, don't worry mister, the police are all our friends. My, wasn't he tempted? And he looked like such a nice, clean gentleman." His voice spread unmercifully through the half-lit concourse. People turned to look at Principato.

"Ain't they somethin'?" It was the colored woman behind the token vendor's screen. She smiled sympathetically. He felt the flush diminish with her absolution.

"Don't the police ever come down here?" he asked her.

"Oh, the police always kickin' them two out. They stays away for a week, then they comes right back. If they embarrasses folks enough, they gets a dollar just to go away. I seen them do it lots of times."

Principato pushed through the turnstile and started down the steps. He realized his limbs were shaking. A long drop of sweat went down his back. He looked up for a last encounter with the bums, but they were gone. Perhaps already playing on the silent fears of another man.

The cars were hot. Beneath them, the wheel flanges groaned in the maze of turnings under City Hall. At City Hall station, his car emptied of everyone but himself, then quickly filled again for North Philadelphia, mostly with sweating, tired-looking Negroes. The only other white person was a girl, a Temple student, to judge by the covers of her books.

Principato watched the girl as the train sped out of the station, and his body lapsed easily into the familiar rocking motion. Her eyes conspicuously scanned first his side of the car, then her own, her head turned critically to the right or left when it came to assessing the faces nearest her. From the movement of her lips, he knew she was counting, computing the odds, he believed. Guarded, fearful lest he somehow tip off the sweating forms around him to their overwhelming advantage, he began his own count. Twenty-eight Negroes and two whites. Some distant part of his mind decided that he and the Temple girl might be snatched up and hacked to pieces and their parts calmly disposed of through the window before the next station could be reached. Really, there was nothing to be done for it if the collective urge to murder them seized their fellow travelers. But some nervous forepart of his mind prayed that it would not happen. He thought unhappily too of the Negro mole men of the track gangs that plodded through the tunnels by night and day, coming upon bits and pieces of himself and the Temple girl, and gathering them up into cardboard boxes, curiously unmoved by the fact that the victims had been whites. In life, Principato was a ready dispenser of compassion. The most he asked of anyone was to be found dead by a compassionate person.

At Susquehanna, where he got off, the Temple girl was at his elbow.

"Were you scared?" she asked.

"Yes, a little."

"I wasn't scared," she piped.

"Well, I guess there was nothing really to worry about. Together we could have fought off the whole car."

"I know karate," she said, not fazed by his levity. "Knee to the groin, and when he's bent over, a chop right here." She demonstrated at the top of the subway stairs, lifting her leg suddenly in the air, then reaching up to touch the back of Principato's neck with her hand. A news vendor and two policemen stood watching them.

Internally, Principato was roaring with laughter: a fat-assed little girl, intense with the notion of her prowess, whose legs of even circumference from top to bottom reminded him of telephone poles.

"I took two night courses at my old high school. Next year they're going to make me an instructor."

"Congratulations. What are you studying in college?"

"Sociology. I'm a senior this year. Next year I go for a master's in social work. Then I'm going to work in Philadelphia. Probably right around here. There's lots to be done," she said, surveying the area wearily. "What do you do?"

"I sell televisions," he answered, waiting to cross the street. When the light changed he waved good-by, walking quickly toward the other side.

"I've heard about your kind," she screamed after him. "The long-term-credit racket that ends up costing three times what the set was worth. But don't worry, the gradual gains of equality for all in this country will put you and your dirty lot out of business."

"No, wait!" He swung round quickly on the other corner to recross the street, frantic to set the record straight. But the light changed and six lanes of traffic intervened. From the opposite side, he heard her scream above the roar of trucks.

"Stay there, you bastard! Next thing you'll try to tell me that you're a social worker!" He watched her turn and march furiously away toward the university. Two puzzled cops shrugged their shoulders.

"What's the matter, man? More trouble with that frigid white stuff?"

Principato turned. It was the friendly black racist who habitually stood on that corner distributing propaganda leaflets. As always, even with today's heat, he was immaculately groomed.

"No, nothing like that. She thinks I'm working a credit racket. What are you selling today? Anything new?"

"Uh huh. Got a choice item. Don't cost us nothin', which is a blessin' since there ain't no more money in the treasury. Some of your white boys prints it up for us and leaves it on the clubhouse doorstep."

"What white boys?"

"The White Nationalist Party of the Philadelphia Northern Districts," the racist read aloud from a handbill so that a few Negroes standing near by turned and began laughing.

"What's their platform?" Principato asked, amused, despite the onlookers, at the organization's name.

"Oh, they warns us that they intends to banish us from our happy ghetto here and reclaim the whole area for the former white-middle-class inhabitants."

"Does it really say that? 'White-middle-class inhabitants'? Let me see," he asked, scanning the print above the man's extended finger. WHITE-MIDDLE-CLASS INHABITANTS was spelled out in huge block letters.

"There it be in black and white."

"Huh. It's probably some little gnome of a guy down in his cellar with a hand printing press. I'll bet he lives right here in the neighborhood," Principato said, trying to recall if he knew any bitter old men left behind in the white exodus years before.

"Might be. Might be. But the best way to find out who the guy is would be to give one of these here leaflets to them Corrigan brother-in-laws of yours. If they thought them four bars they has in here was goin' back to servin' small-time white drinkers, they'd find this guy within an hour and strangle the poor bastard."

"At last! An ally in the fight against complete suffocation by my wife's family! Thanks, you've given me the strength to push on."

"Later, man."

He started along the avenue and in seconds was absorbed in the fantastic rhythm. There was rhythm here: but not the measured, almost martial kind of pedestrians and cars on the downtown streets of the white business world. Instead, crowded and swarming, traffic surged eastward and westward, but always dodging, never colliding, as if the spark of human reasonableness were struck the instant a contest might have begun. Principato was proud of all mankind for this small thing. In the street, everything from cement mixers to motor scooters somehow staggered past in opposite directions. On the sidewalks humans managed to elude humans and uncomplainingly put up with the double encumbrance of moving around fly-covered mounds of watermelons and pecans outside the storefronts.

In a few minutes he came to a restaurant. There were no whites inside. Principato ordered coffee from the red-headed waitress as he sat in the window booth. A funeral was about to take place across the street. Unconsciously, he removed the summer straw hat his father had given him.

From a battered hearse of two-tone gray, its driver and assistant comically somber, a blond-wood casket was being carried into a storefront church. Symbolically, naturally, the color registered in his mind. Behind the coffin, the mourners were waiting: six obese Negro women in a new Lincoln, their huge hats knocking together as if the women lacked the sense or inclination to remove them. From an old walk-in van whose ACE LAUNDRY COMPANY name was faintly visible beneath a new coat of orange paint, about ten men wearing red fezzes appeared. On the back of the hats, when the wind lifted the tassels, the words JOLLY JINGLE CLUB were seen.

On the opposite corner, near the restaurant, a crowd was forming. Principato watched the faces. To a man, they were smiling.

Really, he believed in the dignity of death. But what sacrilege was this? In his mind, Principato saw himself charging out of the restaurant to exhort the spectators to put on mourners' masks and take off their hats. The waitress brought the coffee. Principato's hand shook as he lifted the cup.

"I knew that guy," said the waitress. "He was a real swinger. This here funeral is worthy of him indeed."

Doubtless, thought Principato grimly. The club men and their ladies' auxiliary were lined up and waiting. Laughing and talking. From inside the church, jive music burst forth. The men moved forward in a shuffling dance step, ready to clap their dead brother's soul into eternity. The coffin swayed in rhythm.

"A man ought to be buried like he's lived. Can you imagine puttin' an old reprobate like that into the ground with a big service and choir? I recall once seein' him runnin' from a particular lady's house with his pants in his hand."

Then he remembered the three days after his wedding when Cynthia's father was waked. That poor bastard had been buried as he lived. Abused and despised in life, he lay forgotten and alone in his casket while people filled the rooms about him with talk and only half-repressed laughter. They were still congratulating Cynthia on her catch. Her husband, Principato, sat beside her, watching the party in a kind of disbelief. Occasionally, he got up to stare at his dead father-in-law, who had called him frantically in Florida to warn him not to marry his own daughter. In death, he had changed: his ruddy drinker's face was pale and waxy with the blood removed, and his great, white lion's mane that had given him the look of a patriarch, though he had never actually been one, was combed back stiff and lacquered over his head. Only the nicotine stain of the roots remained.

In the kitchen, broken-hearted Stella wept over deviled eggs and fried chicken, while a strangled Principato, who wanted to cry more in outrage than in sorrow, sat on a work stool beside her.

The last night before the burial, his family had come. The rooms fell silent at the sight of them, and Principato, with a keen sense of theatrics, felt the adrenalin rage through him at the suggestion of the coup about to take place. His mother and Aunt Lucrezia appeared to have dyed their hair an unbelievable jet black. Like his grandmother, who stood between them, they wore black dresses and black shawls about their shoulders. As they approached the coffin, he saw their faces had a deathly gray cast, as if they had spent hours rubbing ashes into them. Three Sicilian priestesses come to raise the body to life and take it with them to a happier land. Behind them, his father was dressed completely in black, a mourning band around his arm, the eternal cigar clamped firmly in his teeth.

They stood for a moment regarding the body, then suddenly, inexplicably, the old man removed the cigar from his mouth, touched his fingers to his lips, then carried the kiss to the dead boozer's face. A kind of gasp went up from the room.

"Requiescat in pace," his mother intoned. His grandmother bent to kiss the cross of the crystal rosary wound about the dead Corrigan's hands. Then Stella came from the kitchen in her black maid's uniform and hung sobbing on the elder Principato's arm. For an instant time froze, it seemed to Principato, and he was suddenly overwhelmed by the odors of candle wax and flowers and perfumed bodies about him. Moths, attracted to the inner lights, crashed against the screened windows. Outside, it was a warm summer night, and strangely, Principato thought of real lovers struggling in the sand on the not-so-distant Jersey beaches. Then he looked down, marveling at how large his wife's feet were. They were cold, also.

Old lady Corrigan broke into the time vacuum. She took the arm of Principato's father, her enemy.

"Won't you stay and have some food?" she said. Her voice had a soft, feline quality to it, incredible in an old woman, and Principato sensed for the first time what a real bitch she must have been in the old days.

"What's the main course? Your husband?" his father had asked, waving his cigar at the dead form. His disgust with these Corrigans was a monster. For a moment, Principato could not believe the old man had come off with such a crude judgment. An angry murmur had arisen in the rooms, and people who had not heard correctly were being told again by their neighbors. He watched as Cynthia's mother's eyes went suddenly large and misty, and he knew the elder Principato had just vanished from her sight. In the next room, brother Matt had stood up, then sat quickly down again after a dark look from the old man, and Principato had felt the familiar jaw-trem-

84

bling pride. No one would dare attack his father! You had to accept the fact that some people were unconquerables. His old man was one of these.

Then the four had left, with Principato helping his grandmother toward the convertible. Outside at the curb, Lucrezia had carefully lifted a jet-black wig from her head. Underneath, her henna hair was flattened and pinned down.

"I thought it was the real thing, just a new color," Principato said.

"Honey, when your hair starts thinning out like mine, you don't play around with too many rinses. It's all chemical, you know."

Beside them, his mother checked out her head in the fender mirror.

"I had to change mine. I couldn't get that wig to stay on right. I hope it goes back O.K." she said anxiously.

"I think I'm going to wear this arm band for a month," his father said. "That would be a nice gesture."

Then they had driven off, leaving a lonely Principato to face the Corrigans, their retainers, and corpse.

Now he drank his coffee slowly, only mildly annoyed that the waitress had put in too much cream. From the storefront church across the street, a woman's gospel-singer brand of voice replaced the jive music and called long and earthily for Jesus. The Savior's name filled the street, grew louder and softer by degrees, alternated, it seemed to him, with the ragged idle of an old truck doubleparked outside the door. Around him in the restaurant conversation had stopped.

The wonder of it, thought Principato, and he smiled dimly into the steaming cup with the half acceptance of a thing that both dismayed and pleased him at the same time. A name so revered, that Principato, a Catholic, never hesitated to bow his head at the mention of it, escaping the funeral singer's lips with a connotation that was disturbingly sexual. Some part of him was sure that this was no way to sing of Jesus. Near the booth, the waitress's body writhed slightly to the call. Her eyes were closed; her lips parted in a smile. Outside, two teen-agers, a boy and a girl, ground out a slow epileptic's dance.

Moments later, Principato rang the doorbell of the house where Myra Phee lived. In a long line put up years before from the same dark-colored brick, it was newly painted and prosperous-looking with aluminum storm windows. The shined-brass address numbers gleamed in the afternoon sun.

In a minute, a wizened old Negroid face peered through a slit in the curtain. Two police locks slid back. A key turned.

"Mista Pato, hello." The voice was kindly, welcoming. Principato tried to disguise his pity. She was bent nearly double over her short length of cane.

"Hello, Mrs. Roberts. Is Myra here?"

"No, she not here, Mista Pato."

Oh, shit! he said to himself. The familiar ache he got from sparring with Myra Phee sprang instantly to his head.

"Did she receive the telephone message this morning, Mrs. Roberts?"

"Oh, she got your message all right, Mista Pato. But she got a new lover man an' she think she almos' got him hooked. So when he call this afternoon, she went right quick to see him. She say you understan' what she doin'."

Principato understood what she was doing, and the old guilt surged through him, crippling him in the doorway. Perfectly he understood. How could he possibly bitch at her not being there? She was still covering up for him, as when she designated one Milton Eisenberg her fled paramour. Trying now to entice a Negro husband to the marriage bed, when she was already the mother of a half-white child. A gift from Principato, her case worker, who had come, shy representative of a benevolent society that sought to aid her in putting her first baby up for adoption. What had he given her? A replacement. A swap even, he sometimes flayed himself miserably. That first child, conceived in Memphis and delivered in Philadelphia, was gone now, thanks to the tireless efforts of her case worker, to approved Negro parents. But where to find approved parents for this one? There would be no end to the tireless efforts.

"What's her new boy friend's name?" he asked. Mrs. Roberts had been standing before him a little frightened, watching him slowly thump his head with a closed fist.

"His name Addie. He have a Cadillac car, Mista Pato. It have big cow horns tied onto the front like this." He watched as she leaned

86

the cane against the wall, then projected two horns from her own head with a wide sweep of her arms.

"Well, if he owns a Cadillac with cow horns, he can't be such a bad bet."

"Yes, suh. That's exactly what I says. Come in for some coffee, Mista Pato. You seems tired. Myra's little baby in here. I watchin' it."

He did not refuse, though truthfully he considered he might enjoy himself more on the roof than in Mrs. Roberts's parlor. The sight of his baby, this love child, fruit of his loins, could be calculated to upset him for days. He followed her into the darkened room.

"Does you wish regular or special coffee, Mista Pato?"

"Special please, Mrs. Roberts, if it's not too much trouble," he answered. Regular was Sanka and condensed milk. Special was a thick clove-flavored brew served in tiny Turkish cups, though Principato could never understand how she came by the custom. It was no ceremonial drink. He knew she took it with all her meals. He watched as she hobbled off toward the kitchen.

Then he crept close to his and Myra's baby girl, who lay sleeping in a crib near the small-screen TV set, her head a Medusa-like collection of braids, each tied at the end with a tiny pink ribbon, and glistening from the oily hair straightener her mother had applied. Principato drew a chair to the crib side and sat watching the small chest in the white nightie heaving with regular breathing and the almost imperceptible flaring of the nostrils as the air passed in and out. It amazed him somewhat that this child did not dribble from the corners of her mouth while she slept. All Principato's Corrigan children were dribblers.

He moved slightly and a light ray came through a parting in the lace curtains at the front window and fell almost squarely on the child's forehead, making a light coppery sunspot. Principato thought of the word "anointed," and reached over to touch the pat of burnished skin, marveling at the final settlement of sallow Italian and dark Negroid chromosomes.

Then he looked up at the sound of Mrs. Roberts's cane tapping its way back from the kitchen. She held a Ballantine beer tray stiffly in one hand with two small cups of coffee on top. He watched her set it on a table.

87

"That child half-white, Mista Pato."

"I know, Mrs. Roberts."

"Myra know who the father is, but she keepin' it a secret. Have she told you who it is, Mista Pato?" the old lady asked, squinting at him through the half light.

"No, she hasn't, Mrs. Roberts."

"Must be somebody 'portant if she afraid to talk. A policeman maybe, does you think, Mista Pato?"

"It could be. Yes, it might be a policeman." He watched Mrs. Roberts reach for her cup on the tray and hoped she had somehow already digested her theory of a nameless, faceless, white propagating cop. Then he stood and walked to the tray for his own coffee. He returned to sit down heavily beside the crib again.

"Myra a good girl, Mista Pato. She take real good care of her baby."

"I know, Mrs. Roberts," he assured her automatically, as he did each time he spoke with her. The old lady was lonely. She viewed Principato with a real fear, believing he could take Myra, her friend and boarder, away from her and lock her—in what?—prison perhaps, or more imaginatively, some sheer-walled, padded tower, staffed by long-gowned, frigid white women, where they somehow cured you of having babies illegitimately. Maybe with sterile, pincer-like instruments that snipped at the life-bearing inner parts. He knew how her mind worked, born not so long after the paper death of slavery: in the great world of the whites beyond her neat, ordered house, anything was possible. Lawful, even. All things to those who held the power. Only it grieved Principato that she should fear him as an agent of such power.

"Myra have fixed up the upstairs rooms where she lives real nice, Mista Pato. Does you want to see them?"

"I have seen them, Mrs. Roberts. Remember?" He smiled at her and her anxious eyes went suddenly calm as if she had just decided Principato was not going to take Myra away after all.

"Does you like the colors, Mista Pato?" There was a small suggestion of disapproval in her voice.

"Well yes, I think so," he answered passively. But like them? He loved them! Especially the Chinese-red bedroom with the lamppost-black trim and floor-hugging bed covered with ultrawhite sheets. There he had lanced Myra to the hilt four times in that single first afternoon, crazed by the clash of her tawny skin against that white pallet, while Mrs. Roberts hobbled obligingly away toward her dental appointment. Principato, sad parent to five sun-despising offspring whose mother had great, cold feet and a freckled belly, in bed with a lioness at last! Adulterer. But, dear Lord, the wonder of that day: the act repeated in full power when he was not chasing her, trembling and erect, following after the fantastic musky Myra odor through the living room with its madras-patterned wallpaper and into the mustard-yellow den with its blazing ninety-eight-cent J. C. Penney Utrillos screaming down from the walls. Heedless of onlookers, they had opened the blinds to intensify color. From her kitchen they had hung back, though, as if by mutual consent. Its walls of cool forest-green were ringed with crisp white appliances: subdued, nonerotic flavors that threatened to break the current of the dream.

"I don't like it so much, Mista Pato. I thinks a room should be like this."

This is even worse than my home, he mused as he looked about. But he kept the thought to himself. This was no room for living in. Instead, it reminded him of that kind of period restoration they put together in museums: the legacy of some turn-of-the-century white family that fled the Negro influx. Aong with their disdain for her race and the smell of their small-minded row-house dweller's fear over devaluating prices and rerooting themselves, Mrs. Roberts was the inheritor of a cluttered assortment of drab, overstuffed furniture. Faded wallpaper, the heavy oak trim and great sliding doors completed the blending. The TV set must have been the only addition to the place in years. Knowing her, Principato guessed she had never changed the original arrangement as a testimony to her belief in that white family's inherent good taste and excellence. It had served them well enough; it would serve her also.

"This a good room for a dyin' old person who waitin' to go to heaven. Does you think so, Mista Pato?"

"Yes. Yes, I think it is, Mrs. Roberts," he answered absently. Then he looked at her closely, watched her lift the clove coffee to her lips with a trembling hand. She was truly dying. But easing out of it: a sweet old matriarch come simply to the end of her days through a process of gradual crumblings and half deaths within her. She had leased fourteen children to the world and so far had outlived six of them and her husband. And, he thought ruefully in a rare unpatriotic moment, she had served the American Empire well, within the limits of her second-class citizenship. The children she had given it were a far-flung essential lot of janitors, maids, and municipal-bus drivers. One even gassed dogs at a city pound somewhere in Louisiana.

Across from him, dwarfed in her huge chair, Mrs. Roberts began to nod with sleep, dreaming perhaps of her dead husband or her distant South or her own colored folks' afterlife she was preparing for. Her heavy stockinged, old lady's legs bent suddenly inward, the knees clutching her cane. The thin ray of light that had anointed the forehead of Myra and Principato's baby had moved only slightly and still cut across the room before him. Particles of dust swirled up and down its length. Otherwise, the room was crammed with shadows, old pictures, old memories, and faded lace doilies on the tops of tables.

A gray mood swept over Principato, but he did nothing to combat it; in fact, he indulged it. Truthfully, he was a secret lover of melancholy. Old rooms like this, murky, dank even, if possible, were a sweet playground for him. That part of his soul inherited from his father, he guessed. From his mother had come the effortless compassion, but also a crippling hysterical trait that he preferred not to think of now. With his imagination darkly fired, he considered walking outside to the street to gaze up into the sky and see the brilliant sun spinning out toward the end of the day. That sight, the continuity implied, might direct his thoughts toward eternity: the much-longed-for exalted reflections in the midst of banal days. Or, failing that, it would simply remind him of time wasted.

But to hell with it. Principato was never one to take himself to task for wasting the day. He only wondered at the succession of events that filled it, was, in fact, amazed by them: meeting the two bums, one who wanted to take him into a men's toilet, the Temple girl who accused him of running a credit racket, the friendly racist, then the funeral. Finally killing off the rest of the afternoon in the parlor of an ancient Negress with a humble slave's mentality. Really, this was

Principato's only art, he decided. To drift aimlessly, but expectantly (always expectantly), through the world on certain days, bumping into some of the half-baked, ass-end people that inhabited it, the same ones that nobody else could possibly become involved with. Alas, he realized, he had been doing this for years.

He stood up and walked across the room to the sofa with its bulging center cushion. There he sank wearily down upon it, stretching out full-length. He watched dimly as Mrs. Roberts, who had come suddenly awake, tapped her way toward him, a patchwork quilt slung over her arm. She rested her cane on the sofa near his head, and unfurling the quilt, spread it over his body. The touch of it on his hands and face and socks (he had kicked off his loafers) was unexpectedly cool. The odor of moth balls clung to it.

"You likes it here, yes, Mista Pato?"

Beneath his covering, he nodded his head.

"You come here to live with us whenever you wishes, Mista Pato."

"Thank you, Mrs. Roberts," came the muffled reply.

"She knows exactly what you need in life," a distant voice said to him, as if it were advising him to grab up Mrs. Roberts and adopt her as his mother. Then the voice diminished and his mind eased deeper into the darkness. Vaguely, he felt the soft, patting touch of the old lady on his shoulder and sensed her hobbling off again. Soon he was asleep.

An hour later, perhaps, he awoke and saw the benevolent, smiling businessman's face looking down from a calendar on the wall beyond his feet. It was Milton Eisenberg, Home Furnishings and Appliances. Principato smiled in return.

"Our child will be a swinger," he told the benevolent Milton. "Her foundations were laid in a tempest."

But Milton only continued smiling.

Refreshed, Principato stood up.

"Mrs. Roberts, I've got to go."

The old lady came awake with a jerk, then put the room and Principato in focus. She arose to lead the way to the front door. There, he shook hands with her.

"Mista Pato, I have somethin' which I must tell you."

She looked at him guardedly and hunched down over her cane as if she expected to be struck. A certainty that he knew what she was going to say welled up in him.

"Myra pregnant again, Mista Pato."

"I didn't do it this time," he shot back at her. Knowing her news in advance had given him time to prepare a response. Normally, he was not so witty.

FIVE

Tuesday evening, after work, Principato ate a Linton's spaghetti special, then stepped into a long, narrow bar for a drink. There was still an hour to kill.

"What'll it be?"

"Bourbon and water."

The bartender pushed a button on a dispenser that held an upended bourbon bottle. The apparatus gurgled forth an exact shot.

"Sorry, mister," said the bartender apologetically, holding up the glass to show the liquid fill to the white line.

"That's O.K. You mean well."

"Ain't that a bitch?" said the boozy-faced man who sat next to him. "It even has a counter that ticks off the number of shots. Automation. Everything is automation. Next year the bartender's gonna be a robot."

Principato turned to look at the man. His nose was swollen and pitted. The veins and arteries stood out in his cheeks.

"What's your problem, mister? Genuine drinker or one-a-day man?"

"For courage," said Principato, holding up the glass.

"Why?"

"I'm going to a meeting tonight to tell a lot of strangers what's wrong with my marriage."

"You got problems?"

It's either all the way or none at all Principato decided: "Yeah, my wife's got the hots for an eighteen-year-old kid. Yesterday I duped him into sending her the most horrible statue ever as a gift. When she saw it was from him, she fell in love with it. Now it's on a table in our bedroom. It even glows in the dark. 'Vengeance is mine,' saith the Lord," he intoned miserably, taking a long swig of his drink.

"I know how it is, buddy. My wife took off with a university professor fifteen years ago. I haven't been off this bar stool since."

"Christ Almighty! It's true?"

"Ask him," the boozy-faced man said, nodding at the bartender. "That's what happens."

Horror of horrors, thought Principato. It happens once in every man's life. I'm sitting next to myself fifteen years removed. He stared intently into the blue-tinted bar mirror; the bartender flicked on a light. The same sallow, wasted look. The same fine, sensitive nose. Under the eyes, the great circles that bespoke incessant worry. Beside him, the jilted husband also stared into the mirror. He turned his head from side to side, as if to admire himself from every angle. There were tears in his eyes.

"Fifteen years ago, I had a nose like yours. Now look at it." It was affixed to his face like a light bulb.

"Touch it!" he commanded.

Principato raised his finger and pressed it to the side of the man's nose. It was hard, its surface a filter of tiny holes.

The single drink had turned his head. He felt he was going to cry, when the bartender kindly flicked off the light over the mirror.

"Was the man's name Kababian?" he asked the sorrowful boozer.

"No, it was Carruthers. Mason Carruthers. Stole my wife," the man suddenly sobbed.

Relieved, Principato slid down from the stool and took a dollar from his wallet. Then he added another to it.

"Buy him a drink," he said to the bartender. The man nodded silently. Beside Principato, the boozer sobbed into his sleeve.

Outside, the air quickly cleared his lightheadedness. He walked to the agency lot, climbed into the De Soto and drove to the Fifth Street address of Neutral Corner. Restored colonial Philadelphia. The front of the house met his expectations: a clean brick façade, with white windowless door and a gold American eagle on the door post. Up and down the street it was the same. Cobblestones and hitching posts and a scrubbed, polished look about everything. The return of Ben Franklin simplicity. He pulled a chain that set loose a jangling of cowbells inside the house.

In a moment the door opened and a woman stood before him, eyes slightly misty, heavily shadowed, right hand extended and beckoning in a kind of studied hostess gesture. The face, covered with make-up, was moon-shaped, the nose small but flared. This then must be Eva Lissome, Nick Malatesta's new playmate and patroness for perfecting marriages.

"Patroness," said Principato suddenly, bending to kiss her hand. She snatched it quickly away.

"Well, I can tell what your problem is all about, Mr. Principato."

"How did you know it was I?"

"The other seventeen are here, all women without their husbands. Nicky Malatesta told us to expect the opposite in your case."

"He was that sure?"

"We have a lot of faith in Nick's judgment, Mr. Principato," she said. Standing there, he resisted the urge to tell her it was Nick's fourteen-year-old son that had done most of the judgment-making so far. He thought of the boy now probably sitting alone among the old carnival ghosts out in the Jersey pinelands waiting for his father to return and wished him a proper misery. The little bastard.

"Please come this way, Mr. Principato."

To get into Eva Lissome's restoration, you had to gimp down two worn stone steps that might be your death in a power failure. The place was austere, paneled with wood that had the look of being pilfered from rural post offices or railroad stations. He followed Eva. She was short and waddled in toreador pants and a man's white oxford-cloth shirt, some perfume that he was too unskilled to recognize wafting back at him. She led the way through another paneled room, cluttered with straight-backed, wicker chairs, then through French doors into a large back garden almost filled with seated women. Silent, they seemed to refuse to talk with one another.

Malatesta sat on the scrubbed-off grate of a fireplace, the heels of his pointy-toed shoes hooked over the edge. Principato thought of his sweat-covered disarray in the trailer on Sunday afternoon, sleeping off a drunk. Now, carefully groomed, he looked curiously chastened, penitent even.

"Hi, Pato." He raised his arm in a greeting. His smile was correctly sheepish.

"Hello, Nick." Then Principato could think of nothing more to say aloud. What he wanted really was to demand in a whisper if Nick had made any contacts in the search for Rocco's woman. Instead, he allowed Eva to take his arm and lead him to a front-row chair between two defiant-looking housewives. Principato tried smiling at one and got a cold stare in return. Affronted, he watched as Lissome took her place beside a tall, middle-aged man with graying, swept-back hair and a dark tan who stood before a sign nailed to a naked rose trellis that read: WELCOME TO NEUTRAL CORNER. The man was Monsignor Allergucci, his father's telephone confessor.

But what was he doing here? And wearing an impeccably tailored but nonclerical sharkskin suit with a white silk tie? The priest nodded to him and Principato smiled in return. Then Allergucci leaned over to whisper something to the short, plumpish Eva, whose legs, Principato noticed for the first time, had a kind of cantilevered look in the toreador pants. She wore faded-blue tennis shoes that reminded him of the kind his mother favored for padding around the house.

In a moment the monsignor stepped forward and began to speak.

"Welcome, ladies and my friend Angelo," he said, pointing to Principato. "This is the beginning of our second two-month forum on marital problems under the patronage of our own Eva Lissome, a woman who, like yourselves, has known a multitude of sufferings, and who, because of her deep humanity is determined to help others find the way to happiness."

He gestured to Eva, who only bowed her head, looking indeed a squat receptacle of all the world's anguish. Beside Principato, one

96

woman began to take notes, scribbling furiously in longhand; his other neighbor fingered a rosary.

Allergucci continued, "We know that it's difficult for you to come here. It takes a lot of courage. You're full of doubts, angry with yourself, perhaps, that you've finally reached the stage where you're grasping at straws. Our contact, Malatesta, catches you in an amusement park, begins to give you the hard sell. He hands you address cards, brochures with schedules and topics."

Allergucci pointed back to Nick on the fireplace, and Principato heard the silence behind him break for the first time. There was a puzzled whispering. One woman said clearly, but low, "It was a little boy who talked with me." The speaker seemed not to notice.

"Why didn't you just throw all these things out the car window? Who was that crazy guy? you probably asked yourself. Why should I get involved in anything like this? But you didn't throw any of it away, and now you're here. Why? I think because you looked at your children and you knew you had to try. For their happiness as well as your own. For this you had to come here and find out if there was any help in it for you. It took courage, but after our great success with the previous series, and many satisfied participants, I'm positive you'll agree it was well worth it."

Around him, Principato could feel the audience loosening up. The monsignor's voice was sugary, the slightest trace of a warm inflection. He knew his hands would stop sweating in a moment. Next to him, the woman with the notebook stopped writing. She twirled the end of the pen thoughtfully in her mouth. His other neighbor, with the rosary, opened her purse and threw it inside. Behind him, muted voices began talking.

"You will each of you notice on the program we've given you that there are Tuesday-evening and Saturday-morning sessions. For Tuesdays we'll follow something of an Alcoholics Anonymous format— that is, public confession. In this, each of our participants will stand and tell us, as objectively as possible, what he or she thinks is wrong with his or her marriage. Make no mistake, we don't try to be nice to each other. We make our criticism as constructive as possible, and sometimes it's going to hurt.

"On Saturdays, there'll be lectures on various topics by people in

97

the marriage-counseling field. Also doctors, legal advisers, and others. Some of the subjects will be divorce procedures and family planning, to name a few. Question-and-answer periods will follow. Now, are there any questions before we continue?"

"Just one," a woman said, obviously warmed to the speaker, "who are you?"

"I am Dr. Allergucci."

"Like hell you are!" a bull voice bounded out of the last row. "You're Monsignor Allergucci of Saint Igitur's parish. And what, may I ask, are you doing with an organization that deals with birth control? Just look here under Family Planning, topic 5C: 'birth-control techniques.'"

Shocked, Principato spun in his seat to see a gargantuan woman in a print dress shaking her brochure at Allergucci. Corpulent but solid-looking, she spoke with a trace of brogue. Principato found her self-righteousness towering. He turned back on hearing the speaker's voice.

"All right, madam, so I'm Monsignor Allergucci," he conceded, addressing the Irish giantess, "but I won't have you censuring me. I thought it would be less embarrassing all around in view of several of the subjects to call myself doctor."

"Huh! I'll bet! And divorce procedures. You, a Catholic priest!"

Allergucci's forte was dispassion. "Are we of the True Church so narrow-minded as to insist that such subjects are absolutely taboo? We're not forcing anyone to accept them. We're only putting them up for consideration."

"Yes, and probably influencing good Catholics here with forbidden topics."

"If your faith is as unshakable as we are to suppose, madam, these subjects will mean no harm to you at all. I hope you will at least show a little tolerance for the interest others might have in them."

"Well, I, for one, will not be here to listen to those two topics."

"You don't have to come at all!" snapped Lissome, suddenly losing her aplomb. She shook a tiny fist in the air at the big woman. Principato had an instant vision of the two squaring off at the end of the garden.

"Ladies! Madam Lissome!" cried the suave priest. "Please let's don't destroy everything on the first night. Sit down!"

Lissome quickly made a comeback, looking more the benevolent patroness than ever. As if to rival her, the print dress sat down too.

Allergucci began again. "Well, with my secret unmasked, it's time to learn a few others." There was an appreciative ripple of laughter.

"Our first confession of the evening will be from Eva Lissome, our own benefactress."

The moment became suddenly strained. Principato watched Malatesta hurry to the control box and turn down the overhead lights to very dim. Looking over the garden walls, he could see the neon glow of hotel and department-store fronts and the floodlit statue of William Penn atop City Hall. Then, dramatically, a small pool of yellow light grew from a pinpoint before the audience. There was no applause as Allergucci guided Eva into the beam.

"I, Eva Lissome, confess . . ."

Fascinating, this woman! Under the yellow light in the dark garden, Principato understood the eye shadow and heavy make-up and the brilliantine-lacquered look of her hair. The hidden actress in the old millionaire's *Hausfrau*. Her face had a gray Ash Wednesday cast to it. The eyes were two black holes in its midst. The hair was fiercely dark by contrast. Around it, moths fluttered in and out of the light like messengers returning fond, then bitter memories to her. Her lips, strangely purple, spewed out the sad tale of Herman and the deceptively perfect marriage. Three sons, a beautiful home, best schools, best cars, best vacation spots. Then, on their twenty-fifth wedding anniversary, after a banquet in a ballroom filled with family and friends, they slipped into a little corner for a glass of champagne. The happy, reminiscing couple. Around them, a dance floor full of beaming, misty-eyed people: the about-to-be-betrayed believers in the possibility of enduring love. In the corner, Herman asks for his freedom. The girl is twenty-five. His lawyer has everything ready for a Mexican divorce.

"Good God!" An anguished shriek went up from Eva and she buried her face in her hands. Instantly, Principato brought a handkerchief to his liquid eyes. He felt her betrayal keenly, like a lance that had passed through him also. Herman became his lifelong enemy. Around him, women sobbed openly.

"Well, he paid for it! He paid plenty!" Lissome exclaimed in a cracking voice. The tiny fists were clenched at her side. Principato's own misery over her betrayal was broken as the women became a mob howling for revenge. Frightened not to, he joined in their chorus.

Eva was off her track. No longer housewife to the millionaire industrialist, three sons married off and gone, she, free and with a still young spirit, went off in defiance of what she knew were clichés to find happiness in Paris. She lived in Montparnasse, discovered she had a flair for painting, and almost died of loneliness.

Then Spain. Then Italy. In Sicily, contemplating suicide, she worked on a nude self-portrait to send to Herman as a conscience lash. It was cold, her villa unheated, her loneliness unabated. Then she met Nicky. The rest was self-explanatory, a category that Principato mentally tagged "interim."

The wronged woman was finished. In a kind of final humility, she bowed her head, pressing the back of her hands against her lap so the palms faced beseechingly outward. Think of me what you will, they said. Behind Principato, the half-weeping, half-raging audience of women began to applaud fiercely. Allergucci walked forward, took Eva by the arm, and led her to a chair. Then he stepped into the pool of light.

"Are there any comments?"

There were none. Clearly, the fault was all Herman's.

"Who shall be next?" he asked.

A number of women raised their hands immediately, but Principato leapt to his feet shouting, "Me! I want to confess!"

Allergucci seemed surprised, then pleased. "Well, Angelo, since you're the only man here, I guess we'll oblige you first."

Principato stepped into the yellow light, wondering how it made him look. The swarm of moths began banging into his head. He thrust his hands resolutely forward, watching his audience closely, and began his own sad tale of Cynthia, her Jesuit uncle and her family, Nikos Kababian lifting weights on the patio next door, and his father who was going into the urn. But from the rows of faces before him, he could tell nothing.

"Shouldn't my father go into the urn if he wants to?" Principato pleaded. "A man should have the right to plan his own dying if he knows when it's coming. This alone above all things. But Cynthia and that clan of hers all say he's a baptized Catholic and should go into the ground with last rites and a funeral mass. Strictly traditional. Stay with the rules. Really," he confessed, "I actually think they're less concerned from the religious angle than they are afraid of what people might say. He's always been a kind of embarrassment to them since I married into that family. I mean . . . Well, you know what he's like," he said to Allergucci, who stood off to one side. But the priest only shrugged his shoulders.

"I'm sorry to air this out in front of you, Monsignor, of all people. But am I going to desert my own father by insisting they read a mass over him and put him in a hole just to please Cynthia and that Corrigan mob?"

It was a near-weeping Principato who asked the question he had seen as a natural, towering finale. But staring out of his yellow light shaft at the stony masks of his fellow miserables, he decided that the issue was irrelevant: they had all aligned themselves with Cynthia, the woman. But then the rows of chairs erupted into turmoil.

"I'd smash that bitch's damn head!" one of the women began screaming, swinging her purse in a wide arc so that Principato feared she might smash the heads of a few of her cohorts.

"I wish I had her here right now! Wham! Dead she'd be for giving this poor man so much trouble!" another promised, turning around in the midst of angry, agreeing faces.

They were his! They were sympathetic to him, ready to fight his fight, and he might have rushed into their midst to be petted and kissed in motherly fashion by each of them in turn, except that he saw through the riot of swirling dresses and flailing arms that one was still seated.

"Are we allowed to ask questions and discuss his problem?" the one who had exposed Allergucci finally stood up and asked.

"Yes, of course," answered the monsignor, stepping forward and edging Principato out of the yellow light. "This is what we hoped for."

"Well, I only wanted to say that I feel sorry for his wife. First on the score of this Kababian fellow. You can imagine what sort of disappointment drives a poor woman to runnin' after a teen-ager. Just look at this one here," she said, pointing a thick arm at Principato. Stricken, he felt her contempt go through him like a knife.

"Thin as a rail, obviously neurotic, he looks like a walkin' persecution complex."

Eva Lissome stormed out of her chair. "Madam, I feel you're making a personal attack on poor Mr. Principato!"

"Poor . . . Mister . . . Principato." The words came back a slow, sarcastic echo. Principato wanted to lunge over the wall and fly away into the Philadelphia night, never to return. He watched helplessly as the gargantuan woman started in on Lissome.

"I didn't say anything when you were finished, lady. But we can just imagine what sort of illicit happenin's was takin' place between you and that one over there in Sicily," she said, pointing now at Malatesta, who abruptly moved his feet from the fireplace and stood up. "You can bet there was never any understandin' between my Cornelius and me until the night we were married."

"I'm really surprised there has *ever* been an understanding between your Cornelius and you," Eva retorted.

"I'd like you to take notice of the fact that I still have him after twenty-three years of marriage."

"Go to hell with your goddam husband!" Eva shrieked. And she sped around the rows of chairs toward the big woman, grabbing a fire iron on the way. Malatesta and Allergucci took off after her, trying to restrain her.

"Out! Out! you bitch!" Eva was screaming. The giantess was running toward the door, Lissome in sneakered feet right behind her. The place was bedlam.

Story of my life, Principato decided, rueful in the midst of the riot. He stepped back into the yellow light, as if from within its beam the chaos would seem corrected and the world sympathetic again and eager for more of his serious monologue. But to no avail. From the front of the house he heard a door slam. In a moment, Allergucci alone came back.

"Ladies, Mr. Principato, I'd like to suspend for the evening because of this unfortunate happening. I hope that none of this will influence your decision to come on Saturday morning. We have the makings of a good working group here, now."

"I'm supposed to go on retreat this weekend," Principato said. "I'm afraid I won't be able to make it."

"All right, we'll see you on Tuesday evening, then. Anyone else?" There was no one else.

"We'll be here," one woman said firmly.

"Thank you, then, and good night." Allergucci bowed. He turned to leave and Principato's women friends surrounded him.

"I think what you're doing is very courageous, Mr. Principato," one said. "After all, a father's death wish is sacred. I should think your wife would realize this and be more permissive. And as to that kid, she must be crazy. Muscles are nice, but I prefer depth and soul personally."

"Three to one over muscles," said another woman with a French accent. Her hair was drawn back into a bun and she wore thick horn-rimmed glasses. Beneath them, her left eye twitched. Principato guessed she might even be winking at him.

The women turned to go, and he found Malatesta at his side.

"Come on inside for coffee, Pato. The monsignor's getting ready to take Eva for a little walk and calm her down. Two more steps and she would have split that dame's skull with a poker. That was a close one."

Eva's kitchen was a gleaming oasis in the colonial austerity. She angrily spooned ground coffee into an electric percolator while Allergucci sat quietly, smoking a cigarette.

"I'll tell you one thing, Monsignor. If that whore ever shows up in this place again, she's dead! I haven't lost my temper since the time we had the argument in Herman's lawyer's office about the settlement!"

Allergucci said nothing, but watched her padding back and forth across the floor. Principato felt he owed an apology. After all, the whole row had started because of him. But the time seemed wrong

103

and he merely took a seat. Beside him, the percolator erupted its first geyser of water. A steady stream followed.

"Mr. Principato," Eva said suddenly, "let me compliment you. You presented your case quite eloquently tonight. You have my deepest sympathy, as well as the sympathy of all the ladies except that moose I chased out. I think you have good grounds for a divorce. Not like what Herman did to me."

At the mention of Herman, she began crying.

"Come, Eva," Allergucci said, rising. "We'll take a little stroll up to Independence Mall. The night air will be good for your nerves. Nick, you know when the coffee will be ready."

"O.K., Monsignor. We'll keep it hot for you."

They watched as Allergucci went into the next room, opened a closet, and took out a light jacket for Eva. He draped it carefully around her shoulders, for a breeze had risen off the river and the yellow lights swung long arcs across the shrubs and walls of the garden. The handsome priest solicitously steered the patroness toward the door. There were small tears on her cheeks, making a slight chromatic trail from the eye shadow. Nick watched them.

"What's the story?" Principato asked after they were gone. He knew Nick would tell from the way he had watched their parting.

"The slickest priest in the service of God!" Malatesta said, getting up to pour coffee. "Even I, Nicky Malatesta, am afraid of that guy. He's out to leave his mark on the world. Father Flanagan's got his Boys Town, so Monsignor Allergucci needs his Saint Igitur's. You've never seen that place? Like Vatican City. Medium-cost cathedral, grade school and high school, neither with enough kids to fill them. An orphanage, a clinic, and two convents. One order of nuns isn't good enough for that guy. He imported one from somewhere. Also cloistered walks, sparkling fountains, and acres of flower beds. Now he's working on the Monsignor Giuseppe Allergucci Memorial Archdiocesan Museum. Not even dead yet! What an operator! If he could find some cripple to drop his crutches up there, he'd turn it into another Lourdes."

Across from him, Malatesta was shaking with a spasmodic anger that had grown suddenly as he spoke of Allergucci. He drank his coffee in long slurps. The cup rattled in his hands.

"I didn't figure this was his game," Principato said gravely. "He hears my father's confession on the telephone. They're both from the old neighborhood. How did he get to know Eva?"

"Easy. That sleuth keeps a black book on everybody in Philadelphia who makes more than twenty-five grand per annum. He was putting the tap on Eva's husband for years before the divorce. Then Herman got a new tax lawyer, and Allergucci of the golden tongue was out in the cold. I guess he was going to cross them off until he heard about Eva's settlement."

"What happened then?"

"Ah, yes, what happened then? Eva goes to Europe, and every week, along with the *Time* magazine, there's a letter from Allergucci. She saved them all. Stacks of them. I've read almost every one. From a priest! I, Malatesta, arch hater of priests, admit that over a can of beer, ninety per cent of these black robes are good guys. But this Allergucci! A gigolo! Worse than me, even. Worse than anyone!

"Why do you think we finally came home? Because Nicky was lonesome for Philadelphia? Never! Because that one came up with the idea of this Neutral Corner bullshit. Constructive therapy he calls it. I can show you the letter. A goal in life for poor, wandering Eva. Also a chance to get her and her money back within working range.

"So I came with her. I admit it, Pato, I was almost starving to death over there in Palermo. The coldest winter on record. We got off the boat in New York in March, and who's waiting for us on the dock with a glowing suntan and violets? Right. Monsignor Giuseppe Allergucci. All set to take Eva back to Philly in that prehistoric Cord roadster he drives. When he saw me, he almost fell over. The only satisfaction I ever got from him. He puts Eva and the luggage up front with the top up and me in the rumble seat. Did you ever ride from New York to Philly in March in a rumble seat? I could have killed that bastard the first day, except that I was almost frozen to death."

Nick stood up and began pacing back and forth, smacking his left hand with his right palm.

"The thing that gets me is the way that he treats me now. Either like I don't exist or like the manservant. I try to tell Eva what he's all about, but she won't listen. You can't touch the guy and he's milking

105

her dry right now. You should go out to that place of his, Pato. He's got his goddam name on everything out there. At the rate he's building, they'll have to tear down Philadelphia to make room for it in a couple of years."

Principato said nothing. Instead, he looked out at the troubled specters of himself and seventeen women seated in the garden and thought sadly how little was actually pure in life. The river of events that had carried them, mere hopefuls, to this confession place, hardly believing that such a place could exist, ran deep and dirty. At its source, Allergucci the monsignor, now sinister to Principato, who feared any intelligence powerful enough to manipulate, had raised Eva to the level of patroness only to keep her in Philadelphia for the sacking of her treasury. And Malatesta, the lesser, dumber gigolo, who thought of Neutral Corner as a lot of bullshit, only stomped about jealous and ineffectual in the mud.

"I'm surprised the monsignor didn't say something about my old man and the urn," Principato said finally.

"What the hell does he care? Allergucci never ruffled any feathers over a little theology. Besides, there's too much at stake. If he plays his cards right, he can get Eva to pay for half that goddam museum of his."

Then the front door opened and Eva came bouncing into the kitchen, as a teen-ager would. Principato gasped involuntarily at the sight of her. Her make-up was mottled, now heavily stained with eye shadow that profuse tears had spread all over her cheeks. The lacquered hair was blown into witch-head formations by the wind. He grasped the sudden notion of middle-aged Eva trying to make time stand still, and his heart overflowed with pity for her. Allergucci was right behind her.

"Hello, boys, Eva's better! Coffee hot?"

"Yes ma'am!" said Malatesta. His change was instantaneous. "Some for you, Monsignor?"

"No, Nick, thank you. I'll have to go. And you, dear Eva, should be getting some rest after that trauma."

"Am I forgiven for being such a bother, Monsignor?"

"Of course, my dear." Allergucci's face was supremely benign. Seated near him, Principato felt something turn to anger inside him.

106

The real admiration he had always had for the sheik priest became dislike. This Allergucci was not worthy to be his father's confessor— by telephone or otherwise. He would warn the old man the first chance he got.

"I've got to go too," said Principato. "Thanks for everything, your help and coffee."

"My pleasure both, Mr. Principato," Eva answered.

Principato and Allergucci left together, going out into the summer night, the former crossing the street to his De Soto after grudgingly shaking hands with the priest. Allergucci walked to an old-fashioned roadster about halfway up the block. It was a gleaming Cord, clerically black, that started in a roar of superchargers and sprang up the cobbled street.

Strange marriage, Principato reflected, standing under a gaslight and looking after Allergucci's vanishing taillights, then at Eva's Ben Franklin house. Just then, a hand touched his arm. He turned to see the woman that Eva had chased out and stepped back from fear. But no need. Her face was stained a blustering red from crying. The heavy odor of some cheap cologne hung in the air about her. She was still breathing hard from running and her armpits were stained with sweat. He forgave her instantly.

"I'm sorry," she said, "it's just that it was so hard to come here. I had to sneak out. If Cornelius ever found out I came, he'd murder me."

"I know how it is," Principato answered, gripping her arm tightly at the elbow. "Come on, I'll give you a lift home."

A light rain started to fall as they drove away, making the cobbled streets look slick and clean. Block-long streaks of yellow reflection from the blinking traffic lights entered and re-entered the car. Beside him, the woman blew her nose into a huge workingman's handkerchief.

"I've got such problems with my marriage," she said, "and Cornelius doesn't even know about them. We were over in Jersey a couple of weeks ago and stopped in that kiddie park with our little nephew, and that boy gives me all that stuff about Neutral Corner. So I didn't say anything to Cornelius, but I kept it all, and thought I'd sneak over here to see if anybody could help me. I wasn't interested in that birth control or any of that business against the Church, though. That's why I got so mad at Monsignor Allergucci for bein' there. I used to go up to Saint Igitur's for a little bingo now and then, and I've seen him up there. Figured he was just a good, holy priest."

"None of that's important any more," Principato said. "What's your problem?"

"Well, it's this way," she began, blowing her nose again. "Cornelius and I are married for twenty-three years. He's a dock worker and used to be a heavy drinker, and every Friday night since we were married until last year, he came home stormin' drunk and beat the hell out of me. You should've seen me on Saturday mornings standin' in front of a mirror checkin' over my bruises and welts, and wearin' black stockings to church on Sundays so the neighbors wouldn't see them.

"It's not like they didn't know about it though. You could hear me over in Camden on a good night. Well, last year we got a new priest at the parish and he persuades Cornelius to take the pledge, and lay off the drinkin' and beatin' me up. Since then, Cornelius hasn't touched anything stronger than Coke.

"I can tell you it's been a misery for me. For twenty years I thought I was the saddest woman alive, trottin' out to church in the afternoon to light a candle and pray for Cornelius to get off the bottle. Now I'm dissatisfied. I don't know how to say it exactly, but I miss those old beatings. The week doesn't seem the same without them any more. I've tried to get Cornelius back into the mood, but without the booze he's meek as a lamb. When I try to start a fight, he turns it into a joke. What am I goin' to do with a man like that?"

Her name was Corky. They stopped for a sandwich in a bright chromium streetcar diner, oblivious to the stares of truckers and cab drivers. She reached over to place her huge paw on the back of his hand and held it there until the waitress brought their order.

"Do you think that Eva woman will let me come again?" she asked.

"I'm sure of it. She felt bad about the whole thing afterward," he lied.

"God, was I lucky! I could feel her and that poker right at my tail when I went through the door!"

If ever I'm to have a real affair, Principato considered in a curious humor, it's bound to be with someone as grotesque as this one. It's in the blood. When gray Uncle Niccolò had his one fling, it was with Gina Del Bisi, a pasta-fattened mammoth who towered over tiny Niccolò by at least a foot. Across from him, Corky wolfed down the last of her chicken sandwich and called to the waitress for a superburger. Then he watched as a sudden apprehensive look crossed her face.

"John Farland!" she said, her face turning into an elaborate deceitful mask. "How are you?"

Principato turned to see a big Irish cop standing next to him. His night stick swung in a slow arc from his arm.

"I'm fine, Corky. Who's your friend?"

"He's a friend of Cornelius's, John," she answered, looking at him with narrowed eyes now.

"He doesn't look like any friend of Cornelius's to me," the cop said as he grabbed Principato's thin wrist between two thick fingers and held it up to her. A terrified Principato watched as she stood up and faced the policeman at eye level.

"I said he's a friend of Cornelius's, John. And if you don't want to believe me, then that shiny badge won't be any protection against me breakin' this Coke bottle over your head." Her left hand had grasped the neck of the bottle and transferred it quickly to the right, then shot down to anchor the end of the cop's night stick. Around them, the truckers and cab drivers cleared off the counter stools. Soft, ironic music came from the juke box. The waitress, frightened, chewed the end of her apron.

"I'm glad to know any new friend of Cornelius's," the cop said after a moment, his voice husky with fear, and reached down to shake Principato's hand limply. Then he turned and went out. Relieved, the customers edged back toward their food. The waitress turned up the volume on the juke box. Corky, trembling with rage, sat down again.

"Aw, you can see why my life is so miserable that it would drive me down to Neutral Corner. Besides cuttin' out the beatings, Cornelius's got the biggest network of spies and squealers in the city. Every time I pass a cop or a street sweeper I have to put on my glasses to make sure it isn't somebody we know. That one'll be on the phone to Cornelius as soon as he gets his voice back. I should have finished him off while I had him here."

"Well, listen," Principato began, his own voice husky, "maybe I should give you cabfare and send you home from here. I don't want you to get in any more trouble because of me." His eyes swept the row of wide-bottomed truckers and cabbies, certain that Cornelius must have at least one friend among them.

"Don't worry," she said, her huge paw going back over his small hand. "I'll protect you."

Outside in the parking lot, she pulled him toward her and kissed him wetly on the cheek.

"Are you Italian?" she demanded, regarding him closely.

"Yes."

"I've decided to give myself to you," she said solemnly.

"How do you mean?"

"I mean sexually. In a bed."

"Oh, that way." Principato only shrugged. Curiously now, he was not frightened. It occurred to him suddenly that they were standing, huge mother and small son, in a well-lit parking lot. He turned back to see the restaurant customers and help all peering through the windows at them. Corky saw them also.

"Let's get out of here. I've got a place for us to go," she said.

Taking her hand, he walked with her to the car, then, following her directions, drove toward the Richmond docks, while she ran her fingers through his hair. A thick fog rolled in from the river after the rain and Principato moved slowly behind the De Soto's weak headlights. They lurched along twisting cobbled streets that passed between endless rows of warehouses and small wholesale businesses, crossing frequent railroad tracks. Occasionally, rats darted out of sewers and scampered along the sidewalks.

"Right here," she said. "Drive up to the gates."

A weathered sign on the front of the old warehouse read DANIEL HALLAGAN, INSTITUTIONAL SUPPLIES.

"Who's Hallagan?" Principato asked.

"That's my maiden name. Danny's my brother."

She got out and unlocked the double doors with a key she took

110

from her purse, then shoved each half back wide enough for the car to enter. Principato marveled at the size of her walking before the headlights, thinking she must weigh at least two hundred pounds. The doors had flown back effortlessly from her strength. She beckoned him inside.

"Park it behind those trucks while I close the gates. I've got a flashlight over here somewhere."

Principato switched off the engine and watched in the darkness until she came skipping back with her flashlight.

"Aren't you excited?" she said. "You're the only man I've ever given myself to other than Cornelius. And that's with being married twenty-three years."

Principato said nothing. Instead, he recalled that Corky would be woman number four for him. The first, the prostitute who had given him that claplike ailment and to whom he doggedly persisted in returning triweekly until graduation: a small price for four years of security. Then Cynthia, to whom he had been married eleven long years. Then the afternoon of faultless erotica spent with Myra Phee. Now he followed his new woman up a rickety flight of steps crammed with boxes of dispenser napkins and canned stewed tomatoes into a room that reminded him of a bridal suite.

"Danny, my brother, gave me this," she said simply.

In the middle of the room was a huge, round bed. The floor was carpeted wall to wall and draperies hung from ceiling to floor all around. There were no windows visible. Corky walked to a cabinet stereo, pressed a series of buttons, and lovers' music came forth after a record clicked onto a turntable.

"Would you like some wine?" she asked.

"No, I don't think I need any."

"You can change in there," she said, pointing to a door marked HIM. "There's three sizes of nightshirt hangin' on the wall. The smallest'll probably fit you best."

Resigned to always fitting best into the smallest, Principato went into the changing room, slipped into the blue nightshirt, used the electric shaver, and slapped on some after-shave lotion.

When he emerged, the room was dark except for the pinpoint of light on a pink Princess telephone. He was reminded to call Cynthia.

"I'm here," Corky spoke softly. She lay in a nightgown atop the circular bed like a walrus on a rock.

"I've got to telephone my wife," he said, starting for the tiny light.

"Oh, what a terrible woman I am!" she moaned suddenly, lifting her legs a short distance into the air, then slapping them down hard on the bed. "Who ever thought I'd be takin' a man away from his wife? What lie are you goin' to tell her? You might say your car broke down and you're goin' to stay at a hotel. After all, you live all the way out in the suburbs someplace, don't you?"

"I'll just tell her I'm staying at my parents'. I do that occasionally. She won't have any reason to disbelieve."

Principato picked up the phone and carried it to the bed, sitting on the edge. As he dialed the number, his new woman wrapped her arms tightly about his waist.

"Hold the receiver away from your ear so I can hear what kind of voice she has," Corky instructed.

After three or four short rings, the phone was answered.

"Hello."

"Hello, Mrs. Phillips, this is Principato."

"Ah, Principato. Where are you? It's almost midnight, you know."

"I'm sorry for not calling earlier. I'll be staying at my parents' home tonight. I've got to be at the office early in the morning. Where's Cynthia?"

"She's sleeping. No need to disturb her." Sleeping? Bullshit. He pictured her, languorous and big-footed, lying in bed watching Kababian's pink-and-blue sequined statue glowing in the dark.

"Make her put your wife on," Corky whispered, jabbing a stiff finger into the area of his kidney.

"Who's that I hear whispering, Principato?" Phillips asked.

"Nobody, Mrs. Phillips. It's only the TV set in the next room. My father's watching the Late Show. Listen, put Cynthia on for a moment."

"I told you she's sleeping. She might not like being wakened."

"We'll have to take our chances. Tell her Nikos Kababian wants to talk with her." Oh-oh. Too much bravado, perhaps? Principato realized it was the first time he had ever made reference to that infatuation with a member of his own household.

112

"Very funny," came Cynthia's voice. She must have picked up their bedroom extension the same instant as Phillips and been content only to listen.

"I'll handle it from here, Millicent," she said to Phillips. Obediently, the housekeeper hung up the kitchen phone. Behind Principato, Corky sat up to hear better.

"What's the idea of that crack about Nikos, Principato? Where are we living? Turkey? A woman can't have a neighborly friendship with a kid next door without her husband turning it into a full-fledged affair?"

"Neighborly friendship? If the President of the United States sent me that horrible statue, I'd find a way to get it into the garbage can before somebody thought I actually liked it. But you turn it into a goddam shrine. Is it still there in our bedroom glowing in the dark? I won't sleep in that place one more night as long as it's there. Do you hear me, Cynthia?"

"Fuck you, Principato! It stays! Even if I have to get one of my brothers to sit outside the door and guard it! Do you hear me? Fuck you!"

Fuck you! Principato heard the words in total disbelief. This was his wife, ultra-Catholic mother of five ultra-Catholic children whom he used as his credentials to buy the atrocious statue in the religious-goods shop? Was she a good woman? the nun had asked. Of course she was a good woman, he had protested. One of the best. She followed the Catholic format for living to the letter. Even had a Jesuit uncle and deceased bishop uncle for extra credits. Now in the middle of the night, lying in full view of her luminous statue she shrieks, Fuck you! at her husband who prepared to go to bed with a two-hundred-pound woman in a dockside warehouse. He could not believe it still. The receiver slammed in his ear.

"My God! Did you hear what she said to me?"

"Oh, you poor thing. I can understand how your life must be. That first character sounded like she works on a barge someplace, and your wife is a real bitch, although I don't figure what she said at the end is part of her standard style. I'll give her that much credit."

"It certainly isn't," Principato conceded, not wanting his new lover to think that his wife was in the habit of liberally dispensing fuck yous to all the world that managed to displease her. Then he allowed himself to be taken into her arms and pressed close to her heavy body while she made primitive dovelike noises that he imagined she used to arouse an unwilling Cornelius. Moments later, summoning some hidden male strengths, he lifted her nightgown. A great odor, not entirely displeasing, rushed out at him. He climbed atop her, trying to surround her girth with his arms, but it was impossible. Magically, his erect member slid into her.

"Do you feel it?" he asked.

"I think so," she replied, a little uncertain. He watched as she raised one arm to bless herself, then urged her body into the suppressed contortions of a sea squall that soon became a full-blown typhoon. A frightened Principato clung desperately to her great ship of a body and saw the light of the Princess telephone across the room pitching and diving like the faraway light of another ship caught in the same storm. After a time, perched on the edge of a fevered seasickness, he felt a rapid change to exultation as the sperm began rushing out of him. For an instant, he thought he might even lift this woman whose body he rode upon and throw her lightly and easily about the room. This, until the first immense convulsion came: so intense that Principato imagined that same ship had arrived to a sudden dead stop in the hurricane's eye and was now being sucked down into some vortex. Down, down, he rode into her, suddenly the whole ocean, instead of a mere ship upon it. Then, without warning, she ejected him with a mighty thrust of her hands against his shoulders so that he yelped with the pain. He was outside, lying spent and lightheaded beside her on the round bed.

"Jesus, Mary, and Joseph," she said over and over again. "Please bring me a glass of water, O.K.?"

He stood up weakly, went into the bathroom, ran the water, and carried a glass back to her. Then he lay down beside her and she caressed his head.

"You said tonight you had five children. Is that right?" she asked.

"Yes, that's right." Five that might be acknowledged. With Myra, he had fathered a sixth. But how could he tell that to Corky, whom he imagined lived in a disintegrating Irish neighborhood already being encroached upon by the Negro districts?

114

"Five children. Isn't that a wonderful thing?"

Principato did not believe it to be such a wonderful thing, but he said nothing.

"Do you think I'll have a baby?" she asked hopefully.

"I'm not sure. Do you want one?"

"Oh, yes. That's what this room is all about. Twenty-three years married and no children. And time is runnin' out for me now. Poor Cornelius, I love him like no woman ever loved a man. And respect him, too. He could lift the front end of a dump truck and drink a whole platoon of cops under the table. But the poor bastard's as sterile as a mule."

Principato raised himself to see her shaking her huge head sadly. Then he lay close to her, pressing his face against her side. Really, the Great God who ruled over us all held the ultimate wisdom. With gifts and talents in the extreme, came faults and detractions in the extreme also. Much balance in the universe. Principato believed it conclusively now. And the Great One had assigned him to a task, balanced the detractions in an incredible way, it seemed: to be pro-creator to self-hallowed, shrinking families who lived in the terrible fear that clan might not be perpetuated. Witness the Corrigans, he thought. Witness the two-hundred-pound woman beside him. Nod-ding to sleep against her, he prayed for Corky's progeny.

SIX

Friday afternoon after work Principato drove with Larkin to the retreat house. As they were leaving the city, it began to rain, a fierce downpour to relieve the muggy day. A good beginning to the weekend, perhaps, the omen of cleansing rain. But, for Principato it took another turn predictably. Its intensity frightened him and forced him over to the side of the expressway to wait for it to pass. On the Schuylkill the wind churned up wavelets as a police boat beat its way upstream—to disaster, perhaps. The notion intrigued him. He decided it would confirm a dismal portent of earlier in the day. He peered intently through the fogged-up windshield, the old vacuum-pump wipers making a sluggish arc across his face. Down below, water sprayed over the police boat's bow as it bounced from the successive waves. In a minute it was gone, disappearing around a bend, still afloat.

The earlier portent had come when Corky telephoned before lunch. Principato took the call alone in the dictation room, prepared to be amused by her.

"Hello, is it you?"

"Yes, it's me," he said. "How are you?"

"Oh, I'm fine. I was thinkin' about you goin' to that retreat this

116

weekend, so I wanted to call and ask you to say a prayer for my special intention."

"Special intention? Oh yes, the baby."

"I made a novena on Wednesday night, and lit a dollar candle after mass yesterday mornin'. Danny said to say hello and ask you if you needed anything. He certainly took a likin' to you."

"And I to him," Principato said. He stretched far back in the desk chair and loosened his tie, thinking of Dan Hallagan. Wednesday morning Principato had awakened hungrily to the sound of truck engines starting in the warehouse below, and telephoned Holy Family house to report sick for the day. Corky slipped into a huge tent of a housecoat and went downstairs to find her brother. Principato, her lover, lying contented on the great circular bed, had a fleeting comic vision of her padding sheepishly across the grimy floor to Hallagan's office until he heard the employees greeting her loudly by name. From the sound of it, she knew them all and stopped to talk with each one. In ten minutes, heavy footsteps returned up the stairs. The door opened and Corky carrying a box of doughnuts, entered first, followed by a gaunt, white-haired man who held a steaming pot of coffee.

"Danny, this is Mr. Principato, my friend."

"Hello, sir, how are you?" Hallagan put the coffee down atop a table and sprinted—it seemed to Principato—to the side of the bed. He took the proffered hand and held it for a long time, regarding his sister's new friend closely. His eyes, ringed with large atrabilious circles that suggested a hidden bile or liver ailment, were hero-worshiping. Principato felt exalted in their gaze.

Then Hallagan stood up and began to pace rapidly about the room as Corky prepared the coffee and doughnuts on a tray.

"I think it's a wonderful thing you're doin' for my poor sister, Corky, sir."

"I'm glad to be of some help, Mr. Hallagan," Principato had mumbled through a mouthful of doughnut. Later, he spent the day with them downstairs in Hallagan's office, its walls covered with photographs of great boxers and race horses. A secretary brought their lunch in a cardboard box, and Principato, cursing the dismal knowledge that he would have to go back to the angry Cynthia at five

117

o'clock, thought how pleasant it would be to spin out the remainder of his days enthroned in Hallagan's leather armchair, eating his lunches from cardboard boxes. At five, when he quit the warehouse, Corky's brother had begged him to take something.

"What sort of thing?" Principato asked, his eyes traveling over the stacks of canned peaches and soups.

"Anything that strikes your fancy." In the end, Principato settled for a case marked SELECT SPANISH OLIVES. Now it was in the trunk of his car, waiting for him to think up a story to tell Cynthia to explain their acquisition.

Corky's heavy breathing came through the phone.

"I wanted to ask you somethin'," she said.

"Ask away."

"If I'm calling you like this, does it mean we're havin' an affair?" Her voice grew tremulous and excited. Principato had an image of her seated on the arm of an overstuffed chair, rubbing her thighs together at the notion.

"Well," she continued, "I never called a man like this on the phone except for the priest or the butcher, or my brother, Danny, of course. I never knew another man I wanted to call for anything. God, if Cornelius knew I was talkin' to you now, he'd probably kill me."

The tone of her voice sobered him quickly.

"No, I don't think we're having an affair, Corky. It involves a lot more than phone calls and helping you out with your little problem, after all."

"Oh." She sounded disappointed.

"Well, listen," she began again, "how about meeting me outside that place on Tuesday night? If I walk in alone, that woman Eva is liable to belt me."

"O.K., Tuesday night at eight." Then he heard another voice, so clearly that he thought someone had picked up an office extension. He realized it was Cornelius, shouting.

"Who are ya talkin' to, Corky?"

"It's . . . it's only a friend, Cornelius!" Her fear was transmitted to Principato instantly.

"Is this a man?" Cornelius demanded of Principato.

118

"Well . . . yes."

"Who are ya, ya bastard? Where are ya gonna meet my wife on Tuesday night? Huh? I'll kill ya!"

Principato dropped the receiver into its cradle as if its temperature had suddenly increased one thousand degrees in his hand. He sat bolt upright and straightened his tie, then walked back into the office, hoping nobody would notice how ashen-faced he was. If Corky gave in and told, he guessed Cornelius would come blasting downtown within the hour, perhaps even knock down the front wall.

But at five o'clock he was still alive and on his way to Saint Malachy's. Beside him, Larkin began paying lip service to the idea of a retreat.

"You know, Pato, a weekend away like this is just what I need every year about this time. A quiet chance for a man to be alone with his God. It reminds me a lot of how it was in the seminary."

A sadness crept into his voice. From the corner of his eye, Principato saw the head droop forward in sorrow or shame at the memory. Larkin had made his sympathy play; Principato guessed it was up to him to lay on the soft, healing hands. His real instinct was to dump salt in the wound while it was open. The whole business disgusted him. He had seen the ex-seminarian pull it off many times before at the Corrigans'. At the mention of the word "seminary" all voices became instantly muted, dismal spirits filled the air, and Principato's imagination was transported to a place of cold, ill-lit hallways, doubtless situated on top of a mountain, where the pious outer shell of Larkin had paced reverently along, rosary wound about his hands, while his inner strength was sapped from the contest with the world and the flesh. Larkin saw it in exactly those terms, too. He had narrated the battle for Principato during many long lunch hours. In the end, he had come out into the world, quested gamely after the flesh.

Dutifully, Principato applied the balm. "Why torture yourself about the seminary, Lark? Maybe God didn't want you in the seminary. Maybe he had a better use for your talents on the outside. Look at the good work you're doing at the agency."

Cars swept past them in the speedier traffic lanes and Principato wondered suddenly if any other vehicle contained two grown men holding serious conversation about the will of God. Or, better said, one excusing the other from failure by agreeably de-emphasizing will to whim. Beside him, Larkin's great simian head began to straighten up. He gave a little sniffle. The lie was obviously to his liking. Inside Principato the Dwarf of Truth began thrashing violently about. The steering wheel started shaking in his hands, and he realized the front end was shimmying because he had pushed the old car too close to sixty. He slowed down abruptly, fearing for his life.

At Saint Malachy's, he parked the De Soto in an almost completely filled lot. Behind the retreat house, the touch-football game was already in progress on a wet lawn. Larkin sprinted quickly around back, leaving his suitcase in the car. Principato, nonathlete, decided to visit Gallagher, the retreat master.

The priest was in his office smoking a cigarette when Principato knocked. For an instant, standing outside the half-open door, he thought of Gallagher lying stretched out on a couch in a cold sweat at the horror of beginning again this task of leading men's minds through a two-day cycle of prayer and meditation. He's been at this job a long time, Principato remembered. He meant to ask him how long.

"Hello. It's Mr. Principato, isn't it?"

"Yes, Father. How are you?"

"As well as can be expected. Sit down, won't you?"

Gallagher looked out the window. The clouds had gone, and a shaft of late afternoon sun came through the parted curtain, falling on the priest at his desk. He had grown thinner since last time, and the sunlight showed his hair to be a curious shade of dull yellow, like a nicotine stain. His teeth, once crooked and discolored, were now gleaming white and even. A recognized miracle of dental science. No other changes were evident. The same ruddy complexion of a man who took cold showers (Principato imagined) in expiation of his sins. The same frayed-looking cassock—or another just like it—with a dried sweat stain in the armpit.

The priest grasped the curtain in his hand, pulling it back to get a better view. Outside, grown men ran screaming up and down the wet playing field. A long pass soared over many heads. On the side-lines, Larkin, in seersucker suit, leapt and screamed. The ball dropped in the end zone. Gallagher smiled benignly at the scene, as if they were a group of parochial-school boys at play. He released the curtain and turned to face Principato.

"What sort of problem do you bring me, or is this just a social visit? No, with that seriousness of yours, you wouldn't waste your time on social visits. You wouldn't trust you'd be welcome. So you'd have to have a business reason for coming to see me."

"Is that the way it works? The jocular bring their anecdotes, the grim their personal problems?"

"Something like that. In any event, it's a nifty balance. It makes my job more palatable. Some men come to be refreshed, others to re-fresh me, weary after refreshing. It almost seems the Lord under-stands Gallagher is getting old. Now he sends them in a one-to-one ratio. After you and your rain clouds depart, undoubtedly he'll hurry one in with a new Saint-Peter-at-the-Gate joke I haven't heard. Then I'll write it down in the anthology of Saint Peter jokes I'm going to publish someday, and the balance will be restored."

Principato watched as the priest opened his desk drawer and pulled out a worn-looking notebook, flashing its pages at him. It was almost filled with dated joke entries in Gallagher's lefty slant. He leafed through it for a long moment, smiling occasionally.

"Yes," he began again, "Pius's encyclicals will lay moldy and for-gotten, but they'll be reading Gallagher right up to infinity."

Principato did not smile. There was weariness and a trace of bit-terness in the old priest's voice. The face was creased with painful lines. He half expected Gallagher to say, "Dear Lord, how long do they expect me to stay on this job?" But nothing came forth. Princi-pato asked the question.

"You've been here a long time, haven't you, Father?"

"Too long, Principato. They give me the bound and captured and require me to perk them up. I wanted to save, not energize. Do you understand?"

There was a sudden piteous intensity in smiling Gallagher's voice. He rose from behind the desk and began to pace rapidly across the carpeted office, his legs making a swishing sound against the cassock. Then, abruptly, he stopped before an embarrassed Principato.

"Jim Corrigan was in here today about your father."

"That bastard!" Principato said. Then he began apologizing to Gallagher, who lit a cigarette.

"No need to apologize, Principato. In part, it's my own sentiment exactly. On the one hand, Gallagher, the priest, hungers to ride into South Philly and find this living, breathing infidel father of yours. Truthfully, he'd be the first one I've ever met, and the whole business smacks deliciously of a deathbed conversion. Forgive me for sounding prosaic. But, on the other hand, Gallagher, the man, rejects being used as a tool by the Corrigans. I've known that tribe for a long time. Their father was one of the most wonderful men God ever put on the earth. He'd give you the shirt off his back. But, like most charming, good-natured types, he was a weak man, and that wife of his was an admixture of vinegar and piss. No better way to describe her. I'm afraid all the offspring have that same combination flowing in their veins. She and that Jesuit brother-in-law of hers must have thought up this weekend for you. Doubtless, you didn't have to pay for it."

"No, Father, Larkin, a fellow I work with, offered me a ticket that someone had canceled out on."

"Ah yes, Larkin. The one who looks like a gorilla. Perfect henchman for the Corrigans. Did he finally get married or is he still trying to decide on going back to the seminary?"

"Still undecided, I guess."

"I hope he gets hit in the head with a lead football out there," said the priest. "It'd save the Church another round of trouble and society at large from the horror of any children he might father if he did get married."

Principato laughed appreciatively and felt Gallagher's hand on his shoulder.

"What crosses we bear, huh, Principato? You, to have married into that clan and given up everything but your name, and your friend Gallagher, who staggers along under his vow of obedience. Twenty years a priest and still stuck in the retreat houses, when I've wanted so badly to go to the missions. You see that old pickup truck out there? I've actually thought of stealing it and driving off to the reservations in Dakota, where my order has its mission centers, and impressing my superiors with the *fait accompli*. Begging them to let me stay. But I'm afraid that old truck wouldn't make it too far beyond Pennsylvania."

The sadness in the voice was immeasurable, and Principato thought they both might sit down on opposite sides of this desk for a feast of weepings. Really, you found your fellow travelers in the oddest places. He only hoped the priest would not demand too much comfort from him. With the revelation of the Corrigan plot, he felt suddenly he didn't have much to spare.

"I'm sorry, Principato. There's a look about you that tells me a lot of people burden you with their problems."

"Forget it, Father. What did you tell Jim Corrigan you would do?"

"I promised to talk with you. And despite my distaste for the Corrigan mob, I'll have to get down to hard earth on this, if you'll listen to me. Have you spoken to your father? As a Catholic, you've got a certain responsibility here, you know."

"I'll just have to forsake that responsibility this time, Father. It's my old man's last wish, and the only thing he wants from me is not to make a mess. Cripes, I feel I owe him something. Look at the set of grandchildren I've given him. Waging a crusade against him now would really be the last straw. Besides, my mother and brother, Rocco, and my sister, Lucy, have all agreed to his decision."

"This Lucy, your sister, she's a nun isn't she?"

"Yes, Father."

"How has she been able to reconcile herself to his decision?"

"I don't know. I haven't seen her since he broke the news to me. I guess she's just looking the other way for this one."

"I hope it's that easy for her, Principato. Please don't be angry with me for saying it, but you seem to come from a most unusual family. Jim Corrigan was here for almost an hour this afternoon, most of the time being exasperated that your father drives a red Thunderbird, and your mother has blond hair when she ought to have gray or white."

"It's gray now. She washed out the dye," Principato answered defensively.

"All these things seem indicative to me somehow—and, admittedly, I love the idea. Could it be that instead of disavowing the Church and her sacraments, your father is actually antiauthoritarian? The eternal rebel type. You know, the Church, because she is also a temporal institution, often manages to antagonize her servant Gallagher, too. And on one occasion or another, probably everyone of her members. Could this be the root of the problem, Principato?"

"I don't know what the root of the problem is, Father. I just grew up with it already in flourish. Everyone who knows my father from the old neighborhood calls it the Defiance, but I don't think anyone remembers how it even got started. I'm supposed to have inherited it a few months back, but I'm not certain what it is I inherited."

"Vague. Mysterious. Too vague and mysterious, Principato. You mean to tell me he never advanced any argument for staying away from the Church for thirty-five years?"

"We Principatos aren't exactly a pack of intellectuals, Father."

"Nor are most Catholics, thank God, or my job could be a hell of a lot worse than it is," said Gallagher, looking out the window again. "But seriously, I worry about the state of his immortal soul about to embark on its journey toward eternity. Do you believe in the immortality of the soul, Principato?"

"I'm a Catholic, Father. I've accepted the Church. I accept the dogma she teaches."

"Very pat answer, and may God reward you if you believe it as conclusively as you say it. But do you ever find yourself doubting anything?"

"No, I don't think about it."

"It doesn't seem right to commend you for not thinking, Principato, so I won't. Look at that mob out there running up and down. There are doubters among them. Serious doubters perhaps. But at this stage of the game, most of them are married and have children

124

hanging around their necks, so they're rather hopelessly wedded to a Catholic way of life. None, I think, has enough courage to break off and start anew. Where would they start? The benevolent trap has already been sprung. I'll confess I rather admire this father of yours for his guts."

There was a silence while Gallagher began pacing back and forth again. Principato resisted the urge to stand up, shake the old priest's hand, and flee the place.

"Principato, the Church teaches of heaven and hell. Do you believe?"

"Yes, Father."

"In the agony of hell's punishments?"

"Yes."

"Have you thought of your father's soul in hell?"

"No!" How could a son think such a thing? In truth, Principato thought only of heaven. Impossible to consider that his father, an honest fat man whom he loved immeasurably, could end up in any other place. He would leave this room immediately if Gallagher did not stop.

"I'm sorry, Principato. But look at the reality. He's going to die. The Corrigans come to me, fools that they are, out of a real solicitousness about your father, whether you realize it or not. It's only their methods that make us dislike them. But I know that family, and above everything else, they fear the outer darkness. I knew Linus, the bishop, when I was younger. A scowling man with a dark mind, who used to scare the hell out of them at Sunday dinners. He was obsessed with the idea that everybody was on his way to the fire. Really, I think he was completely nuts toward the end. And their uncle, the Jesuit, isn't much help either. The last time I saw him was about three years ago, and the first thing he said to me was, 'I think I'm going to die soon.'

"You've got to forgive them a little, Principato. The trouble with that gang is they're completely lacking a sense of humor. Nothing was inherited from their poor, sweet father. Death and eternity are completely out of proportion with them. They're like a bunch of ghouls living in that big house with their burial business."

"My old man sells tombstones, Father."

"And probably chisels scathing verses on them, huh?"

"No, just the usual lies that every family orders up for its deceased reprobates."

Gallagher smiled wanly. Then slowly his face became somber again.

"Principato, why don't you try to bring him to the Church? Look how well she takes care of us on the way out. Do you really think your father is facing up to this without fear?"

"Are you suggesting that I play on whatever fears my old man may have, Father? I promised I wouldn't interfere."

"But your duty, Principato. Consider your duty."

"Father, now are you asking me to choose between my family and my religion?"

"I dread the outcome of any such choice, Principato. Let's try to keep the two separate and distinct for now."

The priest's eyes were suddenly tired-looking and his shoulders seemed to sag forward. From near by a bell began ringing, and Gallagher yanked back the curtain to show an old man toiling on the rope of a bell tower on a low hill beyond the playing field. Now the football game was breaking up, and the players streamed toward some cases of Coke that had been wheeled out of the kitchen. Principato recognized Jim Corrigan down below; he was limping. Larkin, in crumpled seersucker, was at his elbow.

"It's almost time for supper, Principato. Why don't we adjourn this until tomorrow, if you like. I'll see you at the opening address tonight."

"All right, Father."

The two men walked into the hallway, which smelled strongly of cleaning fluid.

The priest said, "You don't happen to know any good Saint Peter jokes, do you Principato?"

"Sorry, Father. I never get the punch lines right, so I don't bother to remember them."

"Yes, you seem to me like the kind of person that would never get the punch line right."

"Thanks."

The retreat master started walking in the opposite direction, his

126

footsteps loud. Principato turned to watch him unlock the first of the two great doors that led to the inner part of the house where the priests lived. How was it in there? he wondered with a child's slow curiosity. The perfect vacuum for the mind to ruminate on God and the things of God perhaps, forcing no one who lived therein ever to choose between two absolutes like clan and religion. Principato wished peace of mind for the frustrated Gallagher, wanted him to enjoy that inner solitude the way it was meant to be enjoyed.

In Principato's room the bed had been short-sheeted, and the sight relieved his low spirits. Strange: this small tradition of inconvenience that bound him wispily to some man who had slept in this bed the weekend before, had thought seriously of his Catholic faith and immortal soul, as his successor, Principato, would undoubtedly do, then gone back to the real task of making a life in Philadelphia. Principato was a firm upholder of tradition. On Sunday, in his turn, he would short-sheet the bed, perhaps even find a little garden snake to include in the fold.

At supper, Principato sat at a small two-place table with a man whose twin sons were leaving for college in a week. The man spoke solemnly of praying for their success, and Principato nodded politely, his mind intent on Jim Corrigan holding serious court at a larger table. Incredible: that bastard had not yet even spoken to his brother-in-law.

Afterward, the man at his side still speculating on his sons' chances, they all walked to the chapel for Gallagher's opening address. Principato chose the last pew, and sleepy from the huge meal he had eaten that lay pregnant in his stomach, he allowed for the takeover of his senses by the place. Despite the Corrigans' pathetic intrigue, he felt curiously at peace. It was sundown; the world was in recline. He gazed through an open window past the retreat house fences to a neighboring field where cows marched homeward, silhouetted against the red band of the sky. The sight positively delighted him. Philadelphia so close that he could just discern the burn-off flames of refineries on the lower Schuylkill, and cows were still being driven toward barns to be milked in the evening.

He heard crickets for the first time since he arrived and wondered if they had not been chirping all along.

Before the rows of pews, Gallagher began to speak, a steady flow of oft-repeated, Latinate words that caressed Principato's mind, then passed quickly beyond. His spine found accord with the hard back of the seat, and he turned his attention toward the chapel itself. A gilt-edged, lacy place full of really mawkish statuary and a special integration of colored lights that seemed to him altogether too feminine for a men's retreat house. But not displeasing either. It had been the gift of some rich old benefactress, who had been given license with her tastes, so the story went, and Principato believed it. Nonetheless, it primed acceptance of the Catholic gods better than the sterile shells of churches they were putting up in new suburbs today. The soul of Principato opted for the flowing curves of angel's wings and the sweet odor of incense that might never be banished by the stink of floor wax. He was a strict traditionalist in this sense. To hell with those bare brick places with the modern weld-art Christs and nubile Marys. The right atmosphere was half the fulfillment when it came to earnest praying. He believed that, also.

Over the pews in front of him, Principato saw Jim Corrigan and henchman Larkin turn stealthily around to check out where he sat. Heads together, they really looked like two kids, and he resisted the urge to stick out his tongue at them. Seeing them shattered his mood, but instead of being angry, tonight's expansive Principato felt only a kind of pity that Corrigan had been unable to share in it. Had he seen the cows? Heard the crickets? Principato guessed not. But as a Corrigan, his brother-in-law was oblivious to so many things. Gallagher had said it right. Death and eternity were a fantastic preoccupation with them and left so little energy to enjoy the effects that moved a Principato: sunsets always, the effortless melancholy of rainy days, the bowel-whirling pleasure (pleasure, even) of fighting traffic into the city on workday mornings. But the Corrigans were, in a sense, dehumanized. They drew the blood from still-warm corpses. Ironically, even the great staggering emotions they permitted themselves on occasion revolved about death.

Kennedy was dead. On the terrible day, Principato had stood dumbly in center city trying to decide between going home to Cynthia, who had voted against him because she was Cynthia, or to his parents who loved the young President dearly. In the end, he found himself moving slowly along the expressway to his own home. Surprisingly, one of the huge funereal limousines was in the driveway—or rather half in the driveway—its front wheels flung hysterically onto his lawn in an indication of the grief being enjoyed in his living room. There, the three brothers wept shamelessly, the long baying wail, like keening, of grown men collapsed at the passing of the emperor. Principato, a ready emotionalist, had no tears to match these. These were broken hearts. He had gone instead into the kitchen, drunk tea with Cynthia and her mother and Phillips, and settled for the deliberate, more controlled sniffling that seemed to suit the three women better. The next day, the brothers had pointed their limousine toward Washington and gone south to move slowly through the Capitol rotunda and then to Arlington also. The ex-President's grave was far from being splendid enough, they reported.

In half an hour Gallagher was finished. He turned to begin some prayers at the altar, and, taking advantage of the restless shifting of bodies, Principato slipped out of the chapel, walked along the hallway, and pushed through the door to the outside. There it was suddenly night, and he could see the Philadelphia lights clearly now. A pale moon shone overhead and he began walking along one of the narrow, flower-trimmed paths that meandered aimlessly about the place, cutting into shrub thickets and an occasional stand of evergreens. They were properly made for meditating, so spaced that it was impossible to bump into somebody for a conversation. Sometimes he came to a saint's statue, ghostly and white in the moonlight, and once (another delight to Principato's soul) to a grotto where a tall Virgin stood looking down at him, her feet warmed by a blue vigil lamp.

His path widened and he passed along the fourteen carved-wood stations of the cross in reverse order. The last time he had been in this place was Holy Week three years before, and on Good Friday, Principato had moved along these same stations slowly and mournfully, privileged in carrying the cross wrapped in black cloth. The weather had been true to the event. Dramatic even. Dark clouds blew over and lightning flashed near by in the north. Principato was excited, keenly on the edge of some inordinate religious experience, though realizing at the same time with the small, protective germ of reason left to him, that the weather was providing the better half of this commemoration. Jesus was nailed to the cross. Around them, the pine trees swayed madly in the wind. A wondering Principato looked about at the other men and saw a kind of fear in some faces. Twigs and bits of paper and red dust from the pathway blew into their midst. They passed the fourteenth station and Gallagher had urged them back to the house, his eyes full of anxiety and doubt as if, as retreat master, he had arranged this show of nature for their benefit, only to have it get mysteriously beyond his control. Rain had begun falling, huge blob drops of it, and Principato had looked down raptly to see it strike the red earth. Rain and red earth formed mud. Not blood. Not blood in any sense. He must remember that always, he told himself then.

A man had poked him in the shoulder. "Don't hold the cross up like that, Pato. It might attract the lightning."

Gallagher had grabbed it from his hands, leaning it against a tree.

"Leave it here for now. Let's get out of here or we'll be soaked."

Then, madly, they had all run back to the house.

His path came out of the woods near the baseball diamond. Principato walked across it, mounting then descending the pitcher's mound, regretting that he had never played baseball when he was a kid. Somehow it seemed an unforgivable omission that contributed to making Principato a person that neither he, nor many others, it seemed, was completely satisfied with. Because of it, he judged, he would always exist many degrees to one side of the reading for mean American excellence. There was nothing to be done for it, really.

Beyond the field was the wing of the retreat house that contained the chapel, and he saw that, except for the red glow of the sanctuary lamp, the place was dark and deserted. It was already lights-out time.

He pushed through the front door and groped along the black hallway toward his room. There he stripped in the darkness, slipped into his pajamas, then stumbled along the hallway again to the toilets. Inside he surprised four men, including Jim Corrigan, who were playing cards on an improvised table. Corrigan skillfully swept the cards and money into a wastepaper basket.

"Whew! It's only you, Pato. We thought it might be Gallagher."

"Sorry to disturb you," said Principato with a rush of apprehension. "I'll leave."

"Now, don't be afraid to take a little pee and brush your teeth, Pato," Corrigan said.

Principato headed for the sink to wash and heard some whispering behind him as the men rearranged their game. Then his brother-in-law stood up in his pajamas and robe and walked over to him.

"Uh, Pato, did Gallagher have anything to say to you today?" he asked. The toothbrush stopped moving in Principato's mouth.

"About what, Jim?"

"Well, you know, about your father?"

"How would Gal know anything about that?"

Principato watched his brother-in-law's hoary face in the mirror, wrinkled in the sudden difficulty of creating a lie.

"Well, Uncle Edward saw Gal in the city last week, and I guess he was telling him about the problem you're having with your father."

"I'm not having a problem with my father, but it seems you are. No, Gallagher didn't say anything."

"God damn it!" Corrigan shouted. He smashed a huge fist into the palm of his other hand. "He was supposed to talk with you, Pato."

Corrigan's reflection in the mirror became dark and menacing. Principato hoped he would not try something like hauling him down to Gallagher's office right now for a supervised conference. He had few defenses against it, he realized, as he warily started the toothbrush moving in his mouth again. Corrigan turned abruptly and started out the door. In a few minutes Principato said good night to the three men who sat around the table exchanging puzzled looks.

He opened the door to his room again, then stopped before entering when he saw a tiny light, the end tip of a cigarette.

"Who is it?"

"Father Gallagher."

"Oh." There was a sudden tired resignation in Principato's voice. The world was indeed closing in on him.

"Why have you come, Father?"

"To ask you a question." Gallagher's cigarette raised to his mouth for a quick, nervous drag.

"Shoot," Principato said. He sat down on the edge of his bed. He was shocked to discover the odor of sweet wine on the priest's breath.

"You're not excessively happy in this life you lead, are you, Principato? I think you're not happy at all. I mean the joy and satisfaction of being a Catholic father and husband must seem rather ironic to you, considering your situation. Confess to me."

"What are you getting at, Father?"

"Run away with me, Pato. We'll go to Dakota in your car. I've got money enough put away for gas and food. In Dakota there's freedom for us both. You might start your life over again. Marry another woman. I wouldn't care. I'm a believer in expedience. I'd be a missionary at least, instead of leading this dismal, unrewarding existence. Did you hear that sermon I gave tonight? I haven't changed a word in fifteen years. There's nothing more to be said. I don't have a reason to switch a phrase until they finally do something like put the O.K. stamp on birth control. Will you go with me?"

Ah, flight of the miserables, thought Principato. One to Dakota to become an approved bigamist and the other a missionary. Even in the darkness, he could sense the hunger in Gallagher's eyes. The militant church trying to shed a yoke. From the dull, repetitive job of guiding the once-yearly spiritual refreshers in Philadelphia, the old priest sought to descend upon some vestigial tribe of Dakota Indians to beat the band for the policy advantages of Catholic Christianity. God help the Indians, he decided.

"Have you ever seen my car, Father? I think we'd stand a better chance with that pickup truck you showed me today."

"Anything, Pato. Anything. Only let's both go before we stop to think about it. If you don't go with me, I'll never leave. I'll be stuck here until the Death Angel arrives. I've had my eye on you. You're the only one I've come across in twenty years with so much reason to kick over the traces. I'm a priest, herdsman of the Catholic sheep. I'm encouraging you to do this with me."

Sure you are, Father, mused Principato. But was it a case of greater desperation or, really, lesser responsibility on the priest's part? He had no family to desert. Only endless flocks of sheep come to graze on the admonitions of his fixed sermon. To hell with them. One priest was as good as another for spewing admonitions. A replacement easy to come by. But where to find a replacement for the tangle of involvements and responsibility that Principato called a life? No, Father, impossible.

"I'm sorry, Father. There have been times I've wanted to escape to paradise before you ever came up with the idea of Dakota. But I just can't. I've got a wife and five children here in Philly and a crisis coming up in my immediate family with my father going to pass on. You'll have to keep your eye open for another partner."

"Alas, there'll never be another," the priest said sadly. "You were the perfect one, Principato. Nobody ever with such a reason."

Gallagher rose to leave. His hand searched for the ash tray on the dresser and he put out the butt of his cigarette.

"Father, it may sound a little childish to ask this, but you're not going to join forces with the Corrigans now that I've put you off, are you?"

"Me get mixed up with that family? Are you crazy? People have been known to die within minutes of being bitten by the mother. She's got worse venom in her than a cobra. And I want to live until I'm at least seventy. Then my superiors will put me out to pasture, and if I'm lucky enough, it might be near my Dakota missions. Say a prayer for my success."

Principato listened as the tired footsteps receded down the hallway. Then he climbed into bed, curiously satisfied with himself. In the past three weeks he had gained supporters and friends at Neutral Corner, made love to a two-hundred-pound woman, and success-

133

fully resisted the invitation to run away to Dakota and become a bigamist.

My life is entering a period of contentment, he promised himself, not really understanding why he felt it. It just seemed that he owed it to himself to be a bit of an optimist on occasion.

SEVEN

Of contentment, of course, he had spoken too soon.

It began Sunday morning during a baseball game at the retreat house after the closing mass, when Jim Corrigan and Larkin grabbed Principato, nonplayer, from the sidelines where he stood watching with a one-armed man, and jostled him into the batter's box.

"But Jim, I don't play," he protested. Really, he knew nothing of baseball; he might flap the cape before a bull with greater skill, he thought. But no matter. Horrifically, the thing had already transcended Principato's small ability to exercise control over a situation. Behind him, men snickered at Corrigan's patronizing instructions on how to spread his feet and hold the bat. He squinted into the already glaring morning sun and seemed to see the pitcher for the first time, a man named Ray Hermans, who stood impatiently atop the mound with one gloved hand planted firmly on his hip. Principato looked down at his feet. He was wearing spikes, which made him all the more formidable. A man who had taken the trouble to carry his spikes to a weekend retreat was there for business.

"You understand there's two outs, Pato, and a man on first and second. For God's sake don't flub this, O.K.?"

"Jim, why don't you get somebody else? I don't even know if I can swing this bat."

"Who else am I going to get, Pato?" he demanded fiercely. "That poor bastard over there with only one arm? Why don't you ask him if he'll sub for you? I haven't got the guts."

Principato turned to see the one-armed man shaking with laughter, safe behind his supreme worthy excuse of having only one arm. Then, miserably, he turned back to face the pitcher. Corrigan had walked off to the side.

"Stand like I showed you, Pato. Don't choke up on that bat," his brother-in-law said. Tittering arose from many separate pockets. Principato squinted again into the sun and watched Hermans begin an exaggeratedly slow windup. Oh, Christ! What in hell was he, Principato, doing here? His instinct was to drop the bat and run to his car and speed home. It seemed to him the most foreign of all things he had ever touched. Its handle slipped in his clammy grip and he waited for it to go limp like a long stick of spaghetti. Before him, Hermans turned suddenly in the windup and whipped the ball at the second baseman, who snatched it out of the air and swooped easily to touch the already safe runner who had been edging toward third. Despite himself, Principato was impressed with these precise, ballet-like motions. He thought of congratulating the pitcher.

He became aware again as Hermans looked to Corrigan for a sign. His brother-in-law signaled a soft, easy movement with the palm turned downward. It would be a slow pitch to point out the absurdity of his being there. Hermans wound up again in the same exaggerated style, brought his arm forward in an impossibly languid arc and flicked the ball from the wrist. Principato watched its creeping progress and secretly wondered what force kept it suspended. Should he go out to meet it? He thought vaguely for a second that the ball would begin a trajectory descent and land at his feet. But it did not, and in the last instant he blinked and swung the bat in a wide circle so that its thrust whipped him around in a colored sweep of summer shirts.

"Strike one!" the umpire called. A judgment on poor Principato. The spectators were grinning, shaking their heads.

"Pato! What're you swinging at?"

Principato turned at the mock dismay in Corrigan's voice and saw Gallagher joining the spectators. The priest was not smiling.

After the next signal, Hermans wound up again, and the ball began its long, dull approach for the second time. Even if he hit it with all his strength, Principato realized, it would go no place far. It would not recoil of its own inner tension like a fast ball and fly off toward the retreat house, vengefully fracturing one of its windows. He watched it coming. A slow curiosity developed in him to trace the infinite line of stitching on the orb as it spun toward him. But: too slow, he swung, eyes closed, and missed, and felt it limp past him into the catcher's glove.

"Strike two!"

Principato looked toward Jim Corrigan to see what sign he had for Hermans this time. Instead, it was Gallagher who called the play, slashing his hand through the air for a merciful fast ball. Obediently and suddenly Hermans whipped the egg toward Principato, who chopped at it frantically, his body turning through a swift half circle. In the instant, it seemed, that he heard the sharp thwack! of the ball against the catcher's glove, he felt the bat handle slip through his sweaty hands, then felt his hands unfold to make way for the hilt. Then the bat was gone. A blunt-ended spear in flight toward a cluster of men, who began dodging in all directions. But not in time. It glanced off the side of Larkin's great simian skull. Principato froze in horror as his coworker collapsed in a heap.

"Lark's dead! Jesus Christ, Pato, you killed him!" Corrigan began screaming. Principato watched dumbly as Gallagher bent quickly over the fallen Larkin, making the sign of the cross, then reached up to grab Corrigan's arm.

"Shut up you fool! He isn't dead!"

Almost at the same instant Larkin sat up, shaking his head and touching his hand to the blood that matted his hair.

"Did I get hit with the baseball bat?" he asked.

"Yes," answered Gallagher, "but no possibility of brain damage. You're too well padded for that." The priest tapped Larkin's head, and around them men began laughing in relief.

"Cripes, he could have been killed," said Corrigan to no one in particular.

"I thought I invited you to shut up," said the priest. He stood up and addressed the others. "Now why don't you guys drive slowly

137

home, and for God's sake don't come back for another year. I've got bad enough nerves as it is. Lark, you come over to the house and we'll fix up that cut."

"Good-by, Father." The words were repeated many times. Respectfully, the men began shaking hands with Gallagher, then departing in twos and threes. Principato was still rooted at home plate when the priest walked over to him.

"Well, it looks like you evened up the score this weekend, Principato."

"I don't even know what happened. It seemed like the whole thing was prearranged."

"It was, of course, by Corrigan and that idiot Larkin. But the rest of them, being human, were just along for the ride. Like watching a hanging or a good dog fight. Only you blew the show by losing the bat."

"I guess I was the dog, huh?"

"Aw, stop pitying yourself, will you? The least you could have done was to kick Corrigan in the balls if you didn't want any part of the thing."

Balls. Principato's mind clung to the word. He believed that hearing that from the lips of a priest shocked him more than anything that had just transpired. Gallagher seemed to sense his amazement.

"Here, Pato, shake hands with me and get out of here. And next year when I see you, I want you to be twenty pounds heavier. And please, trade in that old wreck of a car of yours. I was out looking at it this morning. Anything better would be a shot in the arm."

"Good-by, Father."

"Good-by, Pato."

Principato walked sadly to the retreat house, picked up his suitcase, and drove away from an almost empty parking lot. When he had gone about five miles, he recalled that he had neglected to short-sheet his bed. Continuity was broken. He considered returning to remake it, but what the hell for? The puzzled introspective who would come the following weekend might demand of Gallagher the reason for this lapse in tradition. Principato, the priest would answer wearily: a byword for the eternal fringe case always out of step with the rest of mankind, Catholic or otherwise.

In his driveway at home were the black Ford from the Jesuit motor pool and the Corrigans' black-and-chrome hearse. Brothers Matt and Edward, their mother, and uncle must be tanking up in the midst of one of their orgiastic barbecues. In front of the house was a beige-colored Cadillac convertible. Two huge steer horns projected from its hood. Instantly Principato realized it must be Myra Phee and her new friend. But what were they doing here? At his home? It amazed him to realize his own shock: no Negro had ever been at his home before.

Apparently, his neighbors wondered also. As he pulled up in front of the steer-horned monster, he saw one of the McGinchy sisters' lace curtains move almost imperceptibly and knew they were at the window again. Across the street, an old couple named Hamilton sat on their front-porch steps staring at the Cadillac. As he climbed out of his car, Mr. Hamilton stood up and walked quickly to Principato.

"Mr. Principato, there are Negro people at your home. You're not planning to sell, are you?"

Principato saw the fear in the man's narrowed eyes, knew his pensioned-off mind had been rattled seriously at the sight of those Negroes.

"No, Mr. Hamilton, don't worry. The woman is a client of mine at the agency. They must be here for some business reason."

"What sort of person would want to drill holes in the hood of a fine automobile like that and stick on those things?"

"I'll know in a minute," Principato answered. Then he turned to walk up the driveway and heard Hamilton's footsteps receding loudly across the asphalt street, eager to report to his wife that their way of life was not to be jeopardized through a traitorous sellout by the Principatos, after all.

Coming from behind the Corrigan hearse, he saw Myra Phee and a huge Negro man sitting on the side-porch steps and understood at a glance. There was tension here. The Corrigans sat about the fireplace, studiously indifferent to his arrival. His mother-in-law smiled her eternal half smile into the charcoal flames. His children huddled all on one side of the picnic table, eating greasy spareribs. In the foreground, the eyes of Myra's friend were smoldering, and Principato was sure he could just discern an angry trembling about the lips.

This one was used to rubbing elbows with whites, had perhaps bossed them on some job. Not a man to give too much thought to the propriety of driving from his section of town to Principato's on a Sunday afternoon. And not a man to be told to wait on side-porch steps, either. Too much regard for his own worth to comply gracefully with that request. Certainly an infinitely greater regard for his own worth than Principato, who had begun life with the enormous advantage of being white. But the Corrigans could be expected to recognize none of this. They saw only the color of Myra and her friend, and they swore off their usual elaborate deceitfulness that passed for hospitality when it came to Negroes. In this sense, they could be considered honest.

"Hello, Myra, how are you?"

"Hello, Mr. Pato. I came to see you since I wasn't home last Monday. This is my man, Addie. We have something to tell you."

"Hello, Addie." Principato offered his hand to the man, who stood up to his full height, towering above him. A vengeful iron grip seized his fingers then relinquished them after a second, perhaps realizing that, given Principato's ability to control things, he would not have been relegated to waiting on these steps. On the same impulse, the two men and Myra looked toward the backyard, where the Corrigans were conspiring around the patio fireplace. They seemed actually shocked that Principato held a Negro hand in his own.

"How long have you been here?" Principato asked.

"About two hours, Mr. Principato. We were told to wait here for you if we wished, so we waited like good colored folks would."

"I'm sorry, Addie. Have you eaten? Would you like a beer?"

"No, thank you, Mr. Principato. Until now I've always done my drinking in one of the bars those gentlemen sitting back there own down in my neighborhood. But I'd be the last one to cause any racial imbalance by presuming to take a seat at that picnic table."

Ow! Articulate Negro, thought Principato. The whole painful problem in a nutshell. To avoid the man's relentless eyes he shifted to Myra's softer gazing. If indeed she was pregnant again, as Mrs. Roberts had informed him, she hid it well. Beneath her taut, full breasts, her waist narrowed like a funnel then eased out into a small flare of hips, not like Cynthia's splay hips, bound up now in squarish-looking culottes that somehow emphasized the hugeness of her feet, too. Myra's feet were tiny, graceful, wedged into spike heels that Cynthia could not wear. A tight charcoal skirt clung to her; the near-popping tension of her blouse buttons intimated the struggle with her breasts. But stop! Any contrast was ridiculous. Cynthia, his Corrigan wife, always carried a small football-sized tumor with her between pregnancies that even a girdle was hard pressed to disguise. Freckles grew upon it. Myra's stomach plunged inward, aiming to touch her back bone. Its surface rippled with vibrating muscle. Principato had put his mouth there, run his frenzied tongue along the ripples.

"What was the news you had for me, Myra?"

"We're gettin' married, Mr. Pato."

"I'm sorry," Principato said without thinking. Myra returned a puzzled then hurt look. But Addie, her husband-to-be, grasped Principato's arm.

"I understand, Mr. Principato. I see it in your eyes. That's why I have no qualms about giving your baby my name. No matter what people might say when they get a close look at her. We decided to call her Sylvia."

Sylvia. An ethereal whispering name for Principato's love child after the jig-prompting appellations of his five Corrigan children. Terrance, Sean, Noreen, Aloysius, and Kathleen followed softly by a Sylvia. Much balance in the universe indeed.

The three turned toward the street to watch a neighborhood child leaning across the beige Cadillac's fender, trying to touch the steer's horns.

"Come on, Myra," Addie suddenly spoke, "let's go drown the sting of today's slap by white hands in some pleasant blind pig in our own neighborhood. I'm afraid Myra's a bit disappointed today," he said to Principato. "She wanted so badly to tell you about her going to get married since she says you're her only friend in Philly besides Mrs. Roberts. But there just hasn't been the leaping and festivities she expected." He ended angrily.

"I'm sorry again, Addie. If I had been here when you arrived it would have been different. Believe me, I'm not very proud of this family either."

"I'd sure like to get off a punch at that big son of a bitch over there," Addie said, pointing a thick finger at brother Matt, who scowled over his beer glass. "Hey, Corrigan," Addie yelled, "don't hold your breath waiting for me to come into one of those bars of yours again."

But there was no answer from the tribe beside the fireplace. The heads looked pointedly off in every direction except toward Principato and his friends.

"Huh! Judgment by silence. Come on, Myra, we've got to go."

"O.K. Good-by, Mr. Pato."

"Good-by, Myra. I'll try to see you during the week. Congratulations."

He watched them walk quickly down the slope of the driveway and climb into the Cadillac that started in a roar and lurched away from the curb. When he turned back Cynthia was rushing toward him, like a predator, hungry for an argument.

"What the hell's the idea?" she demanded, gesturing at the retreating convertible. "Where did they get our address?"

"It's on my agency card, along with the telephone number. You know that."

"Boy, if this doesn't end all. I came home from mass with the children and that big coon was laid out on the lawn waiting for you. All the neighbors were out looking. And did you see that car they came in? God! Cow horns on the front of the damn thing! Why do you think my family bought us this house when we were married? Because they knew there would never be any coons around here to worry about. Even the garbage collectors are whites."

"Cynthia, shut up! Where did you learn that word?"

"My family has always used that word."

"Well, you shouldn't use it. Think of the children."

"The children know damn well what that word means. Why do you think I had them transferred to Saint Petronilla's last year?"

"You said it was because they had some lay person instead of a nun as a teacher."

"Not quite, Principato. It was because Terrance came home after the first day of classes and told me there were four coons in his room. In exactly that word."

"Cynthia, I don't believe . . ." But his incredulousness faded quickly. Of course he believed it. She was capable of anything of this sort. Pulling the children out of a local parochial school and sending them off each morning by taxi to distant Saint Petronilla's was merely rudimentary. God forbid a colored nun should have the misfortune to be assigned to that school. Before him, his anger-flushed wife was still spoiling for a row. Declining to thus gratify her, Principato shrugged his shoulders, turned, and walked to the picnic table to pour himself a beer.

"How was dear Father Gallagher this weekend, Mr. Principato?" his mother-in-law asked.

"In rare form, Mother Corrigan. He told me about the time you bit somebody on the arm and he died within minutes." Principato began laughing softly. Some dramatic possibility of seeming to be mad had just appealed to him.

"What went on up there this weekend, Pato?" the uncle asked. The two brothers had put down their beer glasses.

"The best retreat ever attended. I actually clobbered Larkin in the head with a baseball bat."

"Christ Almighty! Why did you do that?" Matt asked.

"Because he was cramping my style."

"Pato, Pato, come and sit down here beside me," the uncle urged, getting up to take Principato's arm. "Tell us all that has happened this weekend. It certainly needs some explaining. Hitting poor Larkin with a baseball bat and Father Gallagher saying that Mother Corrigan bit someone and then those people who came to the house in that atrocious car . . ."

"You know what, Father?" Principato shouted, yanking his arm away. "You piss me off! You more than anyone else right now. You're the priest of a Church that shrieks and screams all poor bastards are equal before God, and you couldn't even make a pretense of hospitality this afternoon when those people came. Did you even offer them a sandwich or a glass of beer?"

"Well, no, Pato. We wanted them to leave. It would only encourage them to stay longer."

"Why did you want them to leave? Were they bothering you?

They came to see me, not you. They weren't going to interfere with your getting vomity drunk all over my lawn."

"Pato! Listen to me!" the uncle said. "What's the cause of your anger? Surely not those people who were here today. Their coming was a mistake. To invite them in, to familiarize them with our family and way of life would only create for them a new level of aspiration. It would only mean frustration and unhappiness in the end. No use disturbing the *status quo*."

"Aspiration? What goddam aspiration? If their stomachs were strong enough to make it through one of these Sunday afternoon booze fests, they'd cross you off their visiting list the minute they got out of here."

"Pato! Your mind is deranged! You don't mean the things you say. The Corrigan family has always striven to do the right thing. We're widely known for our diplomacy and fair treatment of others."

"By whom? Not by my family! My old man tries to shuffle off the coil in his own special style and the Corrigans begin unfurling their nets. Really, that little retreat-house conspiracy this weekend was unbelievable!"

"We only did it for your poor father's sake, Pato. Think of the possibility of his soul's eternity spent in the hell fires."

"My God! My father's soul in the fire twice this weekend! I'm leaving this place. There's only so much a person can stand."

"What do you mean leaving? For good?" Cynthia demanded. A sudden fright he had not seen in years came into her eyes. Beside her, her two huge brothers looked curiously helpless.

"Yes, I believe so, Cynthia."

"Not divorce, Pato," the uncle warned. "Don't ever speak of divorce. Catholic people don't get divorced. The Church sanctified your marriage. It's indissolvable."

"Let's be real, Father. The state is the kind master that grants divorces. Besides, if we looked hard enough, we might even come up with some cagy little technicality and convince the Church to give us an annulment."

"An annulment? Could you actually continue living if the Church decided your marriage of eleven years had been no marriage at all from its very inception?"

144

"I think so," Principato replied evenly. Then he swung about dramatically. "Good-by!"

He began walking down the driveway with Cynthia on his arm.

"Principato, what are the neighbors going to say when they don't see you around here?"

"Well, it couldn't possibly be as bad as what they had to say about our being visited by two Negroes."

"Principato, don't do this to me!" she said. Really, she had gained too much assurance over the years, he decided. Even with her security being undercut as it was now, she could not bring herself to plead.

Climbing into his car, he gleefully watched her standing, morose and shafted on the front lawn, then saw her face brighten suddenly into a wide smile as Kababian shot out of the next driveway in his mother's Volkswagen, honking the horn at her.

"Hello, Mrs. Principato!" he called. Cynthia waved furiously after the small car. Principato only nodded. His victory was not so conclusive after all.

His packed suitcase was still in the back seat and he realized as he pulled away that Principato, deserting husband, was homeless. Where to go? A grudging look in the rearview mirror showed all the Corrigans in a cluster about the wronged Cynthia, peering after him and doubtless wondering also. For one weak moment, he thought of putting the car in reverse and inching humbly backward to beg the Corrigan forgiveness.

But no, returning in reverse was the answer to nothing. Principato tromped down hard on the accelerator, and the old car leapt doggedly ahead and made for the first right turn with a squealing of tires. Then, abruptly out of sight of the house, it slowed and commenced a half hour's aimless wandering along familiar streets while Principato considered desperately what to head for. So desperately that he hoped the wise and knowing ancient De Soto might choose its own way and lead him to his new home. For where, indeed, did a thirty-four-year-old runaway pick up on a new way of life? In some sterile motel room or a suffocating cubicle in a honeycomb of cubicles like a YMCA? Or in his old bedroom in his parents' home? But no, not there. Certainly not there. They did not deserve to have him come back to them weeping and aggrieved at thirty-four as he had been often enough as a kid. A telephone call to inform them of his departure would suffice. Then he thought of church. After a weekend of prayer and comtemplation, he needed still further prayer and contemplation, it seemed. In the Sunday-afternoon quiet he would light a votive candle. Begin his new existence calmly and decisively. All would work out, he assured himself. His eyes searched frantically for a church.

There was one at the end of the next block. But as he checked the rearview mirror in preparation for pulling off to the side, he saw the great black-and-chrome boat, the Corrigan hearse that had been in his driveway, following him at a distance. Slaloming really. Careening majestically from one side of the road to the other, dodging rocks or logs or whatever obstacle the inebriate vision of brother Matt, who was driving, kept encountering. Brother Edward sat on the opposite side from Matt, his nauseous head hung expectantly far out the window, and the uncle between them, gaunt and angular-looking. With the frayed biretta planted squarely on his head, he reminded Principato of an old lithograph he had once owned of the picaresque do-gooder, Don Quixote. Now being shepherded by not one, but two Sancho Panzas. The bastards. Principato suddenly gunned away up the street again, forsaking his appointment in church, hastening to get away. His fear was real. Don Quixote, the honest old fool, he could handle. It was the two drunken Panzas he was frightened of. Foul-tempered and vengeful, they were not above pounding the hell out of Principato in front of a church for abandoning their sister. Then taking him to a hospital in their hearse with its comforting crosses etched into the windowpanes.

Principato hurried toward the expressway, the hearse behind still describing its right- and left-handed elliptical arcs, but at a faster speed. In the glare of sunlight, the great toothy expanse of its grille seemed to be slavering after him. At the expressway entrance he gunned up the ramp then looked behind before entering traffic, to see the hearse stop unexpectedly, turn about on the shoulder, and return defiantly along the one-way lane, oblivious to a pandemonium of blaring horns and curses. As Corrigans they lived, Principato thought. As Corrigans they might die, swimming always against the tide, if something huge and uncontestable like a cement mixer came rolling toward them. But no such luck. He caught a last glimpse of them meanly sideswiping the ONE WAY, NO EXIT sign at the head of the ramp before the same blowing horns and curses forced him into traffic.

He was at the end of the expressway, nearly at the Franklin Bridge when his mind resigned itself to sweeping on to Jersey and petitioning Malatesta for a home, despite the presence of his relentless son, Jon. On the Jersey side, near Cherry Hill, he stopped at a telephone booth to call his father. Outside, the Sunday-afternoon rush flashed past. Inside, he loosened his tie in the stifling air. His mother answered the phone.

"Is Daddy there?"

"Yes, honey. *Momento*."

"What's the problem, kid?" his father's voice asked a few seconds later.

"I've left my wife, Pop."

"Good," came the instant answer. "Maybe we can scout up a new one for you down here in the old neighborhood. What now?"

"I'm going to try to stay with Malatesta for awhile."

"O.K. Need any money?"

"No, I think I have enough."

"O.K. We're with you all the way, kid. Your mama'll be happy to hear this one. Remember the Defiance."

"Right, Daddy. Good-by."

"Good-by, kid."

Reassured, Principato drove on to Malatesta's amusement park. There was only one car in the lot, parked next to the trailer: a gray, unobtrusive Chevy that suggested a state inspector of some sort. A chic, white-haired woman sat at the wheel. Nick emerged from the trailer, a can of beer in his hand. His son followed behind him.

"Hi, Pato."

"Hello, Nick, how's things with you?"

"The usual trembling balance. I got my walking papers from Eva yesterday. But on the other hand my son here is leaving today. This accounts for much happiness on my part."

"I can imagine. What happened with Eva?"

"Ow! A real row there. She caught me completely by surprise, which is why I ended up in the street with so little protest. Your friend Allergucci gave her the word to sack me, I'm about one-hundred-per-cent sure. He's doing most of her thinking for her these days."

"Huh. All the bad guys in the world seem to be priests today. I just had it out with Cynthia's uncle this afternoon and left home. I'm looking for a place to stay now."

"Stay here, Pato. I'll be glad for the company," Malatesta said swigging his beer. "Junior here is taking off with his mother over there as soon as we can find enough bags to hold all his dirty underwear."

"That's Terry?" Principato asked in disbelief. "Terry from college?"

"Same one. She was forty-four then, and she's fifty-eight now. She's the only one of my old associations that looks worse than I do."

"That's only because of her white hair," Nick's son said in defense of his mother. "Otherwise, you're catching up fast. Boy, am I glad I got to see you two together for one last time. The air around here smells of failure," he said, stepping back from the car to sniff the breeze scornfully, though a wounded Principato was certain he could catch nothing more than the odor of hot grease from the rides. The young actor sniffed a figurative breeze. But no less truthful, perhaps, for being only figurative.

"Why don't you go pack your underwear and piss off, Jon," Malatesta said. "I've had enough lashings for the three months you've been here to last the rest of my days. I couldn't commit enough sins to catch up with my stored penance credits if I tried."

"You'll be sorry when I'm gone, Nick," the boy said. "How are you going to manage your life? What will you do with this carnival of yours? It's the only thing you have left in the world, you know. Why don't you try to get some money out of your friend Principato here and fix it up. Paint all the rides black-and-gray and change the lighting to red. Call the place Wasteland Park—Abandoned Gigolo and Deserting Husband, Proprietors. You'll make millions from all the people seeking meaning in their lives."

"If you didn't know he was only fourteen, couldn't you just smash in his head like any other grownup that made you mad?" Malatesta said.

"He's so fucking precocious," Principato heard himself say.

Then they watched in silence as the boy, laughing exaggeratedly, turned and walked back to the trailer, doubtless to apply himself to the menial, undramatic task of collecting all his dirty underwear for the trip.

"Come on Pato," Malatesta said, "you've heard the son, now you've got to hear the mother."

"What's she like?"

"Same caliber as her son. All I contributed to the egg was my intense good looks. The horrors came from her."

Grudgingly, Principato followed Nick toward the Chevy and noticed for the first time that it bore an Illinois license plate. The woman had been eying them all through her son's performance. Now, at their approach she slipped on a pair of sunglasses.

"Terry, this is Angelo Principato from college. Do you remember?"

"Of course I remember, darling. I thought your father was the most obnoxious man I'd ever met that first day at school, but there were too many of you around for me to tell him so. He made me feel like something on a meat hook."

"I'm sure he didn't mean anything by it," Principato insisted. "That's just his way."

"Shit on his way, pal. What did you turn out to be? I'd be interested to know."

"I don't understand, Terry," Principato said.

"I mean what do you do? How do you make your living?"

"Oh, that. I'm a social worker."

"Hmm. Sounds like a gold mine. You two guys have certainly come far along in this life. And you were both so blown full of promise when I knew you years ago. Remember those days, Nick? That's when Terry used to give you anything you wanted. Before you took off for Europe and left her with a baby, that is."

"Yeah, I remember," Nick answered, elaborately casual. But that was all he said.

"Hey, Principato," Terry began again, "tell me, are you married?"

149

"Yes, I'm married."

"With children?"

"Yes, five of them."

"Happily married with five children, huh?"

"I'd rather not talk about it."

"I'm sure, Principato. Tell me, have you finished up the time payments on that car of yours or do you still have a few years to go?"

"My father gave me that car for a wedding present."

"I'm sure he did. Otherwise, you probably wouldn't own one."

Cease, begged Principato. Enough of this. She's made her point. She might proceed next to his worn clothes and haggard mien, and from there to his slim bank account, ignorance of the stock market, and lack of property, since his home belonged to the Corrigans. For what had Angelo Principato of any real value? Only a perpetual-care cemetery plot, and that given to him by his father. Bah. He had heard it was impossible to be judged a failure at so young an age as thirty-four. But why now did he feel so insistently like one?

"I think I'll wait in the car, Nick, until your friends leave."

"I think I'll wait with you, Pato. I've been traveling the circuit and living by my wits for a long time now, but my skin doesn't seem to have thickened up enough to put off this mother-and-son combination."

"It'll never be thick enough for that, Nicky dear. Do you want me to tell you again how I stumbled into a Catholic unwed mothers' home and had your child? An old reprobate of forty-four enjoying her morning sickness with a bunch of loose-living teen-agers. When he finally came out, this sweet-faced old nun suggested I call him John, after your Saint John. That sounded good enough, but for spite I changed it to Jon, spelled J-o-n."

"Why didn't you tell *him* that?" Malatesta asked harshly, gesturing toward the boy who emerged from the trailer carrying a suitcase and two large shopping bags.

"You're the father. Fathers are supposed to let their sons in on the seamier side of life. It's traditional."

"Keep quiet! Here he comes!" Nick said.

They watched as the boy closed the last few yards to the car, looking inquiringly after the sudden silence, then opened the rear door to

150

place the suitcase and shopping bags on the back seat. In a moment he slammed it shut and walked around the trunk to stand before the three adults.

"Good-by, Nick. Good-by, Principato. Try somehow to pull your miserable lives into some kind of shape. I carry you both in my soul." He stood on his toes to kiss his father's cheek. Then he placed a kiss on the cheek of Principato, who reacted with mild shock. No man, or boy even, had ever kissed him in his adult memory. Instantly, he forgave Nick's son all the grievances he held against him.

"There you have it." Terry broke the silence. "The boy inherited all of his mother's good qualities and none of the bad. That's her forgiving nature I'm talking about. You know, Malatesta, if you had just a smattering of brain to go with that sad, much-abused look that makes everyone want to straighten you out when you aren't the least bit interested, you'd own all the land east of the Rockies by now."

"I seem to have acquired at least some of the land east of the Rockies," Nick said, spreading his arms to encompass his small, ugly domain.

"Good luck to you with this piece of land, Nicky dear. With winter coming on, you're going to need it. It's summer's end, you know," Terry said, starting the car. The boy opened the front door and climbed in beside her.

"I know, Terry," Nick answered quietly, touching hands with the old woman as the Chevy moved slowly off toward the trafficless highway, the Illinois J659 plate receding, then suddenly diminishing in a blur as the wheels touched the roadbed sureness of concrete. Nick's son did not look back at them.

"Free again," Malatesta said when the car had completely disappeared over the horizon of highway. Then he wound up pitcher-fashion and hurled his empty beer can into the tangle of scrub pine. It landed with a sharp clink, striking a rock, Principato supposed, after a rustling descent through the branches. The sound hung clearly behind in the silence.

"Christ Almighty, it's quiet here!" Principato said, turning around several times to survey their desolation.

"You'll get used to it, Pato. Come on, let's go get a couple of beers and sit over there in front of the trailer and try to figure out where we are."

They walked to the folding chairs in front of the trailer door, Principato falling into one while Malatesta went inside for two beers. In the West, toward Philadelphia, the sunset had begun. Fiery red with the promise of another hot day on the morrow. The screen door banged behind Nick. He placed a cold can of beer in Principato's hands then took a seat in the other chair.

"You know, Pato, that wasn't such a bad idea the kid had about fixing this place up. A little bright paint and colored lights would draw about ten times as many people. And a guy came by a few days ago and tried to lease me a soft-ice-cream machine. I could give him a call, and . . ."

"Be real, Nick. Terry said it. The summer will be done soon. Bigger and better parks than this are going to have the good sense to close down."

"Just a thought, Pato. Don't get excited. We could always put it under some kind of glass bubble in defiance of cruel winter."

"It looks like it's under some kind of bubble now. Every time I drive up here I'm more convinced that it isn't really a part of this world."

"Aw, there's nothing supernatural about the place, Pato. It's just the location. It takes getting used to. Some nights when we first opened I'd sit here by myself and expect all the rides to jolt into motion and humped-backed monsters to come out of the pine woods. But nothing ever happened. It's all in the dark mountains of the mind, my friend."

"You were just lucky, Nick," he said. If it were Principato sitting alone before this trailer, the rides, short-circuited or otherwise, would find a way to jolt into motion, and something huge and humped would doubtless meander out of the woods. And none of it might be ascribed to the dark mountains of his mind, although he would be the first to admit there were extensive ranges therein. "What are you going to do now?"

"About what, Pato?"

"About making a living."

"Nothing. I've got a little cached away. I'm going to sit around

152

here and regroup for the attack on that bastard Allergucci. I'll admit he's pretty smooth, but this is the first time in my history I've ever been horned out by another operator. Old Eva wasn't the best, but trade is trade, and I'm not slinking off content with the knowledge that he's getting into her."

"What do you mean getting into her? He's a priest."

"Oh-oh, I forgot. Principato the Catholic. Look Pato, when you've been wandering beyond the flock as long as I have, you might realize there are a few propagating priests about. Your friend Allergucci's a man, after all. He's got all the right apparatus down there."

"Nick! Knock it off! He's a priest. There are days I could strangle Cynthia's uncle for his single-mindedness, but he's still a priest. When he comes into the room I stand out of respect. This is the way we were raised. I had a row with him this afternoon, but I'd stand if he drove up here now. I'd take his blessing if he'd offer it to me."

"Well, I don't want to get another row going, Pato, but that seems hypocritical to me. If that guy managed to get under my skin the way he gets under yours, I'd tell him to fuck off. And I wouldn't worry about adding 'Father,' either. There's a man under those black robes who deserves a punch like any other man that's trying to browbeat you into submission. Just because his hands are consecrated or sanctified or whatever the hell they are doesn't mean he couldn't drop you with a good left hook."

"Nick, why are you talking like this? We're Catholics. I've had sixteen years of going to school since the first grade, and all of it Catholic. You've gone almost that far."

"Pato, let me tell you something. That church is a frigging cancer. You're either with it all the way like you, or limping along outside within shouting distance like me. But you never really get free of it. Pato, you won't believe it, but I've awakened Sunday mornings after screwing the pants off some dame I picked up in a bar the night before, and the first thing she asks is, 'Are you going to mass with me?' "

"Nicky, I think you're nuts. Waking up with a strange face on Sunday mornings isn't the Church's fault. What is it you're trying to say to me?"

"The hypocrisy, Pato. It's the Catholic hypocrisy I can't stand.

153

Look at yourself. You're strictly a double-standard man. You sit here and defend that useless old Jesuit because he's a priest, but you've got no reservations about asking me to find a piece of ass for your brother, Rocco. Try that one in confession. Tell the priest how you want to sneak your paraplegic brother out of that home and take him down to Philly for a little bit of woman. Don't forget to tell him she's faceless, nameless, and going to get paid for her trouble, too."

"Shut up, Nick! This is different."

"Different from what? Just because it's a love act on your part doesn't change the name from illegal prostitution to anything else. The guile of a thousand Jesuits at a Vatican Council won't find another name for it."

"Prick!" screamed Principato, winging his empty beer can at Malatesta and missing. The last drops rained in his own face. A vicious slap followed instantly afterward.

The angry sunset provided elaborate background for Principato and Malatesta on this cruelest of Sundays in the oiled-down lot between the merry-go-round and miniature train as they attempted to clarify with flailing fists and crude polemics an important theological question. Not the first two friends in history, certainly.

EIGHT

On Monday Principato awoke to the unlawful persistence of a single horsefly that returned audaciously many times to his swollen lower lip. Irritated, he brushed it away, then raised his head to peer bleary-eyed through the trailer's ripped-screen window at the expanse of scrub pine beyond. The sight shocked him into complete awareness. Where was the view of lightning rods on the McGinchy sisters' house that he came alive to each morning? Fiercely pointed, shafting the atmosphere, defiantly calling down the lightning of summer storms, he often half-expected to see a man impaled upon one of them, his face, a bug-eyed, frozen mask of the terrible agony of his death, turned toward Principato's shared bedroom to warn him of the terror contained in the day ahead. And where was the troll voice of Millicent Phillips pounding on their door to launch him into the familiar routine of rising, dressing, and eating before he climbed into his car and gratefully fled from his house and family to his job?

Patting his painful lips where Malatesta's blunt, heavy ring had slashed the night before, he lay back on the pillow and pulled the woolen covers over his head. On signal, his stomach tightened and jets of acid sprayed its tender lining. Where was Principato's precious security? His familiar lightning rods that had yet to show an impaled man and Millicent's troll voice that grated yet reassured? After

155

a long moment, during which he failed to stop the high-pressure acid jets, he felt the trailer shake and heard the main door open and realized that Malatesta, his polemic enemy, was up and about. Then he listened to a gentle spattering sound and uncovered his head to look out the window again at Nick, his long nightshirt raised in front, urinating on the nearest trees in great sprinkling arcs as if the alkalinity of his water were intended to check their encroachment on the trailer.

See what your new life is, Principato thought miserably. They were as bachelors again. Both of them roughing it. From the raw comfort of his great house with four gurgling bathrooms to pissing on the heads of dwarf trees in the face of the rising sun—for Nick had broken the toilet the evening before. Principato did not relish his freedom so far.

He slid out of bed and staggered in his pajamas toward the kitchenette, intending to put together a breakfast of Corn Flakes and instant coffee, as Malatesta re-entered. By mutual consent, it seemed, neither spoke, Nick merely turning his back and making again for his room, then falling heavily into his bed so that the trailer springs bounced. Angrily, Principato yanked up the wide leaf of the collapsible table and began loading it with breakfast dishes, only to have it fall minutes later as he poured boiling water over his spoonful of instant. Broken china littered the floor and his leg was burned through the pajamas that instantly sopped up most of the water. From Malatesta came the sounds of muffled laughter, as Principato ripped off his pajama bottoms.

Disdainful of cleaning up the mess, Principato hastened to shave and dress, then left the park after a grudging good-by to Nick, deciding he would stop in a diner on the way to the city for a quick breakfast. But by the time his third slow cup of coffee had brought on the bowel-whirling sensation he usually experienced from battling morning traffic, it was nine-thirty, and he conceded that he had not really wanted to work this day, anyhow. Instead, he stepped into the restaurant phone booth to call Jedda McMahnus and report sick. An unfamiliar buzz carried along the wire as the switchboard operator connected him with the supervisor's cubicle.

"Good morning, Miss McMahnus. This is Principato."

"Good morning, Principato. I'm very sorry to hear about your trouble."

"Yes, I have the flu," he began, prepared to spin out his favorite excuse.

"That's elementary. I'm talking about your leaving your wife."

"Oh, that. How did you know about that?"

"Larkin was in here bright and early at a minute after nine with the sordid details. Apparently, one of your brothers-in-law called him last night. From the way he's desk-hopping out there now, he must be trying to turn office opinion against you. I think I'll find a sudden emergency in his case load and dispatch him for a home visit."

"Ow! Larkin's got it in for me on two counts, then. We had some trouble at a retreat this weekend."

"Yes, one side of his head is neatly bandaged. He said you hit him during a baseball game."

"Not me. It was the baseball bat."

"Too bad it wasn't a harpoon," said the supervisor. Principato, disbelieving, held the receiver away from him, looking into its filter of tiny holes as if he might piece together Jedda's calm, kindly features and be assured that she had not really made such a judgment on Larkin. Not that anyone else's vindictiveness toward his coworker could normally upset Principato. In fact, he welcomed it. But look who had spoken the words in this case. If Thomas Butler, biology teacher, was Jedda's symbol of hope, then the motiveless Jedda herself was Principato's own symbol. Yet somehow she had just managed to fail him. The unfamiliar buzz filled the gap of silence between them.

"How was your weekend, Miss McMahnus?" Principato asked finally.

"As usual. All alone and lonely. An enormous hulk of a woman driving about in a tiny Volkswagen, willing to stop at the sight of anything that might relieve her boredom or be an occasion to speak with someone."

"But Mr. Butler . . . ?" he asked, dreading the answer.

"Dead. But never having lived really, Principato. He was a figment of my imagination. A gesture on my part, I think, to show my belief in the inherent virtue of man. He could not exist," she said bitterly. She began to weep softly.

157

"Jedda, make sure your door is closed," Principato cautioned her, then was astounded to realize that his only reaction so far was to dispense this calm advice.

"Yes, thank you, Principato. Wait one moment, please."

He heard the muted click as she placed the receiver on her desk, and listened as she walked across her cubicle to close the frosted-glass door. Then she returned, sniffling, and picked up the receiver again.

"I'm here, Principato."

"Jedda, listen to me. Is it because of me that Mr. Butler is dead?"

"Partly you, Principato, and partly Larkin and my own despair also. But I'm keenly disappointed in you. I'll confess you were the closest living person to my Mr. Butler for me. The irreproachable good conduct always. But, in addition, you were patient and quietly long-suffering, as Mr. Butler would certainly be, in the face of adversity. I know about your marriage. I've coaxed enough out of Larkin during our conferences. He's in the Corrigan camp, so to speak, but by reinterpreting most of what he says I get the picture. You've put up with quite a bit, but Mr. Butler would have stuck it out, Principato."

"Impossible, Jedda. Or else Butler was not meant to exist. You cast both him and me in the role of some traditional saint, wearing the yoke patiently on earth with the promise of heaven and happiness. But I haven't got the strength. I'm not up to wearing the yoke. I simply admit to having failed the Church's and your own expectations."

"Don't connect my expectations with the Church's, Principato! And don't speak to me of our Catholic tradition! Butler was real to me. Perfectable modern man, if you will, but nondenominational. He was not a Catholic. As for the Church . . . well, mass is something I tell people I go to, to make sure I can keep my job with this agency. There's too much shit in the bottom of the Catholic vat for Jedda McMahnus to go on participating. You should have heard Larkin in here earlier denouncing you in the name of our poor outraged religion. Principato has left his wife! He plans divorce! I actually ended up defending you, though I don't approve of what you've done, just to wipe the savage righteousness from his face. I even told him to go back to the seminary. The world was obviously too damned impure for him."

"Jedda, Jedda, what's wrong with you? You're the one the world sounds too impure for. You've been my supervisor for eleven years, but you've never spoken like this. What's wrong?"

"I'm despairing, Principato." She sobbed openly. "Really despairing. I had long ago given up on the willingness of anyone to become personally involved with someone as grotesque as myself. But the events of yesterday afternoon and this morning have brought everything to a head. Yesterday I was driving along a highway in Delaware looking for any place to stop—a gift shop, tame bears in a pen, anything—when I saw a baby crawling right at the edge of the road. I stopped to pick it up and carried it to the nearest house, where a woman came screaming out onto the lawn, cursing at me for daring to hold her child. I tried to explain that I'd found the baby on the roadside, but she wouldn't listen. She pushed me, Principato, and I fell down because of my high heels. Then she kicked me in the thigh twice before I got away to my car."

"Jedda, don't cry like this. The woman was obviously mad. Why else would anyone act like that?"

"But it's merely symptomatic, Principato. The whole world seems mad to me. Last night I became so frightened driving home in traffic that I pulled off the road and sat there for two hours. There were accidents everywhere, and people cursing and growling through their windshields like animals."

"Jedda, listen to me. Don't let them hear you crying out in the main office. You're their supervisor. You must make sure they don't see or hear you crying. Do you understand me?"

"Useless words, Principato," she sobbed. "I can't stop crying."

"Then cry as long as you need to. I'll stay here on the phone. Only keep it low."

Principato remained on the phone for forty-five minutes, conspiring with a teen-age waitress to supply him with additional dimes and keep other customers from trying to use the booth. Someone on the other end of the line was having a nervous breakdown, he told her simply, and he held the receiver close to her ear so that she might hear Jedda's sobbing. It was enough. Convinced and sympathetic, she left her work abruptly several times to head off potential intruders, requesting that they use another phone. Each time, Principato saw her lips form words "nervous breakdown." Curiously, no one protested, all turning away without a second glance at Principato in the booth, except one woman who observed him for a long moment, then shook her head sadly, swung around, and left.

"I haven't cried in a long time, Principato." Her phlegm-coated voice came to him over the wire at last. "I'm not a crying kind of woman. Forgive me."

"Forget it, Jedda. The important thing now is to pull yourself back into shape."

"Into what kind of shape, Principato? I haven't got the energy to rise from this chair. The brittle façade is stripped away and my supporting rib of a Mr. Butler has died. I feel like a pliable wet sponge."

"Then put the façade back and resurrect Mr. Butler, Jedda." He spoke furiously, lecturing her. But really he was trying to bang his familiar Jedda back into the mold. "That damn agency couldn't run without you. If you're not there tomorrow morning at nine, then I'm handing in my notice. You've got a responsibility to a lot of people out in that office who would be left floundering around if you were suddenly to take off. Do you hear me?"

"Yes, Principato, I hear you," she answered, then began crying anew.

"And, Jedda . . ."

"Yes, Principato?"

"When I ask you tomorrow how Mr. Butler was this weekend past, what are you going to say?"

"That Mr. Butler is quite well. That we drove along a highway together in Delaware on Sunday and rescued a child from almost certain death, and that the child's mother clung to us, weeping with gratitude. That's what I'll tell you, Principato. But how will you respond, knowing it to be a lie?"

"With another agreeable lie. The way most people do to soften up reality. That way we'll both stay in our jobs. Now what about that sudden emergency that was going to stop Larkin from smearing my name around the office?"

"I'll get right on it, Principato," the supervisor promised with the last echo of sobbing before she replaced the receiver. Principato hung up and then tried to tip the waitress a dollar. She refused.

"It was the least I could do. That poor woman on the other end of the line was losing her mind. I hope she gets better."

Principato bent to kiss her forehead and was gratified that she did not shy away. He hastened from the restaurant, the inquiring glances of its customers following him, and drove to a liquor store that stood solitary and oasislike on the edge of the great expanse of scrub pine and purchased three fifths of scotch. Then he continued on to the trailer to make peace with Nick, whom he found sitting, still in his nightshirt, over a late breakfast.

"Let's get drunk," Principato said, holding up a bottle.

"O.K.", Nick readily agreed.

It was not yet noon.

Tuesday he made it to work, spoke briefly with Jedda McMahnus in the morning, asked after Mr. Butler, was assured that he was alive and well, then sat out the rest of the day in anticipation of leading the corpulent Corky into Neutral Corner that evening.

At eight o'clock he found her, clad in black stockings, on a bench near Eva Lissome's home.

"Cornelius beat the hell out of me on Friday night, and he's back on the booze like a trooper," was the first thing she said. "But he'll never find out who you are. I promise you that."

"Thank God!" Principato muttered, still mindful of the problem of getting his friend into Eva's confessional place. Moments later it was the patroness herself who answered the jangle of cowbells at the door. She was heavily made-up, her hair stiffly lacquered again, as if she meant to go on stage tonight if things became overly dull. From the mean cast of her face, Principato knew they were unwelcome.

"Yes, may I help you?"

"Good evening. Corky here figured you might still be angry with her, so I agreed to come with her and smooth out the way."

"Well, she's right, I am still angry with her. And you're not in any position to be smoothing the way for anybody."

"What do you mean, Eva?" Principato looked beyond her through the house and saw Allergucci in his nonclerical sharkskin suit lecturing a group of women in the garden. Almost at that instant the priest ceased speaking and turned to look at them curiously. A white carnation graced his lapel.

"What I mean is that you, bosom buddy of Nick Malatesta, are unwelcome after what that creep did to me!" the patroness said, lapsing easily into the vernacular to make her point.

"What *he* did to *you!* You were the one who threw him out!" Principato said.

"Yes, after he attacked me! You should have seen him! Like a madman! Smashing me around like a . . ."

"Bullshit, Eva. Nick's too smart for that. He wouldn't yank the carpet out from under himself. The first salvo had to come from you."

"Are you calling me a liar? Get out of here, you two! I don't need either of you!"

"Obviously not, . . ." Principato began, only to have Eva slam the door in their faces, so hard that a small jangle of cowbells erupted from the vibration.

"Let's go for a sandwich, O.K., Angelo?"

"O.K.," Principato said, smiling wanly. The unexpected sound of his own Christian name after the unpleasantness helped restore him somehow. He was so rarely called anything but Principato or Pato. They walked slowly toward his car in the twilight, Corky wincing from the pain of Cornelius's beating.

"What I'd like to know is how Monsignor Allergucci gets mixed up in all of this business," she said.

"Nothing simpler. He's boss in that house. She makes the speech then pays him for the privilege." He made the information he had gained from Malatesta seem like routine perception.

"So that's the story. Boy, when you live in a tight little neighborhood like mine, where everybody's pretty much the same and you can't even remember why you hate some of the people you hate, it takes gettin' out into the world like this to find out what real bastards there are afoot. That twosome, Eva and the monsignor, will end up drownin' in their own piss. Mark my words." She shook her head sadly.

162

Oh no, Principato thought. Not another despairing, after Jedda McMahnus yesterday. But he saw the truth of her words. Principato had come out of his own tight little neighborhood to discover the same betrayal. Believing in the great humanity of the patroness, the unquestionable good intentions of the priest, they had been deceived. Instead of a working partnership of priest and patroness, they had unearthed another sort of relationship. A kind of symbiosis, really, to which the participants at Neutral Corner were only incidental. Allergucci and Eva fed ravenously on each other until they should be done with each other. Until they ended up drowning in their own piss, as Corky had aptly put it.

"Let's go to the same diner, O.K., Angelo?"

"Are you sure they'll have us after what happened last week with that cop? I'd hate to have two rejections on the same night. It would begin to look like conspiracy to me."

"Don't worry about anything," she said. "If they refuse us, I'll stage a sit down in the doorway and they'll all be trapped on the inside."

They climbed into the De Soto and drove quickly to the diner with its brightly lit parking lot. As they entered, it all seemed to Principato to be too repetitive: the same long row of wide-bottomed truckers and cab drivers on a break, the same waitress, who turned, frightened, to whisper, "They're back," to the same short-order man, then stuck the end of her apron in her mouth. Even the same record on the juke box.

"We don't want any trouble here," the waitress said in a shaky voice, as she stood ready to take their order.

"There won't be any trouble," Principato promised. In five minutes, when she returned with their superburgers and Cokes, she seemed assured.

"I think it's terrible what that cop started last week," she said. "I mean taking a sneak out to meet your lover is one thing, and I'm not going to pass judgment on that. But I don't feel that anyone has the right to butt in unless it's a close relative of the jilted husband, like a brother or sister, do you?"

"No, of course not," Principato replied, curiously unmoved by the offhand charge of adultery.

"I mean that cop was just a friend of the jilted husband, I found out later. And . . . Oh, my God! Here he comes again!"

Principato turned swiftly. Farland, cop and friend of Cornelius, strolled toward their booth and sat down, uninvited, beside Principato, as the waitress hastened away. The counter customers turned to watch.

"Is Tuesday your regular meetin' night, Corky? Because this diner is right in the middle of my patrol and I can arrange to skip takin' coffee here if it'd be more convenient for you."

"Look," Principato said, "I don't think you should concern yourself here. The waitress feels the same way. You're not her husband's brother or even a relative, after all."

"You shut up, pal. I intend to concern myself here if my best friend of forty-five years doesn't know his fool of a wife is runnin' around with some dark-skinned gypsy. And there isn't much to stop me from takin' off this badge and invitin' you outside for a beatin', you skinny weasel. Are you game?"

The great hoary face of the cop, not unlike his Corrigan brothers-in-law, hung before him only inches away. Beads of perspiration stood out on the forehead. The strong odor of something consumed at an earlier coffee break—Principato guessed it was anchovy pizza —crept toward him on the man's breath. His eyes were narrowed: the face of an ultimatum.

No, Principato was about to answer, conceding he could not sustain another beating after the one Malatesta had given him, when Corky broke silence.

"With what hand were you figurin' to take off that badge and maul my friend here, Farland?"

"With this one," the cop responded, brandishing a clenched right fist in the air, then laying it palm downward on the table as before. As if by reflex, Corky raised her Coke bottle and came down on the hand so hard that a geyser of dark liquid shot into the air. Somehow the bottle did not break.

"Jesus, Mary, and Joseph! My hand is broken! Call the police! I'll have you booked for assaulting an officer!" he roared at Corky.

"Keep quiet, Farland," she said, grabbing the injured hand the cop was waving in the air and squeezing hard. "You call any more law in

164

here and the Democrats won't pick up a single vote in that ward of ours when I get finished canvassin' the place with a few tales about that politician brother of yours. Do you understand?"

"Ow! Yes, Corky, I understand. Only please let my hand go."

Principato felt a rush of pity for the cop. As before, the other customers had edged off the counter stools and huddled in knots at either end of the diner. The frightened waitress chomped furiously on her apron end.

"I didn't telephone Cornelius last week, Corky," the cop moaned. "I figured you'd get scared and stop this foolishness and everything would be back to normal."

"Well, I didn't get scared and I'm not goin' to stop my foolishness until I've got what I want. Now why don't you go peddle your police car around town for a while. You can pick up coffee someplace else."

"I hope there are no bones broken in this hand," Farland said, standing up.

"You've got Blue Cross, I'm sure." She turned to Principato. "Isn't it ironic about cops? A poor woman could be raped and robbed and left unconscious on the street and there wouldn't be one around for miles. It's just when you're sittin' down for a quiet sandwich somewhere that you can't get rid of them."

"Who the hell would ever try to rape and rob you? There's no man in Philadelphia could even get his arms around you," Farland said.

"Now you've made me mad!" Corky rushed out of her seat and herded the cop toward the entrance. Obligingly, the pale waitress held open the plate-glass door. Principato craned his neck to see his friend give her adversary a mighty shove that rocketed him across the asphalt pavement into the side of his police car. Then Corky waddled back to the diner as the car with Farland and his partner inside drove quickly away. Warily, the counter-stool customers returned to their food.

"Bring me another Coke, honey," Corky called to the waitress as she sat down, breathing hard. In seconds, it seemed to Principato, the girl was at their table.

"I had it all ready for you, ma'am." She spoke in a trembling voice.

"Thanks, honey. I'm sorry about the mess I made."

"That's all right. Uh, ma'am?"

"Yes, honey?"

"Do you think you're coming here next Tuesday again?"

"I'm not sure, why?"

"Because if you were certain, I could arrange for Tuesday to be my night off. I just couldn't go through this again."

Principato watched as Corky's eyes became suddenly liquid. She raised a lacy handkerchief to them.

"Oh, what a terrible woman I am. Disturbin' poor people at their honest labor. Rest assured we'll never come back here again, honey," she told the waitress. Then she broke down into sputtering sobs. Principato reached across to take her arm, anxious to lead her out of the place and save further embarrassment.

They walked across the parking lot, this time large mother being comforted by small son, to the De Soto. As before, the restaurant patrons ganged the windows to watch them. Principato started the car and began to drive along the cobbled street toward Hallagan's warehouse near the Richmond docks, when he saw the red police car, its dome light whirling, come up quickly behind them in the rearview mirror. Corky saw it too.

"Oh, damn it! It's that Farland again. Don't stop for him."

"Are you crazy? You have to stop for a police car. He'd really be able to get even if we didn't."

"Well, you stop for him. I'm gonna get out and keep right on walkin'. You come along and pick me up after he gets finished givin' you a hard time because your license plate is on crooked, or whatever excuse he's plannin' to use."

Principato pulled over to the side against a line of parked vehicles and Corky climbed out and began walking away. But not before Farland's driver neatly angled the police car in front of Principato's to corral her. She stood huge-busted and defiant, hands planted on hips in the metal triangle, while the arc of the dome light played over her angry face.

"Corky, will you just tell me why." Principato heard Farland demand from the car.

"Why *what*, Farland? Why don't you mind your own business?"

"Why you're doin' this after twenty-three years of marriage? How do you think Cornelius would feel if he knew about this? I know how

166

I'd feel if I ever heard my Alice was out runnin' around with some greaser like this."

"How many children has your Alice had, Farland?"

"Six. You know that, Corky."

"Then I'd say she doesn't have any reason to do any runnin' around."

"What are you talkin' about?"

"Your dear friend Cornelius doesn't have a sliver of lead in his pencil," she said, shaking her head sadly. "Why do you think we haven't had at least one baby in all these years? Because we didn't want one?"

"God Almighty." The cop whistled. "He could carry a horse down to Atlantic City if he had to."

"A lot of good it would do him," Corky said quietly. She seemed to Principato suddenly wearied and years older standing in the harsh glare of inquisitor Farland's dome light. He got out of the car to lead her from her pen.

Instantly, the cop extinguished his light. They were left standing, Corky and Principato, her lover, in the weak glow of the De Soto's headlamps, Corky weeping softly, as Jedda McMahnus had the day before. In their car, the two policemen instinctively pulled the peaks of their caps low over their foreheads. Then Principato felt a hand grip his.

"Shake," said Farland. "Only don't squeeze too hard. It hurts like hell where she clobbered me with that bottle."

Principato took the hand, squeezing with all his force. But the cop did not wince.

By Wednesday, when he arrived late to work from Hallagan's warehouse, he was sure this was the real week of Principato's women. There was a message for him to telephone his Aunt Lucrezia.

"Hi, sweetie," came the silky voice, "your old aunt is up from Florida for a month. I've heard you've gotten rid of that wife of yours. Your father's been thinking about making a new match for you down here in the old neighborhood. How old do you want it?"

"Aw, knock it off, Lucrezia. I don't know if I've left her for good, anyhow. I've got five kids, you know."

"Yes, darling, those five are really going to miss you. To heck with them all, I say. You still have a little juice left in you. The world is waiting, love."

Principato bit his lip. Really, Lucrezia could infuriate him sometimes. A bona fide millionaire, and she had never spent one dime to improve herself. Not even to acquire a veneer. Since his early teens, when she took him shopping to buy his occasional expensive clothes, she considered it perfectly natural to converse in her soft vulgar flow, speculating on the promiscuity of women they encountered in the streets. Later, gliding slowly home in her huge limousine, she would instruct her chauffeur to stop and ask meaningless directions of some policeman. Lucrezia had a vaunted passion for cops, especially the young ones on the motorcycles.

"Listen, Angelo, I can tell you're angry with me. How about letting your aunt buy you a nice lobster tonight, huh? Besides, I've got something to tell you, baby."

"Tell me now."

"Tonight. With the lobster. At that Italian sea-food place I like. Otherwise I won't tell you."

"O.K., eight o'clock."

At eight o'clock, Principato waved to Lucrezia's Negro chauffeur standing near her limousine outside the restaurant. A patient man, he thought. But he would have to be to put up with Lucrezia all these years.

Inside, his aunt sat, thin and faintly Oriental-looking, at a table for two, her lips fantastically reddened, noticeable from across the room. He peered at her closely for a moment to see if she were wearing her favorite shantung pajamas. A prim couple at the next table stared at her unabashedly. They wore convention-delegate badges stamped UTAH.

"Hi, honey. Got a kiss for your old aunt?"

Principato bent to kiss his aunt on the cheek. The welter of smells that totaled Lucrezia rushed up to smother him.

"What's new, Lucrezia?" He sat down across from her.

She raised her drink to her mouth. The narrow half moon of her lipstick was stamped on the glass.

"Want a drink?"

"No, I don't think so."

Over snapper soup, she told him that his mother was coming to live with her in Florida when his father died.

"It's just as well," Lucrezia said. "Your mama would want to be near the old man anyhow."

Principato heard the news dully and realized that he actually had not considered what would become of his mother after his father died. The idea of closing the house in South Philly staggered him. He had fled to it so many times for comfort.

"What are you thinking about, Angelo? A little depressed, yes?" Lucrezia asked quietly.

"No, not depressed, Lucrezia."

Around them, low music played and the male of the Utah couple spoke knowingly of Alaskan King crab. Glasses tinkled. Lucrezia's rhinestones sparkled under the lights. Principato noticed for the first time that his aunt's eyes looked green. New contact lenses, apparently.

"Is that what you had to tell me?" he asked her.

"That's only the baby part, honey. The rest is a little more difficult."

"Shoot."

"Lucy's coming out of the convent."

"Oh, Christ, no!"

The words escaped him with fierce intensity and he dropped his lobster claw and closed his eyes. Some deep, totally secured part of himself had just been reached with a long-bladed, extra sharp knife. The shrine to Lucy, his sister, who walked among adoring children in a nun's veil, patting at their heads. Inside, he began bleeding profusely. Then he opened his eyes. The Utah couple stared at them. Across from him, tears began gouging down through Lucrezia's mascara.

"I'll tell you the truth, sweetie, your aunt Lucrezia's just a plain questionable woman. I must've had every motorcycle cop from Jacksonville to Miami in that house of mine for a drink. But the one thing in life I always thought was beautiful and pure was our Lucy. All the more for a person like me. I always said, 'Imagine her being my niece.' I couldn't believe I knew someone so perfect. I'm a fool for saying it this way, but when I look at Lucy I think of the Blessed Mother."

"Everyone does," said Principato. He had understood long before what was the spell Lucy had been able to cast over the Corrigans and their retainers from the very beginning.

"When, Lucrezia?"

"The end of November. They received the letter at the house today. Your father really took it hard."

"Did she say why?"

"No."

A waiter came to clear the table. Young, with the dumb-blond handsomeness that Lucrezia favored. Principato's aunt smiled reflexively at him through her tears.

"Didn't you like your lobster, ma'am? I can bring you another." The notion that he had connected Lucrezia's tears with a perhaps poorly done lobster set Principato to laughing despite himself.

"It was fine, honey. I'm not very hungry," Lucrezia answered. Her voice was now deep and husky.

"Excuse me, darling, I'll be back in a minute." She rose to go to the ladies' room, keeping a handkerchief to her face, as the waiter brought coffee. Inquiring glances followed her. The Utah man reached over and touched Principato's arm.

"Say, is that poor woman in trouble?"

Principato resisted the urge to say, 'Mind your own business.' But the man looked genuinely kind and well-meaning. His wife's face was a mask of concern.

"We found out today that her niece, my sister, is coming out of the convent. She's a nun."

"Oh," said the man. He seemed disappointed somehow. Not Catholics, evidently.

"Well, it comes on top of another problem," began Principato, anxious to assure him there really was trouble. "I left my wife and kids this week."

170

"Oh, dear," the woman said, "that's terrible. Dr. Thorn and I have been married for thirty-seven years." Behind her horn-rimmed glasses, her eyes were large and honest.

"What happened exactly, son?" Dr. Thorn asked.

From the aisle, Principato told the couple about his father and the Corrigan conspiracy at the retreat house the weekend before. Mrs. Thorn had taken a handkerchief from her purse and touched it to her eyes on hearing of the elder Principato.

"Son, a father's last wish is sacred!" Dr. Thorn pronounced a bit too loudly perhaps. His wife gave a double emphatic nod. The doctor's face was creased with sorrow.

"And as for your wife and this Kababian fellow, well, it wouldn't go on for long out in Salt Lake City, where we live. Do you remember Sarah Eldridge and that Mexican delivery boy?" he asked his wife. She nodded again. Apparently, she knew exactly what he meant. Principato saw her give the room a kind of nervous, uncertain sweep, as if she were seeing Philadelphians for the first time. Notorious inhabitants of the East Coast Sin Town. This sort of thing could never happen in Salt Lake City. But that was the classic line for Philadelphia, too. Or anywhere. You took security from knowing it was home, Principato decided. The woman sighed. Probably with longing for their home and its Mormon-desert purity.

"What happened to Sarah Eldridge?" Principato asked.

"Oh, she had to leave town. Ran away to California. The last time we heard, she was making her living as a prostitute." Dr. Thorn shook his head sadly. Certain paths were inevitable, Principato supposed. Either a prostitute or an illegal abortionist. There was a long silence while they mused.

In time, Lucrezia returned. Candles glowed in the watery orbs of her eyes. Her cheeks had a freshly powdered look that failed to blend with the whole of her complexion. As Principato got up to leave, Dr. Thorn grabbed at Lucrezia's hand.

"Everything is going to be all right, dear lady."

"Really? If I were to find a nice motorcycle cop waiting outside the door for me, I might agree with you, dear." But she smiled after saying it. It was the loving kindness in the eyes that got her, too.

171

Outside, they walked toward Lucrezia's limousine. Her driver opened the door.

"Honey, why don't you take a day off tomorrow and go out to Pittsburgh and see Lucy. She's probably having a hard time of it right now. You were always her buddy."

"I think I'll do that, Lucrezia."

"Good. Need any money?"

"It wouldn't hurt."

"Here's a hundred," she said, removing the rubber band from a wad of bills in her purse.

"Where to, Miss Lucrezia?" her driver asked.

"Let's go check up on some cute cops, Georgie."

"Yes ma'am." He winked to Principato as Lucrezia ducked her head through the door.

Abruptly the car moved away, looking from behind like the limousine of any other rich woman who favored such comforts, except that it bore his henna-haired, tinselly aunt who harbored a secret mania for motorcycle cops. For an instant Principato was bemused, despite the revelation about Lucy. But then he remembered the warning given him by his father, a man to be heeded since he dispensed such warnings so infrequently. When it came to business, Lucrezia was a rabbit puncher. The old man distrusted her mightily.

In the morning, early, he telephoned Pittsburgh and made arrangements with Lucy's Mother Superior for an afternoon visit.

"You may come any time after one o'clock. The children have only half-day sessions this week," she told him in a very correct, British-sounding voice. She gave no clue to what she thought about the idea of Lucy's leaving the convent. Somehow he expected her to offer an opinion, perhaps even flood the tiny aluminum cubicle of his telephone booth with sobs from all the way off in Pittsburgh. But in the end she simply hung up, the voice still crisp and controlled.

Moments later he called Jedda McMahnus to report sick.

"You're not sick, Principato," the supervisor said.

"All right, Jedda, a little more trouble in the works. You know how it is. It doesn't rain that it pours."

"God, and I had the nerve to cry to you. How long do you think the trouble's going to last?"

"I'll be in tomorrow."

"All right. See you then."

Good mother Jedda. Who else could possibly be counted on to put up with the uncertainty of being a Principato? he considered as he crossed the bridge into Philadelphia from the Jersey side. He drove quickly along the morning's sparsely traveled outgoing lanes of the expressway to the turnpike and swung into its western extension that cleaved through the mountains toward Pittsburgh and ended eventually at the Ohio pike.

Except for an occasional large truck, the way west was practically deserted. Passing through the neat, godly fields of Pennsylvania Dutch country with their look of practiced economy, he noticed for the first time the subtle nature changes taking place. It was already mid-September. The long fields of corn were beginning to show that yellowed, brittle look. The trees were changing too. He saw it especially when he drove through the first long tunnel and found himself in the mountains. The edges of the maples were turning to reds and browns, and Principato, moving slowly in the old De Soto, seemed to see everything with insistent clarity for the first time in months.

He recognized now how gravely his problems were preoccupying him. Normally he was attuned to change, excited by it: the gathering of events that ushered in another sweet, melancholy autumn. But this year he had missed the symbolic return of his children to school only days before, had been somehow unaware of the great normal influx of students back to the Philadelphia universities. He lived these days in an expanse of three-foot Jersey scrub pines that reflected no change so far, breathed the incessant sea smells that blew across the land from the Atlantic only fifteen miles off. No place to divine the trembling edge of a new season. That was for certain. It was necessary to transport himself to these mountains and see the first beautiful flush of a maple's decay to realize that autumn had indeed come again.

Then, sadly, he thought of Lucy. Trying to guess the reason for her impending departure from the convent had kept him awake for hours the night before. In truth, his mind still only half-accepted the news Lucrezia had given him. To be convinced, he had to see Lucy in a properly deplorable state: her lovely skin mottled, with dark, deep circles under her eyes to show she had fought the host of torments and finally given in to them, was indeed ready to shuck off the flowing blue habit and don the modern garb of a woman on the outside. Thirteen years a nun. Why should she choose to revoke her woman's Orders now? The time for that, he had believed, was the testing days of her postulancy, when she had worn a simple, dark dress and learned to walk quietly with hands clasped and head bowed in humility. Each time he was permitted to visit her at the mother house of her order and saw her approach him softly from out of the shadows of a long, dark hallway he expected her to announce suddenly and angrily that she wanted to leave. This Lucy, his sister, who played baseball when he did not and was forever laughing at being thrown into swimming pools by gangs of boys, gone into the convent to serve the Christ with all her heart and soul as nuns promised, and allow her spirit to be tamed. It did not seem possible. He had not really believed it until the day he saw her in a wedding dress taking her final vows. Then the acceptance had flooded into him and he realized that Lucy, a Principato, daughter of a man who did not go into churches, was indeed a cleric. He had come to have an immense faith in her vocation: she would always be a nun. He had erected a shrine to her within him.

He ambled with surprising ease through Pittsburgh's center city, stopped for late lunch at a diner, then drove to Lucy's convent, a cluster of well-kept, gray-stone buildings in a prosperous-looking suburb. They loved Lucy here, he knew. Twice before when he had come to see her he had found her in a ring of worshiping children and young mothers, that same circle, unhappily, fraught with the small jealousies of children and mothers when it came to gaining attention from a nun. The dark, warning looks were unmistakable.

He rang the front doorbell. An old nun opened the heavy door and smiled out of the dimness, blinking against the outside light.

"Yes, may I help you?"

"Is Lucy Prin—, I'm sorry, is Sister Veronica here?"

174

"Yes, come in. You must be her brother."

At the mention of Lucy's clerical name, the old nun's face had fallen suddenly, it seemed to Principato. She knew of Lucy's choice then. They must all know. He imagined this convent was in mourning.

"Come with me, please."

He followed her down a long passage that reeked of cleaning fluids. The walls were newly painted, the tile floor highly polished. Their footsteps echoed down its length. In front of him, the small, old nun seemed to be running, her rosaries clacking against the coarse cloth of her habit.

"In here, please."

She pointed into a tiny, windowless room with two hard-backed chairs and a spindly-looking table that held a single ash tray. He entered and sat down. The nun walked quickly away, the swish of her habit receding down the hallway in the same direction they had come. In the silence, Principato noticed his heart was pounding and his palms emptying rivers of sweat. From far off, upstairs in the great house, came the muted, monotone sound of prayers in the chapel. Then the prayers ended and were replaced by a beatific singing, in Latin, of many sweet voices.

> *"Veni Creator Spiritus,*
> *Mentes tuorum visita. . . ."*

The words drifted toward him, stopped in his mind for an instant of translation, then quickly passed on, unable even with their implication of caress to silence his heart or dam the rivers in his palms. Then he heard again the sound of stubby-heeled nun's shoes coming to him along the hallway, the habit swishing, the rosaries clacking. A form filled the doorway, the face still hidden in the shadows. Principato sprang to his feet.

"Lucy?"

"Hello, Angelo."

He advanced to touch her, remembering at the last instant to kiss her only on the cheek. He looked down to where he held her shoulders in his hands and saw to his embarrassment that there were two sweaty prints on the black linen of her veil. She pushed him away gently, closed the door, and sat down opposite him. Her beauty was incredible.

"Somehow I expected to see you all aggrieved and afflicted-looking," he said.

"Not a chance, with the beauty treatments we get here. What happened at home when they received the letter?"

"I really don't know. Lucrezia told me about it, last night in a restaurant, then went off on a crying jag to the ladies' room. I couldn't get anything out of her after that."

"Hmm. That sounds bad. The only time Aunt Lucrezia ever cries is when she's trying to get someone to drop his guard so she can deal him out of something."

"This time was real."

"I can guess." She smiled faintly at him, then lowered her eyes. Her body seemed to him to slump almost imperceptibly in the chair and she began to twirl the large crucifix at the end of her rosary beads in a slow circle. Then abruptly, she pulled herself up straight; the beads dropped with a clatter against the leg of the chair.

"What's new with yourself, honey?"

"Well, I've left Cynthia."

"Oh no. Is everyone discovering his vocation's been a mistake?"

"Cripes, what do you expect, Lucy? You couldn't see this coming, all along? I've been nothing but a stud to that family for eleven years. It's time to start taking some kind of hard line with those Corrigans. You should hear the business they're giving me over Pop's refusal to have anything to do with the Church before he dies. Let him die if he must, but make sure it's in approved Corrigan style."

"I didn't know this, honey. The old lady, Mrs. Corrigan, always sends a nice check here every year."

"Huh! Conscience money. They figure if they pay out to you here in Pittsburgh, they can go right on belaboring me in Philadelphia. That's a typical Corrigan attempt at balance."

"I'm sorry, I didn't know it was this way with you until now. How long until the end for Pop?"

176

"The doctors say February or March. Lucy, is this why you're coming out? To try to get Pop to relent?"

"I wouldn't dare. Pop never tried to stop me from joining the order. I wouldn't presume to interfere with his dying."

"Why then, Lucy?" He leaned toward her, sitting now on the edge of his chair and watched her shrug her shoulders in a sudden gesture of hopelessness.

"It's because of a man, honey."

"A man? Who? Where?" Principato was shocked. Searching his own mind for Lucy's motives, he had not even considered the possibility that a man was involved. Dishonor to his sister to think such a thing.

"Who is he, Lucy?" he demanded fiercely.

"A doctor. He's a widower with two children."

"Where the hell did you meet him?"

"At the hospital. Sister Margarita was dying there, and Mother Superior sent me over a few afternoons each week to read to her. His rounds were in that ward. Angelo, it was terrible when I realized why I was going there after the first month. It was . . ."

"Lucy, why?" he interrupted. "There were a hundred ways you could have put him off. Why didn't you ask your Mother Superior to relieve you and send you to another city?"

"Because I didn't want to. I wanted to keep going back. Honey, he kissed me. I didn't resist him."

"He kissed you! But how? You're a nun! In that habit he kissed you?" Principato's voice was trembling.

"Yes, in the elevator at the hospital. Angelo, stop looking at me that way! I think you've gone and made some kind of deity out of me. There's a human being under this habit, whether you recognize it or not. Human beings make mistakes. I admit it now: going into the convent was a colossal mistake."

"A mistake! Suddenly now, after thirteen years?"

"Stop screaming at me! You've all gone and loaded a kind of moral responsibility off on me. Pop hasn't been to church in thirty-five years, but it appeases something inside him to know he's got a daughter in the convent. I even sense it with Rocco in his wheel chair. I don't know what his reasoning is, but . . ."

177

"Forget it, Lucy. I'm sorry."

Principato stood up and weakly circled the rickety table, then leaned heavily on one hand against the wall. The small, unventilated room was becoming stifling, and he loosened his tie, wondering vaguely why the architect who designed this convent chose to include a room without a window. Functional, no doubt: an unemotional cubicle for highly charged confrontations between accusing siblings. Then he pulled away from the wall and saw a perfect sweaty handprint, a dark-yellow outline against a beige background. Lucy looked at the form curiously.

"It's too warm in here. We ought to go outside for a little walk," she said.

"All right."

She opened the door and led him down the hallway again and through the front door into the blinding light outside. They turned into a small path that wound through the convent garden.

"What are you going to do when you come out, Lucy?"

"Marry him."

"How soon?"

"In the spring. And don't look at me that way. I'm not going to sit around in the sad afterlife of a spoiled nun until people get used to my being outside. He's been a widower for four years now and he's got two wonderful boys who need a mother. We've got this all planned out."

"But how, Lucy? How were you able to see him beyond a few minutes at that nun's bedside or getting into an elevator with him?"

"When I was sure, I told my confessor, and Mother Superior made arrangements for permission to have him come and visit me here at the convent. He's come at least ten times already."

Beside Sister Veronica, her brother smiled ruefully. A courtship worthy of a Principato. The girl in the dark-flowing garb of a nun and her widower-doctor-suitor sitting stiffly in the convent parlor, where festoons of saints' pictures hung on the walls. In the next room, doubtless, was the sad duenna, a confused Mother Superior forced to cope with a crisis of the Church in the modern world, but praying fervently, perhaps, for an old-fashioned resolution to the inconsistency of two vocations' trying to overlap. Principato shook his head slowly at the image. They continued on in silence.

"Where are you staying now?" Lucy asked him.

He tried smiling for her. "In Jersey. I'm living with Nick Malatesta in a house trailer at a crummy amusement park he owns now. It's a classic of a place to flee to from your wife."

"Strictly elementary." She laughed. "We're Principatos, remember? The only thing that shocks me about our family is that we're still able to be astounded at some of the things we do. The first time I ever saw Poppa in a pair of Bermuda shorts, I just gave up. Remember the Sunday of the centenary when he came out with Mama and you to see me?"

"Yes," Principato said, also laughing. The parish had celebrated with a block party, and the Principatos had come in the Thunderbird to visit Lucy, the old man in glaring madras Bermudas and his henna-haired wife in her favorite culottes. A bishop had been there, and city dignitaries and the Mother General of Lucy's order. Children in little blue uniforms had come to watch the trio disembark from the red convertible. Lucy and another young nun howled hilariously at the sight of her parents. Anxious to preserve his Sunday-afternoon image of wheeler-dealer, the old man had written out a check for the Mother General.

"How's Rocco?" Lucy asked.

"All right, I suppose. I haven't seen him for a couple of months now."

"You ought to try going more often. I can imagine he gets pretty lonely out at that home."

"Well, Mama gets up there two or three times a week. Besides, every time I go, I'm on the receiving end of a barrage from him without any apparent reason. I think it's kinder to stay away and not get him excited."

"Does he know I'm coming out?"

"I don't think so. I only found out last night. Mama'll probably tell him on Sunday."

"I want *you* to tell him, Angelo. Very calmly. You know how emotional Mama is. She'll start crying and get him all upset. Is it possible to stop there tonight on your way home?"

179

"Yes, it's possible," Principato said. But highly undesirable. He guessed Rocco would be less interested in Lucy's departure from the convent and impending marriage than a progress report on the search for his woman.

"Do it for me, all right, Angelo?"

"It's a long drive back, Lucy."

"Please. It'll only take you fifteen minutes. Just get to him before Mama does. It's important that he doesn't find out about me in fragments between her crying fits. And tell him I'm sorry."

"All right, I'll go. I see your point."

Later, they walked slowly about the school and church. Little girls, still in their uniforms, had stopped their playing and run up to Lucy, hailing her by a title still unfamiliar to her brother: Sister Veronica. She joked with them, calling each by name in the special lilting voice she reserved for children, even stopped to play jacks with them. Principato watched, his heart swollen with a real sorrow at the thought that all this would soon end. Married to her doctor, if it ever happened, she would always be Lucy the nun, Sister Veronica to himself and many others. She was right. Everyone in the family had traded something off on her.

At four o'clock she went back inside and Principato began the drive home. The sun seemed to go down abruptly as he entered the mountains and a sudden chill reminded him again that it was September. He fumbled with the knobs that were supposed to bring on the heat, heard the soft roaring of a fan somewhere, then felt the warmth curling about his legs. Faithful servant this car. The last vestige of security left to him when the squat tower of his familiar existence was showing up such large cracks. He had a keen sense of their size now after the events of this week and he babied his aging security along the dark highway toward Philadelphia.

At nine o'clock he was at the gates of Good Shepherd Home for Paraplegics, an hour past visiting time. He asked the gatekeeper to get Sister Winifred on the phone.

"Who is it?" asked the familiar brogue.

"Hello, Sister Winifred. How are you? This is Angelo Principato, Rocco's brother."

"Ah, yes. Don't think I've forgotten what ya did to me a few months back."

"What *I* did to *you!* You were the one who stomped all over my foot, if I remember correctly."

"Yes, but I wouldn't have had to do it if it wasn't for ya tellin' me I didn't know how to take care of your brother."

"I'm sorry about that, Sister," Principato said, "and I hate to disturb you, but I've got an urgent message for Rocco."

"So urgent it couldn't wait until the mornin'?"

"Yes, Sister, very urgent. It's from his sister, Lucy, the nun."

"Lucy? The one out in Pittsburgh? What order is she with?"

"The Agnines. Sisters of Saint Agnes."

"Oh, yes, I know about them. They're not such a bad bunch. What's wrong with her?"

"I'm afraid it's a bit private, Sister."

"Hmm. All right, I'll be right down to take ya in to him."

Principato watched the front-staircase lights go on, illuminating four storeys, and saw Sister Winifred begin her descent from the top, her veil flying as she hurried across each landing to the head of the next stairs. Then a door opened with a clang and the white of her habit rushed at him through the darkness to the gatehouse.

"I really shouldn't let you in," she said. But her curiosity had overridden that conscience struggle. Doubtless, she would begin working on Rocco for information the minute he left.

"Thank you, Sister," he said gratefully. He followed her into the building and up four storeys in an elevator, then along a half-lit hallway where red and blue vigil lights burned before an occasional statue. Rocco sat in his wheel chair in the game room, apart from the other boys, engrossed in his eternal box of Pepsi-Cola caps.

"Poor lamb," Winifred said, holding Principato back with a tight grip on his arm. "Always alone and amusin' himself with his Pepsi lids. You'd think there was never another thing on his mind. Wait here and I'll bring him out to ya."

Principato moved farther along the dim hallway from the game-

181

room door and watched Winifred walk up to Rocco and begin speaking with obvious disapproval in her face. He guessed that, to her mind, it would be the ultimate victory in their small war if she were able to return to him and tell him that Rocco was unwilling to see him. But instead, a great flash of a smile came into his eyes. He held the box to his lap with one hand and propelled himself into the hallway with the other. Miffed, Winifred did not follow.

"What's wrong with Lucy? Did you get my woman?" he demanded in the same breath, coming to an abrupt halt before his brother.

"Let's go over there. I want to sit down," Principato said quietly, pointing to a bench halfway along the wall.

"You got my woman, right?" Rocco pleaded as Principato sat down.

"Lucy is coming out of the convent in November, Rocco. She's going to marry a doctor from Pittsburgh."

"Angelo, did you find my woman for me?"

"Aren't you even interested to hear what I came here especially to tell you about your sister?"

"Listen, Angelo, it's too bad she's coming out of the convent and nice she's going to marry a doctor. But it's her life. Nothing I can tell her is going to change it. I thought you came here to tell me about my woman."

"I haven't found one yet."

"What the hell have you been doing? It's months since you promised you'd get me one."

"Do you think I've had nothing else to do but look for your woman? Besides, I wouldn't know where to start. I've got Nick Malatesta working on it now, but it's slow going. His contacts from years back are rusty."

"Rusty-fusty, you fucker. I knew this was going to happen. You're one of those guys that everything they touch turns to shit. If I get a woman it'll never come from your help."

"Rocco, stop it! I want to help, believe me. But everything's in such a mess lately. I've left my wife, and Pop's going to die, and Lucy's coming out of the convent, and . . ."

"Don't tell me your problems, Angelo. There's nothing I can do to help you in this wheel chair. You've got two legs to walk away from them at least."

"Don't start that again, Rocco, please."

"Why not? If I had two good legs like you, I would've passed you out in life by now. I wouldn't get tied up with a mess of a wife like you've got, or be flat on my ass depressed every time the wind shifted. If Lucy wants out, that's her problem. And Pop has to die someday. Better now than flying from doctor to doctor looking for a cure for all those things he's got wrong with him and spending piles of money."

"You can talk that way about your own father and sister?" Principato said.

"Aw, shit with you, Angelo. There has to be something wrong with you the way you get upset over other people. Fuck them all, I say. If it doesn't affect me directly—like you not getting my woman for me—then I don't give it a second thought."

"That's not the way we were raised, Rocco."

"Well, sorry I've failed the Principato tradition, brother," he said. Then, casually as always, he dumped the box of bottle caps on the floor. Some tricolored buttons rolled nearly the length of the hallway from them. Winifred's face appeared suddenly at the game-room door, a question mark upon it.

"I won't pick them up this time, Rocco," Principato said.

"You'd better pick them up or you won't be allowed in here again."

"I'll take my chances then."

Sister Winifred moved slowly toward them, her stubby-heeled shoes stepping occasionally on a cap.

"What happened, Rocky?" she demanded.

"Him again, Sister," Rocco answered with disgust.

"I knew I shouldn't have let ya in here. I was a fool to be kind to ya. Well, get pickin' them up."

"I didn't do it, Sister, and I have no intention of picking them up."

"He says ya did it."

"He tells lies, then."

"Out! Get out of here! Slanderin' your own poor brother bound to a wheel chair." She grabbed Principato's arm and shoved him toward the staircase, while Rocco laughed vengefully from behind.

The real week of Principato's women indeed, he decided, as Winifred maneuvered him hastily down four flights of steps and toward the gates.

NINE

Autumn in earnest.

Time passed swiftly for Principato, lover of melancholy and dark, brooding moods. Joyfully he embraced the real autumn of chill days and blowing leaves that came with a vengeance after the late Indian summer. Around himself and Malatesta, in their sea of scrub pine, the ends of the needles turned yellow and the cold winds howling in from the coast brought frequent rains that changed the cleared area of the amusement park into a mire so that Principato was forced to leave the De Soto on the highway shoulder and walk a narrow path of planks to the trailer. The abysmal look of the place, with the rides all sinking precariously into the ooze on one side or another and the tattered ends of the canvas coverings flapping in the wind, delighted Principato's soul, helped make this the best and dankest autumn ever.

He settled in for long months of sweet sadness and chose to go to work only sporadically, vaguely realizing that Jedda would, in conscience, have to ask him to leave after a time. In the evenings he took to sitting in the trailer with Nick, sipping straight Scotch (a previously unknown vice) to the accompaniment of FM music out of a Newark station for night drivers and ruminating on the three discords that troubled his waters.

One, his halved marriage, was not actually a tragedy for him. Rather, more and more he tended to look upon it as a relief, had no real thoughts about rectifying it immediately. In truth, he played it out for all it was worth: to his fellow case workers at Holy Family House he assumed the immense proportions of protagonist. The Corrigan henchman, Larkin, had lost a round in the attempt to defame him. Kind mother Jedda had seen to that. He knew it from the rows of dim, pitying smiles that greeted him when he made work on occasional days and the muted whisperings about his five children. Accordingly, he hung his head for their benefit.

But the other two—Lucy's impending leap from the convent and the ugly promise of his father's death in February or March—these were real sorrows. Concerning Lucy, he had acted out in his mind at least a hundred times the events of a day still more than a month off when he would drive with his mother to the novice house of her order to pick her up and bring her home. The thing that worried him most was her hair. How would it be? Did they cut it off periodically under those veils? The question plagued him endlessly, but each time in the past, confronting her, he had forgotten to ask—for no reason he could remember. He envisioned her standing pathetically in a thin raincoat holding the small satchel of her personal belongings, her bald head turbaned in terry cloth against the cruel laughter of children who had known her only as the lovely wearer of a veil. His vision of her in this condition drove him to silent, alcoholic tears.

As to the old man, these days he began calling him again each afternoon at the same time despite the former's protestation, either from the office or driving the ten miles from the trailer to the phone booth at the nearest traffic circle. His father was taking drugs against the pain, and Principato could sense the pain and knew the killer was advancing. Like a battery running down, the great, quiet strength was flowing out of the old man, being replaced by a supreme tiredness. His voice fell frequently, going into a dry, choking rasp, which was followed by a small silence during which Principato imagined he spent the time somehow soothing his vocal chords. Ironically and almost desperately, he had much to speak of now, and mostly it was Lucy. Listening to the old man in his loud whisper remembering how she had been each year of her life until she entered the convent, Principato realized with a sudden monster guilt that Lucy had named it. They had all loaded something onto the thin shoulders of Sister Veronica. He was not sure of his own tradeoff, but he thought he understood his father's with perfect clarity. Despite himself, he was often testy with the old man.

"Rocco called from Good Shepherd the day after you told him about Lucy coming out," his father said once. "He's coming in for a few days when she gets home."

"What's he going to do that for?" Principato asked, angered that Rocco, of all people, should want to share Lucy with him in her time of duress. Perhaps he even meant to slander her.

"He's her brother, too, isn't he?"

"Yes, but . . ."

"But nothing. One more cry around this house isn't going to matter much. Don't be so selfish. Do you hear me, kid?"

"I hear you."

"Good, then call me tomorrow."

Another time, Principato decided to tell his father about Allergucci.

"I found out your friend, the monsignor, is playing a con game on some rich woman in the city."

"So what?" his father said. "Once an operator, always an operator. When we were young he was hustling down the Jersey shore. Just because he decided to become a priest doesn't mean he lost the old touch."

"That's all you can say? He's a clerical Rubirosa and he gets to hear your confession over the telephone every week. He's unworthy."

"Look, kid, don't always slam head first into the pillar of the principle. He may be slicing a little bit off some rich baby's bank account, but he's also feeding three hundred orphan kids up at that place of his, they tell me."

"Like hell he is. Or not with that money, at least. He's using it to build some memorial archdiocesan museum with his own name on the cornerstone, Nick Malatesta informed me. And who are you to be telling me how to get around a principle? You haven't been to church in thirty-five years because you couldn't find your way around something."

"Kid, don't lecture me. I'm a dying man. Allergucci gives the absolution the way I like to hear it. This is no time to switch. Where the hell am I going to find another priest who'll listen to me over the telephone? Nowhere, that's where. There's nobody in the world can bend with the wind like Allergucci. If the only way I'd agree to confess my sins was in a rowboat in the middle of the Delaware, he'd be there. Right on time, too."

"He's sinister, Pop," Principato said. "There's something dark and ominous about him."

"Well, if you don't want to give him any satisfaction, don't tell him you think so. That hammy actor's been dying for somebody to say that since he became a priest. You should see him when he wears his big black cloak on a rainy night. He's scared the pants off more than one poor bastard in a dark alley."

"He manipulates minds, Pop."

"Who wouldn't if they had the chance? Now stop trying to change your old man's mind when there's only a little life to him."

Each time he placed the receiver back in its cradle it was with the awful realization that one day less of that little life remained to his father. Then finally, on the last day, in a bedroom at home, in another scene that Principato had acted out and wept over a hundred times, the old man would die. But die roughly and stubbornly, for, in spite of himself, this was the way Principato still saw it: without the cushioning hand and soft voice of the Church to propel him into eternity. The old man's soul moving gratingly toward the Particular Judgment. Unlubricated in every sense. But this was only Principato's view. Who knew how his father, a man who did not go into churches, saw his eternity? A long darkness perhaps, to be cleaved through by the bright beams of his Thunderbird for a restless, short time until his henna-haired wife appeared suddenly by the side of the road.

In the trailer, Malatesta was the ideal companion for this sweet, sad season. In the mornings, on rising, he grew instantly depressed with the bad weather that would not allow him to go fishing in Beach

188

Haven, spoke prophetically of moving into Philadelphia, then descended easily into an alcoholic daze that rattled the conscience of Principato, who had received a surprise letter from Jon urging him to ride herd on his father's battered liver of which Principato had no previous inkling. But to no avail. These days he was a confirmed fellow traveler who leapt blithely into that same fog. It seemed to him altogether ludicrous to be handing out lectures on the evil of straining alcohol through a diseased liver. Instead, he sat back and listened to Nick's self-castigating musing on his past, dragging out old stacks of photographs from a cardboard box. Always, from year to year, from the Riviera to the Basque coast, were the unmistakable signs of decline that Nick seemed to be seeing for the first time only.

"That year I was Mr. Ibiza," he said mournfully, handing Principato a muscle beach photo of himself. Days of the golden boy. Ibiza, a Mediterranean island, paying tribute to his incredible good looks. But mock tribute, really. The year before there had been a different Mr. Ibiza. Another to follow the year after. A short, trembling reign of twelve months implied perfection for Nick. Transitory, strictly transitory. But Principato could not scoff at the obvious folly of Nick's choice—or even call it folly, for that matter. Had he done any better? Hobnobbing with a leftover *contessa*, trading nimbly on your beauty, waiting for the one important contact, was the easier way when hard work would have stood you in better stead. Nick had been a whore: no other word for it. But at least he had tried something, aimed at the illusion of fame, craved it indeed, though never really sure how it might be arrived at. His codrinker, Principato, had opted for precious and immediate security, leapt into a marriage, and seemed now, at thirty-four, to be tasting the larger life for the first time. Though from a bottle. Across from him, Nick reached over to retrieve Mr. Ibiza, handed him in return a snapshot of himself and three matronly-looking women taken at Cannes. The women were oblivious to the camera. Nick, however, was never caught unawares.

But autumn, the season for beginning to board up the mind in a dark house, was made cruel and real after a time. The first incursion into the alcoholic daze came in early November from the Corrigan mob when Principato drove home late one afternoon after work to pick up some winter clothing before returning to the trailer. Until then, he had not seen Cynthia since the Sunday he left her, only heard her voice growling at him occasionally over the office phone, informing him of the need to have certain forms from the children's school signed by both parents, and that she would send them to him by mail. As he parked the car in the driveway, Kababian and his mother hurried along the sidewalk to speak with him. It was already dark and chilly. The squat Armenian woman's breath smoke came out in harsh gasps. She had Nikos's red varsity jacket pulled about her head like a shawl.

"Mr. Principato, is it true you've left your wife?"

"Yes, Mrs. Kababian."

"Well, I wish you'd hurry up and go back to her," she said. "She's bothering my poor Nikos in an awful way."

"I didn't even know what she was doing, Mr. Principato, until Mama told me," Kababian said. Suddenly, Principato felt pity for his rival. Standing before him, the usually kind, doe-eyed Kababian looked haggard, frightened even.

"I'll speak with her, Mrs. Kababian."

"Something has to be done, Mr. Principato. She started coming over when the weather was still warm and sitting on the patio watching my Nikos lift his weights. I didn't think anything then, because, after all, we've been good neighbors for years. But when she insisted on going into my Nikos's little gym, I knew something wasn't right."

"Does she still come over?"

"Yes, and everyone in the neighborhood knows about it, too. Mr. and Mrs. Hamilton are always out raking the leaves when Nikos gets home from school and they can see her hopping the hedge to go to our house, with a drink in one hand and a pack of cigarettes in the other."

"Cynthia doesn't smoke," Principato said.

"Well, she does now. You must speak with her, Mr. Principato. We've always been good neighbors. Of course, things couldn't possibly be the same after this."

"I guess not."

Principato watched the mother and son turn about and walk sadly back toward their home. This, then, was the end of poor Kababian's innocence. His shoulders seemed to Principato somehow stooped

190

under the burden of his new knowledge, as if he would never again be able to walk erect and totally secure in his old world of football, weight lifting, and mother love. Principato climbed slowly up to the front porch of his own house. Mrs. Phillips opened the door for him; her huge frame protestingly filled the opening.

"What did that witch have to say?" she demanded.

"She only wanted for Cynthia to stop trying to put the make on Nikos in his private gym. I think she's got a pretty good case myself. She says all the neighbors are on to it now."

"And you'd actually believe such a thing about your own wife?" Phillips said. "Think of her stanch Catholic background. No moral lassitude was ever permitted there."

"Come now, Mrs. Phillips. Let's be real, huh?"

"Why did you come here, Principato?"

"To pick up a few things I'm going to need for the winter. I'll be all right. I remember where most things are."

"Good, because I've got work to do."

Just then Noreen appeared in the hallway.

"Hello, Principato." She waved to him.

"How are you?" He smiled and patted her small Corrigan head absently.

"Come on, child, let's go into the kitchen." Phillips grabbed at Noreen's hand and yanked her along the hallway.

Principato went upstairs for some clothing, carried it outside to the car in two separate trips, then went downstairs to the basement treasure cabinet for his bags of hair and his football. He unlocked the double doors and was startled to see rows of canned vegetables lining the shelves. The cardboard box containing the bags was gone. Also the battered football. An instant panic seized him.

"Mrs. Phillips!" he screamed. Almost immediately, the door to the kitchen flew open and the housekeeper's fat legs appeared at the top of the stairs.

"What's wrong, Principato?"

"Where's my box of hair? Where's my football?"

"We needed room for the vegetables, so we threw those old things out and burned them."

"You burned my hair!" Principato lunged to the bottom of the cellar steps to confront her. "Why did you burn my hair, you old bitch? Where's Cynthia?"

"Well, we didn't think it was good for anything. And we needed the space," she said, frightened now.

"Where's Cynthia, you whore? Where is she?"

"She's over at the Corrigans'."

"Call her and tell her to get the hell over here! I want to see her now!"

As Phillips lunged up the steps, an enraged Principato raced back to the cabinet and, wedging a shovel between it and the damp wall, pulled it over. It fell to the floor with a crash, cans of mixed vegetables and stewed tomatoes rolling across the basement toward the front end of the house. He stood for a moment vengeful in the havoc he had created and considered what to do when Cynthia arrived from the Corrigans'. He decided resolutely he would smash her across the face. For the interim he sat down on the bottom of the staircase and tried to weep over the loss of his hair. But tears would not come. Trembling with rage, he went up to the living room and paced back and forth, smashing the fist of one hand into the palm of the other. He could hear Phillips in the kitchen whispering guardedly into the phone. Soon she ventured into the room.

"Cynthia is coming right over, Principato, although neither she nor I can understand what's got you so upset. It was just a lot of old hair. I'd never even seen it before. And the boys tried playing with that football and it burst the first time they kicked it."

"Phillips, for your own safety get out of this room!" He watched the housekeeper edge toward the door, then resumed his pacing, hoping his anger would not somehow run down. In time he heard a car turning into the driveway and looked through a window to see one of the Corrigan limousines. Cynthia and her three brothers were inside. Principato started out of the house.

"Cynthia!" he yelled, running across the lawn toward the still moving car, "why did you throw out my bags of hair?"

"Stop shouting! How did I know you wanted them? You haven't been around here for two months."

"You knew I'd been saving that hair for eleven years now! You knew damn well!"

"So what? It's the stupidest thing I've ever heard. I could never understand why you had to go to Bisbing's symbolic barbershop, anyhow. He gives the worst haircut in Philadelphia."

Boldly, she opened the car door and stood in the driveway looking at him squarely. Taking advantage of the added height afforded him by standing on the small slope of the lawn, he wound up to strike her, only to have Matt Corrigan stop his arm abruptly in mid-motion.

"Don't have me get rough with you, Pato. Nobody's going to smack our sister while we're watching. Now get into that car of yours and get the hell away from this house."

Brother Jim grabbed his other arm. Edward spat disgustedly onto the lawn. "I don't like to criticize anyone in our family, but Uncle sure picked a winner with this nut."

"Don't call me a nut," said Principato. "You don't know how she is! Ask her about Kababian. She's trying to put the make on an eighteen-year-old kid. His mother came to me tonight to beg me to make her lay off!"

For a moment there was a stunned silence, then Principato saw Edward's great scarred brawler's fist hurtling at his face through the early darkness. It connected with the side of his nose, flinging him back onto the lawn, suddenly free of the steel grips of his other two brothers-in-law. He sprang quickly to his feet, tasting his own blood flowing from his nostrils, and began swinging wildly at the three Corrigan men who danced about him. Cynthia laughed cruelly. His fists made hollow, ineffectual sounds against their chests.

"You dirty sons of bitches! I'll kill you! I'll kill every one of you!" he screamed, lunging at brother Jim and trying to take a choke hold on his neck. Calmly, almost amusedly, Jim forced him to the grass and planted a heavy knee on his chest.

"Now settle down, Pato. You're going crazy. Do you hear me?"

From ground level, Principato tried swinging at Jim and got off one weak punch against the side of his head. Then Matt and Edward each pinned an arm against the lawn, and he folded back exhausted. A sudden quiet intervened and Principato could hear his own raspy breathing, saw the smoke rise jerkily from his mouth in the streetlight illumination. He tasted again the blood from his nostrils. Vaguely he wondered if his children were watching. Cynthia leaned against the side of the Corrigan Cadillac, regarding him narrowly.

"I think he's all right now. Let him up," she said.

"No, wait a few minutes until he settles down completely," Jim said.

Then they heard the shouting and saw the Kababian and Hamilton porch lights go on simultaneously.

"Mr. Principato, is something wrong?" Turning his head, Principato saw the two old Hamiltons descending their front porch steps in heavy coats. Mr. Hamilton held a baseball bat in his hands.

"It's perfectly all right, Mr. Hamilton," Cynthia called, "these men are my brothers."

"Yes, all three of them," Hamilton said, continuing across the road. At the same time, Kababian and his mother came hurrying up the sidewalk again. This time, the woman had taken care to slip into her son's varsity jacket, giving her free leverage for the clothesline pole she was carrying. Kababian swept onto the lawn and took in the situation with one short glance.

"I don't think you should be doing that to Mr. Principato, sir." He addressed brother Jim, still in kneeling position. The voice of a clean-cut kid trembling at what he sensed to be an injustice.

"Now, this is none of your problem, kid," Matt said. "Pato here is all worked up and we had to quiet him down."

"Does it take three of you? He looks like a steer ready for branding," Hamilton said. He raised the baseball bat to shoulder level and handed his glasses to his wife.

"Nikos, punch that man who's holding down Mr. Principato," Mrs. Kababian commanded.

Immediately her champion knight flew to the task and caught Jim Corrigan with a powerful uppercut. Below the action, an astonished Principato actually saw a tooth fly from his brother-in-law's mouth. Jim lurched backward, his head slamming resoundingly into the Cadillac's side. Matt and Edward leapt to their feet, thus freeing Principato. Both rushed at Kababian, pinning him across the hood of the limousine. Principato jumped up and scaled Matt's broad back, trying to hold his right arm from punching at Kababian's face. Beside him, brother Edward had a grip on Nikos's throat.

"Mr. Principato, watch out!" Principato turned to see Hamilton nimbly swing the baseball bat at Edward's lower back, connecting hard right where the kidneys should be. Edward bent over with a sudden fierce yelp, releasing his grip on Kababian, and collapsed to the ground. Seeing an advantage, Principato wedged one foot against the car's fender, and pushing off, pulled Matt over on top of him onto the grass. Kababian leapt from the hood and began swinging vengefully at Matt, while Principato slid out from beneath his brother-in-law.

"Help! Help! For God's sake, help!" It was Cynthia, still standing near the trunk of the car. Her eyes were wide with fright. Brother Jim was knocked out against the door panels, Edward writhed on the lawn with old Hamilton standing over him with the bat. Kababian was finishing off Matt with slow deliberateness.

"Help! Phillips, call the police!" Cynthia screamed. From the corner of his eye, Principato saw Mrs. Kababian suddenly lurch into motion after standing fixedly watching her son work on brother Matt. She raised the clothesline pole above her head, then brought it down with a fierce whack on Cynthia's hand which gripped the edge of the small tail fin for balance.

"You shut up! No police here!" Mrs. Kababian ordered.

"My fingers! You've broken my fingers!" Cynthia moaned, pressing the gloved hand to her mouth.

"Let me see," Principato said, running up to his wife. He felt her hand, but nothing seemed broken to him, no fingers loose or dangling. Cynthia yelped with the pain.

"You shouldn't have done that, Mrs. Kababian," he said to the stout woman, who still held the pole threateningly. She advanced toward him.

"Mr. Principato, we've been good neighbors, yes?"

"Yes, Mrs. Kababian."

"And my Nikos has helped you with these men, yes?"

"Yes."

"Then why do you get mad if I hit her? She's not a good wife to you, anyhow. Every day she comes over to see Nikos in his bathing suit lifting his weights. But she won't come any more."

"I only went over to count for him when he did his arm curls," Cynthia protested.

"I know why you came," Mrs. Kababian said. "A mother can feel it here." She thumped her breast with dramatic savageness, so that Principato, an American, but with an alien flair for drama, was keenly impressed.

"You're right. I'm sorry, Mrs. Kababian. But she won't come again. You heard his mother," he lectured, turning to the brothers Corrigan. "You heard what kind of woman your sister is. Believe me, the fault hasn't all been mine."

But there was no answer. Only the glazed look of the eyes that said the Corrigans had fallen back on their nimble ability to see only what they wanted to see, to hear only what they wanted to hear. Wearily, Principato shrugged and turned to thank his neighbors as Phillips ventured down from the front porch.

"Well, isn't this a fine scene for a supposedly respectable neighborhood. If I'd known the kind of people I'd have to live near, I would never have taken this job years ago."

"You should hear the tales this woman has been dropping around the supermarket about you, Mr. Principato," Hamilton's frail wife piped up suddenly. "I've never heard anything so unkind from a Christian mouth."

The Hamiltons were Lutherans. They believed excessively in loving kindness toward fellow white Christians as a duty. Even Principato thought them naïve at times.

"I have never said one thing, Mrs. Hamilton. I would consider it undignified to divulge any secrets about this family to someone I met by chance in a supermarket."

"Oh, yes, you have, Mrs. Phillips. I clearly heard you tell one woman that the Corrigans decided to approve Cynthia's marriage to Mr. Principato because they were afraid he might commit suicide if he were refused. He was that much in love with her."

"You said that?" Principato asked, incredulous. "You told that to someone you met in a supermarket?"

"You go into the house!" Mrs. Kababian commanded Phillips. Then she swung her clothesline-pole staff of justice in a wide arc and caught the housekeeper squarely in the stomach. Bent almost double, Phillips retreated toward the porch.

"The rest of you go in, too," she ordered, brandishing her pole above the wounded Corrigans. Immediately, they moved off after Phillips.

"Your wife is not a very Christian woman," Mrs. Hamilton said.

"Not very Christian," Kababian's mother echoed. Then, for no reason at all, it seemed to Principato, she slashed her pole against the limousine's front windshield, smashing at it until only tiny fragments of glass remained about the edges. Mr. Hamilton went to work on the narrow rear window with the blunt end of his bat.

"'Vengeance is mine,' saith the Lord," Mrs. Hamilton intoned. The Corrigans stood watching on the front porch, unprotesting. For the first time, Principato took out a handkerchief and pressed it to his still bleeding nose. Breathing heavily, Hamilton stood before him.

"When do you return to us, Mr. Principato?"

"Never, I think now." Really, he had thought previously that he would certainly return someday. Now he was almost resolute about not coming back ever.

"I am truly sorry, then. I have always thought of you as a man of much good will."

"Thank you," Principato said. He shook hands with each of his four neighbors, then opened the door of his car and climbed inside. He looked sadly at his reflection in the mirror. His face was smeared with blood. Two rivers of it congealed thickly above his lips. He started the car and drove off, watching his friends and allies still standing near the limousine, waving their staves and cudgels in the air.

"Dark season for a dark priest," Principato said aloud, surveying the storm clouds above the pinelands after the Western Union messenger had departed. Then he turned and made his way, in his inebriate's shuffle, back to the trailer door, careful not to spill his drink.

"His sinister excellency Monsignor Allergucci sends me a telegram," he announced to Nick.

"Let us hear the charlatan's words."

"He says: Wish to see you today p.m. at Saint Igitur's. Allergucci. I wonder how he got my address."

"Dame Eva must have given it to him. She knows you're here. Are you going? You're pretty plastered."

"Of course I'm going. I'll hang my head out the window until I hit Philly traffic and let the cold air clear the cobwebs. I wouldn't miss finding out why Allergucci would send for me."

"It can't be your money," Nick said, taking a long swig of his beer.

"I guess not."

"Well, give that one my fondest regards and tell him to prepare for my counterattack."

"When shall I say it's coming?"

"Late-spring offensive. When it's warm enough for madras. Can't expect to turn that bitch Eva's head when the only thing I own for winter is a peacoat."

"O.K., I'll pass it on," Principato said thickly, disappointed somehow that the endless plans for counterattack were now postponed until spring. He had enjoyed the idea of the monsignor's effortless existence being plagued by a gnat, no matter how small and distantly irritating.

An hour later, having neglected to hang his head out the window to brush away the cobwebs, Principato urged the De Soto toward Philadelphia through lanes of more wary vehicles that seemed willing enough to clear out of his way. He crossed the Franklin Bridge, then headed uptown to the end of Broad Street, cunningly discovering the rhythm of the lights by gluing himself to the rear of a police car.

Following the broad lines of Nick's shakily drawn map, he turned toward the vast sprawl of northeast suburbs and promptly lost himself along the tortuous way of narrow, constantly right-angling lines that honed in on the cross that Nick intended for Saint Igitur's. Around him, everything was fantastically uniform: rows of red-brick development houses, not one of whose owners appeared to have a small devotee's courage to change even one of the everywhere-white front doors to another color.

He stopped perhaps ten times to ask for directions only half understood, sputtering ahead a scant few blocks between requests, until he drew alongside a gnomish man in a blue station wagon for a second time.

"Follow me or you'll be driving around in this maze for the rest of your life," he said. "It all looks the same to an outsider. If you're an insider, the important thing is never to get drunk. Then you'll miss the little tip-off signs everybody has for knowing where they are and you'll have to find a Saint Bernard like me. O.K." The man drove off with Principato following.

Fifteen minutes later the man in the blue station wagon said, "It's up there." He shuddered, though it may have been only the cold, pointing to the collection of gray-stone buildings grouped around a spire on the top of the only sizable hill in the area. A tall fence with spear-point pickets enclosed the buildings and extensive lawns.

"Some call it Bald Mountain and others say it's a Catholic church. It's a pretty joyless place to be near on Halloween or any other night is all I can warn you."

"Thanks," said Principato, watching the station wagon move quickly off, as if toward safety. Secretly, he wondered what sort of parishioners Saint Igitur's claimed. He supposed they lived about in the expanse of brick development houses through which he had fumbled for the past hour, and which seemed to him now to be all converging upon this hill, some in desperation even attempting to struggle up its sides to the level of the tall fence, as an indication of their owner's craving for the dark graces that Allergucci, their pastor, dispensed.

He slipped through the front gates and moved first past some barracks type of buildings, where large-eyed, frightened-looking children peered at him from ill-lit rooms. Doubtless the orphanage of which Nick had spoken. He cruised twice about a large plaza before the demicathedral church, searching for Allergucci's Cord as a sign as to where the priest might be. Then he saw a nun walking away from a classroom building and drew along the sidewalk to speak with her.

"Sister," he asked without looking at her face, "where is Monsignor Allergucci, please?"

She turned slowly and he was startled at her severe Oriental features beneath the wimple. This, then, was one of the monsignor's imported nuns. From Formosa? Or Buddhist Japan, perhaps?

"He is there." She pointed an incredibly thin finger toward a figure in a black cloak who walked slowly across a grassy hill beyond the last buildings. The low rounded contours of the hill were reminiscent of the moors.

"He is thinking," she said.

"Is it wise to disturb him?"

"Only if you are in his thoughts. Then he will turn toward you and beckon. This is how we know that we may approach to speak with him. It is a rule of our order."

Holy shit! thought Principato, fearing that instead of being merely high, he was completely drunk. A nun, pragmatic servant of the institutional Church, depending on telepathy for her right to speak. Instinctively, he whirled about to check the gates behind him, fully expecting them to be shut and knitted together with an appropriate growth of vines. But they were open still, calling him toward safety.

"He has turned and signaled," she said. "It is you he is thinking of. Park your car and walk out to him."

Obediently, Principato parked and wobbled past the outermost, castigating himself for not having postponed the audience until a more sober day. Now his knees were weak and a chill in his bowels warned him that he might become ill. A cold wind swept him up toward Allergucci, who stood beneath a naked tree, the cloak draped around him and pulled closely about his chin. The great lion's mane of white hair whipped in the breeze.

"Welcome to Saint Igitur's, Angelo."

"Who was Saint Igitur, Monsignor?"

"A martyr. He died a ghastly death. Flayed and roasted and his eyes plucked out, I believe."

"Um," was Principato's only reply. But it figured. Either an Igitur or a Stephen or an Agnes. The memory of some martyr's agony had to be the inspiration for naming this place.

"Come, Angelo, let us walk. I have many things on my mind."

"Why did you call me here, Monsignor?"

"To speak of your father."

"My father is a pure man," he said. "I told him you shouldn't be his confessor."

"Why? You think I am not also a pure man? What is pure anyhow? Because you think your father arrived at the conclusion thirty-five

200

years ago that some principle was at stake in his life, and has clung doggedly to that conclusion ever since, refusing to vacillate, does that make him a pure man? No, Angelo, not to my way of thinking. This is the Defiance of which I speak. A log jam your father has lived behind for thirty-five years. Another man, more broad-minded, would have extricated himself by now. Broad-mindedness can be commended as a virtue, too."

"Is that how you explain your lack of scruple about bilking Eva out of her money? I wouldn't try something like that."

"You're not intelligent enough to try something like that, Angelo. And don't attack me. I am a good priest in that I do the Lord's work. To some, like you, my methods may be offensive. But Eva is a curious woman with a special set of needs, and to anyone who understands those needs, the money is there for the taking. Besides, is it more just for that clod, Malatesta, to take it for Malatesta, or Allergucci to take it and apply it to God's works?"

"Poor God. All sorts of injustice done in His name. Is that one of God's works, Monsignor? That nearly finished museum of yours?"

"That is another thing. A lofty tribute from my parishioners. It's just that their funds were not equal to their ardor. They needed some help toward the end."

"I'll bet. You sound almost contemptuous of them, Monsignor."

"Please, Angelo, why so testy? But I'll excuse you since you've obviously been drinking. I asked you to come here because I need your help. This is a very difficult time for me. Your father is going to die and I bear an immense guilt on my shoulders. I am the cause of thirty-five years of the Defiance and now, in the closing moments, I can't get him to relent."

"You're the cause of the Defiance?" Principato asked, surprised. The Defiance was so old that it seemed no one remembered the cause. His father had never taken pains to explain it. He had grown up with it always in existence, accepting it with as little protestation as he accepted the Catholic faith he was reared in. Simply, his father did not go into churches. But at long last to discover where it sprang from. . . . Somehow it seemed fitting that the dark priest was involved in the old mystery.

"Yes. It happened years ago when I was first ordained and assigned to a parish in your father's neighborhood. It was a poor Italian parish during the Depression, and I was furious for being stuck there. If you think I lack humility now, you should have known me then. Anyway, I thought of upgrading the place. Culture clubs, the whole works. They must be still laughing at me back there, the way I charged into action. But my real folly involves your father. Once when I was reading announcements during mass, two little girls walked right to the front of the church, late and not wearing any shoes. Well, the young Allergucci couldn't have that in a parish he was trying to upgrade, so I told them to leave, not once considering that perhaps they had no shoes to wear at all. The children began crying from shame and embarrassment and ran from the church. Your parents were sitting right before me and your father stood to give me hell. Did I really care what anyone wore to mass? he asked me. That wasn't the issue, I told him, there were other factors involved. Did the Italians come to America only yesterday so that we might condone their coming barefoot into a church? Tit for tat. If it were anyone else in the parish, I could have shouted him down, but your father . . . well, 'trenchant' is the best word for him perhaps.

"Then he asked me if I were speaking as a priest of the Church or was it just the vain man Allergucci talking. I remember it now as if it were only days ago: so stupid. Your father standing there with that little spark of anticlericalism that's in every Catholic growing into a bonfire, and myself too proud to retreat and douse the flame. I replied that, yes, I was speaking as a priest of the Church. So right there he swore if that was the case he'd never set foot in church again, and out he stomped, as your mother stayed behind. *Voilà*, the Defiance. The congregation was calling it that before mass was even ended. They almost clapped for him when he walked down that aisle.

"Later, when I realized what I'd done, I practically got on my knees to him. The only concession I obtained from him was confession by telephone, but not even that—a dialogue really, unsanctioned by any church authorities, so that I wouldn't lose contact with him. But he never told you that story?"

"No."

"But then why would he? That father of yours whom you love so immeasurably and whom everyone defers to because he has never re-lented on a vow he made before the altar, has a Satanic vein that he wouldn't want you or anyone to know about," Allergucci said. "No, he wouldn't tell you. He's clever. For thirty-five years he's been pun-ishing me for my sin of pride and enjoying every moment of it. Rarely has one man held the ax over another like that. Raising my hopes that he might relent and return to the mass and make his Easter duty, then alternately dashing them. A sadist, Angelo."

"No, never. My father is an honest man. He's lived in defiance be-cause a principle could never be made pliable for him as for other men."

"Wrong, Angelo. All wrong. It is not the principle the old man lives for, it is the joy of punishing. He understands I bear a guilt for his leaving the Church like the cross of the other, and he's tortured me each time I've tried to expiate that guilt. False hope, like dan-gling the carrot before the rabbit, then no hope at all. Now soon he's going to die. Angelo, you must help me! If he goes to his eternity, my guilt still unrelieved . . ."

Principato stopped walking and turned to regard the priest. He winced from the headache his earlier drinking had brought on. Aller-gucci's suave looks had become intense. He looked as if he were on the verge of crying.

"What do you want from me, Monsignor?"

"How coldly you ask that, Angelo. True son of his father, I believe. What I want from you, what I beg from you, is to make him recant. To allow me to hear his confession, give him absolution, viaticum, and the last rites. He loves you, Angelo. You're his favorite, even more than Lucy, your sister. He's told me this often. You might in-duce him to change his mind."

"No. Absolutely out of the question."

"Huh, what a family you are. A flat no, after three minutes, from Lucy when I drove all the way to Pittsburgh to see her. A flat no from Rocco, plus fifteen degrading minutes spent on the floor picking up a box of bottle caps that I'm now quite sure did not fall by acci-dent. I believe that when God infused the lofty pride into hiſ serv-ant, Allergucci, he also caused the Principatos to find their lives' work."

"Only your interpretation, Monsignor."

"Yes, you would say that, not wishing to hear the truth about your father. Angelo, I seem to remember you angry and aggrieved at Neutral Corner over the entrenched minds of your in-laws, the Corrigans. But you, in your own way, are infinitely worse. In revering your father, you revere a false god. You think you revere his Defiance because it takes strength and integrity to maintain an old vow. But it's not that at all. The Defiance, the name applied years ago to his righteous anger, is only a veneer. Deep down he's mocking us all by having us believe in a falsehood, and enjoying every moment of turning the screws into me."

"You're lying, Monsignor. I must go now. I won't listen to you slandering my father. We have a right to expect priests to tell us the truth above anyone."

Principato began walking quickly back toward the car, Allergucci following close behind, his cloak flapping in the wind. When he climbed behind the wheel, the priest was at the door.

"Why not just fade out from now on, Monsignor? He's only got a short time. It will be unpleasant enough as is."

"Impossible, Angelo. At the hour of his death your father will make sure that Allergucci, of all people, is at his bedside. If he chooses to reverse and re-embrace the Church, then I have suffered enough and he is done with humbling me. If not, then he makes the final, irrevocable turn of the screw. But I'll have to be there. He'll see to it."

"It's true what he says about you, Monsignor. You have a flair for drama. You love the sinister viewpoint. The obvious is too easy for you."

"Laugh. I'm used to abuse from Principatos, Angelo. Only I warn you not to be surprised when you find me in the death room. I'm just another pawn like yourself."

"Bullshit." Principato started the car. He moved off without a backward glance at the black-clad figure, descending through the gates to the miasma of look-alike development houses, bravely turning into the first right-angle street and depending on his sense of direction to take him toward the broader recognizable lanes of his familiar Philadelphia. Away from this dishonest corner of the city, where the dark Allergucci spun lies about his poor, honest, dying father.

A week later when he heard his mother's low voice creeping toward him through the office phone, he realized his disturbing visit to Allergucci had somehow managed to occlude many of the problems his mind normally sparred with these days, including Lucy's leaving the convent.

"You didn't forget we have to go and pick up Lucy tomorrow, did you, Angelo?"

"No, Mama, don't worry," he lied. "I was going to call you tonight. What time do you want me to come for you?"

"Early. Around five o'clock so we can get there before noon. It takes about five hours, huh?"

"About that much time."

"Your daddy says you can take the T-bird if you want to."

"No, I'll take my own car. It's slow but sure."

"O.K., Baby. Does the heater work?"

"Yes, of course it works."

"Good, I just wanted to make sure. Don't get mad if I bring a blanket to cover my legs. It doesn't mean I think your heater doesn't work right."

"I understand, Mama."

"I'll bring money for your gas and turnpike tolls."

"Don't worry, I have money."

"Look, fair is fair. I'll buy the meals then."

"O.K., Mama. Five o'clock. Good-by." He closed abruptly, cutting her off as he had learned to do in recent years. Lest she fill his morning by leading him through a conversational labyrinth that seemed to him always to have no real beginning and could be ended only by the God-sent interruption of a third party. Then, ashamedly, he reflected that he had cut the henna-haired, blindly loving mother of his youth down to sentence fragments of late. With the old man he had filled entire volumes since learning of his impending death. But tomorrow alone with her in the car for at least five hours on the way to Pittsburgh, he guessed he would be able to make up for it.

In the morning he arose in the four-o'clock darkness, breakfasted quickly, drove to the city, amazed at the bumper-to-bumper truck traffic pounding across the bridge, then turned abruptly off toward the docks on the Philadelphia side. There were no other passenger cars about. The sights of the hour, weakly illuminated, and for which he could not remember being awake at any time in his life, excited him despite the sad mission of his day. He advanced, chancing his way among the mobile mountains of tractor trailers, then swung away from the bridge into Eighth Street, moving across the cobblestones toward his parents' home, his eyes watchful. The denizens of the Shadow World whom Principato imagined slept by day, hiding against any light, preferred this hour. The ones who waited concealed for nurses coming off duty and menaced small businessmen opening early. But he saw no one, except an occasional police car, its dome light assuring the neat array of items in jewelers' windows, until he spotted his mother standing alone on the steps in front of her home, a blanket folded across her arm. She seemed to him suddenly more diminutive in one of Lucrezia's cast-off fur coats than his old image of her. Less flamboyant also: her hair was a mousy gray now, tied back into a bun; she had washed out the henna rinse in keeping with the measured advance of her husband's dying.

"You shouldn't be standing out here all alone in this darkness, Mama," he told her.

"Why not? There's nothing to worry about, Angelo. No bogeys are living down here yet."

"Mama, don't use that word," he chided her as he had done for years.

"I'm going to use it if I want to. All of a sudden I'm glad I'm getting out of here and moving to Florida with Lucrezia. They'll be coming into this neighborhood fast enough. The day I'd see them going into my church over there would be the day to pack up. There's a bogey playing the organ now, but he doesn't get a chance to pray so that's not so bad."

Principato kept silent, guessing that her arthritis was causing pain in her knees and sponsoring the senseless outburst. As he guided her toward the car door and seated her inside, she hobbled slightly, confirming his guess. In another moment he climbed inside himself.

206

She was already unfolding her blanket and wrapping it tightly about her legs.

"See, Mama, the heater works fine."

"Thank God for small favors." Then there was unexpected quiet from her as he drove away from the house toward the expressway entrance, and along its length to the westbound turnpike. As before, there was the surprisingly heavy truck traffic in and out of the city. Occasionally he glanced toward the east, past her pain-creased face, for the first sign of dawn, but there was no suggestion of brightness yet.

"I'm sorry for calling the Negroes bogeys, Angelo. I know you work with them a lot and you like them," she said. They were on the turnpike now, the old De Soto choosing a steady, manageable sixty in a vise of two trucks.

"There's good and bad, Mama, like anybody else."

"Your daddy always liked Joe Louis. He used to bet him all the time."

"I remember."

"There's three Negroes who work at the plant for your daddy. He says they're good workers."

"I know, Mama. But what's the real problem? The arthritis?"

"It's everything, Angelo. My regular life is falling apart on me. Lucy's coming out of the convent, Daddy's going to die, you've left your wife and I don't know what's going to happen to you, and Rocco won't come with me to Florida."

"Why won't Rocco go to Florida?"

"He wants to stay at Good Shepherd. He says all his friends are there and Sister Winifred takes good care of him. I'm his mother. I could take better care of him than Sister Winifred, but he won't let me. Angelo, do you think Rocco's a little crazy?"

"No, Mama, why?"

"Everytime I go up to see him he drops his box of bottle caps on the floor and I have to get down and pick them up before Sister Winifred comes. When I tell him not to hold the box so he won't drop it, he always says he'll be careful then ends up dropping it anyhow. It's hard with my arthritis."

"It's just a game he plays with everybody, Mama. He even did it to Monsignor Allergucci one time."

"Some game. It's not nice to make a priest get down on his hands and knees like that."

"Why not, Mama?" Principato said angrily. "Allergucci's no friend of Daddy's, after what he did that time years ago." His mother turned toward him, a look of surprise on her face.

"I kept my mouth shut about that business for thirty-five years, Angelo. Daddy was right for getting mad at Allergucci at the time, but he shouldn't have stayed away from the church for so long. He hasn't got the faith like you and me," she said sadly, "and he's a tough old bird when he gets an idea in his head."

"What do you think about him dying without the priest, Mama?"

"I don't want to think about it. If you're ever around when I'm dying, Angelo, make sure the priest is there. I could never understand how he grew up in the religion, then could live without it like he did and not want the priest at the end. And who the hell gets cremated? I was sure we'd all end up in the Italian cemetery where we belong. But he has to go into a little vase down in Florida."

She sighed: a long wind of exasperation over the mystery of her husband's choices while her son pondered the riddle of his parents' marriage. With the old man into his sixties and his wife not far behind, they were a tightly knit pair of lovers still. But supremely respectful of each other's idiosyncrasies. She would talk for five hours at a clip. The old man simply did not listen. He had not accompanied her to mass in thirty-five years. She made no demands on his Sunday-morning time. An easy balance completely lacking in Principato's own marriage.

"The Corrigans are pretty mad, huh, Angelo?" she asked suddenly.

"They're a pain in the ass, Mama. I don't want to talk about them."

"When do you think you're going back to them? You can't live with Malatesta the rest of your life. He's only a bum anyhow. If you knew his mother, Giulietta, in the old days, you'd know where it came from. She ran a chain of bordellos until Hoover started cracking down on the gangsters. So you should go back to the Corrigans and not stay with Nick. Besides, you've got five kids."

"I don't think I'm ever going back. Cynthia threw out my bags of hair and her brothers tried to beat me up a couple of weeks ago."

"What bags of hair?"

"The ones I've been saving for eleven years now."

"Oh, those." She clearly did not understand what he was talking about. She fell silent again as they drove into the still dark Pennsylvania Dutch farmlands and removed a rosary from her purse. In the dim glow from the dash, he could see her lips moving through the changeless list of her morning prayers. An hour later, perhaps, when the first weak light appeared behind them in the east and he was sure she had finished, he spoke again.

"Do you remember the way to the novice house after we reach the city, Mama?"

"I have it all written down, Angelo. But we don't go into the place. We wait in a drugstore across the street for her to come to us."

"Why? Doesn't she want us to help with the luggage?"

"No, it's not allowed. You wait in the drugstore and watch this black door that opens out into the street. Lucy showed it to me once before. When it's time, she comes out there and she's all ours again. She doesn't belong to them any more." His mother wept softly.

"Don't cry, Mama. Not today. You'll upset Lucy."

"How can I help crying? She's going to walk out that door in the same dress she wore in thirteen years ago and carrying that little leather suitcase I gave her. Just think how funny she's going to be in those old clothes. And no lipstick either."

"That's all you're worried about, Mama?"

"No, there's more."

"What?"

"What about this doctor?" she asked, her tears suddenly ended. "Did you meet him yet?"

"No, Mama, did you?"

"No, but what kind of guy can he be going after a nun like that?"

"I'm sure he's a very fine person if Lucy thinks so," Principato said—and he wished he believed it.

"I don't know. It's all such a mess to me. In the old days a nun was a nun, and anybody who wasn't was trying to get married. Why does

209

she do this at her age after thirteen years in the convent? She's no spring chicken, you know. She's older than you are."

"So what? People get married at eighty. There's no law says you have to be married at twenty-one. I wish I had waited, the way things are now."

But she did not answer. They stopped twice at Howard Johnson's restaurants for long coffee breaks and arrived in Pittsburgh later than anticipated, at eleven-thirty. Principato was surprised that the written directions were clear and precise. When they pulled up at the drugstore, his mother nodded toward the opposite corner at the novice house.

"There's the door."

He turned off the engine and sat for a long moment regarding the narrow black-metal door set in the blank-faced stone wall of the building that had windows only above the second storey. Something about the sheer aspect of black portal in gray wall suggested to him that the door had massive proportions behind, like the door to a bank vault, perhaps, that could be opened only grudgingly through combinations and a timer to allow Lucy back out into the world.

"How do we know when she comes out?" he asked.

"We telephone from the drugstore to let them know we're here. She comes out then. You telephone, Angelo. I'm afraid I'll start crying in the phone booth. Here's the number."

"Let's go inside and have something to eat, Mama, while we wait."

"I couldn't eat anything the way my stomach is jumping now. I never thought I'd see the day Lucy would come slipping out the back door of that place into this crummy life," she said, looking about with distaste, as if all the offal of the earth had somehow managed to collect suddenly into this particular Pittsburgh intersection.

"God damn it, Mama, she's not leaving prison! There's nothing to be ashamed of. She's simply quitting one life and taking up another."

"Yeah, aren't you the calm old fox? Lucrezia told me how upset you were when you found out about Lucy. Don't go treating me like a hysterical old woman. Since when do nuns leave the convent to get married? Since never, that's when. I said it before: a nun is a nun. I don't buy this mistake baloney."

210

"You'd better buy it, Mama," he said evenly, placing his foot on the brake pedal and pushing it hard toward the floor so that he imagined he could hear the hiss of hydraulic fluid being pressed out of the cylinders. In moments the pedal was squarely on the boards. He began pumping it rapidly to restore it to life.

"You'd better buy it," he repeated, "because Lucy's going to come through that door with enough problems without needing a hard time from you. I'll tell Daddy you were nasty to her."

"No, Angelo," she whined, "don't tell Daddy anything like that. I'll be good. I won't say a thing."

"Promise?"

"I promise. Don't even tell Daddy I was thinking about it."

"O.K., let's go inside for a milkshake while I make the phone call. It's good for nervous stomach."

Obediently she opened her door and stood waiting on the sidewalk for him to take her arm. In the drugstore they chose a marble-topped table near the window.

"Black-and-white shake for me," he told her, then walked off toward the wooden phone booths. He dialed the novice-house number, his heart thumping so loud he could hear it. He wondered if Lucy herself would answer his rings.

"Yes, may I help you?" a voice not unlike Phillips's asked.

"Will you please inform Sister Veronica her people are here," he said. The words came forth as a throaty whisper. He wondered a second afterward why he used "people" instead of "family."

"Yes, I will. Allow her fifteen minutes to come out, please."

"All right. We're waiting in the drugstore."

"Yes." He heard next the loud click of her receiver being replaced, then the afterbuzz of a broken connection that he listened to for perhaps thirty seconds before he hung up. He turned and saw his mother through the glass plate of the booth. She had begun crying again, staring at the black square of door in the wall across the street. A matronly-looking waitress came up behind her with his milkshake and a cup of coffee on a tray. The easy sounds of her sympathy flooded the luncheonette area. Thank God there were no other customers but the Principato twosome, he mused. He continued watching as the waitress set down the tray and removed the fur coat from his mother's shoulders, slipping it over the back of the chair. She placed the coffee before the old lady and the milkshake across the table, thoughtfully arranging a chair in the best viewing position. The milkshake was in an old-fashioned heavy glass instead of the now usual waxy containers. A thick foam sat on top. He emerged from the booth, thoughts of Lucy momentarily banished by the rumble of his hunger.

"I'm sorry for your trouble," the waitress said as he sat down behind the milkshake.

"We're not calling it trouble," Principato corrected, anxious not to have this woman of great sad eyes prompt his already overemotional mother. "She's simply decided to change horses. Lots of people do it."

"Well, call it what you want, but it certainly turns out to be the saddest of events. The last time was three years ago, and this old man and woman sat here and cried themselves dry. I remember the old guy especially because he reminded me of my own father. When their daughter finally came out, he couldn't lift himself from the table. She wouldn't come in here, so I finally helped him out to the car."

"Look, there's only ten minutes left and I'm not interested in having this become a sopping tragedy. Don't you have something you could do?"

"Angelo, this woman is only being sympathetic," his mother said through her sobs.

"Don't worry about me, lady. I've seen enough of these leaps to know it hits the men harder than anyone. He can't help it, the way he's acting. A man who puts a woman on a pedestal is always going to live long enough to see her fall."

"Take off!" Principato said. He did not lift his head from the milkshake glass, but he sensed that the woman shrugged her shoulders, exchanged a glance with his mother, then moved away toward the lunch counter.

"You shouldn't have said that to her, Angelo. She's right, you know."

"Who the hell asked her to pass judgment? Not me."

212

"Yeah, but what she told you about the men, she's right about that. I thought your daddy was going to cry when he read the letter from Lucy. He was moping around for a couple of days after like a sick dog."

"Mama, I don't want to talk about it, all right? What time is it now? Why the hell does it take fifteen minutes to get through the door?"

"I guess she has to say good-by to all her friends."

"I'm sure it's not all that easy." He had a sudden blurred vision of Lucy running a gamut of dissociation before reaching the door, being stripped of each clerical item by a separate stone-masked nun in her turn, who then symbolically about-faced, showing only the fantail pleats of her veil to the deserter. Finally, she would stand naked and ashamed, trembling helpless in complete detachment before hooking up to the umbilical cord of a new life, donning the undergarments, slip, and dress, albeit thirteen-year-old versions, of a woman beyond the walls. Then the emergence: the massive portal creaking open, resisting to the last, to emit her blinking into the light of the banal intersection of two streets in Pittsburgh. Commence the new Lucy, Principato thought dejectedly, watching two slow-moving Negroes shovel spilled garbage into the jaws of a grinder. Perhaps if she came out in time for the sight, she would turn and claw frantically at the door to be readmitted.

Then the door across the street swung open, abruptly and easily, long minutes before he willed it to happen. He was not yet done with imagining Lucy's new condition when he saw the reality of it. A sellout. She wore a tan, belted raincoat and spiked heels, and carried the small suitcase his mother had mentioned. Her hair, which had so preoccupied him, fell long and dark and incredibly straight to her shoulders, framing the bright sepia flesh of her face. She was beautiful, then, in her own right. And supremely confident. He saw it all in an instant. He watched, unwilling to believe, as she marched quickly across the street, disdainful of waiting for the traffic light to change. When she entered the drugstore, he was only halfway out of his chair. His mother was riveted to her own, a handkerchief placed squarely across her mouth as if to suppress a scream.

"Hello, Mama, hello, Angelo." Lucy swept past them toward the phone booths. Speechless, Principato only stared as she opened the door, dropped a dime into the coin box, and hastily dialed a number, not thinking to close the door.

"Hello, Martin?" They could hear her excited voice. "This is Lucy. I'm sprung!"

TEN

The man who knocked Lucy from the pedestal of her brother's making was not such a bad guy after all, came Principato's first collected thought on New Year's Day when he awoke. Otherwise he was capable of only scattered observations: that his head throbbed; that his mouth was unbelievably dry and sandpapered; that the normal tonus of his muscles had given way to slack rubber bands. Also that he lay in his old bedroom in his parents' home on the great sagging mattress of his youth. Accordingly, his back pained him with that recognition.

He moaned once, loud and self-pitying, for all the troubles his life encompassed on the first day of a new year and pulled the covers back over his head, feeling instantly nauseated, with nothing in his stomach after last night's vomiting. He vaguely considered resolutions. But for him, resolutions were impracticable now.

"Where the hell am I going?" he asked out loud, sitting up in real wakefulness after banging his head on the bedstead. Opposite the bed was a wall mirror, and as he spoke he used elaborate theatrical gestures.

"In the most basic terms, I'm hung up somewhere between these extremes. On the one hand, I'm the bringer of life. A new love child, inheritor of my melancholy nature, prepares to spring from my huge woman, Corky. Blessed be my virility." He smiled at his reflection. "But on the other hand, I'm the attendant on death. My father, whom I also love, will soon die. Cursed be my propinquity." He spoke to the now bitter image.

Then, suddenly, the idea came to him and he said it out loud, half with incredulousness: "Would I exchange one for the other? Leave Corky fallow so that by some basis of trade the old man might live?" But in turn deprive Corky and Cornelius of their incredible joy? Wipe the tears from Dan Hallagan's eyes when he kissed Principato in his office before Christmas on hearing the news of his sister's pregnancy? Hallagan had pointed to a ferocious Max Schmeling in his collection of famous boxers and race horses and said simply; "He couldn't have done better himself." Deprive Principato of his life's highest tribute then? Nuts: no solution there. And what of the rest?

Between Principato's kinship with life and death was a casual mess he preferred not to think of, though today was a day for taking stock. He had already ended it with his job, bid a sorrowful farewell to Jedda McMahnus, most well-intentioned of all women, who had been forced to ask for his resignation. Blatantly incompetent, Corrigan henchman Larkin had vengefully told everyone in the office. But from the Corrigan mob itself he had heard nothing since his neighbors had turned a massacre into a rout on his front lawn in early November. For that family, such a silence was incredible. Lately, instead of enjoying his standoff with them, he was becoming fearful that he had somehow altogether passed out of the Corrigan memory, never having been, never having existed. The five sallow-skinned, russet-haired children he had fathered by Cynthia were only Corrigan wish fulfillment, then. At Christmas, obsessed with the notion, he had debated charging his home with presents for his five offspring, not because he loved them particularly, but simply to see if the Corrigans had allowed them to remember who he was.

As to his own private existence, he still lived in the trailer, despite the frequent protests of his mother, who warned him of the bad blood Nick had inherited from old Giulietta Malatesta. But it was merely existing, he saw clearly at that moment, and it would soon somehow have to end. They spent most of their days huddling with glass in hand around the wood fire, sinking blithefully into the fragrant ooze of their own self-pity, and leaving the trailer only occasionally for periodic foragings for fuel in the scrub pine about them.

"It's got to end! Something's got to take its place!" He smashed a fist into his palm for emphasis. Then he sank down again into the bed, pulling the covers over his head.

In a moment there was a slight knock. The door opened and his mother appeared with a large cup of black coffee.

"Here, Angelo, drink this and try to have a little breakfast downstairs. You were really stewed last night. Your papa's over at the plant and he wants you to come over as soon as you can."

"How did I get undressed?" he asked, reaching shakily for the coffee. He was wearing one of his father's long nightshirts. His clothes were piled neatly on the dresser.

"Everyone got into the act. You started throwing off your clothes as soon as you hit the house. Your papa and me got you into a nightshirt and Lucy and her friend held Lucrezia, who wanted to dance with you while you were naked."

"I was naked in front of five people?"

"Uh huh. In the living room." But he sensed the sight had not fazed her in the least. She lay her hand across his forehead as he sat higher in the bed, testing for fever. Then, apparently satisfied that all was normal, she walked toward the door and turned uncertainly before opening it.

"What do you think about this boy friend of Lucy's, Angelo?"

"He looks like a good bet to me."

"She could have done worse, I guess," his mother said. "Lucrezia likes him fine."

"He's a man, isn't he? Lucy had better watch out or Lucrezia will try to buy him and take him back to Florida."

His mother seemed to enjoy the joke. She gave one of her short, trilling laughs, heard so infrequently these days. Then she became serious.

"It's funny how Lucrezia and me are sisters and are so different, isn't it, Angelo? Your daddy never had to beat me for running after the boys. If Lucrezia was his wife, she'd be permanently black and blue. She's a real nymphy bitch, isn't she?"

"It's just her way of going about it, Mama."

217

"Yeah, honey, but at her age . . ." She shook her head sadly. "I didn't miss the way she was hanging all over you last night. I mean— you're her nephew."

Oh, Christ, here we go on New Year's Day, and with a hangover to boot, he thought.

"Did you go to mass yet this morning, Mama?"

"No, honey, I was going to go to afternoon mass at five o'clock."

"You've never done that before. Slipping a little, huh, Mama?"

"Angelo, I'm not! I was so tired after last night that I couldn't get out of bed this morning. Oh, I'm not going to argue with you on a holy day. I'll be downstairs in the kitchen. Hurry up. Your papa is waiting for you."

She closed the door angrily, then opened it seconds later. "Try to get rid of your bad mood before you go to see your father. He's very happy after last night and I don't want you creating any arguments."

"All right, Mama, I'll try." He was mildly ashamed that he had resorted to intrusion on the high-walled preserve of her sanctity. Then he struggled out of bed, still nauseated, remembering piecemeal the events of the night before.

On New Year's Eve the Principatos kept tradition. As always, they drove across the river to Jersey to his father's favorite, the Ochre Club, for the festivities. This year, along with himself, there were his parents and Lucrezia and, for the first time, Lucy and her doctor from Pittsburgh. Principato had snubbed the young widower, only three years older than himself, on Christmas Day. But last night Lucy's fiancé had been positioned next to him at the table. Principato had turned covetously to his father on his other side. The old man had regarded him a long moment, his gray, haggard face looking curiously menacing in the dim light. He puffed on a now-infrequent cigar.

"Talk to him or I'll break your neck," his father had rasped. Frightened into obedience, Principato had swung about and listened for an hour through the din of dance music and a floor show as the man spoke haltingly of his first wife, who had been taken away by meningitis, then of Lucy. In the end, easily conquered, he had mentally given his sister to this halting-voiced future brother-in-law.

"There are people in my family, too, who are a bit reticent about this marriage," the man had said.

"This isn't the place I figured we'd get to talk about it," Principato answered. "I wanted to be joyous and shrieking tonight."

"Then why not be?"

Why not indeed? Cynthia, separated from her husband, would be doing her own chaperoned shrieking at whichever of her brothers' bars they had chosen to grace at midnight. Even Malatesta had quit the trailer on receiving an emergency telegram from Eva Lissome, anxious not to spend the evening alone. But Principato felt no spontaneity until his father, grabbing suddenly at his arm, provided the occasion.

"Look, Angelo, there's Lola!"

He followed the old man's pointed finger to the end of the bar where the manageress, Lola Fabresi, had appeared and begun talking with some customers. His father had taken the cigar from his mouth and grinned at the sight of her, a huge, dark woman in a sequined dress who had laid claim to a legend in her lifetime. The old man worshiped the legend: a long series of fervently practiced impieties that could not keep her from being photographed with the mayor and visiting dignitaries. In the old days she had been a vaudeville chorine, then long-time mistress to a gangster in Jersey City. She had been endlessly subpoenaed as a grand-jury witness, his father had told him. With all the grandeur of her living-legend stature, each New Year's Eve at the sound of midnight she kissed one man in the place and canceled that table's bill for the evening. Out of the shifting motives of her mind the elder Principato's number had come up three years before and the old man recalled it constantly. A picture of joined lips and faces blurred by the glare from a spotlight hung on his bedroom wall. Real triumph of a man who had never cared enough to seek the standard bowling-league and golf-tournament trophies.

"I wonder who she's got in mind tonight," his mother said.

"Remember when she kissed me?" the old man said hoarsely. "Was I surprised. I saw her snaking over to the table, but I never thought it was me she was aiming for. But three years ago, I wasn't such a bad-looking guy."

Principato looked at his father. If it were in his power, he would press the tired, lined flesh of the face smooth again, and order the glaze away from the old man's eyes. He took a long sip from his drink. Then he excused himself and went to talk to Lola Fabresi.

"Hello, Lola."

"Hello, kid. You look sweet tonight. Who are you?"

"I'm a Principato."

"Then have a drink on me."

"Thanks. Listen, Lola, I want to ask you something."

"Shoot."

"Tonight, for the kiss, could it be my father?"

"There's a lot of important people here, kid."

"He's dying."

"That's dramatic, kid, but Lola got to be what she is by hard work and planning."

"I'll give you fifty dollars, Lola."

"I've already turned down a fifty-dollar offer. Money isn't everything."

Suddenly his mother was at his elbow.

"How much does Lola want?" she asked.

"I don't know." Principato said before he realized that it was his own mother he was talking to.

"I wasn't trying to pay her anything," he lied quickly.

"Like hell you weren't. It cost me a hundred dollars that time three years ago. What's the rate now, Lola?"

"For a hundred and fifty bucks I could just manage to remember who your husband is and where he's sitting."

"How much do you have, Angelo?"

"I could go fifty, Mama."

"I'm good for another fifty. Wait here and I'll take your Aunt Lucrezia for a walk to the ladies' room. My sister could buy this whole chintzy place if she had to." She sneered at the huge Lola.

"Maybe. But she couldn't guarantee Lola's splendid kisses on New Year's Eve for some lucky man."

"Ugh. And I'm paying this woman to bring a little happiness to my poor husband. Hang on to her, Angelo, before somebody with a bigger purse gets here." He watched as his mother walked off angrily to get Lucrezia. Then he started drinking the free one provided by Lola.

"Sometimes I think no one's motiveless any longer," he said to her.

"You were naïve to think you could have it for asking."

"I actually believed your choice was a real whim."

"Almost everyone does, and I'd be the last one to take the hope from all those eyes." She gestured toward the noisy tables. "But the fact is that most decisions get made by a select little group of back-stage manipulators. That's you and me and your mother with the money she's going to get from your aunt. And when you get finished paying up, you know something that nobody else out there knows."

"What?"

"That I'm going to kiss your old man at midnight."

"Oh, that."

At two minutes before twelve the staccato drumming of a count-down began and Lola Fabresi urged her sequined bulk away from the bar and moved about the room in a grotesque, hip-swinging shuffle: across the dance floor and whimsically through the jungle of tables, where men grabbed at her arms and women shrieked with laughter, until she reached the Principatos. A hundred and fifty bucks' worth of impious legend advancing on his father, a man invio-late. Forgive me, then for defiling you, the son suddenly thought at the stroke of midnight. He watched Lola pull the old man to his feet, saw the spotlight sweep suddenly across the haggard fat of his face and the eyes blink shut against the glare, then open in a full smile as he removed the cigar from his mouth. While the band played "Auld Lang Syne" and the patrons clapped and cheered, his father kissed Lola on the lips, but ardently, fiercely, as if he were taking his last great draught of living from the act. His arms pressed into the naked flesh of her back, locking their two bodies tightly together. Lola backed off for an instant, clearly surprised, then pecked the old man again on the cheek as a bonus and waddled quickly away. Spent, per-haps giving up on his hunger for life, the elder Principato sank into his chair and exchanged a quiet kiss with his wife. Their son watched the legend, Lola, snake off through the midst of kissing New Year's revelers, performing her splendid lonely dance before oblivious eyes.

For Principato, there was no one to kiss. Beside him, Lucy clung to the doctor who would be her husband in the spring. Somehow, the sight still pained her brother, though he had finally given his blessing. Lucy had done it all too quickly for him, dispensed with even the shortest mourning interim and plunged into the world beyond the convent walls. But what could he do about it? It was the old man, as always, who provided the wisdom: it was her life to live. Then he saw Aunt Lucrezia leave her seat and walk toward him.

"Give your poor aunt a kiss, Angel, and let's dance. We're the loners here."

Dutifully, he stood to kiss his aunt, then led her to the dance floor. She threw her thin arms around his neck.

"I wonder what your father would say if he knew somebody had to give that doll money to kiss him," Lucrezia said.

"Don't say anything to him, Lucrezia, or you and I aren't going to be friends much longer."

"I wouldn't say anything, Angel. I'd lose my only friend. It's nights like tonight that make your old aunt want to get good and drunk. All the motorcycle cops in Florida wouldn't be enough to get rid of the loneliness. Do you miss that wife of yours tonight?"

"No. We never spent New Year's Eve together anyhow. She always goes with her brothers to their bars. You know that."

"I guess I do. I just felt like sticking the shiv in a little. I'm bitchy that way. While I'm in the mood: what do you think of Lucy's boy friend?"

"I wouldn't give you any satisfaction, Lucrezia. If Lucy likes him, that's all that counts."

"I suppose so. But doesn't it anger you just a little to see how happy everyone else is sometimes?"

"Well, I wonder about it at times."

"Angel, let's get happy. We'll go to the bar and stand there until we drop, O.K.? Tonight I've got to have a friend and you're elected. The tab's on me."

Principato suddenly felt an immense pity for his sad, shrunken-faced aunt with the tears ready to dart through her mascara.

"Come on Lucrezia," he said, dragging her toward the bar.

It was hours later, it seemed to him, when the weeping outline of Lucrezia rocked toward him for a last provocative time, then finally fell into him. Vaguely he remembered being led through the door to the cold outside, yoked between the faithful horses that were his parents.

Now he dressed quickly, taking a thimble-sized portion of breakfast in the kitchen and drove cautiously over the slippery streets to meet his father. An inch of new-fallen snow covered everything and would be coming down all day the weatherman promised. At the plant, the steel gates lettered AGOSTINI AND PRINCIPATO, CEMETERY SUPPLIES were open a crack and he pushed through, walking past two large trucks whose doors bore the same lettering, though it was flaking. He stopped for a moment in the dimness, listening for some sound to locate his father in the incredible silence. Neat rows of polished coffins ascended on shelves against two walls, looking already as if they had been positioned for eternity in a mausoleum. On the concrete floor beside him, a small forest of identical low-priced grave markers stretched away to a dark corner. It registered in a distant part of his mind that the inside of the barnlike building was colder than outside. Then he heard his father's coughing resounding from the small office.

"Pop?"

"I'm in here, kid. Come on in."

The old man sat at his desk, wrapped in his great black fur-collared coat, watching the flame of a gas heater on the floor beside him. Through a small window, Principato could see the larger monuments in the yard outside. Snow blanketed the arms and shoulders of two life-size Jesus statues and formed a serrated landscape on the neck of a Virgin where the head had been knocked off.

"How do you feel, kid?"

"A little hung-over."

"What did you have to go and get potted for?"

"Lucrezia and I both got pretty morbid around midnight. It seemed like the right thing to do."

"It didn't take you too long. We hauled you out of there at one-thirty."

"Never much of a bar fly, I guess."

"I guess not."

There was silence while his father looked out the window. The old

223

man prepared to light a cigar—bit off the end and spat it into the corner—then seemed to decide against it. Principato moved closer to the gas heater, trying to warm himself. But the blue flame made little headway against the cold. There was an actual frost on the cinder-block walls.

"Why did you come here, Pop? It's as cold as an igloo."

"An igloo is warmer, I bet. But it doesn't matter. Today's the last for me. I just came by to pick up a few things I want to take home. After today, Agostini can sit here on his fat ass by himself and freeze to death." Then he began coughing. Principato, alarmed, hastened to pummel his back. The old man raised an arm to stop him.

In a few moments, the spasm was ended. "That's not where the cough comes from, kid. It doesn't do any good. It comes from here," he said, putting his finger to his throat. His father opened a desk drawer and took out a framed photo of Principato as an altarboy in cassock and surplice.

"Where did you get this, Pop?"

"That's you when you were eleven years old. It was the first time you served on the altar and your mama and Lucrezia took it in the backyard of the priest's house."

"You have a good memory, Papa. I didn't recognize it."

"I used to like to look at it when I talked to you on the telephone. I got one of Lucy, too, and one of Rocco in his crib."

The old man took out two more photographs in identical frames and handed them to his son. Lucy in a wedding dress as the bride of Christ, and Rocco, too young to realize he was permanently crippled. His father's children, then, in their respective moments of perfection. Without a word, Principato returned the mocking likenesses.

"I brought 'em out here years ago when Agostini started plasterin' the walls with his kids. Cripes, that's an ugly bunch he has."

Principato frowned. Above his father's head was a line-up of profile shots of Agostini's offspring. In the center, framed in a black band, was Bruno, whom the children had called Bruto when he attended parochial school years before with Principato.

"How long is Bruno dead now, Pop?"

"About ten years, I guess. You were just finishing college when it happened."

"I felt bad for Agostini then. He really took it hard."

"Everybody else was happy for Bruno. The old lady wanted him to be a priest and his father wanted him to be a doctor. They were both on his neck all the time. He wouldn't get too far along in either of those lines with a puss like that. I don't think it was an accident that his car ended up against that telephone pole."

Principato said nothing, examining the sad, ugly face of Bruno Agostini, who had perhaps usurped the ultimate privilege and driven his car into a telephone pole. On either side of him, in twos, were his four acned sisters. Somehow, incredibly, they had all managed to grab husbands. Principato looked down and saw his father regarding him closely.

"Angelo, did we talk about everything you wanted to talk about?"

"What do you mean, Pop?"

"I mean when we talked on the telephone all those afternoons, did we say everything we had to say to each other?"

"I guess so."

"What I'm trying to say is, is everything O.K. in your life?"

"I've got a few problems."

"Yeah, I can see that. What are you gonna do about your wife and those kids of yours?"

"I'm not going back to them on their terms."

"You oughta figure out some arrangement, Angelo. You can't go on living in the woods over there in Jersey. And what about a job?"

"I guess I'll have to get one pretty soon, huh? I can't live the rest of my life on handouts from you and Lucrezia."

"Agostini would give you a job after I'm gone."

"This isn't exactly my line. I'm melancholy enough as is."

"You're a hard man to please. A job is a job. You go to it for eight hours a day then leave the damn thing alone. Not like that social-worker business you were in before. I used to see you after work and I could tell how many interviews you had that day from the lines in your face."

"It wasn't that bad, Pop."

"No, but nearly. Tell me something else: are you all squared away about Lucy now?"

"Yes, I think so. Her friend seems like a pretty decent type."

"Good. One plus for Lucy and two minus signs so far—one for your marriage and the other for your job. You're not in such bad shape as I thought. Answer me one question, Angelo. You got a lot of problems now, but did your religion help you out much? I mean did you go to church a lot to pray and talk to some priests about things?"

"Well, no, Pop. I didn't get to talk to any priests about it. I went to mass every Sunday like I'm supposed to . . ."

"But didn't you pray, Angelo?"

"Well, yes. I prayed for you and for Lucy. . . ."

"But did you pray for yourself?"

"No, I forgot."

His father looked out the window again, but at a distance that was beyond the brick outer wall. He pulled the fur collar closer about his neck. Then he spoke slowly, his breath wheezing between words: "I think when you get your life rearranged, you aren't going to need the old Church so much as you used to. It'll be good to get rid of that crutch if you can. And something else, kid, if you can't come to terms with the Corrigans then get moving on a divorce. Nobody's got the right to force two people who hate each other's guts to live together. Now, is there anything else we have to talk about?"

"No, I don't think so."

"I just wanted to make sure," the old man said quietly after a moment. "I won't be doing too much talking from now on, the doctor says. It'll all have to be by notes after a while until the end."

Principato said nothing, hearing the words drift past him, but unwilling to accept their implication. For a moment he thought of making a protest, but that would be futile. He watched the old man reach for some papers on his desk. They rattled in his hand as he held them out.

"Think you're steady enough to sign these?"

"What are they, Pop?"

"Title transfer for the T-bird. I want you to take it and do some howling with it. You need some kind of booster shot."

"You're giving me your T-bird?"

"I can't take it with me, can I? Now don't give me any tears, kid. Just sign and go back to the house for dinner. Your new car's sitting out front there, and the keys are on the telephone stand. You can take it out for a test drive any time you want."

Principato reached over to sign his name in four places, guilty because in truth he felt no staggering gratitude. Instead there was only a kind of fright. He had an instant vision of a worn, anemic Principato cowering behind the wheel of the sleek, powerful car, surging along an open highway. Of the old De Soto he was the gentle master. But the T-bird was the car of his father, a great burly man who easily controlled its impulses and puffed his cigar defiantly at the competing traffic.

"I don't think I'm ready for a car like that," he said.

"It takes a little growing up in the mind, maybe. But it's about time you started. Come on, let's get the hell out of here. I'm supposed to be dying of cancer, not exposure."

His father slammed the desk drawer shut, gathering up his pictures, then bent over to turn off the gas heater. It sputtered for a moment, then fell silent. Touching it gingerly, Principato was not surprised that it had barely been able to heat its own reflector in the intense cold. He followed the old man out of the office and through the forest of identical grave markers. Instead of turning at once toward the door, his father headed for a polished coffin that sat atop a dolly awaiting delivery the next morning. A piece of tape held a name tag labeled LAMPMAN to a handle. The old man lifted the lid. Inside, a pink silk lining covered the padded sides and bottom.

"I've been in this racket for thirty-five years, but I never could get used to all the waste. I must've decided the very first day I wanted to get cremated."

Gently, his father lowered the coffin lid, looked closely at the name tag for a moment, then swung about and began walking toward the doors.

"My car is parked up the street, Pop."

"That's O.K. I walked here this morning and I'm going to take a slow walk home. You drive on by yourself."

"But it's snowing heavily."

"It doesn't burn, does it? Don't worry about me."

Shrugging, Principato turned and moved in the opposite direction toward his car. He climbed inside and started it, making a U turn through the cobbled street's level covering of snow that had been creased only by his own tire tracks. To his left, the old man marched along the sidewalk huge and swaggering like a Mussolini, carrying the three framed photographs of his children in his naked fingers. Principato honked the horn. It rolled, loud and clear, toward the black-clad figure through the crisp air. But his father did not respond.

When he arrived at the house minutes later, there was an urgent message to telephone Malatesta.

"Hello, Nick, Happy New Year. What's up?"

"You'll never guess what I ran into last night at a party."

"What?"

"A tip on a lay for Rocco."

"You're kidding." Principato lowered his voice. His old promise to aid in vanquishing Rocco's virginity had recently moved beyond the wide circle of his thoughts. Not through his agency would it ever come to pass, he had decided.

"Yeah. I called her this morning and she's going to meet you in Independence Mall at three o'clock, which is a half hour from now."

"Independence Mall? That's a big place. How will I know her?"

"If there's anybody else in Independence Mall on New Year's Day in a snowstorm wearing a tan coat and green scarf, then call me down and I'll help you figure out which one it is."

"But what will I say to her?" he asked. There had never been an occasion to deal with a paraplegic's prostitute before.

"You say, 'Big Blackie sent me,' then you start discussing where, when, and how much."

" 'Big Blackie sent me'? Does it have to sound so much like a detective story? Couldn't I say something else?"

"Look, say, 'Big Blackie sent me,' and make the poor creature happy. It's not for the money alone whores go into business. Everybody's got their needs."

"O.K., thanks, Nick. I'll get right on it now."

He put down the receiver and hastened back into his overcoat, anxious to leave the house before his father arrived. Ahead of him the

228

kitchen door swung open and his mother emerged, holding a large spoon. Cooking odors rushed out in her wake.

"Aren't you staying for dinner, Angelo?"

"I can't, Mama. I have to meet a friend of Nick's."

"Who is it, that Big Blackie I heard you talking about?"

"How did you hear? I was whispering."

"I was standing near the door, honey. I wouldn't go to see this guy. Nobody decent would have a friend named Big Blackie. Only somebody like that bum Malatesta. It's probably a pal of his old lady's from Prohibition days. Why do you have to meet him?"

"Private business, Mama," he told her. Private indeed. But how to tell a mother what he was up to, when in truth he was only trying to gain a small measure of Rocco's approval? His hand moved nervously over the telephone table until his fingers stumbled upon the keys to the Thunderbird. He lifted them up to examine them.

"Those are your father's keys, Angelo."

"They're mine now, Mama. He gave me the car this morning."

"He did?" She looked at him a long moment, then shrugged her shoulders indifferently. "I wondered what he was going to do with it," she said simply. Then: "Don't you forget about mass, Angelo."

"I won't, Mama."

Principato dropped the keys into his pocket, then went out. Warily, he approached the T-bird, trying each of the three keys until the door was unlocked by the last. He sank into the bucket seat, sniffing the odor of new car that his father lived with always, since he traded in on a rigid schedule. Principato's other car had no intrinsic odors. It was neutral except for the occasional whiff of hot grease that came to him when the moving parts had been turning for a long time. He sat familiarizing himself with dials and buttons on the T-bird's dash, then switched on the ignition and pressed the gas pedal. The engine started instantly.

His spirit rose to the occasion as he released the hand brake. He would sweep through the quiet, snow-covered streets to Independence Mall and impress the paraplegic's prostitute with the brilliance of his arrival. In the midst of the whitened patriotic landscape, then, would suddenly appear Principato astride a Thunderbird.

He fed gas to the motor cautiously and eased the car away from the curb. It stood for a moment squarely in the traffic lane, then leapt ahead of its own impulse, many miles per hour in excess of Principato's shy footwork on the accelerator. Frightened, he clung to the wheel in fulfillment of the vision that had come to him when he had signed the title papers. Accustomed to the lavish play of the De Soto, he wrestled with the power steering, moving drunkenly from one side of the street to the other, praying to the Saint Christopher medal on the sun visor to keep the way clear ahead of him. He could not stop. In a moment of lucency he remembered the brake and stomped frantically on the wide pedal, but the effect was only a token slowing. The engine at full charge was too powerful to be halted. Then, two intersections ahead, he saw the massive black figure of his father crossing the street. Hurtling down upon him, he realized the old man had a sudden fearful look on his face that must be equal to Principato's own. His father leapt onto the sidewalk.

"Put it in neutral!" The command flew toward him so loudly that for an instant Principato guessed the old man's lungs had been seared by the effort. Instinctively, his hand found the gear stick and moved it to neutral. The engine noise became a high-pitched scream turning now on nothing, as he braked the car to a halt.

"Take your foot off the goddam pedal!" his father ordered, panting as he ran through the snow.

"It's off," Principato said. "It's running by itself."

"Get out. Let me see."

He slid out from behind the wheel and his old man put his head inside, then bent far down to grasp the accelerator with one hand, suspending himself from the steering wheel. He pulled hard and abruptly the engine settled into a low idle.

"Nothing supernatural," he said, breathing heavily. "The gas pedal was stuck halfway down."

"I was frightened. It was just going by itself. I didn't know what to do."

"You could've put it in neutral right away like any other dumb bastard would've done."

"I didn't think of that."

"I guess you aren't ready for this car yet, kid. How old are you now?"

230

"Thirty-four, Pop."

"Hmm." That was all he said. Sighing, he dropped heavily into the driver's seat, stacking the three framed photographs on the dash; his son sat beside him. Then he drove calmly back to the house, disavowing any claim of the supernatural to the running of his car.

"I'm going to leave it right here until you're big enough for it, kid. The keys'll be on the telephone stand."

Principato did not answer. Instead, he climbed out and walked wearily toward the De Soto under the old man's cold gaze, resigned sadly to encountering the paraplegic's prostitute in his typical naked state.

He saw her immediately as he approached the Mall from the south side and parked the car before the empty Bourse. Snow had collected on her motionless head and shoulders as if she were a statue. He approached her bench from behind, making a slight depression in the level whiteness that he assumed was a pathway. Suddenly he imagined that, in her overtime of waiting for him (he was already fifteen minutes late), she had frozen into hard statuary, lifelike even to the pearls of tears descending her cheeks. Today, all alone in a public place on a day for the gathering of families, face to face with the specter of loneliness that always haunted her old trickster's life, she had relinquished.

But she was young, or about his age, and specially bred, looking like a girl who had stomped out of a family dinner somewhere on the Main Line and come to Independence Mall to sulk. A beauty with long blond hair that rolled out from beneath her scarf to the shoulders of her camel-hair coat.

"Big Blackie sent me," he said weakly, embarrassed.

"Sit down," she said, dusting the snow off half of the bench with a gloved hand. He sat on the cold wooden slats, looking straight ahead, toward the dim outline of buildings that began abruptly where the Mall left off north of Market Street. Turning sideways, he watched her cheeks move slightly in the beginning of a smile.

"Can you hear the snow, Principato?" she asked him.

"Yes, I can." It seemed to be falling more heavily now, the low hiss sound of its descent loud against the quiet of the city around them. Then he realized she had called him by name.

231

"How did you know my name?"

"The insincere voice that spoke to me on the telephone this morning told me a man named Principato would meet me this afternoon wherever I wished. Despite the insincerity, I was happy to leave my lonely rooms and come here. One should be giving of one's self on a day like today, don't you think?"

"Yes, I suppose . . ."

"But you sound uncertain. Really you are giving of yourself, you know, in arranging this servicing for your poor brother. Will it be his first time?"

"Yes."

"I must be extra gentle then. How old is he?"

"Nineteen."

"It's time he has known a woman then. Because he's a cripple doesn't mean he should be excluded from the experiences of whole men. But you understand that, of course, or you wouldn't be sitting here with me today."

"Yes, I understand."

"Have you known women, Principato?"

"Yes."

"What kind? Are they a single type?"

"No, all different. Cynthia, my wife, different from Corky, my gargantuan woman, as snakes are different from puppies, I guess would be a good comparison. Then there was Myra . . ."

"Were any as beautiful as I?"

"Myra was in her special way."

"What was her special way, Principato?"

"She was a Negro."

"Oh, that doesn't count, does it?" the girl asked, suddenly beginning to laugh coarsely. He had not expected it of her.

"No," he agreed. "Now, when, where, and how much?"

"I see the dialogue is ended. All right, here's my address. Come there at seven this evening and bring fifty dollars. There's an elevator for the wheel chair, so you won't have to worry about getting up steps."

"I'll be there," he told her, standing to leave.

"Principato . . ."

232

"Yes?"

"You've been typically hard on me, but I'll be gentle with him to-night."

"Good. Anything to make him happy. That's all I ask. See you at seven."

He turned and began walking away quickly, his shoes making squeaky noises against the snow. As he reached his car, he looked back for a moment and saw her slumped outline still on the bench. Then, angry that she had not been a hard old trickster, he started the engine and drove toward Good Shepherd Home, squinting through the windshield past the sluggish wipers.

At Good Shepherd he asked to see Rocco and was instructed to wait while a nun went to a theater at the end of the hallway where the paralytic fraternity was watching a film. In moments she returned to ask if the visit were merely social or did Principato have something important to tell his brother.

"Please tell him I bumped into the woman whose address he asked me to find, Sister."

A minute later she came back, pushing Rocco's wheel chair. At his end of the hallway, he heard his brother urging the nun to move more quickly. Laughing, she deposited him before Principato, then went back to her reception desk.

"When?" Rocco asked as soon as she moved out of hearing range.

"Tonight at seven. We have to hurry back into the city. Am I going to have any problems getting you out of here?"

"No. Tell the one at the desk that you're taking me out for dinner and we'll be back at nine or so. Winifred's got the flu today, so it ought to be easy."

Grateful for the small godsend of Sister Winifred's flu, Principato easily talked the young reception-desk nun into giving him a pass while Rocco ascended in the elevator to his room to dress. After about twenty minutes, the elevator doors opened and his brother appeared in an abnormally long Loden coat, the dangling ends of his legs just visible beneath it. The heavy odor of aftershave surrounded him and his hair was lacquered back with a white tonic not yet completely absorbed.

"You look fine," Principato said.

"Thanks a lot. Let's go get me laid," Rocco said. Wordlessly, Principato pushed him out to the car. The snow came down only lightly now, and it was possible to see a long distance across the low hills that merged eventually with the National Park at Valley Forge.

At the car, Principato held open the rear door while Rocco, unassisted, hoisted himself with his powerful arms into the back seat. Then he folded his light-aluminum wheel chair and put it on the floor.

They drove silently along the already plowed road from Good Shepherd and into the suburbs, where they could see actual Christmas trees or their reflection through the front windows of houses. Occasionally, Principato looked back at Rocco in the rearview mirror, but the other seemed content to watch out the window and said nothing.

"Are you excited about this?" he asked Rocco, finally.

"Yes. Thanks for getting her for me, Angelo. I thought about it a lot. What does she look like?"

"She's young and has blond hair and she's very pretty."

"Is she tough though?"

"What do you mean?"

"I mean does she have a real hard face and big hips and knockers?"

"No. She's got a very sweet face and she's slim like a college kid. Nice."

"Oh, like that," Rocco said. His disappointment was obvious.

"Well, what did you expect, Rocco? For your first time, a girl like this is best. She'll be very gentle with you."

"I don't want her to be gentle, Angelo. I want her to be like those girls in that book I showed you that time. You know, the ladies from Hamburg."

"You're kidding." Principato laughed. "You mean those hags with the whips and toe crunchers?"

"Yeah, like that. When I thought about it, I used to picture them in my mind. Ask her if she'll do something like that for me tonight, O.K. Angelo?"

"No!" Principato pulled over to the curb and stopped the car. He turned around angrily to face his brother. "No, Rocco! No! Never!

234

That's not normal. It's a perversion. A distortion. Making love to a woman isn't like that."

"What are you talking about, Angelo? Paying money for some whore to lie down on her back and take it from me doesn't have anything to do with love. Besides, let's face it, brother, I'm a distortion. I don't want any motherly type staring down at my two shriveled legs with pity in her eyes."

"Rocco, if you've changed your mind we can go right back to Good Shepherd now. But this girl isn't going to be anything like the babes in that book. Do you understand? Now, what do you want me to do?"

"Keep going. I'll do it your way, Angelo."

Principato started the car again and pulled out into the traffic. Fifteen minutes later they arrived at the apartment building in midtown. Silently, Principato helped Rocco into his chair, then wheeled him into the dimly lit lobby and onto the elevator. On the sixth floor the girl answered the ring of the door bell almost immediately. A short sigh from Rocco showed she did not match his criterion.

"You can wait in the living room," she said to Principato. "There are plenty of magazines in the rack."

He removed his coat and watched as she wheeled the still wordless Rocco into her bedroom. The thought suddenly came to him as she closed the door that she was preparing to change from fully clothed, motherly solicitude to the reality of nakedness and paid-for-lovemaking. How would Rocco react to the switch? He tried quietly to picture them undressing, but his mind had no images, refused to consider the sight of his brother unclothed, the misshapen tendrils of his legs dragging along behind him.

Principato sat down on a sofa and began nervously leafing through a *New Yorker* magazine, seeing only dimly the succession of modeled clothes and liquor ads. After a time, he put it aside and began considering his responsibility. If Rocco failed in this attempt, he might have to bear a weeping tragedy back to Good Shepherd later in the evening. Perhaps he ought to have left well enough alone and forgotten about his promise to Rocco. He blessed himself quickly, muttering beseeching prayers.

Then, in the blank second between the end of praying and the act of retrieving his magazine, he heard screaming. After a moment, in which he realized the frightened cries came not from somewhere outside in the snow-covered night but from within the apartment, he rushed toward the room into which the girl had wheeled Rocco. She hung back, naked, against a wall, one hand spread across her breasts, in an attempt to cover them, and the other to her face, half blotting out the sight of Rocco, also naked and sweating, planted firmly on his buttocks on the low bed, his phallus huge and stiff from between the wispy extension of his legs, swinging a thick leather belt in a wide circle in the air.

"He tried to beat me!" she told Principato incredulously. "He tried to beat me with that belt! Get him out of here! I wanted to be gentle and understanding with him, but he's a monster! He's not fit to live with human beings!"

"Why did you get me this kind of mushy broad?" Rocco demanded, the belt still whizzing about his head, the buckle whistling from the speed. But Principato gave no answer, instead dived at the figure of his brother on the bed, tipping him over like a kingpin. His life's single greatest act of rage, he flailed at the heavy arms and torso of Rocco, who, with his useless legs, had no leverage to throw his brother off. The girl, against the wall, screamed throughout the mauling, changing the name of Principato to monster now.

ELEVEN

Principato saw his chance for a unique vengeance on the Corrigans after learning of that family's involvement in the elaborate preparations for his father's approaching death.

The news came to him one afternoon in January when he drove to South Philly to sit inside the Thunderbird gift car, and run the engine to keep up the charge. Previously, in a dream, it occurred to Principato that, sitting unused before the house, the T-bird's battery would continue to run down until it would be ingloriously dead and inoperative on that day he must assume his father's full powers. Now, at least three times a week, he took pains to guard against that risk. Often his mother joined him, bundled up in her fur coat, taking a few minutes respite from watching over her now bedridden husband to leaf quickly through her *Daily News*.

"How's Papa now?" Principato asked.

"Not doing any talking, just a little whispering. Sometimes he writes me notes. He's been writing some letters to different people and sealing them up in envelopes. He wants them handed out as soon as he dies."

"What kind of letters?"

"Just good-by letters, I guess. He's getting everything ready now

237

because the doctor told him he won't be able to do it toward the end. There's a nurse going to start at the beginning of next week taking care of him."

"That's good. It'll give you a chance for a little rest."

"Angelo, there's something else I have to tell you that you might not like too much."

"What, Mama?"

"He told me yesterday he wants Monsignor Allergucci in the death room when he goes."

"Why?" Principato raged. "What does he need that guy for?"

"Don't ask me. Maybe he's changed his mind, Angelo. Maybe he's going to make his confession and let Allergucci give him the last rites," she said hopefully.

"If Daddy wants to go back to the Church, there's three priests living in that house," he said, pointing to the rectory only twenty yards from where they sat. "Allergucci is unworthy."

"Your papa told me what you told him about Allergucci conning money out of that divorcée. But she's fair game, Angelo. Better the monsignor should get her money to feed all those kids up there than some bum like your pal, Malatesta."

"He isn't feeding any kids with her money, Mama. He's building some kind of museum to his own memory with it. You've never been up there so you don't know what it's all about. He's created his own little domain and put a fence all around it to keep out the world."

"I don't want to hear any more, Angelo. That's not what your papa told me. Allergucci's got his faults, but he's a good priest. I have to go now," she said, noisily refolding her tabloid and opening the door. "Your father might need something."

"Mama . . ."

"Good-by."

Principato watched as she slammed the car door shut and hobbled up the steps of the house, entering, then quickly closing the door behind her. In an instant she reappeared and painfully descended again, motioning for him to lower the window.

"You might as well hear the rest now," she told him, her breath smoke rushing through the opening.

238

"What rest?"

"The Corrigans are coming, too."

"What? Is he crazy? That's no way to die. That family'll be casting nets for his soul till the second he goes. He'll never have any peace."

"Some of our side is going to be there too, Angelo. There'll be you and me and Lucy and Lucrezia and Agostini and some of the men from the parish Holy Name Society who don't mind the Defiance as much as the others, and . . ."

"Where the hell is he going to die, Mama? In a football stadium?"

"That's the best part, Angelo. De Marco, the construction man, is lending us his whole house for the end, so there'll be enough room for everyone. He's even throwing in a band and caterer. You know how De Marco thinks your father's the greatest man alive because of the Defiance. He comes by every afternoon now to plan it. The two of them are having a great time. They're even having a special high bed built and set up in that big room downstairs with the marble pillars."

De Marco! Gnomish worshiper! He was a spiritual coward! Craving to spit in the face of the Church but fearing the consequences of his act. Like a Corrigan, he believed excessively in hell. Principato understood this. So the construction mogul took his pleasure vicariously, having the old man spit for him.

"Will there be dancing?" Principato asked, furious with his mother that his father was planning to debark in the midst of an extravaganza in De Marco's *palazzo* when he had already laid jealous plans for a quiet bedroom finale.

"I don't know. There's certainly space enough. That's the room where they had the wedding reception for De Marco's daughter. Do you remember? That was some bash he threw. There were a lot of people in that place."

"Mama! Mama! This is madness! Don't you see anything wrong with it?"

"Angelo, what can I do? I can't change his mind. I never could. Thank God he doesn't want to die someplace like City Hall courtyard. That's the way I look at it."

239

"Or a barge on the Delaware," he said, slumping down in his seat. He turned to regard his mother. Her ungloved hand that gripped the window frame seemed gray from the cold. Her teeth chattered occasionally. "I'm sorry for yelling," he said.

"Forget it."

"Mama, did Pop write a good-by letter to me?"

"One for you, one for me, one for Monsignor Allergucci, and one for the Corrigans."

"He didn't say what he wrote to us?"

"Nothing. We'll have to wait until the end to find out. I'll bet it's an explanation of why he did everything in life so strangely. Anyhow, make sure you come to see him in the afternoon a few times a week, all right, Angelo?"

"All right, Mama. You don't have to ask me that. How long until the end?"

"It's hard to tell, but the doctor thinks about six weeks. These sicknesses usually go the same way, and he's at the writing stage now. . . ."

So the talking stage was ended. And after the writing stage, when he no longer had strength enough to guide the pen across a pad of paper? But Principato left the question unspoken and watched his mother climb the front steps and close the door behind her. Instead, he resolved the very next day to begin invading his parents' home each afternoon, taking frantic advantage of the remaining writing time before his father's decline advanced to the rattling gasps and pleading eyes of a really dying man with much to say and no means at all to say it.

But, to his surprise, there were long periods when the old man played idly with the magic marker he favored for printing. Ironic: reams of paper and a pen to underscore the urgency of last thoughts in thick red lines, and there were suddenly few thoughts to impart. Thirty-four years the parent of Principato, added to his own youth, made sixty years of a life in which he had married one Angela Medico, fathered three children, left the church of his upbringing and stayed defiantly away, embraced the Communists during a fling in the thirties, then quit them to work for the Republicans and Democrats, made money in the interment racket, played the horses, driven expensive cars, made handouts to his married son, seen his daughter enter and leave the convent, accepted the judgment that his young son was permanently crippled: all this, and he seemed to have no more memory of any of it. Or cared not to remember perhaps. Beside him, on the bed, the old man shrugged his shoulders occasionally and gave him a sad smile, embarrassed, Principato believed, at having no lines to write.

Daily now he made a catalogue of the room's effects, but he did it half consciously (his mind easing slyly beyond the task of concentrating on his father's fingers poised above the writing pad). So the sudden removal, between two visits, of all the props of religiosity—the Virgin's statue with the red vigil before it, the picture of Saint Theresa with the woven palm rope around it—registered with only small shock. If this was the wish of his father, if his mother had agreed, uncomplaining, to carry her favorite gods off into exile for the approach of her husband's death, then it was enough. Principato made no mention of it.

But the purge of his mother's Christian symbols in one corner of Philadelphia somehow prompted him to recall that wily Catholic tribe, the Corrigans, in another. Doubtless they were plotting. Mending their nets for a final casting, as it were. He grew incensed at the notion that they must be meeting nightly now in his own home. The old Jesuit would be laying the groundwork: lengthily extemporizing for the mob on the immortality of the soul—even a Principato's soul —and picking his shredded memory to serve them up precedents of deathbed recantations. Then the old lady, master tactician, would plan the assault. Cynthia and her three brothers were the storm troopers. Fanatical and useful, Principato knew, even to the point of holding down his father until the Jesuit could plaster him over with holy oils and water. The Corrigans had a low-brow approach to theology. For them, a good bath in the symbols of easy departure would be nearly as valid as if the Defiance had actually consented to crumble, be absolved, and shuffle off the coil with a consequently peaceful smile on its face.

But Principato would have none of it. With that family at the bedside, his father's reconversion—for which he had once fondly hoped —would now seem a flight to dismal parochialism and the furnished apartments of their minds that had no place for ecumenicalism, a hearing for birth control, or even English masses. He would fight them. Condemn his own father's soul to the endless void in which he believed as much as they, rather than see them triumphant.

"Why did you invite the Corrigans to De Marco's, Papa?" Principato demanded testily.

The last thing I want to see before I go is "loser" written all over their faces was printed on the sheet he handed his son moments later.

"How did you get them to agree to come?"

I wrote them a letter that I was planning a brink of death return and needed strong spiritual kinship. They wouldn't miss that chance for anything he penned out next, laughing as he showed it to his son.

"I don't trust them, Pop. You shouldn't have invited them. You don't know how it'll be that day. You might weaken toward the end and they'll win. And that's the one thing you can't do."

Let me worry about that. I bet I fix them yet.

"Are you sure? You can't give in, Pop. You've got to help me with my plan. After being married to them for eleven years, I need some kind of revenge."

And I'm the sacrificial lamb? Who the hell told you to marry her? Not me! Another sheet was thrust at him angrily after a full minute of furious brittle scrapes with the magic marker that set Principato's teeth to grating.

"I'm sorry, Pop. I was pleading like a jackal."

You don't worry about anybody. Allergucci or the Corrigans. Everybody's going to get their just due on the last day. Me included, I guess.

Then De Marco came into the room, as he found time to do nearly every afternoon these days. A diminutive Caesar with intense dark eyes, small like a weasel's. Principato knew him to the soul: nervous and rich from presiding in singular tyranny over his burgeoning construction empire, his mind was intensely stimulated now at the prospect of the Defiance soon to be tested against an absolute like death.

242

The old man hopefully standing firm was becoming some version of everybody's sacrificial lamb, Principato thought ruefully. He smiled falsely at the mogul. Today's toga was expensive cashmere, his scepter an ivory-headed walking stick reserved for Wednesdays only.

De Marco went directly to a chair on the opposite side of the bed from Principato.

"Joe," he addressed the old man, "I wanted to talk to you about inviting some more priests for the end. It's been on my mind for a couple of days now."

Wearily, it seemed to Principato, the old man began scratching out a reply. De Marco took the proffered paper, scanned it, then handed it to Principato. *Allergucci and the Corrigan priest are the only ones important to me.*

"Joe, I had a vision in a dream," De Marco pleaded. "Acres of priests! Hundreds of them, all shuddering in their goddam cassocks because somebody's soul had the guts to plow on into eternity without their magic act. Don't you see what it'll do to them, Joe? It denies their *raison d'être,* mocks their whole ministry!"

De Marco's eyes were wine-drunk at the notion. The old man calmly wrote his response, fracturing the mogul's glee: *Maybe they're shaking because they're afraid for me.*

"No, Joe, that's not the way it was in the dream. I insist. It wasn't anything like that. We defeated them. And that's how it's going to be at the end. Now what about music? I've put off booking a band because I wasn't sure what kind you wanted. How about something nice and religious like the "Ave Maria"? Can you picture it, Joe? You're dyin' in the middle of my salon on a high bed surrounded by layers of priests. From one side of the room comes the "Ave Maria," real soft and sweet. On the other side is Ricci the caterer's layout: yards of caviar and cold cuts and a nice long bar all hung over with some of those truck-driver hoods who work for me and who'll take a drink at any time of the day. Real secular types, Joe. Can you see the contrast?"

On the bed, the old man smiled wanly, nodding his head. The slight motion of acquiescence caused Principato to check his fury at the cashmered pariah.

"Or, if you don't like the contrast angle, Joe, how about a complete blanket technique? This one appeals to me best, the more I think of it. Nothing left to chance. We get a colored band and have them play Charleston music from the twenties. Irreverence and worldliness pelting them from every angle, you in the middle calmly dying a heretic's death. . . . Joe, it'll be magnificent! They'll strangle. It'll go down in diocesan history as the event that everyone wants to forget. And I had the privilege to be part of it," De Marco ended softly, somewhere off on the higher plane of his reverie. Then there was a silence while Principato watched his father, who regarded the tycoon with frank disbelief. Seconds later the magic marker began slashing across the pad of paper. Impulsively, Principato reached for the message before it got to De Marco: *Impossible. In my life I can account for only two priests who'd be interested enough in my dying to come.* De Marco read it too.

"Don't worry, Joe!" he begged. "Don't worry at all! I'll have priests there by the bus load. I'll find a way. Nothing is too good for your death scene, Joe!" he said, scooping up the old man's hand and kissing it repeatedly. "You're the martyr to our cause. You can't know how I love and respect you, Joe. I was in that church thirty-five years ago when you stomped out. Did you see me? I was standin' in the back next to the confessional tryin' like hell to keep from going to sleep. I was you, Joe. All of a sudden, I was inside your skin. I still remember how you turned around halfway down the aisle and thumbed your nose at Allergucci. 'Fuck you, Allergucci,' you said. . . ."

The old man raised his arm to stop De Marco. The magic marker slashed again, and the note was handed directly to Principato.

I didn't say fuck you Allergucci. His father seemed concerned that Principato believe this. De Marco read, then crumpled the paper.

"All right, Joe. You didn't actually speak it. But we all knew what you were thinkin'. We were thinkin' it for you. I've got to go now. Take care of him," he commanded Principato. "There's still a lot of planning to be done."

The mogul rose hurriedly, planted a parting kiss on the old man's cheek, then left the room without another word to Principato. On the bed the elder shrugged his shoulders and wrote another note.

Maybe we're being too theatrical?

TWELVE

At the beginning of Principato's third week of afternoon visiting his father wrote, *Does Niccolò know I'm dying?*

Principato held the pad out for his mother to read. She shrugged her shoulders. Niccolò, the gray, shriveled brother of his father lived only blocks away but had long since been forgotten. The choice was Niccolò's. His only gesture toward maintaining ties was the small Christmas gift he sent to the house each year for Lucy. Otherwise, to meet Niccolò on the street implied no certainty that he would speak. To Principato, the real relationship of his father and uncle was less a question of their being siblings than that each was a kind of hand-servant of death. The old man prepared coffins and tombstones; Niccolò dug graves in the Italian cemetery.

Don't come to see me tomorrow, his father wrote. *Go to Niccolò. Tell him I'm dying.*

Obediently, Principato drove the next afternoon to Niccolò's apartment on Sixth Street. His uncle had no phone; refused to consider the expense. In the apartment-house foyer he pushed the button under NICCOLÒ PRINCIPATO and waited for a voice from above. There was none, but the release buzzed almost immediately, and Principato pushed through and climbed the steps. At the top, the door next to Niccolò's opened suddenly and blind Ardico, the flower seller, stood facing him.

"Niccolò's at the cemetery. He has a grave today. Do you want to leave a message for him?"

"No, Ardico. I'll drive there and see him myself."

"Who is it?"

"His nephew, Angelo."

"Is something wrong, Angelo? You don't come here so often."

"My father is going to die. I have to tell Niccolò."

"Angelo . . . ?" The voice grew excited. Ardico moved a few cautious paces out of the dimness of his rooms and Principato was able to see the spatterings of the blind man's last groping meal etched across his shirt front.

"Yes, Ardico?"

"Did his brother leave Niccolò any money?"

"I don't know. I haven't heard anything about a will. Why? For what reason do you want to know?"

"Niccolò said if his brother left him money we'd get out of here. We'd get a nice apartment together near the sea. At Asbury Park maybe."

"He shouldn't have told you that, Ardico. Niccolò and my father were never so close. There's a good chance the old man didn't leave him anything."

"How could he do that, Angelo? They're brothers, aren't they? Brothers are supposed to be generous with each other."

"When was Niccolò ever generous with anyone?"

"I don't know. There had to be at least one time. But I prayed your father would leave him money, Angelo, so we could get out. Look inside at my apartment and see how ugly it is. It smells bad and I can't get rid of the stink. There are roaches, too. I can't see them, but I know they're crawling around."

"You should open the blinds and windows and let some sunlight in, Ardico. I've told you that before."

"They stay shut, Angelo," he said flatly. "You know that already."

Principato knew. He had long since learned from Niccolò of Ardico's incredible fear: that people might observe him through the open windows without his knowledge in his daily stumbling routine of washing, eating, and dressing. These people might include children with pellet guns and slingshots. So the windows stayed closed and the air was befouled. Impulsively, Principato moved closer to the door. The dark rooms were rife with the odor of mildew.

"Tell your mother I'm sorry for her trouble, Angelo," Ardico said unexpectedly. "Give her this for me."

Principato took a card that the blindman had removed from his shirt pocket and read quickly a formula for gaining an indulgence printed on one side. On the reverse was a saint's relic housed behind a cellophane window. Looking at the dark speck, he could not be sure whether it was a scrap of cloth or a sliver of bone or a bit of coffin wood. Perhaps it was only a parcel of earth completely unassociated with the good saint who, from her picture, had certainly been a nun. Principato suspected there were chiselers in the relics trade too, like anything else.

"Thanks, Ardico. I'll be sure to give it to her."

He left the building and drove to the Italian cemetery, cruising slowly along its winding roads, looking for the telltale sign of fresh earth. Here and there, he saw wilting flowers atop the small rise of a newly covered grave. Listening closely, he heard the sound of Niccolò's pick before he actually saw him, since his mound of dirt was hidden behind a large tombstone. Principato parked the car on a low hill and walked across the frost-hard lawn toward his uncle.

"Niccolò."

His uncle was four feet down in a squared-off hole that had obviously been hard going. He swung the pick high over his head.

"*Buon giorno*, kid. What did you come to see me for?" Above the gravedigger, Principato smiled faintly to himself. Niccolò always tried to put you off; suspected everyone of wanting to borrow money from him.

"I don't need money, Niccolò."

"Then have a seat."

Niccolò handed him that morning's tabloid newspaper and he spread it over the cold of a low, flat gravestone and sat down on it. The spiders of frost between the markers reflected a weak sun. His uncle returned to swinging his pick, his breath escaping in even clouds of smoke.

"How's business, Niccolò?"

"Huh! With February comes the death season. Never seen a slow February yet. The rush is on after the real winter, and the bastards are droppin' off like flies."

"Who's dead here?" Principato asked. Niccolò had gone down exactly on a line between two stones, it seemed to him. One was marked AGNELLI, the other LA BELLA.

"Old La Bella, the rich dog. Owned a finance company and a used-car lot. Sold the same cars six times to some of that trade in West Philly. Racketeer," he said, screwing up his face in an elaborate Latinesque gesture that implied that whatever else old La Bella had been, he was a shrewd one. It amazed Principato when he worked with Niccolò during college vacations that his uncle always seemed to know the most intimate details about the people he was burying. He watched as Niccolò threw the pick out of the hole and began shoveling the rocky earth onto the pile atop a piece of canvas that was stretched out on the other side of the grave.

"I saw Lucrezia was up from Florida last month," he said between grunts.

"Yes, she was in for Christmas and New Year's."

"I'd like to know how she made her money. She goes ridin' around in that big Caddy with the nigger driver like she just bought Philly the day before." Suddenly furious, Niccolò thrust his shovel onto the pile, then shuddered as it stopped abruptly, clanking against a stone. He continued with his perennial lament. "I can't figure out how it all passed me by. Look at me, a gravedigger! Old La Bella had the money, Lucrezia, that family of your wife's, your old man. Everybody I know. I never had a single chance to make any."

"Come on, Niccolò, everybody in South Philly knows you've got millions socked away."

The shovel stopped in mid-motion. Niccolò's fearful mask appeared above the edge of the hole.

"Who says that? I ain't got any money. I only hope I live longer than your old man so he'll leave me some. I'm his only brother. Who else can he leave it to?"

"You get part of your wish, Niccolò. He's dying now."

"What are you talkin' about? When?" Before Principato, the face went suddenly cautious and slit-eyed.

"In about a month, Niccolò."

"What's wrong?"

"Cancer."

"He was a good man," Niccolò began, already spinning out a eulogy. "I'll have to hire somebody to dig the hole, though. I don't think it's right a man should dig his own brother's grave."

"He's going to be cremated, Niccolò. No grave to dig."

"Why the hell's he gonna do that? That's against the Church, ain't it? Hey kid, he's not still carryin' on that private war of his is he? He's gonna have the priest, right?"

"There're going to be two there that I'm certain of, though hundreds are promised. But I'm almost sure none of them is going to get a chance to do anything."

Niccolò threw the shovel out onto the grass and climbed out of the hole.

"What's wrong with that old man of yours? Isn't he scared? It's dark out there," he said, pointing past the cemetery fence, as if to eternity. "I'd be scared to die without the priest. But that's something I could never understand about your old man. Are they gonna have a mass for him?"

"No. The mortician will fix him up, then he'll be cremated."

"I don't get it. Your family's got a nice plot here. Do you know where it is? Come on, I'll show you."

Wordlessly, Principato followed his uncle, for miles, it seemed, over thousands of dead to a gravestone on the other side of the cemetery marked simply: PRINCIPATO.

Principato observed it curiously, recalling that he had seen it but once before. Only his paternal grandparents, two old people that no one seemed to remember very well and who died before their grandchildren were born, were buried in the plot. A slight depression in the lawn marked the spot.

"Your grandma and grandpa are buried here. That's all. There's plenty room. Your father ain't that big a man."

"That's O.K. It's all been arranged. Mother and Lucrezia are going south with him after he dies."

There was a long silence while Principato waited for mention of the will. But Niccolò only shrugged his shoulders in endless consternation. His nephew turned to leave.

"Did you see my monument?" Niccolò demanded.

"No, but I've heard about it."

"Come on. I'll show it to you then." They marched off in the opposite direction and Principato began thinking of something warming against the cold, like a shot of whisky. After a time, they came to his uncle's monument, an atrocity of a concrete nubile Virgin looking down on a marble slab that bore Niccolò's name. Two life-size angels prayed for his immortal soul on either side.

"It's the biggest in this goddam place," Niccolò said with a tremble of pride. "Everything's ready. I got it set up with the priest and undertaker, too. I gave the priest money for a lot of masses after I'm gone. How do you like it?"

"You deserve it."

"I worked hard all my life. I never had a Thunderbird car like your old man."

"You wouldn't know what to do with it if you had one. You don't have any friends to take for a ride anyhow."

"I could take Ardico. He's my friend," Niccolò said.

"He's blind. He couldn't see anything."

"Never mind. If I had a car like that I'd have plenty of friends all of a sudden. You know how cagy people are when it comes to something like that."

"Maybe," Principato said, starting toward his car.

"Kid"—Niccolò pursued him—"the will?"

"They'll read it as soon as he's dead, I suppose. But there won't be any point in showing up." He easily created a lie: "He left everything to Charlie, the locker-room man at the San Giorgio Baths."

"What? Angelo, what are you sayin'?" Niccolò screeched. "Why would anybody leave all their money to that goony bastard?"

"The old man liked Charlie. He always kept up a good head of steam."

"Just for that? Just for that alone? It ain't human, Angelo. Where's my brother dyin'? At the hospital or at the house?"

"At the house."

"I've gotta start visitin' him. I've gotta talk to him, Angelo. That Charlie has an air-conditioned apartment and his own car. Look at me livin' in that dirty old apartment in an old building. Never owned a car in my life. Who needs it more? Me or Charlie?"

"Charlie. The shock of sudden, new wealth might be too much for you. You'd go to pieces. Charlie would handle it better."

"Yeah? Who decided that? Your old man? He was a Communist during the thirties, Angelo. Bet you never knew that, did you? If that father of yours would leave me as much money now as he gave to them Wobblies during the Depression, I'd be a rich man, sudden or not."

"I'll tell him you said so, Niccolò."

"No, Angelo, wait. Don't say anything. I'll talk to him myself."

"Yes. I'm going to tell him, Niccolò."

"Then I'll get nothing for sure, Angelo." Niccolò spoke quietly. "One thing is for certain. That old man of yours don't like to be reminded of any mistakes he made in his life."

THIRTEEN

De Marco played God with the ragged end of the old man's life and made certain all the props for the death scene were on hand before he called up the star cast. Principato was advised of his treachery ten days after his visit to Niccolò by a three-a.m. phone call to the small South Philly hotel where he had taken a room to be near his parents' home for the end. The ringing on the night table near his bed woke him to an instant consciousness from a tossing sleep, and he knew before the desk clerk's voice spoke what was required of him.

"You have a call. Hold on a moment, please."

After a few loud clicks and a long ripple of static, he heard his Aunt Lucrezia, who had come up from Florida the week before.

"On your horse, kid. The old boy's going. Hurry over. De Marco's secretary thought she had phoned you over an hour ago and just realized she hadn't." Behind Lucrezia, the *West Side Story* overture rushed about; glasses tinkled; muted voices could be heard.

"That bastard De Marco! Who else did his secretary just realize she forgot?" Principato asked, instantly sensing manipulation.

"The Corrigans and Monsignor Allergucci."

"Doesn't it start to look like anything to you, Lucrezia?"

"Yeah, a nice party. Hurry over, Angelo. There's plenty to eat and drink."

Ten minutes later Principato saw the extras for De Marco's death scene: the mogul had somehow enticed forty-one priests to the event. Tall and short, hefty, dumpy, or slim, some in cassocks and some in black clerical suits—though none as perfect as Allergucci or dissipated as the ancient Jesuit Corrigan—they spilled out of the marble-columned salon of De Marco's *palazzo* and into the foyer, blocking Principato's way in to the deathbed. Most of the priests had drinks in their hands. They stood in little clusters, puzzled whispering filling the air about them. Above their heads, Principato saw the saxophone player, who was rendering a solo of "With a Little Bit of Luck." His body and instrument faced telepathically toward the band leader; his eyes, bug-wide at his notion of sacrilege perhaps, were directed toward the raised imperial pallet that held the dying Principato's bulk. Purple bedclothes covered the form. Principato the son pressed inward, apologizing heavily all the way. Then he saw Lucrezia in the midst of the mob. She was clearly excited in the presence of so many priests. Henna-haired and eternally tinseled, she waltzed giddily amid their perplexity with a cocktail tray, urging drinks upon them.

"I don't know what this is all about," Lucrezia whispered conspiratorially into his shocked face, "but we almost lost all these guys until De Marco broke down and gave them a drink."

"Lucrezia, Pop is dying in the next room."

"I know, Angelo. But what can I do? He lived a long time and made enough money, and he'd be the first to tell you not to suspend hospitality on his account—if he could still talk. Now why don't you go in there and do what you have to do, and let me take care of the guests?"

Rebuffed, Principato pushed into the death room, passing the caterer's tables that bountifully lined the length of one wall. An element that he assumed was De Marco's hoodlum truck drivers mixed freely with some members of the Holy Name Society from Saint Theresa's parish, distinguished by the black bands on their arms. De Marco was everywhere among them, pushing sandwiches from the tables into protesting mouths, heaping cole slaw and potato salad on their plates, even thrusting a drink into the hand of an occasional wayward enemy priest detached from his fraternity. The mourners dipped and jived to the "Luck" lyrics.

Niccolò stood bent over the victim at the topmost of the three steps leading to the deathbed. Not bothering to remove his coat, Principato ascended the opposite side. Beneath his feet, the purple carpeting was inches thick.

"Joe," Niccolò was pleading, "how much? Nod your head yes when I hit the right amount, O.K., Joe? Is it five thousand?"

Intrigued at the final communication of brothers, Principato did not interrupt. The old man's head was propped up slightly on a pillow, the two arcs of light from tall candles positioned on either side of him converging on his face that was incredibly pale and glistening with sweat. For a moment his eyes were closed, the baggy puffs of skin beneath them gone gray for the hour of his death. Then the head moved slightly to and fro, telling Niccolò negative.

"Eight thousand, Joe?" Niccolò beseeched, gripping the old man's hand. Principato looked beyond his wizened uncle to the line of gilded chairs that already contained his mother, Lucy, and Rogansky, the nurse. The old lady, dry-eyed and pensive, as he had not expected her to be, leaned heavily on the arm of her chair, cupping her chin in her hand. She did not acknowledge him. Lucy, beside her, cried softly, staring at the floor and moving a rosary through her fingers. Rogansky alone favored him with a brief trace of a wondering smile, then went back to her unabashed contemplation of the blaring band and the feasting mourners three rows deep at the caterer's tables at four in the morning. Principato wondered why she was not making some token professional gesture at the end of his father's life, like wiping his sweaty forehead with a cloth.

"Eight thousand, Joe?" Niccolò repeated.

On the pillow, a brief trace of smile came into the corners of the dying man's mouth. The head swung a slow negative again.

"How much, Joe? More?"

Still smiling, the old man nodded an affirmative.

"Fifty thousand?" Niccolò blurted, louder than the music.

The elder Principato nodded yes again.

"Joe . . . sixty thousand?" Niccolò asked slyly, leaning closer to the old man. He had released his brother's hand and clasped himself tightly now. Principato's arm shot across the bed to grip Niccolò's lapels.

"Piss off, Niccolò."

"O.K. Joe, good-by," he stammered, frightened now. "Thanks for leaving me money." He turned and moved quickly down the steps away from his brother's dying to the caterer's tables.

The old man opened his eyes for the first time to regard Principato, who saw that his father was actually embarrassed. He rolled his eyes from side to side, from the band to the bar, then shrugged his shoulders slightly.

"Pizzaz," Principato said. "You're going out like a Caesar." He moved closer in response to the elder's smile and took the old man's hand in his own, surprised at its clamminess. Impulsively, he spread open the fingers and placed them against his cheek. The cold touch alerted his senses. He sniffed the ammonia odor on the hand, heard the barely audible whistle of air entering and receding through his father's nasal passages. Beside him, the old man opened his eyes and stared at him for a long moment before closing them again. After months of accelerated dying, chagrin in the real presence of death, then. Who had guessed things would get this big? the old man seemed to be suggesting.

The band played "On the Street Where You Live."

Then De Marco slipped through the row of gilded chairs and hastily climbed the steps to the opposite side of the bed from Principato. The proxy rebel's weasel eyes were wine-drunk with happiness.

"How many priests, De Marco?" Principato asked him.

"Forty-one so far. Can you believe it, Angelo?"

"How did you get them here?"

"I sent a form letter to fifty priests in the diocesan directory. Here, Angelo, look at this." De Marco removed a folded sheet of paper from his pocket and handed it to Principato who read:

Dear Father ———:

I am writing you on be half of my beloved friend, Joseph Principato, who is about to pass from mortality to immortality. (He is dying of cancer.) Often in the past my friend expressed sentiments of admiration concerning the good work you were accomplishing in ——— parish. Although he was not known to you personally, he was in a position to receive favorable reports concerning you. Therefore, it is his stated wish that you be present at the final hour of his life to offer him comfort and administer the sacred last rites of our holy religion. He has spoken of this so pointedly and often that I have taken the liberty of writing you in the certain hope that you will be available at the anxious hour. He has also spoken somewhat less pointedly (in keeping good taste) of the unspecified amount of money he intends leaving you in his will for the continuance of your excellent work. I will make every effort to contact you when the end is at hand.

> Respectfully,
> Isadoro De Marco, afflicted
> friend of the dying
> Joseph Principato

"Good God!" said Principato, looking off toward the knots of priests, who were growing restless now in their perplexity. "Do you mean they all got the same letter? If these guys get serious about that hint of money they could wreck the place."

"Relax, Angelo. They got finished comparing letters in the first half hour. Nobody's got a hope for money any longer since they figured your old man is just some kind of eccentric crank. It's food and curiosity keeping them here because I've got the word leaked out that there's a grand finale coming. They're going to stay for this one," he said, patting the dying man's stomach.

"Nobody tried to find out who Isadoro De Marco is and ask about their money?"

"A few did, but nobody knew the guy," De Marco chuckled. "For the most part good taste is prevailing. These guys aren't all like Allergucci, you know. I'll say that much for them."

"When does the Prince of Darkness get here?" Principato asked, warming at least to this aspect of De Marco's madness.

"He's here. Haven't you seen him? He must have been camping out somewhere in the neighborhood he got here so fast. He's sulking over in that corner behind the bar. I'll get him for you," De Marco volunteered, descending the steps toward the cloak-draped figure of Allergucci, who sat staring into the floor. De Marco touched the priest's shoulder, then spoke. The monsignor nodded and rose slowly to begin walking, splendid in a new black cloak, toward the center of the room. At the foot of the carpeted steps, he motioned Principato into one of the gilded chairs beside Lucy and his mother.

Joining him, Principato saw the rheumy glaze of frustration in Allergucci's eyes.

"The final confrontation, Angelo, and he's as intractable as ever."

"So what am I supposed to do? You should have known better, Monsignor, than to expect him to change. He's made his decision. He'll stick by it."

"Yes, until death he'll stick by it. How commendable. But where does that leave me?" the priest asked wearily, arising to walk slowly before the row of chairs. He paused for a moment to gaze relentlessly at the trombone player in the midst of his solo. "Rhapsody in Blue" spilled into the room. Around Allergucci's legs his cassock still swayed from the rhythm of his walk. Its hem was newly torn, perhaps in his haste to get to the old man's bedside.

"The Church teaches heavily of conscience and guilt, but it seems the lesson has consumed the teacher this time," Allergucci spoke distantly, peering now at the form on the bed. From below, the old man's chest rose and fell, shifting the purple cover. The priest turned toward Principato's mother, his eyes lit up with a sudden anger.

"He's your husband, Angela, but I don't think you really know him. Thirty-five years ago, in the folly of a youthful priest, I drove him from the Church one Sunday morning. But since then I've begged and pleaded with him to come back to the mass and sacraments. Any other man, seeing my contrition, would have relented and returned to the Church. But not him, Angela. No priest was ever humble enough for him. The reason he walked out of mass that day has long since ceased to be important. He's retained that as an excuse to punish me for my pride and vanity.

"And he has punished me, Angela. Thirty-five years of throwing out the bait then hauling it back when my hopes were highest. But he understands conscience and guilt very well. Not that I believe he's ever been conscience-ridden or guilty about anything. Simply he understands the responsibility I feel for his immortal soul and makes me pay for it. This is the diabolical thing about him. He has disavowed

258

the concept of soul. It amuses him, in fact. Your husband is lying there dying, completely certain in his own mind that there's no judgment or reward or eternity to cope with. This gives him his power over me, Angela. He has no fear of dying."

"Stop slandering him, Monsignor," Principato said.

"I'm not slandering him. I'm telling you the truth about him. And if I seem to be exacting a small vengeance of my own after all these years, then it's due me," the priest said, poking his chest with his thumb.

"You're not gaining any small vengeance at all, Monsignor, because no one believes what you say," Lucy told him, her tear-coated voice erupting suddenly against the background of music. "He hasn't spent years punishing you either. Just running away from you. Some people aren't made to be good bedfellows with the Church."

"Not in this family at least," Allergucci said. "How long were you a nun before you decided to leave and get married, Sister?"

"Now you're acting like a spiteful child, Monsignor. You're making a mockery of my poor father's dying. Remember, you're here because he wanted you to come for some reason. If it were up to any of the rest of us, I don't think you'd be invited."

"Ah, my poor Principato children. You don't understand his reason?" Allergucci said, his arm extended toward the bed. "It's to see me in this agony of knowing I'll never get him to relent now. Look at him. His eyes are open. He sees and hears it all. Right at this moment he's laughing at us, laughing at me for my desperation and at you because he's duped you so cleverly all your lives by making you think he's the very symbol of integrity."

"That's not his reason," Principato's mother said flatly. "He's afraid of dying like anybody else would be afraid of dying. I'd be afraid to die. He just called you here in case he changes his mind and wants you to pray for him."

"Then I humbly wait on his whim, Angela. But he won't change his mind," Allergucci said. Then he unbuttoned his cloak and removed it, placing it over the back of his chair. He walked away from them, past the knots of priests, toward the front windows and stood looking out, his shoulders drooping perceptibly after releasing a sigh that Principato imagined he could hear.

"Angelo," De Marco jabbed him unexpectedly from behind. "Here comes the other priest!"

Principato swung toward the doorway to see the Corrigan mob taking in the scene with undisguised incredulousness. Rows of priests, sensing their common evangelical purpose perhaps, fell back at their entrance. Cynthia stood in a triangle of her brothers, while the old lady and the Jesuit clung together. Then, at the familiar click sound from the mother, they all began marching toward the deathbed. The band hammered out a jazz rendition of "Summertime."

"As he lived, so shall he die," the Jesuit intoned mournfully beside the carpeted steps, shaking his head at the musicians and caterers.

"There was plenty of food around when your brother, Cynthia's father, died, Father," Principato said, standing to meet him.

"Yes, but at least we waited until the old buzzard was dead, and we never even considered having a band," the mother retorted. "I can see by the heaving of his chest that your poor father is still alive, thanks be to God. Hello, Mr. Principato, do you remember me?" she demanded loudly, hastening up the steps to the bedside to take the old man's hand. Principato dashed up behind her. Something like a weary smile of recognition flickered over his father's face. His head nodded slightly.

"We've come to aid you in your deathbed return to Holy Mother the Church, Mr. Principato," the Jesuit told him. "Remember the letter you wrote to us?"

"You're taking a lot for granted," Allergucci said, ascending to the bed, obviously annoyed at the real possibility of being muscled out by a new priest.

"You're taking everything for granted," De Marco said. He was now standing by the dying man's head and gripping his shoulder. "No clutching at the cross for this one! He's got the Defiance in him. To hell with Rome and Jerusalem! He's said it himself. This one doesn't need that business."

"He told us in a letter that he was going to return to the Church," Cynthia protested. "That's why we're here, for God's sake."

"It was a trick," Principato informed them, facing triumphantly

260

toward the six. "My father's not doing any such thing. He's just called you here to see you strangle on your own spleen in payment for the eleven years of horror you've put me through in living with Cynthia. He's avenging me."

"Too damn bad for you, Pato," shouted brother Matt, advancing upon him. "Do you think it was easy for our family to put up with a mess of neuroses like yours all those years?"

"Stop it, all of you!" Lucy ordered. Principato could see from the look on six Corrigan faces that it suddenly dawned on them who she was.

"Sister," said Mrs. Corrigan, "what are you doing here dressed like this?"

"I've left my order, Mrs. Corrigan. Since before Christmas. Hadn't you heard?"

"Oh no, it's not true, Sister," the old lady moaned, real tears springing to her spaniel eyes. "You were so pure and angelic-looking in your habit. I had trouble most times believing you were Mr. Principato's sister. And, oh dear, I just sent off a check to the Mother House of your order."

"Lucy, Lucy, my child," the Jesuit exhorted, "go back inside the walls! Take up your real vocation. Don't you see how mean it is out here? Look at all this. Would anyone in the religious life choose to die like this?"

"Don't be so dramatic, Father. My decision is made and I'm not going back. I'm getting married in a few months."

"Holy Mother of God! Let's kneel down in that corner," the Jesuit pointed toward the bandstand, "and pray a rosary for Sister Veronica and her poor damned father who prepares his soul for hell."

Splendidly, outcast and offended, the six Corrigans moved away to the bandstand corner and knelt down simultaneously, the rosaries rushing from their pockets and purses as the old priest began the Sorrowful Mysteries. Respectfully, the band leader reduced volume for a moment, only to have De Marco cry to him, "No! Louder! Louder! Drown the fools out!"

Appeased, Prnicipato watched them for a moment until he saw his mother rise, remove her rosary from her purse and make her way across the room to join the Corrigans on their knees.

"Mama! Mama!" he begged, hastening after her. "You can't pray with them!"

"I'm not praying for the same thing they are. I'm praying for something else. Besides, I just want to pray. I'm so confused about what's going on here."

"At least pray over near us, Mama. Get away from them. Come on, I'll pray with you."

"Oh, Angelo, leave me alone. Go talk to Daddy for a while. Ask him if the pain hurts. Or go to the bar and have a drink or something."

Abruptly she chimed in on the Corrigan chant, and Principato, defeated, returned to holding his father's chill hand. Soon the band put aside their instruments for a break, and moments later, above the drone of praying, church bells began suddenly to ring from across the street. Loud and booming, chasing the familiar flight of pigeons out of the belfry and into the first weak light of dawn that could be seen through the windows. Principato watched them: their wings flapping violently for the short ascent, then halting abruptly as they glided to the macadam of the schoolyard basketball court to wait for silence.

"What is it?" Allergucci asked. He stood near Principato at the bottom of the steps.

"Six o'clock mass. It always rings at five minutes to," Lucy told him.

"They get a nice crowd," Allergucci said. "When I read an early mass there's nobody but the nuns."

"A lot of women stop in on their way to work in the morning."

"It's very strange, Lucy, but I think I've seen these women going into mass from this window before. I knew somehow, from a dream perhaps, that I would be standing in a room glutted with people and a band and a bar waiting for your father to die on a gray morning with church bells ringing and streetcars moving along past the house, completely oblivious to us here in the central drama. *Déjà vu.* There was even an old Jesuit like that relic over there." He jerked his shoulder at the Corrigan prayer huddle. "And a church burner by proxy like our friend De Marco here. And even in the dream I believe I was amazed at the notion that one man's soul had become so very impor-

262

tant to everyone present when an entire world went chugging by outside the window. I think I called him my cross in the dream."

"Yes, you probably did," Lucy said. "I'll say one thing about you, Monsignor—and God forgive me for speaking to a priest this way—but my father was a hundred per cent right every time he said you were the biggest ham he knew. Look at you being persecuted! Why don't you admit it's not his soul you're worried about? It's your own."

"Lucy, you don't understand. I drove all the way out to Pittsburgh to ask your help. . . ."

"I understand plenty now. You either shut up or take off out of here right away!"

"Lucy, don't shout at a priest like that!" her mother commanded. The old lady had grown tired of praying with the Corrigans, who would not admit her to their pact, and had returned to the bedside.

"I'm not under any vow of obedience any longer, Mama. I want him to keep quiet or leave. That's all."

"She doesn't understand, Angela. The issue here is . . ."

Allergucci stopped talking, his eyes fixed on the nurse, who had just taken a sudden step from the place she had been standing since the Corrigans' arrival and placed her ear against the old man's chest. Then, on the opposite side from Principato, she lifted a hand to take his pulse.

"He's going," she said to no one in particular.

"He's going," De Marco spoke in a loud whisper to the band and the revelers at the bar. Respectfully, the latter lowered their drinks and sandwiches; the priests crowded forward; the musicians rushed back to their resting instruments; the Corrigans started from their knees in unison toward the soul about to flee from the room.

Then the march strains broke loose from the bandstand. Principato listened closely for a distracted moment but could not identify the music. The same consternation showed on every other face. Except for De Marco's.

"Giuseppe! Giuseppe!" He ran deliriously up the steps to the old man. "Do you hear it? Do you remember? The 'Internationale,' Giuseppe. Remember it from the thirties, when we used to meet in my basement? Religion was finished . . ."

263

"Joseph! Joseph!" yelled Allergucci, "kiss the cross!" He whipped a small crucifix from the pocket of his cassock and pressed it toward the prostrate gasping form while Principato and De Marco tried to hold him off. Abruptly, the old man rose up, eyes wide and fearing, arms extended as if to clutch at Allergucci's crucifix, but he missed and tumbled from the side of the bed, through the hands of the nurse, bouncing off each carpeted step in its turn till he crashed to the floor like a log. It was a concussion that got him in the end, Principato supposed dimly, still holding tightly to the monsignor's arm. It was taken for granted he was dead.

"Angelo! Angelo! Did you see?" his mother implored. "Your father was going back to the church!" Beside Principato, the six Corrigans actually began clapping in a union of delight. The *"Internationale"* fell off in a disjointed wail of horn sounds.

"Yes," the old Jesuit exulted, "it was obvious enough for us. The full intent was there."

"Go to hell, priest! Go to hell, all you priests!" De Marco yelled from the floor, trying with the aid of some of his truck drivers to reassemble the old man for lifting to the bed. "Go to hell, I repeat! He was tryin' to knock that cross out of your hands, Allergucci! Wasn't he, Angelo? You tell Monsignor Moneybags here what he was tryin' to do!"

"Yes, De Marco is right," came the muted answer. With more than a hundred others, Principato watched as his father's body was returned to the bed. After De Marco's rantings, there was the absolute silence of disbelief in the place, broken only by the enormous grating creak of the nurse's shoes as she moved about the room with a new, post-mortem efficiency, released now from her lethargy of waiting. She arranged the dead man's arms by his side and closed the eyelids. Then she propped a small pillow beneath the chin to hold the mouth closed. Principato saw the shock on his mother's face melt into sudden, incredible tears. She rocked back and forth on her chair, but did not attempt to leave it to go to her reinstated husband. Beside her, Lucy took hold of one of her arms and began rocking in rhythm. After a moment, her head sagged down against the old lady's shoulder. Lucrezia, beside Lucy, wept into an organdy hanky.

Allergucci had not moved. He stood with the crucifix inserted now

264

in his cincture, his hands clasped behind his back, frowning, annoyed, Principato thought: as if he considered the old man was only pretending, to gain a respite from the priest's battling for his soul. Then, slowly, he advanced to the dead man's side.

"He's really dead, then?" he asked Principato. The question seemed to inject life into the audience again. A rash of whispering broke out among the priests and they divided into their conversational knots. Absurdly, the band began playing "Stout-Hearted Men"; De Marco's lackeys headed back to the bar.

"Yes, Monsignor, I'm afraid he is."

"I'm very sorry, Angelo," Allergucci told him.

"You've stolen the moment from me, Monsignor," Principato said quietly. "You hurried his death with that ridiculous salvation act of yours."

"Perhaps it was better that way. What did you expect from him? Some wrenching final moment of communication? It was not possible. You've given him enough of yourself already. Besides, he came back. The Church accepts this. The intent was plainly visible, as this old Jesuit says. Everyone saw he wanted to embrace the crucifix."

"He didn't, Allergucci! He wouldn't! I'm his son and I know him. And I think I'm happy that now, wherever he is, he's free of your dark presence."

"My dark presence? What are you talking about, Angelo? It's been more like my poor sniveling presence seeking an end to being punished all these years."

"Nevertheless, Monsignor," the old Jesuit spoke, "I feel certain that we're all vindicated, no matter what the nature of our past entanglements with the poor deceased. He stood on the brink of his eternity, viewed it with fear, and rushed back to the Church. It was evident in his eyes when he sprang up to embrace the Cross. The grace of salvation had entered his soul by the time he cracked his skull on the floor."

"You listen to me—" Principato began, only to have the nurse interrupt.

"I hate to break up this argument, but there are some letters to be handed out. Mr. Principato asked me to hold them until after his death to make sure that his wife, his son Angelo, the Corrigan family, and Monsignor Allergucci received them."

"What kind of letters?" Allergucci asked. He looked first toward Principato, then his mother, who only continued her silent, shuddering sobs, not bothering to look up. Then he took his envelope from the nurse. "I'm going outside to read this," he said.

"We'll take our letter to the safety of our own home to read it," Mrs. Corrigan said, advancing to snatch the one for her family from the nurse's hand. Then, abruptly, the six Corrigans pocketed their rosaries, took up their coats, and hurried through the lines of priests, not even pausing to look another time at the dead man. As the last of his in-laws slipped through the front door, Principato accepted his letter from the nurse. Silently, he took it, not remembering to mumble a thank you.

The envelope was white, unlike Allergucci's light-blue that had come from his mother's stationery. Principato passed it before the bedside candle and saw the blur of reverse writing done with a red magic marker. Then, abruptly, he walked out of the room, through the priests, into the hallway, already tearing the envelope flap with the same fevered lack of patience with which he opened any letter he knew was not a bill.

He looked for a secret place and chose a powder room, locking the door, then sitting down atop the lid of the toilet. He pulled the letter from the envelope and began to read his father's ragged printing. Each sentence was underscored.

Dear Angelo:

I write you this letter now because I want you always to suspect for the rest of your life that everything may not be as it seems. Right now, you take everything at face value, and at thirty-four, you're too old to take everything at face value.

Search for the rot, and if you can find it, that puts you one up on the next guy. I'll give you an example. For years you've respected me for some stanch defense of principles that everybody calls the Defiance. This is a bunch of bullshit. Thirty-five years ago I got angry at our friend Allergucci for yelling at some kids in mass one Sunday and stomped out of church, telling the congregation I wasn't coming back. This began a convenient hoax.

266

On the one hand, I didn't have to go to mass any more. I only went until then because I loved your mother at the beginning of our marriage and I didn't want to upset her. Also because I was a Communist Party member (along with that crass millionaire De Marco) and wanted to keep up a good front with the peasants in the old neighborhood.

And on the other hand, though I never had any use for the institutional Church, I couldn't stand Allergucci. He was (and is) a vain bastard. Every time I saw him passing out Communion to the flock with that patronizing look on his puss, I wanted to punch him. But, by walking out and refusing to come back that Sunday, I had a much better and more long-term device for humbling him. Allergucci, of course, as a priest, is concerned with the soul and the hereafter. In the beginning, he made the bad mistake of admitting he was guilt-ridden over chasing my uncaring soul out the door and would do anything to atone for this. I suppose you could say by then that I had him by the balls.

So, for the last thirty-five years I've put out the bait and snatched it away, torturing him with telling him I was on the verge of returning to Holy Mother the Church, then changing my mind. This business of confession by telephone was his idea, and although Allergucci has been all over the city in different parishes, and changed his number seven times, he hasn't missed a Friday night yet.

I've been a bit sadistic with him at times. Once I told him I wanted him to meet me at Barnegat Lighthouse and he drove down there, but I couldn't make it. You understand. Another time it was Atlantic City Race Track. Another trick was to invite him for one of our silent dinners in a restaurant on Friday, then feed myself a big steak (in the old days, before Vatican II, of course). Just little things, as you see, but enough to keep him reminded there was a smudge on his ledger.

Finally though, when I die, Allergucci will have his satisfaction, because I intend going back to the Church. I have always intended this, fearing an eternity in hell as I do. Thirty-five years spent punishing Allergucci was a calculated risk, as you can imagine. What if I had been hit and killed by a car, for instance? No confession or absolution. Ow! It gave me cold sweats at night just to think of it. My fear was real, no matter how hard I reasoned with myself. I guess you can't peel off the layers of a Catholic childhood just by wishing it.

But Allergucci doesn't really matter. Let him strangle on his new joy if he takes it all that seriously after I'm dead. What matters is you, Angelo. After you read this and know disillusionment, get angry, kick walls, curse yourself for being duped, then toughen up! Lay down the law to your wife's family and stop running into churches to light candles every three minutes. Your old man had clay feet. Never forget it.

> Eternally,
> Joseph T. Principato,
> your father.

Slowly, Principato folded the long sheet of paper, then stood up from his seat, raised the toilet lid, and began tearing off small pieces, watching them descend like flurries to the water, the red ink running instantly as they became sodden. Then he flushed: the incredible testimony of his father's betrayal circling rapidly on the sudden flood, then disappearing into a maelstrom. Principato turned to regard himself in the wall mirror. There was no suggestion of sorrow in his face now. Only a sudden hardness about the eyes that was not at all theatrical.

He left the powder room and made his way slowly back into De Marco's salon. Priests exited now by twos and threes into the March-morning grayness like tired revelers after a dance. The musicians dragged their instruments behind them. The catering staff sat resting at one cleared end of a long table, breakfasting on sandwiches and coffee. Some of De Marco's drivers lingered, devouring plates of food on the bar. In the center of the room the traitor lay entirely covered with a purple shroud, two candles burning low beside his head. His wife, Lucy, and Lucrezia had left the room. De Marco also. Only Allergucci sat in the line of gilded chairs. The priest looked up as Principato joined him.

"Did he tell you what I think he told you, Angelo?"

"Yes, and you?"

"He merely confirmed what I suppose I already knew. That he had no intention of coming back to the Church. That the efforts of the best part of my priesthood would be a waste."

"He wrote that to you?" Principato instantly saw the possibility that the dead man had left behind him an enigma. "I wonder what he wrote to Mama?"

"Something short and ambiguous, no doubt. Just enough to confuse the poor woman for the rest of her life. He was well aware her intelligence is limited. He used to complain to me about it constantly on confession nights."

Principato said nothing, instead arose and moved into the foyer to open the front door at the sound of marching feet. Outside, on the opposite sidewalk, uniformed children moved by twos from the church around the corner to enter the school for classes. A creeping streetcar cut them momentarily from his vision. Then he was aware of Allergucci at his side.

"I would like to know how many potential Joe Principatos there are marching along in that line right now," the priest said.

"It suddenly occurs to me for the first time that, from the way they're being dumbly marched along, they might all be secretly nursing a spark down there," Principato said.

"Yes, but happily not too many of them will ignite and cause the Church any harm. Only one in a million little schoolchildren anywhere could grow up to have your father's sadistic genius."

"Hmm. Curious. He used that word himself: 'sadistic.' But in an almost humorous sense. He told me about the time he asked you to meet him at Barnegat Lighthouse, then couldn't make it himself. Considering it's you, that must have been pretty funny. Monsignor, I really believe you'll miss him. Having him around to lash you for thirty-five years has probably kept you from drifting into excesses."

"Miss him, Angelo? Never. He was an odious, horrible man who gave me nothing but nightmares. I failed to get him to relent, but sitting inside, reading his letter, I was suddenly filled with a kind of relief that I'm sure no priest ought ever to feel about a man's death. But I'm goddam good and happy that your father is gone."

Allergucci crumpled the letter in his hands, flipping the ball of paper into the gutter beneath the Cord roadster, then turned fullface into Principato's fist that caught him squarely in the forehead, knocking him down the low flight of steps to the sidewalk. His head resounded loudly against the Cord's side and for a moment of passive horror, Principato thought he might have killed the priest. But: wide-eyed and head shaking in disbelief, Allergucci sat slowly up, lifting the end of his cincture to place it childlike in his mouth. Principato hastened down the steps to help him to his feet. The priest pushed him away.

"What have you done, Angelo? With a single punch at a priest you've put yourself further away from the Church in an instant than your father could have done in all his years as nonpractitioner. Seek an act of redemption, Angelo. Seek an act of redemption for this."

As Allergucci backed slowly away from him, the cincture returned to his mouth, Principato became aware that the line of shuffling children across the street had come to a halt and stood staring at him. But not in fright: only a diminutive imitation of Allergucci's own open-mouthed disbelief that someone had done the limit and punched the priest. Two nuns wrapped in shawls stood side by side, the round, unadorned lenses of their eyeglasses reflecting a strong morning sun like twin gold pieces scotched across their eyes so that Principato could not see any expression of horror. One of them stepped down into the street between two cars.

"Are you all right, Father?" she asked Allergucci. "Shall I call the police?"

"No, Sister, everything will be O.K. Please continue taking the children into school."

"Yes, Father." Obediently, the two nuns began the line moving again. Rows of children, gradually ascending in height, marched on, each twosome's eyes glued to Allergucci and Principato for a pro-tracted half block, then suddenly turning the corner. When the last had passed, Principato turned to see his mother standing in the open doorway. There was a look of uncertainty on her face connected with the letter she held out in front of her. He realized she was not aware that her son had punched the monsignor.

"Angelo, what kind of letter did Daddy write to you? Was it funny or was it serious?"

"It was funny, Mama," he said automatically.

270

"Boy, that's good!" she sighed with relief. "I didn't know what he meant here for a minute. Look at this."

She handed the letter to Principato, who opened it as Allergucci stepped to his side.

Dear Angela,
    You have been the best of all my women.

                                    Eternally,
                                    Joseph T. Principato
                                    your husband.

"What do you think of that, Angelo?"

"He was only joking, Mama."

"What did he write to you?"

"He told me to go out and get a nice girl friend with my new Thunderbird."

"He was a very comical man if you knew him long enough," his mother told Allergucci. "What did he say to you, Monsignor?"

"He said he hoped they made me bishop of Las Vegas, Nevada. That was the only diocese worthy of me," the priest responded.

She laughed, although it was the day of her husband's death. "He was a real crackajack. Playing games right up to the end." Then suddenly her face melted into tears again and she turned quickly to re-enter the house, forgetting to take her letter back from Principato.

"Playing games right up to the end," Allergucci echoed. "That bastard put a worm in every piece of wood he ever touched. He couldn't even leave your poor, simple mother in complete peace. He was a beast," the priest raged.

Principato said nothing, instead raised his head at the sudden ringing of bells in the church opposite for the second mass of the day and saw the expected flight of pigeons charged out of their roost, circling the belfry once, holding themselves majestically aloft like the illusions in which Principato had believed until this morning. Then they began their spiral gliding descent to the macadam basketball court to wait for an end to the booming. A savage wish entered him: to have them crash supersonically to the earth, blinded eagles about to spread themselves over the banal space in a carnage of blowing feathers and bloodied meat. So his illusions had died. He walked silently away from the priest and headed toward his car, neglecting to take his coat from De Marco's house.

FOURTEEN

By the next dawn his remorse was intense. He awoke sweating and whimpering from the nightmare of pulverizing Allergucci's face with a bloodied mallet to demand of himself an act of redemption. Then for two hours afterward he walked the streets, wondering what form it should take. Over breakfast he thought of simple confession, leaving it to the impersonal imbiber of sins beyond the screen of the confessional to mete out his punishment. The solution was suddenly so easy that he assailed himself for being always a Principato, a seeker of complexities, and walked into an obscure center city church where a priest was continually in service.

He sat in a back pew for perhaps fifteen minutes thinking up a format. He decided to put the report of punching Allergucci third in line in a gradual build-up in grievousness.

"Bless me, Father, for I have sinned. It's been two weeks since my last confession. I accuse myself of . . . cursing at least thirty times during that period, Father."

Through the screen Principato watched the faint outline of the confessor's head. It nodded twice, swiftly, as if to imply impatience. He was unimpressed then. Everyone curses in our modern, tense society, overburdened with traffic jams and all manner of deadlines. Next.

"Also, Father, I've committed adultery with a married woman." The priest seemed more interested in this. His outline turned slightly toward Principato.

"One time or several times?" he asked.

"Many times, Father," Principato told him. Now he was rehashing his affair with Corky, whom he had seen only once since New Year's. The sin (?) had been confessed and reconfessed from September to January. Principato seized on it now as a stepping stone.

"Have you confessed this sin before?"

"Yes, Father."

"Then what have you done to put an end to it? Are you married yourself?"

"Yes, Father. I have a wife and five children."

"I see. And the other woman, do you continue to see her?"

"Yes."

"Why? How long do you intend letting this thing drag on?"

"Oh, I don't know," Principato spoke impatiently. "Until it's finished, I suppose. This isn't what I came to tell you anyhow."

"What did you come to tell me?" the lips in profile asked through the screen.

Principato took a deep breath, noticing for the first time that the white body of Christ on a crucifix above the screen was stained with penitent women's lipstick.

"I punched a priest," he said very rapidly. Through the screen came a gasp an instant later. The head turned completely toward him. There was a silence while a shaking Principato assumed the confessor was somehow trying to piece together his criminal features.

"But how did you come to punch a priest?"

The shock in the voice was unconcealed. Considering another word futile, Principato began rising from the kneeler, when the screen was whipped back and a thick-veined hand shot through the opening to anchor him down by his lapels.

"Wait a minute! Just a minute, penitent!" the voice said. "I've got to hear more of this story. After years of waiting since the seminary for the big one to walk into the box, I'm not letting you go that easily."

"That bad, huh?" Principato judged as the priest withdrew his

274

hand and slid closed the screen. He became instantly calmer on realizing the cleric was not about to exact an Hebraic vengeance for his transgression against the priest cult. A fist of that size would have spattered his face, he believed.

"I had a murderer in here about five years back."

"Do I fit into that same category, Father?"

"He knelt right where you're kneeling now."

"The priest I punched needed punching."

"It was the same way with the other one. He insisted the guy he murdered needed murdering, right up to the bitter end. I couldn't give him absolution, of course."

"Stop drawing parallels, Father. It's not the same thing. This priest hunted my father's soul for thirty-five years. Yesterday, when the old man died, his last act was to spring up in bed and try to knock the cross from his tormentor's hands. Afterward, this priest even slandered the dead. He deserved that sock he got."

"Is this the real truth?" the confessor asked. "Could your father, raised a Catholic, I take it, be so contemptuous of his eternity that he wanted to die without the sacrament and absolution?"

"Yes. . . . No. . . . Well . . ." Well, what did it matter? The old man had left three versions of the truth behind. Principato knew his own, and was reciting Allergucci's in the confessional. And who knew what the Corrigans had been willed?

"Do you feel contrition then?" the confessor asked.

"Yes, for violating the office of priest, but not for hitting the person in it. Can you see your way clear to making a distinction in this case and giving me absolution?"

"No. The person is the embodiment of the office. You must see the two as one. I can't apply absolution to higher and lower planes as it were, allowing you forgiveness for meddling with the sanctity of holy orders while you went right on hating the man who fulfilled these orders."

"If you knew this particular priest, you'd go on hating him, too."

"That's irrelevant. You're in mortal sin. You'll fry in hell for this if you don't expiate your guilt."

"Then I've got to leave you, Father," Principato ended, springing neatly off the kneeler and through the door as the screen zipped back and the hand rushed through again, grasping futilely in the air for his lapels.

He paused for an instant at the church entrance to look back, and saw the confessor emerging from his cubicle to confront a line of startled penitents.

"You are all forgiven and absolved," he told them, making the sign of the cross on the run, now forward toward the door where Principato stood frozen. In a moment he sprang through to the outside, flying down the church steps to touch the sidewalk as the priest plunged through the door.

"Penitent! Penitent, wait! I want to talk to you!"

Principato tore north toward Market Street with the confessor in pursuit. At Walnut, he ran against the light, neatly dodging between two cars, convinced of the possibility of his escape until he saw in a storefront reflection that the priest had hiked his cassock up to his waist. The thick-veined hand descended on his shoulder between Chestnut and Market. Principato idled to a stop, his breath coming out in great, heaving gasps, and he turned to face the confessor. The man was six-one at least, and in his late thirties, with rugged good looks that suggested that he did off-season jobs as a lumberjack or construction worker. His only concession to exertion was the slight flaring of the nostrils as the quickened air passed in and out. His gaze rested coldly on his captive's face. Curious pedestrians gathered about them now.

"I was with the Marines in Korea," the priest told him. "I played four years of football in college."

"Yes," Principato answered, not doubting.

"Which way were you going, penitent?"

"The other way, actually. My car is south of the church."

"Let's walk there," the priest said, releasing Principato and slipping into a jacket he carried with him. They marched militarily back along the route of the chase, turning off one block before the church in case anyone was out looking for the confessor.

"Aren't you violating the secrecy of the confessional, Father?" Principato asked. "You're not supposed to leave the box and chase after someone like that."

"Let's worry about the technicalities later, penitent. I don't even want to know your name. My concern is to learn why you can't muster up sufficient contrition to leave that box on your own with my absolution. You've got a soul there to worry about, buster," he said, jabbing Principato's breastbone with a backward thrust of his thumb.

"All the world trying to nail down a Principato's soul."

"What was that, penitent?"

"Nothing. My family motto, that's all. Here's my car, Father. This is where we part."

"Not so fast, fella. My time is yours and God's. And I'm working to get you back on his team. Where are we off to now?" the confessor asked, springing into the unlocked De Soto before Principato himself.

"To a crematorium then, if you insist on coming along. My father's body is being disposed of at one o'clock this afternoon."

"You're kidding. Cremated? Who decided on that?"

"My father himself."

"Hmmm. This guy must've been some fumbler."

"He was better on the long passes than the short ones," Principato said, sliding the car out into traffic and not really knowing what he intended in saying this. But the priest found meaning in it, and as they moved west on Spruce Street, he extemporized in a sports commentator's lightning jargon about carrying the ball for God: the playing field equaled life; the opposition was the satanic host; a touchdown, external happiness. Crossing the Schuylkill, he spoke of the pollution of the spirit. At the Penn campus, the wolves of secularism. Beyond this, in the West Philly Negro districts, indifference to salvation came up for its turn. By the time they reached the crematorium, Principato decided the only level on which he need fear this priest was the brute physical. The man was a nut.

"So, this is what a crematorium looks like," the confessor said, a keen edge of wonder coming into his voice for the first time as Principato halted the car. "Pretty fancy, let me tell you."

It was 12:45. They stood a long moment before the massive façade of mourning-purple stained glass splashed across with a confusion of Biblical imagery in inlaid bands of copper on brass, then decided they had time for a walk about the near-by New Testament gardens. Principato found himself disquieted. Some Catholic forepart of his mind had no use for this place. The dead went into the ground. The sheer white aspect of the crematorium behind the façade, with its two far-reaching, rocket-shaped stacks trickling a gray smoke suggested to him somehow that fitful spirits got launched from this place, ever to roam the Philadelphia atmosphere, never to settle down in peace again. Apparently, the confessor thought so, too. He discoursed upon the Ash Wednesday ritual and seemed to long petulantly after the missing dust.

They strolled past a plaster reproduction of Capharnum and a shoulder-level elevation, nondescript except for some resemblance to a camel's hump, that was labeled the Mount of the Beatitudes. Beyond this, in Gethsemane, Niccolò and the blind Ardico sat side by side on a bench. The gravedigger stared morosely at a concrete sleeping Jesus. Ardico tapped his cane steadily on the flagstone, his head turning at the sound of their approach.

"These two guys look like they were sent back to the showers a long time ago," the priest whispered.

"I know them. One's my uncle and the blind guy's his neighbor. They're both on God's team," Principato said drily.

"I don't doubt it. Not for a second. What I mean is that not everybody's tough enough to play offense ball. The meek are also blessed. Somebody's got to be water boy and medic, you know."

"I know. Hello, Niccolò. Hello, Ardico," Principato greeted them.

"Angelo, Angelo," Niccolò mumbled, lurching to his feet to face them, his eyes dilated and atrabilious in the gray mask of his face. "Why didn't you show up this morning for the reading of your old man's will?"

"I was busy in church."

"Angelo, that father of yours, he was insane. I mean it, Angelo. He didn't leave money to Charlie, the locker-room man at the San Giorgio. He left every goddam thing he had to the Archdiocese of Philadelphia, except for that car he gave you. Even the house he gave them. Not a dime for your mother or Lucy or Rocco, much less me. Can you imagine it, Angelo? Those priests live in air-conditioned houses and drive big black cars. Ardico and me are doomed. We'll never get out of that hole we live in, now."

"I used to dream about our apartment in Asbury Park," Ardico said in a phlegm-coated voice that suggested he had been crying. "I could even hear the surf pounding down on the shore. And when you opened the door, it would smell fresh like the sea, instead of like everything was rotting."

"I'm sorry for you, Ardico." Principato spoke mutedly, somehow unaffected by the news that the old man had left nothing to him.

"Angelo, how could he do it?" Niccolò begged. "How could he go on for most of his life firin' a cannon against the Church, then turn around and leave them all he owned?"

Niccolò was crying now: lavish squeezes of the gall and bitter within him streaking down his gray cheeks while he shuddered with sobbing. Blind Ardico wept beside him, leaning heavily on his cane. Principato was conscious for the first time that the two wore identical red hunting caps with the ear flaps tied beneath their chins.

"How blameworthy can the dead man be?" the confessor asked. "It sounds to me like he ended up on God's team, after all. As a booster. It takes money to keep God's boys in uniform, you know. They need transportation to and from the games, good grub, et cetera. You ought to rejoice in this new addition to the Booster Club."

"Fuck God and the Booster Club!" Ardico spat savagely.

"What did you say?" the jock priest demanded threateningly, advancing on the blind man.

"You heard him, padre," Niccolò spoke. "If you knew the four-flusher that just got into that Booster Club of yours, you'd probably decide it didn't mean much to belong to it, after all."

"I thought you said these two guys were on God's team," the priest turned accusingly on Principato. "They are like hell. They're spiteful bad losers. A clear example of poor sportsmanship. Stand up straight, you two, and dry your eyes!"

The confessor stepped between Niccolò and Ardico and, grasping each one by the upper arm, yanked them into ramrod stiffness. "Now you guys come along with us to the front of this factory, and when the dead man's coffin arrives, I want to see you both smiling at the sight of it. You might've lost the game, but you lost out to God's team, and that's no third-rate outfit, you know. You can be proud you even made it to the finals. You too, penitent. Come along."

Stupefied, Niccolò and Ardico allowed themselves to be urged out of Gethsemane, past the Mount of the Beatitudes and the Temple at Capharnum to the broad sidewalk before the mourning-purple façade. Principato brought up the rear. Almost immediately, a gray limousine swept up beside them, unloading the old lady and Lucy and Lucrezia and De Marco. An unobtrusive black station wagon bearing the old man's coffin edged across the background and to the side of the building. The newly arrived four arrayed themselves against the limousine. Predictably, De Marco spoke first.

"Who's this priest, Angelo?"

"He's my confessor."

"He's not needed. Old Joe Principato, the Defiant One, is going into the flames just the way he wanted. Nice and quiet. Send him home."

"You send him home if you can," Principato responded, smiling.

"Who's this guy?" the confessor asked, releasing Niccolò and Ardico. "Which team is he on?"

"Who's playing?" De Marco asked, his eyes narrowed. Principato saw that the construction mogul was unafraid.

"God's boys and the satanic host. Who are you with, fellow?"

"Today we're betting the satanic host, priest. The dead man was a long-time team member, by the way."

"That's not the way I heard the story. Any man who leaves all his money to the archdiocese is playing for God, in my book."

"Yeah, he's the whole goddam team," Lucrezia said. "That crumb! Not a dime for his wife or kids! We ought to dump his body in the river and let it float out to sea so we can at least save some money right here. It costs a fortune to cremate somebody."

"It certainly is a very impressive place anyhow," Principato's mother said. Her son had watched her closely: she had accepted the jock priest immediately on debarking from the car simply because he was a cleric. The nearness of priests always comforted her. Now her mind ranged unaffected somewhere beyond the passion of the argument, her awed eyes traveling slowly back and forth across the façade.

"It's worthy of him," De Marco said. "It's worthy of any man who kept his anger fanned for thirty-five years like old Joe Principato."

"His thirty-five-year anger doesn't hold a candle to mine right now," Lucrezia turned on the mogul. "It isn't hard enough trying to make a living down there in Florida, so now I inherit the responsibility for my sister and her three kids because of that hero of yours."

"You're free, Lucrezia," Principato told her sharply. "You're not responsible for anyone. Why don't you get in that car and leave now, and we'll carry on with the cremation."

"Angelo, forgive me. You know me. I'm such a dramatic woman," she purred, instantly changed, advancing to kiss his stony cheek. Today's contact lenses were mourning-purple, like the crematorium front. They rode high on the angry waters of her eyes, and Principato half-expected them to pop outward from the pressure of her furies. He felt a hand slide into his overcoat pocket and instinctively—a vestigial memory from childhood—followed after it. Lucrezia had deposited twenty dollars this time in the midst of his manhood. Without a word, Principato handed it back to her.

"You're becoming so strong, Angelo," she said. "It seems like since the old man died you've received all his . . . well, 'bigness,' is the best word."

"Now that's the Christian way," the confessor said. "Shake hands and make up. Let's all go inside as teammates of God and pay homage to the dead Booster Club member."

Magnificently, pastorally, he swept the four Principatos, Lucrezia, Ardico, and De Marco up the crematorium steps with the momentum of his charge, and through the bronze temple portal that was held open by a pin-striped receptionist who led them toward highly burnished, also bronze doors set in a sheer marble wall that suggested the inner sanctum lay behind. Real torches burned at either side of the doors. At the touch of a button they opened onto an elevator.

"In what parish was the funeral mass read for the deceased?" the priest asked when the panels closed behind them. His voice boomed and echoed in the bronze cavern with the quality of a monologue in space. The elevator lurched and started almost imperceptibly upward toward the slowly changing projection of a universe of stars that hovered over their heads. Eternity, doubtless. Principato's mother, holding his arm, gazed raptly upward.

"There wasn't any funeral mass, Father," Niccolò told him simply.

"Wha-a-a-t? No-o-o m-a-a-ss?" The long vowels bounced and ricocheted furiously about their container. The confessor turned a slow circle at the center, holding them all in an incredulous stare from the advantage of his height.

"He didn't want any mass, priest!" De Marco boomed and echoed in his turn. "No mass, no last rites, no priests, no nuns, no confession, no Rome, no Pope, no Jerusalem, nothing. He had the Defiance in him. He didn't need the Christian myth like the rest of us cowards. He kept the Gregorian calendar because it was convenient. That's all. Jesus Christ was just another John Doe to old Joe Principato. He was a free thinker, and he wasn't afraid!"

Slap! The sound of the priest's flat hand striking De Marco's leathery jowl was like the crack of a rifle fired in an intense cold. The mogul reacted reflexively, the far-gone remembrance of some old boxing ability lashing out at his assailant. The confessor dodged the fist, then grasped the old man tightly by the wrists. The only noise in the elevator was De Marco's sudden harsh breathing. Disbelief had muted everyone else. Even blind Ardico seemed to understand what had happened.

"I could have you bumped off for that, priest," De Marco said.

"I could bump your head on this wall a couple of times, imp! How dare you slander the worthy dead! This man left all his money to the archdiocese, didn't he? That redeems him completely in my book. I'm going to preach the best damn eulogy over his coffin that Philadelphia has ever heard."

"No eulogy was called for," the pin-striped receptionist reminded them from the open doorway. The elevator had halted, the universe of stars disappeared, and the doors parted to reveal a high-ceilinged, white-walled room broken irregularly by slashes, spheres, and Rorschach splats of more mourning-purple stained glass, clustered with a menagerie of religious symbolry, intended, Principato supposed, to show the nondenominational inoffensiveness of the place. The old man's coffin stood atop a carved rock altar that connected to a long chute sloping gently into a double bronze portal like the outer door of a tabernacle that was set into the wall. Clusters of grapes and sacrificial lambs bulged on its surface. Behind was the cleansing fire, then.

"I'm still going to preach," the jock priest affirmed. Then, facing Principato, he was instantly apologetic. "Unless, of course, you didn't want me to, penitent. After all, the deceased was your father. Do I have your permission?"

"Yes, if you like, Father," Principato told him. He was not afraid: his certainty that the confessor could physically terrorize the mismatched mourners with impunity was transcended by his intuition that some great hand, spry with vindictive humor, was sketching out this scene now. De Marco, the maggot, was catching his; Lucrezia, Niccolò, and Ardico were about to suffer through a sportscaster's panegyric over the object of their hatred, or face possible pulverization at the hands of the priest. Only his mother seemed appeased: Principato could tell she was eager to hear her husband eulogized.

The pin-striped mortician seated them in a row of chairs before the coffin. He seemed suddenly rattled and effeminate, his voice quivering whole octaves over this lapse in perfection. "I'm sorry. I was made to understand there was no last service intended. Nothing has been prepared."

"Then what were you going to do?" the confessor demanded testily.

"Well, in these odd cases, the usual procedure is for the mourners to contemplate the coffin in attentive silence for, say, ten minutes, before it's caused to move along the Bridge to Eternity rampway and through the Gate of Heaven portals to its final disposal.

"Hmmm," the confessor grunted, visibly impressed. "I knew it was all symbolic. But if the ramp is the Bridge to Eternity and the doors the Gate of Heaven, what's the rock under the coffin?"

"That's the Altar of Living Attrition."

"Slick. Very slick," the confessor said, walking slowly the length of the rampway toward the doors. "How is the coffin caused to move toward the Gate of Heaven?"

"The ramp is actually a conveyor belt. Three quarters of the way along the coffin intercepts an electric eye that opens the gate. You can see from the imagery on the doors that we've done everything possible to encompass all religious denominations so that the passing out, as we like to call it, would have no heavy overtones of any favored group.

"Today's passing out is Roman Catholic," the priest said flatly. "Do you have any Catholic music to play before I begin preaching?"

"The 'Ave Maria'? Is that O.K.?"

"No, too common. What else?"

"Not much else. Not too many Catholics do it this way," the receptionist shrugged. "Wait! How about 'Pavane for a Dead Infanta'?"

"What's that?"

"Spanish, sort of Catholic, very morbid. You'll like it, I think."

The attendant moved mincingly off to the record closet while the confessor took a chair, moved it apart from the mourners and sat down to stare fixedly at the coffin. In moments the melancholy coils of the "Pavane" began a slow unwinding on the room. Principato's mother was instantly affected. New tears rushed happily down her face. Beside her, Lucy, ever silent, now gazed into the distance far beyond the limits of the crematorium. The curtain of her black lace veil, half drawn, bisected the sepia smoothness of her cheek. Principato noticed for the first time that his sister had gray hairs among the dark.

Lucrezia poked his arm. "Boy, you live long enough with this family and you see it all," she whispered. "Whatever happened to the simple wops of yore? Look what we've come to: an everybody's-religion crematorium run by a faggot undertaker where we're going to hear a eulogy given by your pal, Superpriest. Where did you pick this guy up, anyhow?"

"He was hearing my confession this morning and he chased me out of the box and all the way uptown to Market Street."

"I don't believe it. No, wait! I do believe it. I know who's son you are, Angelo. I'll believe anything you tell me now. Old 'Viva la Defiance' is dead and somebody has to inherit the family madness after all."

"Have you no shame?" the confessor demanded of Lucrezia. He stood and silenced the "Pavane" with a wave of his hand, then positioned himself behind the coffin, still glaring at Principato's aunt, resting one arm on its burnished surface.

"Dearly beloved in Christ," he began. "We are gathered together in this place of indiscriminate leavetakings to bid good-by to one

284

who, though not an actual rough-and-tumble player on God's team, still found his place before his death in the no less honored rank of avid supporters. A generous Booster Club affiliate lies here being eulogized then. Trust that the Great Coach is well pleased in this man.

"During his lifetime, it has been said, he entertained a particular devil who thrashed about madly in his soul, overpowering him at times, causing him to be known to his perplexed family and friends as the Defiant One. Certain rebellious acts, anticlerical, even anti-Christian, have been alluded to at the mention of his name. Hissing, rancorous blasphemy came from within him, though his lips did not move.

"Yet here, today, we find him in peaceful repose. Is this not strange, dear brothers in Christ? Truly the workings of God are unfathomable and unaccountably slow. But the case is clear: this tortured soul, once in the power of a malevolent spirit, has left all his worldly possessions to God's one, holy, Catholic, and apostolic church at the end of his life. God's players will get their new pads and whirlpool bath, so to speak. The deceased is truly redeemed.

"But how do we see him now at the hour of his particular judgment? He waits along the avenue of the afterlife until the old athletic-department station wagon picks him up and carries him swiftly to the fieldhouse; the driver, brilliant in angelic radiance, is silent for the entire drive, giving the dead one neither reason to hope nor reason to despair. Arrived at the fieldhouse, he passes into the stadium and sees the game in progress. He is alert, tremulous over the notion of judgment, noticing everything about him. God's boys are uncommonly beautiful and well-made. Their eyes are stoically calm with the certainty of their righteousness. Their uniforms are white, as are their projecting wings, and both are unsullied and sparkle even though they hustle the ball back and forth through a slough of offal that the field has become. So foul and tainted is this field, dearly beloved, that it must be confessed even the yard-line markings are only a guess, despite the fact they are constantly being limed.

"He sees also the satanic host. How different they are from God's players, my fellow mourners! They are dark and wizened, fiercely ugly, dangerous little dirty fighters with horny projections springing from their shoulders, elbows, knees, and calves. Imagine in horror with me to what use these lethal spikes are put on the line. The deceased is appalled. His sense of fair play scandalized, he wishes suddenly that all of his willed wealth might be used to buy new shoulder pads, helmets, and jocks for God's boys. He stands and observes a play at the forty-yard line: the heavenly host loses yardage. Despite himself, the dead man weeps at the outrage. Need we ask further to know where his true feelings lie?

"Then his guide's hand touches his shoulder and he turns to see the Great Coach himself pacing worriedly back and forth only ten yards away. Michael the line coach, and Peter the backfield coach, are in a tight huddle, also wearing intent faces. Imagine then, beloved, the deceased's sudden new fear. Will the Great Coach choose to acknowledge him? Will he proffer his hand for the traditional grip test, in view of the dead one's past reputation for slandering God's team? The moment is tense, the real action shifted from the field to the sidelines. Across the scrimmage, the opposition coach, too horrible, brethren, to describe, leers at the shaking deceased. Peter and Michael, understanding the importance, raise their huddled heads to watch. Suddenly the Great Coach stops his pacing, holding the newcomer in his fearsome manly gaze. Then the corners of his mouth relax their tension. He marches smiling toward his booster: 'I'm glad you made it, pal. We got a tough game on our hands today.'"

The jock priest was finished. Dramatically, he lay his hands palms downward atop the coffin, staring deeply through the wood at the man he had never met, his lips moving in a silent good-by. Beside Principato, the black-clad Italianate chorus of his mother, Lucy, and Lucrezia howled furiously into raised handkerchiefs. Ardico wept. Niccolò wept also in real sorrow or at the hopeless irony this day's events contained. Only Principato and De Marco were dry-eyed, though admittedly milked.

Then the confessor slashed his arm through the air, and the now red-eyed attendant re-entered the record closet. The "Pavane for a Dead Infanta" continued from mid-note. Somewhere a motor, high-pitched and whirring like a far-off dental drill, sprang to life, and the coffin edged slowly from the Altar of Living Attrition onto the rampway. Eight pairs of eyes watched vacuously as the priest, walking ponderously beside, with one hand resting on the casket, escorted the new booster toward the Gate of Heaven. Smoothly creeping, the box moved for an eternity before Principato until its passing tripped the electric eye that caused the bronze gates to spring open. Inside the furnace, instead of the expected purity of white light, was an incredible blackness. The coffin head inched through the doors, settling with a small lurch on some platform perhaps. The confessor relinquished his grip, standing still now, gravely waving farewell to his friend. Then the doors began their slow closing over the inner darkness.

Clunk! Good-by, you fraudulent old bastard, Principato thought distantly.

FIFTEEN

"Viva la Defiance!" De Marco screamed against the background of funeral music. He leapt suddenly from his seat, jumping and cavorting before the line of mourners like a stubby, overweight cheerleader, flailing the air with his fist. But his attempt at firing their bloods was ineffectual: the jock priest did not even bother to turn around.

"Knock it off, De Marco," Lucrezia said.

"We should never forget him for what he was! He was a great man!"

"A prince," Lucrezia commented, then quietly rose, aiding her sister to her feet. The others followed, moving toward the star-domed elevator. The attendant walked after them, waited a moment to ascertain that Principato and the confessor would descend later, and eased the doors closed.

"Viva la Defiance!" came booming and echoing up the shaft twice in quick succession followed by the cymbal-clashing effect of communal abuse being heaped on De Marco. Someone actually hammered the cabin wall. Afterward the construction mogul was silent.

"I can't stand that expensive-looking little guy who was doing all the shouting," the priest said to Principato.

"I haven't got much use for him either."

288

Both were standing now, leaning on opposite sides of the Bridge to Eternity, studying the inoffensive lambs and grape clusters on the Gate of Heaven doors.

"He reminds me of a gangster. The type you could pretty well figure was doing a little game fixing," the confessor continued, convinced of his own reasoning.

"That was exactly his racket after a fashion," Principato said.

"Well, it had to be something like that. How did you like my preaching, by the way?"

"It was a fine eulogy."

"He was a great man. Left all his money to the archdiocese after all."

"Yes."

The elevator returned abruptly and the attendant beckoned them inside. Principato heard the long-expected muted woosh! sound of the pyre flame being turned on as the doors closed behind them and they descended.

Outside, the old Jesuit Corrigan stood beside a new white Thunderbird convertible studying the mourning-purple façade. Inside the car sat one of the beefy Corrigan lackeys.

"Pato," the priest called, hobbling across the broad sidewalk, the frills of his tattered biretta flouncing in the wind.

"Your poor father is gone then?" the priest asked sadly. His Corrigan spaniel eyes were dark-ringed with fatigue.

"Going," Principato guessed, looking toward the tops of the twin stacks where a light-gray smoke began belching into the overcast sky.

"That's what it looks like, huh?" the Jesuit asked, as intrigued as Principato.

"It's my first time too, Father."

The three watched through a long silence. The smoke rose sluggishly, actually curving and spreading as it reached the layers of smog overhanging the city.

"I wanted to talk to you about something, Pato," the Jesuit said.

"What's on your mind, Father?"

"Can we be alone? Who is this priest?"

"This is my confessor, Father. He stays. He's a participant to all my affairs."

"Very well," the old Corrigan conceded, favoring the other priest with only a glance. "The family wants you to accept the keys to this new automobile as a reconciliation present, Pato."

"I already have a T-Bird, Father. My old man gave it to me before he died."

"We knew that, Pato. But this is newer and consequently better. Two years newer in fact."

"What's going on here, Mr. Pato?" the jock priest demanded. "Which team is this guy on?"

"On God's team, obviously. Can't you tell by his uniform?"

"That doesn't crack any ice with me. I have a difficult time believing a priest of God would go about offering Thunderbird gift cars as a bribe. Where does he get his money?"

"None of your business, Father," the old Jesuit said. "There's something unfinished-looking about you in that cassock that makes me suspect you may not be a priest at all."

"How dare you, Jesuit!" the confessor snarled. His lips trembled, veins stood out in his forehead.

"*Introibo ad altare dei?*" the Corrigan asked, his voice adding a question mark to the now unused Latin of the mass.

"*Ad deum qui laetificat, juventutem meam,*" the jock priest responded instantly. Principato drew away from the contest.

"*Kyrie eleison*": Corrigan.

"*Christe eleison*": confessor.

"*Christe eleison*": Corrigan.

"*Kyrie eleison*": confessor.

"*Suscipiat Domine sacrificium . . .*" the Jesuit invited.

". . . *ad manibus tuus, ad laudem et gloriam nominis sui. Ad utilitatem quoque nostrum totiusque ecclaisiae suae sanctae,*" they ended in unison, the one narrowly watching the other for a slip-up. The jock priest spoke a better-accented Latin, though, and Cynthia's uncle conceded with a shrug of his shoulders and turned to Principato. "What do you think of our little offer, Pato?"

"Just like that I'm supposed to accept your present, Father, and come back to living with Cynthia?"

"There's more."

290

"What more?"

"The family has decided you should know about Raymond."

"Raymond? What happened to Raymond, Father?" He was keen with the hunger of eleven years to know of the closet skeleton's deed. Instinctively, he looked skyward again to the stacks where the gray smoke still moved sluggishly out, somehow regretting that his father had not lived long enough to satisfy the curiosity that had restlessly gnawed at him, too.

"Raymond was not an ordained priest, Pato. He was only a brother of the order. And he had the terrible misfortune to fall into the clutches of a Belgian trollop over there in Africa. She was an atheist, Pato," he said gravely, looking straight into Principato's face as if the matter might be already completely understood. "She attacked and destroyed to Raymond's satisfaction all the tenets of our holy religion: the divinity of Christ, the Immaculate Conception, papal infallibility, and so on. The real problem was that poor Raymond's faith had never been tested. I daresay before he met this woman he had never personally known a non-Catholic. And he had no intelligence, Pato. I remember those letters he wrote to us, a man shedding off his thirty years of Catholic upbringing like clothes before a bath simply because this woman told him his beliefs were erroneous. No counterarguments came from him at all.

"Anyhow, he left his mission area with this woman and went to South Africa, where they were married. Both became South African citizens and occasionally we received photographs of their children from Durban. That's the story, Pato, as far as we know it. He is, I guess, still living, though he'd be somewhat older than myself. At least we haven't heard any news to the contrary."

"The sad tale of a weak link in God's line," the jock priest said immediately, shaking his head in pity.

"Shut up, you," the old Jesuit ordered.

"It's lucky for you, Father, that we're both clerics with a common cause," the confessor said.

"Common cause or not, I've got three nephews, any one of whom could probably pound the hell out of you, that I'd like to unleash at this moment."

"You don't scare me, Jesuit. As Mr. Pato's confessor, I think I have a perfect right to interpret for him an obvious moral lesson. Isn't that right, penitent?"

Right, mused Principato. There would be no way of shutting him up anyhow if he had something on his mind. But the moral lesson hardly mattered. What did matter was the Corrigan secret, kept from him with incredible skill for eleven long years. Not even an inkling of what it involved. His father, floating on high, would have been pleased to know he had partially figured it out: there had been a woman, only she was white instead of black; there had been a runaway as the old man suggested, though it was to near-by South Africa instead of France.

"Why did you decide to tell me all this, Father?" Principato asked.

"Partly because of the events of the last several months and partly because of the letter we received after your father's death, Pato. There is a need to build a bridge of trust between our two families."

"What did he tell you in his letter?"

"He told us he had no intention whatsoever of returning to the Church. A strange man, Pato. A strange thing to write also since his invitation to his death extravaganza gave us a promise that he would make his peace with God."

"Then it seems you Corrigans have lost, Father," Principato said, a smile at the corners of his mouth.

"Not so, Pato. Not so at all. We saw the end. The intent was there. When your father lunged for the cross in the monsignor's hands, there was the fear in his eyes of a man who had looked across the brink of his eternity for the first time."

"That's not right, Father. He wanted to knock that cross from Allergucci's hands. I know my own father. He wouldn't back down on his word. He told me he wouldn't in his letter to me and he didn't," Principato lied.

"As you choose to believe, Pato. We're satisfied at any rate with our interpretation."

"An old Corrigan dodge, Father. You see what you want to see and hear only what you want to hear. I know your tribe."

"Nevertheless it's comforting, Pato. Now will you be coming back to us?"

"Not as long as you believe that my father recanted."

"Pato, why be difficult? You believe what you want to believe and we'll believe our side, and let the marriage go on. The family has bought you a nice new Thunderbird automobile for your return. Cynthia and the children are so anticipating your arrival."

"Not until I get a signed, notarized statement that all of you, my children included, are convinced my father was trying to knock down that cross, had no intention of rejoining the Church, and, in accordance with the expected rewards of our Catholic rigidity, is now roasting in hell."

"That's not possible, Pato."

"It's the reconciliation condition, Father."

"Take the car at least, Pato. Think about it for a while. More presents are possible."

"Take the car," the jock priest nudged him. "We can always give it to the Church if you don't need it."

"No—keep your car. Good-by, Father," he told the old Jesuit, whose spaniel eyes were suddenly filled with the rarely seen Corrigan incredulousness that the white jewel of a Thunderbird had not brought down its man. Principato marched abruptly off toward the De Soto. The confessor followed him, mumbling that impracticality had no place on God's team either, along with a lot of other things.

SIXTEEN

There was no getting rid of the jock priest.

Principato offered to drop him off again at his confessional box, but the cleric refused, intending to cling tenaciously until his penitent, newly estranged from God and the team, might be safely returned to the bench. For the price of one soul, he seemed willing to let his pastoral duties slide indefinitely. That night he slept in Principato's hotel room, rolling himself wearily into a blanket on the floor for the sleep of the just after an hour of vigorous preaching, and a second hour of even more vigorous calisthenics, in part of which a brittle Principato was obliged to join.

The next morning they drove to the North Philadelphia Station to say good-by to Principato's mother and Lucy and Lucrezia, who were going to board a train for Florida. They found the three women standing alone on the platform, the old lady turning a slow circle in her preoccupation with surveying the North Philly ugliness. Perhaps for the last time, Principato thought as he solemnly kissed her cheek. She greeted the jock priest effusively, grateful for his eulogy of the day before.

Above the repetitive row housing hung yesterday's gray smog, this day's atmosphere still too humid to move it away. Below them, a slow river of traffic moved up Broad Street behind a huge crane riding a flat-bed trailer. The five watched silently to see if it would pass beneath the station bridge. In moments the boom appeared, unretarded. The majestic lumbering procession continued.

"Whew! I didn't think he was going to make it," Lucrezia said.

"Yes, but they always do, Lucrezia," his mother told her. "Every time Daddy and me would be out riding in the car and we'd see a tractor trailer heading into an underpass, I'd cover my eyes. But you know they always make it. Do you ever remember seeing a truck stuck under a bridge like that, Angelo?"

"No, Mama, I don't."

"I don't either." Then she turned and looked off toward the row of rusted storage tanks near Lehigh Avenue. "I haven't been up here in a long time, Angelo. Daddy and me used to go to see the baseball games over there at Connie Mack Stadium. Not any more, though. You know, when you get to be a certain age, different things help make you die a little faster, I think. Like when the Athletics went to Kansas City. Your papa really took that hard."

"A tragic moment in Philadelphia sports history," the confessor assured her.

"I didn't know the old man liked baseball so much, Mama," Principato pressed on.

"Well, he really didn't like the game, but he liked to go and watch the crowds. He could put a cigar in his mouth and watch a mob longer than anyone I've ever met. And he liked to bet the games, too. He used to bet football and the horses and basketball and hockey. And the elections. He was mad for betting the elections."

"I remember," Principato told her.

"There's nothing wrong with betting, as I see it," the priest said. "It's fixing a game that boils my blood."

"He didn't have anything to do with that, Father," the old woman insisted. "We didn't know any gangsters, anyhow."

"How about that little guy that did all the shouting at the crematorium yesterday, Mrs. Pato?"

"No, he's construction, Father. De Marco and Company. He might have used a little shoddy lumber in his day, but he never had anything to do with the rackets."

"That's hard to believe, Mrs. Pato. What with racketeers and crooked politicians all about us, it's a wonder your friend De Marco didn't get his thumb into the pie, too."

"Impossible. De Marco doesn't trust politicians," she said simply. "By the way, Angelo, do you still belong to the Young Democrats?"

"No, Mama, not for a couple of years now."

"Well you ought to join again," she said, reaching up to brush something from his cheek. "I wouldn't let the Republicans get their pointy-toed shoes in the door of this town again, Angelo."

"Yes, Mama," he answered dutifully. Not to "let the Republicans get their pointy-toed shoes in the door to Philadelphia again" was a private campaign slogan she had come up with during the last mayoral election. Principato guessed that, of all things in Philadelphia, his mother would miss her committeewoman status most.

"How do you usually vote, Father?" she asked the priest bluntly.

"Usually Democratic, Mrs. Pato."

"But not always?"

"No. Occasionally I have voted Republican."

"Hmmm." She regarded him narrowly for a long moment. "Anyhow, there were other things I wanted to advise you about, Angelo. Do you remember what else I said I wanted to tell Angelo, Lucrezia? Lucy?"

"Something about the Thunderbird, I think," Lucy said.

"Oh, yes. What are you going to do with Daddy's T-bird, Angelo? If you don't want to drive it because it's too close to his death, then at least have it put in storage someplace. The house is up for sale and there won't be anybody to keep an eye on it. Some kids might slit the top and try to steal the radio."

"All right, Mama. I'll have it put in storage."

"Good."

She lifted her eyes to the platform roof, fingers to her temples, perhaps trying to recall what else she meant to tell him. For his part, Principato thought of going, fleeing the station and leaving his mother to the care of the jock priest who had preached the eulogy that so pleased her, before her departure included hysterics at the sudden sight of the gleaming silver cars that would bear them off. And there must be hysterics: Principato was certain of it. Not even the special magic of the confessor could waylay that.

"That's a nice bag, Mama. What's in it? Your bathing suit?" he joked. The sight of the red-flowered straw beach bag against the background of an ugly March day had distracted him all the while. She sat now on a baggage truck.

"Daddy's in there, Angelo," she told him, surprised that he didn't already know.

"What do you mean, Mama?"

"I mean his ashes. The mortician brought them over early this morning. Look." She lifted the bag from the baggage truck and opened the top to show him a nondescript gray container like a small pretzel can swaddled in a black shawl.

"Mama! Mama! Holy Jesus!" His eyes suddenly flashed with tears. "He can't have come to that! Not to a can of ash that you're carrying off in a beach bag to Florida like a lunch box!"

"I couldn't believe it myself, Angelo. He was such a big man and look at what he ended up in. I was still sleeping when the mortician came and gave it to Lucrezia. She left it on the dining-room table, and when I came downstairs, the first thing I thought was that somebody sent over a can of cookies until I opened it. I didn't even know what it was at first."

"Mama," he wept now, fiercely, as he had when a child, "doesn't it seem sacrilegious to you in any way, carrying him off like this? Look at all he was to us, Mama! We waited in whispers for months for him to die, even paid a woman a hundred and fifty dollars to kiss him on New Year's Eve, and made big plans for him to go like a Caesar at De Marco's place. He was a great man, Mama! He was defiant for thirty-five years and now look at him! Ashes are supposed to go into an urn. Why couldn't they have put him in a nice urn and sent him to Florida in a plane? What if you put the bag down somewhere and forget it?"

"I won't forget it, Angelo. And what am I supposed to do? Go all the way to Florida by limousine with motorcycle cops in front of us and behind us so everybody'll know the dust of the Defiance is passing through their little town? He's dead, Angelo. Gone. The mortician brought him to me in a cookie can and the best thing I could find to put him in was my beach bag."

"I don't know, Mrs. Pato," the priest interrupted, his own eyes watery now. "My feelings are mixed on this business although I kept silence yesterday. It doesn't seem like the right ending for a Catholic. I know it's approved and all that, but it smacks of irreverence. I once heard tell of a man who slyly scattered his father's ashes all over the floor of a barroom and had them tracked out into the great world by the shoes of alcoholics and B-girls. How's that for a story?"

"I don't go into bars and I'm going to keep his ashes in an urn in my sister Lucrezia's house, Father," she told him belligerently.

"Lucy, Lucrezia, is this the right way?" Principato implored, turning to his sister and aunt, who had been silent thus far. "He can't have ended up like this!"

"The train is coming, Angelo," Lucy said tonelessly. "Dry your eyes and try acting like a man. We have to go."

He watched mutely, offended, the jock priest beside him, as the three women swept up their bags and edged gratefully away from him toward the train that eased into the station. Leaving their suitcases to a porter, they forced their way aboard in the face of descending arrivals and disappeared into the entrails of the chromium serpent, leaving behind a last vivid impression of the red-flowered beach bag on his mother's arm being crushed and jostled in the play of opposing bodies on its way up the steps. Then they were not seen for long minutes.

"They're hiding from me," Principato lamented. "My own mother, sister, and aunt are hiding my father's ashes from me."

He and the priest ranged swiftly back and forth along the hissing line-up until they found the women seated at a window four cars nearer the engine than the one they had boarded. Their smiles were collectively dim and pitying. The old lady supported the beach bag in her lap, the red flowers pressing close against the pane.

In moments the departure signal was given and the train inched forward, the groaning of wheel flanges against the rails louder for the instant than the roar of traffic on Broad Street below. By reflex, the confessor swung into action. Pacing alongside the moving car, he raised his arm and first solemnly blessed the old lady, then Lucy, then Lucrezia. Principato sprinted beside him and saw the three women cross themselves in unison each time. Then he stopped, leaving the priest to trot, his cassock billowing out behind him toward the end of the platform, while he waved in response to his mother's fluttering handkerchief. This, until the car curved out of sight behind the angle of an advertisement sign. Good-by, Mama.

The confessor returned, still trotting. The new, absurd look of sheepishness plastered over his face, so different from the stern, athletic Christianity of a moment before, somehow warned Principato that the admission was forthcoming.

"Not a bad act for an impostor, huh?" he said.

"Are you an impostor?" Principato asked vaguely, realizing it did not seriously matter.

"Yes. I'm not really a priest," he admitted, his great shoulders drooping now with shame or self-pity. "But still, it doesn't seem so bad. I think I was a great comfort to your poor mother."

"She really fell for you." Principato smiled.

"She was a fine woman. Very Catholic. Are you angry with me?"

"No."

"You're generous in your own way, Mr. Pato. Others have been furious. I once got carried away and married two people. Very strict, doctrinaire Catholics they were. The woman had been a virgin up to her wedding night. You can imagine what hell broke loose after that one. But I can't contain myself. I have such a need to minister unto others."

"Then why not become a priest?" Principato asked simply. They were moving across the platform now, ready to descend the steps into the station waiting rooms.

"Can't. I'm an epileptic. I've already tried to bluff my way onto God's team through three different religious orders. But each of them found me out after a couple of months. Now I think every order in the world has a mug shot of me posted to its admission director's desk, waiting for me to walk in the door. No chance any place."

"I'm sorry. How did you come to be in that confessional box when I walked in yesterday?"

"The regular confessor leaves for lunch at that hour. That's why there was nobody in the church. I drop in there about once a week and pretend. I just slip into my old Jesuit cassock that I carry around for emergencies and sit in the box until about ten minutes before the other priest is supposed to return. Every once in a while somebody like you makes a mistake and comes in to confess. You're the first one I couldn't give absolution to, though."

"You're not empowered to give absolution," Principato reminded him, growing suddenly testy.

"Well . . . no. But I know all the prayers from seminary, and the intent is there even if the authority isn't. At least no one's ever been suspicious. I give good and wise counsel, too. I can tell by the sighs of satisfaction when they leave. Especially the women. For me, this more than makes up for my sin of impersonation."

"Not in my case, it doesn't. You didn't give me any satisfaction," Principato said angrily.

"Don't be annoyed with me, Mr. Pato," the jock priest begged. "Let's go into the restaurant and talk this out over a cup of coffee."

They stepped into the restaurant, stopping at the cashier's desk while the confessor bought a pack of cigarettes, then sat at the marble-top counter and ordered two coffees. The imposter inexpertly broke open the cigarettes and, lighting one, puffed clouds into the air with the furious concentration of a nonsmoker, his cheeks inflating and deflating like a guppy in a fish tank.

"I don't mind a bit that you took over the show at the crematorium yesterday and delivered that ringing eulogy over my old man," Principato told him. "So much the better, I guess, since he turned out to be a bunch of shit at the end of his life anyhow. But your compromising the secret of my confession is the thing I find myself suddenly angry about."

"Understand my need, Mr. Pato," the jock priest pleaded. "Please understand!"

Heads turned at the suggestion of desperation in the voice. Beside Principato, the imposter was growing flushed and red, as if the Roman collar had begun suddenly to choke him. The calm certain eyes were bloodshot now. The Negro waitress stared at him, her hands unconsciously beginning to fill a glass with water.

"Are you all right?" Principato asked warily.

"My need to minister unto the faithful is so intense. I have commands to fulfill. Once I thought it was possible. I joined the Trappists. We never spoke; we lived in our individual cells. If I had a fit in my cell, I was sure nobody would find out about it. But one night during Lent I flipped out in the community dining hall. It was weird, Mr. Pato. Nobody spoke a word except the reader at the lectern. He didn't even miss a syllable. Such inhumanity. Two brothers scraped me up off the floor and carried me out. I was finished. The others didn't even slow down one spoonful. . . . Now, do you forgive me?"

"No," Principato said, standing down from the counter stool. "You made me believe you were a priest with the authority to absolve sins."

"Forgive me!" the impostor pleaded once more before the ramrod stiffness overcame him and he toppled hugely to the floor, his skin incredibly white now and the eyes bug-wide. Then the stiffness fell prey to a twitch that caused the giant to slither back and forth across the pattern of filthy tiles, upsetting magazine racks and toppling a suddenly vacated table and its two breakfasts, as the restaurant patrons hugged the walls.

"Aaaggggh. Forgive! Forgive!" came the jock priest's rattle. His slitherings had worked the lower half of his cassock up above the cincture and Principato saw for the first time that his black slacks were actually new Wranglers. A cowboy galloped his horse on the paper label still stapled to the confessor's buttocks.

"It's 'lepsy! It's 'lepsy!" the waitress shrieked. "My brotha have the same thing. That bad! You gotta putta pencil in his mouth so he don't swolla his tongue! He kin die!"

Principato looked on fascinated, not searching for a pencil: the epileptic's eyes had gone far back in his head so that only the whites were visible like the eyes of a blind Negro he had once seen. Now the afflicted worked his way toward the cashier's counter, and raising his legs, neatly kicked in the glass panes shielding the chewing gum and candy bars. Then, the motion remembered, he flipped back across the floor and went after the remaining tables, covering himself in a rain of flying sugar, catsup, and half-eaten breakfasts. Concentric rings of terrified white and black faces watched him move out of that destruction, his hands still tugging at the tightness of his collar, and reverse himself to attack the unattackable marble of the lunch counter.

That was when Principato left him.

The new Corrigan Thunderbird was parked in the small lot beside his hotel when he returned from the station. Along with his room key, the desk clerk handed him an envelope bearing the Corrigan family seal. Principato took a seat in the lobby and opened the letter.

Dear Pato,

After a family council last night, it was decided to present you with this fine automobile as a frank bribe in the hope that you will return to us with proper haste. Also, there are more things to come. Mother Corrigan suggested that a complete new wardrobe might be included in the package as a means to revive your spirits after your long absence from our Cynthia and the particular anguish of your poor father's passing on. Matt, your brother-in-law, has proposed an adequate expense account until you are able to find work again; brother Edward is offering you a gasoline credit card for a minimum of two years' time; brother Jim, an unlimited tab at any of the family bars you should choose to patronize. (Since your leave-taking, the boys have opened a desirable new club in a white suburban area, although it seems a poor business venture to Mother Corrigan and myself on the basis of past experience in any white neighborhood.) I, for my part, will offer five masses for your particular intention.

Also considered at length was your insinuation that dear Cynthia was attempting some sort of illicit relationship with the Armenian boy, Nikos Kababian, who lives next door. Though we rejected this opinion as utterly unfounded, still we thought it might somehow comfort you to know that since Christmas this young man has become engaged to a girl from his high-school graduating class, and they are to be married in June. Cynthia is joyously happy for him, of course, which certainly tends to erase any miniscule doubts that might have crept into our minds. *Nous avons fini ce petit problème, j'espère.*

Otherwise, what remains to be discussed is your demand that we acknowledge your assertion that your father died accepting his damnation. In truth, we cannot, Pato. Six Corrigans saw the man leap up from his bed to embrace the cross of salvation. The intent was there, never mind by what means motivated. No Corrigan could proceed confidently to his own eternity, if, for reasons of conspiracy to get you back together with Cynthia and your children, he agreed to sign a testimony that he did not see what he did, in fact, observe. We are not a race of conspirators and false oath takers, Pato.

So you must recognize our position. We want you to return to us, ready to assume your sacred duties as Catholic father and husband. Accept our proffered gifts and recognize that, in good faith, we cannot present you with the particular piece of testimony you've asked for.

Yours sincerely in Christ,
Aloysius Corrigan, S.J.

Principato refolded the letter and telephoned Malatesta at Eva Lissome's, where he had been securely encamped despite Allergucci since their New Year's Eve *rapprochement*. After fifteen minutes of consultation he replaced the receiver and left the hotel with the address of a West Philadelphia junk dealer.

Within a half hour, Principato maneuvered the Corrigan Thunderbird through the gates of Rifkin's Junk Yard. Inside a tall wooden fence, mountains of chromed bumpers and grilles and used tires pressed closely upon each other. He passed slowly along avenues of stacked engine blocks toward the sound of metal being tortured at the center of the lot, where a bailing machine, a collection of blunt steel plates pneumatically driven, hammered away at the almost unrecognizable shape of a car. As he watched, the plates stopped their movement abruptly and a square block was ejected from the end of the machine and fell rudely to the ground. Immediately, the boom of a magnetic crane swooped in to lift it and place it bricklike in a neat stack.

"Nice, huh?" a voice asked. "This machine is the answer to the poets and all their piddling over how this green and grassy world of ours is being buried in rusted car bodies."

Principato turned. A grimy gnome of a man who wore a new Phillies cap stood before him, chewing on the end of a thin cigar. Beneath the peak, the man's eyes were directed to the Thunderbird. Their covetous look was unmistakable.

"What can I do for you, friend? You buyin' junk?"

"No. I want to get rid of this car," Principato said.

"Tell you what," said the gnome, "I'll give you fifty bucks for it. I'd like to make it a little more, but it's a house policy. We never go above fifty for a junk car."

"No, I don't want any money. I'm serious. I just want you to put it into your machine and destroy it."

"When? Now?"

"Yes."

"Friend, what do you think those heaps behind you are waiting for, a paint job?" he asked, pointing to the neat stacks of wheel-less wrecks, one of which was being lifted now by the magnetic crane for its turn in the crusher. "This thing won't be due to go for two months yet. If you really are serious, why not sell it to me and let it wait its turn?"

"Look, I'll pay you twenty-five dollars if you'll feed it into your machine now. This is very important to me," Principato said, advancing toward Rifkin (he presumed), the diminutive junkman who held a sudden incredible power. Rifkin looked frightened, began retreating backward. He regarded Principato for a long moment.

"Listen," he spoke finally. "I think I understand this. It's something sacred to you, isn't it? Some men have a peculiar religion. They don't like to leave any loose ends around after they've gone. You're going someplace, aren't you?"

"Yes," Principato answered, because it seemed easiest.

"I knew. It's the same thing with my son. He kept talking about going someplace, then he killed himself. The morning he did it I came here and found his sports car in that machine, all mangled up. Only he didn't finish it off right, because he couldn't take the engine out. It's like that with you, I think."

"No," Principato protested, "it's not like that at all."

"Yeah, it is. The signs are all the same. All right, I'll help you. You've got the twenty-five bucks, right?"

"Yes."

Principato took the money from his wallet, handing it to Rifkin, along with the new owner's card and title papers that he had signed only twenty minutes before. The junkman scrutinized the cards for perhaps two minutes, raising his head frequently to look at the T-bird. Apparently satisfied, he instructed Principato, "Take whatever you want from the heap then come into the office. There are some papers to be signed."

The small man marched off toward his office and Principato strode to the car, searching for anything worth salvaging. In the glove compartment he found only an unopened package of Clorets. In the trunk were a spare, a hydraulic jack and tire iron that he decided not to remove, and far back, unexpectedly, with one foot caught in the lid spring, a black-skinned doll that he remembered belonged to his daughter Noreen. One arm was ripped completely off and a tuft of white cotton spewed out of the wound. A rueful smile crossed his face at the notion that he was regarding some appropriate imagery, and he lifted the doll gently, placing it in his coat pocket, patting the stuffing back inside. In a minute he stood beside Rifkin in the office.

"Sign here," the junkman pointed to a series of X marks that glared upward from the multipage run on of small type. Principato complied, signing his name in full: Angelo Xavier Principato, while Rifkin watched him narrowly.

"I'll have this notarized later today. Where shall I send your copy? To your parents? Or do you have a wife and family you're leaving behind?"

"Send it to this address along with what's left of the car," Principato instructed, writing the address he had not used since November.

"Are you serious?"

"Yes."

"Wow! You're really getting even with them, whoever they are. What shall I say to them when I deliver?"

"Nothing. Just wrap up the remains in a bed sheet or some white cloth, back your truck into the driveway and dump it on the lawn."

"Hey, how about a gift card? I can get some nice ribbon from my wife and we'll write out a card and attach it to the bow."

"Whatever you like."

"Good. I'll do a fine job, buddy. Count on me. By the way, a delivery is twenty-five bucks extra."

After paying the additional money, Principato stood silently in front of the office with Rifkin as two disbelieving workers siphoned gas from the tank, then removed the T-bird's wheels so it sat tortoise-like on its frame. Next the radio came out, and the spare and jack, and the upholstery—with a brittle, ripping sound that made Principato think of muscle and sinew being torn. The windows were shattered with a crowbar and the unblemished blue motor unbolted and lifted swiftly away to the avenue of stacked engine blocks.

"O.K., haul it away!" Rifkin shouted to the crane operator. The boom swung round and the magnetic disc dropped with a plop on the car's roof and lifted it smoothly into the machine between the steel plates. The junkman stepped into a small shed and pushed a series of buttons and the monster lurched into motion, the plates moving forward and back like a giant's arms mashing the Corrigan gift car between them.

"That's one beating the bastards never recover from," said Rifkin. Turning, Principato saw that a gleam had suddenly appeared in the man's eyes. He hammered a fist into an open palm each time the plate struck home. In five minutes, still hammering to the rhythm of destruction, he re-entered the shed and pressed another series of buttons so that the plates stopped moving, and a block of metal, so pulverized that they could not even tell from it what color the car had been, was flipped onto the earth.

Slowly, Principato advanced toward the lump, finally squatting down beside it. He reached out to touch it with one finger and was not surprised to find it was warm. Battered but still breathing, then. For a time he felt he might cry again as he had done that morning: flood the immense auto graveyards with the echo of his sorrow: lamentation at last in the midst of old car frames like skeletons and fenders like arms and engine blocks that were hearts and viscera once before. But his tears were too late in coming, their privilege usurped suddenly by the incredible whine of a saw passing through metal somewhere among the avenues of grilles and chromed bumpers. For him, the ultimate sound of sadness; the keening of an entire high-voiced chorus. Rifkin found it so, too, Principato decided. The junkman stared dumbly at the oiled-down earth, perhaps remembering his son who had committed suicide.

Then the whirring blade stopped abruptly and Rifkin's face returned to the living. "Come on pal, you're slowing up production here! I've got a business to run! We've wasted enough time around here today! You go someplace else and do what you have to do! Here we bust up old cars." He slammed his fist furiously into his open palm.

Shrugging, Principato walked quickly from the junk yard, crossing the street to a bus stop, the loud hammering of Rifkin's machine already begun again. While he waited for the bus, the junkman, visible only from the top of his Phillies cap to the lower rim of his eyes, watched him steadily over the tall fence.

It was then that Principato resolved, for no reason at all, that he would spend the rest of the day at the movies.

SEVENTEEN

"My father did not relent."
"He never had any intention of relenting."
"My father did not relent."
"He never had any intention of relenting."

Sitting across the street in his father's T-bird, Principato began this day's instructive chanting through his megaphone at his former home. He had been doing it each day for weeks now. But he was talking into the wind: no one acknowledged him or had done so since he began.

In the driveway sat a Corrigan Funeral Service limousine, which meant that at least one of the brothers—and probably the old lady—was inside the house. The black Ford from the Jesuit motor pool behind it spoke for the uncle. Three of his children played in the front yard, chasing about and miraculously dodging the canvas-wrapped lump of mangled Thunderbird that Rifkin had dumped on the lawn near the porch steps. For them, Principato thought sadly, the lump did not exist. The special Corrigan ability to see and hear the selective flowed in their young bloods also.

In time, the Jesuit left the house, descending the front-porch steps and making his way near enough the lump so that for an instant Principato prayed his cassock might snag on some sharp extension of it and force the priest to admit it existed. But he by-passed it deftly, started his car, and drove away from the place without a flicker of recognition for Principato.

Moments later Nikos Kababian descended the front steps of his house with the small thermos of coffee his mother prepared for Principato each afternoon now.

"Nothing today?" he asked, climbing into the front beside Principato.

"Nothing," Principato answered. He stopped his chant to sip the coffee.

"There's something wrong with them, Mr. Principato. I watch them a lot, and your wife and her family go out and come in a few times every day and never even look at the thing. The kids play in the yard, but they never touch it or even look at it. It just sits there. How long do you think they'll leave it as it is?"

"Until it dissolves, Nikos," Principato said morosely.

"Are you going to keep coming here every afternoon for the next couple of years, Mr. Principato? They might finally call the police and have you arrested for public nuisance or something."

"Never, Nikos. That way they'd be admitting a nuisance existed."

Mr. Hamilton tapped at Kababian's window and the young god pressed a button to lower it.

"It will do you no good, Mr. Principato. I don't know the nature of your transgression, but firing a shotgun point-blank at that house would not get them to admit you are seated out here in your car. They are a curious family, made unto their own images, and not likely to bend to the instruction of another once they've made up their minds. I think you're only wasting your time."

"Yes, Mr. Principato, Mama says you have to make a new life and forget them. Don't go back and live with them or it'll be just like it was before."

"Yes, you're both right," Principato admitted sadly.

"My father did not relent."

"He never had any intention of relenting."

"My father . . . oh, what the hell . . ."

Principato set the megaphone on the back seat. Nikos left the car and stood beside old Hamilton as Principato drove away.

EPILOGUE

One day months later, in August, when he had just returned from a half-hearted job interview, the Corrigan brothers invaded his lonely hotel room with an invitation to an evening of home movies in their mansion. How could he resist? A Corrigan invitation was next to a command.

As soon as the children had been properly delighted with the feature attraction, and then packed off to bed, the brothers showed him several hundred feet of infrared film of himself and Corky entering Hallagan's warehouse on several different occasions. The Corrigans also had had a friend in that tempestuous diner, an obscure relative whom Principato should have recognized after eleven years of Corrigan wakes and weddings. But he had not, and the unintended snub prompted a phone call to Cynthia's brothers.

The shots were skillfully done with telescopic close-ups of the mismatched lovers giggling and kissing as they worked at moving back the great sliding doors. Principato made no defense again. What could he say? The viewing completed, the three brothers ceremoniously took him outside on the soft August lawn and beat the hell out of him. Cynthia had coldly watched the event from the front porch. There were no Kababians or Hamiltons available.

"Our sister is petitioning Rome for an annulment, Principato. Do

310

you understand?" brother Matt, the eldest, demanded, his knee planted squarely on the victim's chest. "She will most probably remarry."

"Who?" Principato asked faintly, incredulous, even through his pain and bleeding. "Who would?"

"We'll cross that bridge when we come to it," Matt declared. "Now you'll hereby cease to refer to the Corrigan family as being in any way related to yourself."

Thus began the time of his real wanderings away from the Corrigan tents. Months of patient waiting on Rome's pronouncement that, because of some conveniently discovered technicality, his marriage of eleven years had been no marriage at all from its very inception. But the case had gotten itself lost somewhere in the cogs of the Church's creeping bureaucracy, and despite frequent and generous Corrigan handouts to greater and lesser clerics on the way to the Holy City, nothing was heard. Principato had long since given up real hope, deciding it was a dead letter.

In the time of his loneliness thus far, he had seen only two really bright sunrises. The one, the day that his and Corky's child was born and named Angelo, regardless of Cornelius's protestation that it did not go well with Gallagher. The other, the day of Nikos Kababian's marriage to a girl of his own age, when Cynthia was carried faint and weeping from the church.

Otherwise, there was only Corky to encourage an occasional beautiful day, faithfully mailing her one-time lover a box of chocolate brownies at the beginning of each week.